The
Nursemaid's
Secret

KT-220-137

9030 00006 2604 5

Sheila Newberry was born in Suffolk and spent a lot of time there both before and during the war. She wrote her first 'book' before she was ten – all sixty pages of it – in purple ink. Her family has certainly been her inspiration and she has been published most of her adult life. She spent forty years living in Kent with her husband John on a smallholding, and has nine children, twenty-two grandchildren and six great-grandchildren. Sheila retired back to Suffolk where she still lives today.

Also by Sheila Newberry

Angel's Secret
Bicycles and Blackberries
The Canal Girl
The Daughter's Choice
The Family at Number Five
Far From Home
The Gingerbread Girl
The Girl With No Home
Hay Bales and Hollyhocks
Hot Pies on the Tram Car
Molly's Journey
The Poplar Penny Whistlers
The Punch and Judy Girl
The Watercress Girls
The Winter Baby

Sheila Newberry

The Nursemaid's Secret

ZAFFRE

First published in Great Britain in 1996 as *Tilly's Family*
by Piatkus Books

First Zaffre Publishing edition published in ebook as *A Home for Tilly* in 2016

This edition published in Great Britain in 2018 by

ZAFFRE PUBLISHING
80–81 Wimpole St, London W1G 9RE
www.zaffrebooks.co.uk

Copyright © Sheila Newberry, 1996

All rights reserved.
No part of this publication may be reproduced,
stored or transmitted in any form by any means, electronic,
mechanical, photocopying or otherwise, without the
prior written permission of the publisher.

The right of Sheila Newberry to be identified as Author of this
work has been asserted by her in accordance with the
Copyright, Designs and Patents Act, 1988

This is a work of fiction. Names, places, events and
incidents are either the products of the author's imagination or
used fictitiously. Any resemblance to actual persons, living or dead,
or actual events is purely coincidental.

A CIP catalogue record for this book is available from the British Library.

ISBN: 978-1-78576-455-4

Also available as an ebook

1 3 5 7 9 10 8 6 4 2

Typeset by IDSUK (Data Connection) Ltd
Printed and bound in Great Britain by Clays Ltd, Elcograf S.p.A.

Zaffre Publishing is an imprint of Bonnier Zaffre,
part of Bonnier Books UK
www.bonnierzaffre.co.uk
www.bonnierbooks.co.uk

For my Father and Mother
and for John.
With my love.

LONDON BOROUGH OF WANDSWORTH	
9030 00006 2604 5	
Askews & Holts	22-Nov-2018
AF	£6.99
	WW18011275

PART ONE

1894–1897

ONE

Tilly set down the flat irons in the hearth with a satisfied little sigh. The kitchen was steamy, her forehead damp from her exertions, her back aching, but she hauled the airer aloft with a light heart. It was always a pleasure to press Mrs Augusta's fine linen, she thought. There had been even more ironing than usual for they would be departing from Brixton very shortly for the Christmas visit to Norfolk. Tilly was really looking forward to that. It would be almost a holiday for her, too, for she wouldn't be expected to clean and cook in the family farmhouse – mind you, she would still have to look after Mrs Augusta and her young daughter Gussie.

'Maid-of-all-work' the servants in the neighbouring houses dubbed Tilly Reeder. She knew, but it didn't worry her. For hadn't Augusta Quayle, her autocratic employer, given Tilly that vital chance to make something of her life when well aware of the painful secret in Tilly's short past? The pale, undernourished, bewildered fifteen year old of almost seven years ago had become the tall, shapely, confident young woman of today. Tilly might possess sore, chapped hands – for the soda in the washing-up water did not only dissolve grease on pots and pans, she often thought ruefully – but her crown of golden hair, as bright as a new penny, and her pretty, smiling face, turned many heads although she was quite unaware of it.

Her mistress had been a teacher for many years; she had recognised Tilly's quick intelligence, fed and encouraged it too. How often had Tilly bitten her lip and blinked away the tears in the early days, when Mrs Augusta had been forever correcting her slipshod speech or pouncing upon the incorrectly laid cutlery with a sharp: 'Will you *never* learn?' What a tartar she must have been at that school, Tilly often thought. Books were thrust at her when wearily she made her way up those winding attic stairs to bed. Obediently, she had yawned her way through a chapter each night for she knew that she would be questioned as to what she had absorbed the following morning. But to her joy the educational tomes had at last given way to the novel, and Mrs Augusta had catholic tastes in literature. Tilly had read *Jane Eyre* compulsively, until her candle flickered and died at dawn. Jane Eyre had suffered as a child too, and Tilly just had to make sure that there was a happy ending after all.

She hung her Holland apron on the hook on the kitchen door, smoothed down her black dress and donned her frilly apron. Time to serve afternoon tea – ten minutes later than usual.

She paused in the vast hallway to check in the ornate mirror that her cap was straight. Then she smiled spontaneously at the huge portrait of Mrs Augusta's revered late husband, George. 'I do wish I'd known *you*, Mr George,' she whispered. 'I just know you wouldn't have terrified me as Mrs Augusta does sometimes. Thank goodness Gussie takes after you!'

Pushing open the double doors, she wheeled the trolley into the drawing room. It was a grand room with much ruby-red plush, spindly legged, uncomfortable chairs and a stiff-backed sofa, where Mrs Augusta sat, clearly waiting for her refreshment. Several occasional tables, draped in lacy cloths, displayed small pieces of valuable porcelain. Gloomy dark pictures in massive frames jostled for space on the flock paper which covered the walls. Tilly never felt at ease in this room.

Gussie was curled up in the basket chair by the window, her head bent over her sketching block as usual. She was a quiet, dreamy child and Tilly was very fond of her.

The fire needed making up, Tilly saw immediately, the curtains must be drawn, and then the pleasure of pressing down the switch to illuminate the room with the wonderful new electric light.

'You're late, Tilly,' Augusta observed sharply. Big-boned she was, tightly corseted, handsome in her sweeping deep-blue velveteen dress which showed off her startling auburn hair and pale skin. She possessed curious, hooded eyes, appearing blue now because of the colour she wore, but more often grey.

Tilly lit the spirit lamp immediately. First things first. 'I filled the tea kettle with hot water from the range, Mrs Augusta,' she said soothingly, 'it shouldn't take long. I wanted to finish off the ironing, to get everything aired before I start the packing tomorrow.'

She shovelled coal onto the fire from the brass bucket then crossed to the window. 'You'll strain your eyes, the light's almost gone,' she pretended to scold. Gussie was nine years old, slender and delicate, with a cascade of crinkled red hair tortured into tight ringlets. How Tilly felt for her each morning when she observed Mrs Augusta smacking the backs of Gussie's raised, protesting hands with that painful bristle brush! Poor fatherless child, Tilly thought. It hardly seemed surprising that after all those years of a childless marriage, Mr George Quayle had been so startled at their unexpected production that he had succumbed to a heart attack soon after Gussie's birth. While Augusta was still confined to bed, he had expired. Well, that was how Mrs Augusta herself had described his demise to Tilly. At least his death had left her a very wealthy woman.

Glancing through the window as she was about to draw the curtains together, Tilly saw that the street lamps were already sputtering, casting yellow pools of light on the dark pavement. The fog was thickening; it was a typical early December afternoon. Someone was pushing the front gate open, leaning a bicycle against the dense privet hedge. It was a telegraph boy, coming whistling up the path to hammer on the heavy door.

'Oh dear!' Tilly exclaimed. Everyone knew telegrams brought bad news.

'We'll have our tea first,' Augusta told them firmly. 'It's silly to get upset on an empty stomach. You may join us at tea, Tilly. Sit down for five minutes, you've been working extra hard,' she told her graciously.

The fruit cake fortunately passed muster, for Tilly had knocked it up hastily whilst waiting for the irons to sizzle. The griddle scones had already gone down a treat, dripping with butter. Tilly really appreciated the reviving effect of the strong tea, even if the cups could have been larger in her opinion. But small cups, she had learned, were in good taste. In her old home there had only been used tea leaves, given to her mother, a washerwoman, by her generous employers. Tea had either been very weak, despite no added milk, for that was a luxury too, or tasted horribly stewed, the teapot remaining on the hob night and day. Mrs Augusta was never mean regarding the housekeeping, which had been entrusted to her maid since she'd turned twenty-one, and Tilly enjoyed the same good food. Still, Mrs Augusta liked to remind Tilly how much things cost in order that she should appreciate how lucky she was to be so cosseted.

She waited until Mrs Augusta dabbed at the corners of her mouth with the linen napkin Tilly had just ironed – now she would have to wash it again – then she fetched the ivory paper knife and placed it unobtrusively by the telegram. Augusta read it in silence.

Then: 'I knew it!' she cried wrathfully. 'This is from my sister-in-law Rosa, Tilly – from the Isle of Sheppey. I advised her not to go back to that isolated damp cottage this winter when my brother went overseas, as you well know. Now she thinks I should know that young Joe is gravely ill – oh, why didn't she leave him with me for a few months, as I suggested! How *can* I help when we are going away in three days' time?' Bright spots of scarlet appeared on her cheeks, as they always did when she was agitated.

Tilly knew Rosa and her three children, Nandy, Maud and Joe, of course; Rosa was married to Augusta's favourite brother, a naval officer. Tilly had often listened to the story of how Augusta had brought her baby brother up when their mother died. She had also deduced for herself that Mrs Augusta envied Rosa her sons. Only yesterday she had said of her sister-in-law: 'Impetuous, Tilly, following her husband from port to port when he is in this country – must be that foreign blood in her veins! With those little children in tow, too.' Tilly thought that having a Spanish mother was really rather romantic, but naturally didn't say so. Tilly considered that they were two strong determined women, always at odds, when they should think of all they had in common, both being left to cope on their own.

She said placatingly, 'Mrs Searle must have forgotten all about us going to Norfolk, what with the worry and all.'

Augusta demanded: 'Fetch my writing things, Tilly, then you can go and pack. For yourself, girl. *You* shall go and help with the nursing. Tonight. I'll send you by cab to Victoria.' She checked her fob watch. 'There's a train around five o'clock as I recall – didn't *they* catch it last time they called in here on their way back from Southampton? Oh, leave the trolley, Gussie can see to that. Hurry, Tilly!'

She could not know that this errand of mercy would change her whole life once more.

Tilly was about to join the family under the sea wall.

TWO

The friendly, dark-jowled driver, reeking of horses, tobacco, beer and masculinity – which made Tilly feel a little nervous, as she was travelling on her own – swung up her basket case and left her to step up by herself into the hansom.

Augusta, standing by, extracted some coins from her purse. 'Here you are, driver, *I* am paying the fare. Make all speed but be careful in this wretched fog. Your passenger must not miss her train.'

'Goodbye, dear Tilly – and good luck! Hug little Joe for me,' Gussie called tearfully from the doorway of their square double-fronted house in that long street of identical Georgian residences. This was the select part of Brixton, of course, where cabs were often to be seen.

'I will!' Tilly called back. She had managed to give Gussie a swift kiss in the hall before Mrs Augusta came out.

'You must join us in Norfolk just as soon as you can,' Augusta told Tilly, 'but not until you are sure, naturally, that Joe is well on the road to recovery. Tell Rosa I expect her to keep me well informed of his progress.'

'I will,' Tilly promised again.

So began her journey through the London streets to Victoria. They seemed to be enveloped in acrid, choking fog. The cab wheels ground noisily on slippery cobbles; dark, hurrying shapes disappeared into the welcome warmth of the illuminated shops. As they trundled along, Tilly muttered to herself: 'Change at Sittingbourne, the dockyard train, take another cab to Cheyney . . . '

Once delivered at Victoria Station there was an anxious, echoing walk ahead, and such a cacophony reverberating from the vast dome overhead that Tilly felt as if her head would burst. She bought her ticket and ventured onto the crowded platform, as directed. The pungent, nostril-dilating smoke billowing from the approaching train seemed to swallow up the waiting passengers, to suck Tilly into the nearest carriage and deposit her on to the hard seat, for she was saving Mrs Augusta's money by travelling second-class.

She sat straight-backed, aware of the muddied hem of her best dark-green serge skirt, the one she wore to church on Sundays, and her soiled boots which she had not had time to polish.

At last the train emerged from the fog into the open countryside, where the feeble evening light tinged the silent, stripped fields and hedgerows with a faint, eerie glow.

Later, she sat apprehensively in the waiting room at Sittingbourne Station, the first stage of her journey successfully completed. It was like a toy station, Tilly thought, compared to the vastness of Victoria. Here, the station had a yellow brick facade, arched windows and even a tiny garden confined behind black iron railings. She was the only one, it seemed, waiting for the Island train.

The porter poked energetically at the fire, sending up a shower of sparks which hung for a moment, suspended and glowing, then floated down as sooty flakes into the hearth. He emptied the bucket with a flourish, straightened up and dusted his hands on his trousers: 'Another fifteen minutes, miss, before the Sheerness train. This should warm you up; it'll soon burn through.'

'Thank you, porter; that is most kind of you.' Tilly unconsciously repeated one of Augusta's stock phrases.

It was a blackened monster of a train, belching noisily, coming towards her as she stood on the platform with such a rush that Tilly was terrified it would steam past and leave her stranded. But it ground to an excruciating halt and the majority of those aboard disembarked to the porter's cheery bellow: 'Sittin'bourne Stashun!' There was much slamming of doors and cheerful shouting.

'No need to hurry,' Tilly's friendly porter advised, coming alongside the train with a lighted taper. 'I've got to light up first. Go along a bit, I should.'

She watched, fascinated, for a moment or two, as he stepped lightly along the tops of the carriages, lifting the trap doors, trimming and lighting the oil lamps inside. There were three golden lights to each coach.

Then a helpful stout gentleman swung the door wide for her and helped her aboard. He looked quite elderly, so she supposed it was all right.

The wooden seats were exceedingly hard. 'Quite a relic, this train, must be at least fifty years old,' remarked the man who had assisted her. 'I suppose they think it's good enough for old Sheer Necessity,' he added drily. He had an accent, but Tilly could not place it.

She was intrigued, despite remembering Augusta's final admonition not to speak to strange men on the journey. But this one had noted her look of interest at the strange name.

'That's what the sailors call it, when they are forced to stay there in port for a while.' He smiled. 'It's not as bad as it sounds; I've lived and worked there for a good number of years.'

Tilly favoured him with a dismissive nod, as she had seen Mrs Augusta do when accosted by those to whom she had not been properly introduced. She was aware that Sheerness was a naval port, of course. Mrs Augusta often said darkly that it was no place to bring up children. Tilly imagined it to be like the London docks. Not just cockneys, but a mixture of nationalities.

It seemed rather like the journey in *Pilgrim's Progress* to a bemused Tilly. Fortunately she was not really aware of the water swirling deep and black as night as they passed safely over the bridge. There were numerous stops and starts to allow passengers to step down and disappear across the fields before the official halt.

The stout gentleman held on to the bulky portmanteau on his lap. As if it contained something precious, Tilly thought. Then he brought out from the pocket of his travelling cape a small box. 'You would like a lozenge, perhaps? Against the chill air?' The beam he bestowed on Tilly quite disarmed her, although she had reason to know that kindly middle-aged men were not always as they seemed.

'Thank you,' she said. The lozenge was indeed warming, and loosened her tongue.

'I was afraid, you know,' she confided, 'of crossing over the railway bridge over the sea – but I didn't realise we had until we stopped to let people off.'

His smile broadened, but Tilly did not feel that he was laughing at her.

'Here on the Island, my dear young lady, you are still in the county of Kent – a mere fifty miles from London. You did not realise the geography of Sheppey, eh?'

Tilly shook her head.

'The Island is at the mouth of the Thames, where that great river joins with the Medway. We merely passed over the waters of its tributary, the Swale. But you shall surely see much of the sea while you are on the Island – the cold North Sea, that is – and your feet will tread that same London clay which you know.'

'How did you know I come from London?' Tilly asked, surprised. Having ironed out her cockney inflection, thanks to Mrs Augusta's prompting, she did not realise that her voice still betrayed her origins.

'Ah, I do,' he said. 'Don't forget,' he added cheerfully, 'that this Island is still regarded as a fortress. Has been for centuries. The people here are always ready for an emergency.'

These words sent a shiver down Tilly's spine.

'Emergency?' she exclaimed fearfully.

'Oh, there is always the fear of invasion here – old enemies become friends, but are not entirely trusted. Like the French, the Dutch – and we Germans. Ah, we are here, I shall call a cab for you. Myself, I shall walk. It is my pleasure to stroll home along the sea wall when I have been away on business – I enjoy watching the lights of the ships at sea. I'll give you my card, my dear. You may wish to make use of my services while you're here.'

Tilly tucked the card into her bag. She was glad he had not said he would share her cab, but his parting words were: 'I go another way. Goodbye! It was most refreshing to talk to you.'

'Goodbye,' Tilly said, wondering if she would see him again.

The journey from Sittingbourne had taken barely twenty-five minutes, but she was immediately aware how much colder it was here on the Island. She didn't realise that there was usually a strong, blustery wind off the sea.

The cabbie hummed as the horse clopped along. They passed terraces of houses with lower windows lit to reveal folk at their supper. As Tilly swallowed the last fragment of the lozenge, she was pleased to see the rows of shops, reminding her of Brixton. Sheerness, it was obvious, was a bustling town. But the shops were closed for the day. Not many people about, she thought, just the occasional sailor strolling along with his arm around his girl's waist, and a stray dog darting out into the road to bark shrilly after them. They were making for the very outskirts of the town.

When they reached the unmade road which led to the cottage and its few neighbouring properties, Tilly found herself shivering convulsively. What a desolate place this was! Yet when they stopped and she had paid the cabbie, she was comforted by the glow from the front room of the cottage. The glow of oil lamps, of a fire leaping in the grate.

The cottage was just as Augusta had disparagingly described it: some eight feet below sea level, with its back braced against the sea wall. In rough weather, Tilly would shortly learn, the spray smacked violently against the bedroom windows, which were exposed to the sea.

She climbed the three whitened steps which led to the stout, studded front door. She put her case down at her feet and knocked, hesitantly the first time, then firmly. At the other side there were the unmistakable sounds of a scuffle.

Then the door was flung wide by Maud. A small, stocky child, with raven hair complementing her lustrous dark eyes – that Spanish legacy again, Tilly thought, just as Nordic looks and blonde hair recurred in her own family. Maud had always been creamy-skinned but now she appeared positively pale and unsmiling. She stared in disbelief at Tilly.

'Yes, Maud, it's me,' Tilly told her. 'Mrs Quayle sent me to help you all – we received the telegram at tea-time. Aren't you going to ask me in, then?' And she instinctively put out her arms. Seven year olds were not too old for embracing, she knew.

Maud hugged her tightly, crying: 'Oh, Tilly! Joe's so ill – we really do need you so! And Nandy has burnt the pie Grandma Isabella brought round earlier, and now we won't get any supper – and Rosa – Mother! – hasn't eaten anything all day – and *he* wanted to answer the door –'

Standing in the background was Nandy. Tilly took in his rebellious pouting, sensed the impatience he felt with his younger sister. At the best of times, Tilly knew, from observing them at Mrs Augusta's, they still clashed, for they were both stubborn. He was ten, long and loose-limbed, with curling fair hair and deep-set blue eyes like his father, but was much more like his mother in temperament, which was probably why *they* did not hit it off especially well either.

'That's enough of *that*,' she said firmly, closing the door behind her. 'Nandy, I've been travelling for a long time and

I need a cup of tea. Will you make one for me, please? And I've got a bag of muffins which your aunt sent for you; you can toast them by the fire . . . Maud, will you let your mother know I'm here? I imagine she's upstairs with the invalid?'

Maud nodded. 'She hasn't left him today.'

Tilly followed Nandy into the kitchen, which led off the parlour. It was all so different from Augusta's house that she felt a wave of confusion for a brief moment. This morning, she thought wonderingly, she had woken as usual in Brixton, done a really good day's work, and had had no idea that she would not be sleeping in her own bed at the end of it.

Here, the old piano stood against one whitewashed wall; the high-backed hide and horsehair sofa, spilling some of its stuffing from holes poked, no doubt, by idle little fingers, was drawn up to the crackling fire. The ceilings were low, bulging and black-beamed. The inner doors, of pitted black wood, were fastened with a latch. Against the other wall was a big table, crowded around by chairs, next to a long dresser with cupboards and deep drawers with big round knobs. Tilly had an impression of pots and willow-pattern china, of saucepan lids hanging decoratively on either side of the dresser.

There was a dreadful smell of burning in the kitchen, and a blackened pie still smouldered on top of the range. Nandy indicated the three large earthenware jars beneath the deep stone sink.

'The water supply is limited to four hours daily,' he said, 'from the stand-pipe in the yard. From six to eight in the morning, and four to six in the afternoon. And the butt's full,' he added importantly. 'Plenty of rain this past month.' He looked at Tilly. 'And the privy's out in the yard, too. No proper WC like Aunt A's, you know, Tilly – or bath with a gas geyser. That's why Aunt A never visits us here. It's even more primitive than it is in Norfolk.' His voice was challenging. Had she come to interfere?

'It doesn't worry me,' Tilly told him. No different from where she'd grown up, she thought. She took off her coat and hung it on a spare hook. 'Make a big pot of tea, Nandy, and bring it up to your mother.'

Tilly felt the tiredness leave her. She was needed here, that was all important to her. She went as quietly as she could manage, for the stairs were uncarpeted, up the steep steps to the bedrooms. Just two rooms up here, she observed, one either side of the stairwell, two paces apart across the minute landing.

Through the open door on the left she saw Rosa's slight figure bending over the brass-railed double bed. From the heaving of her shoulders, Tilly knew that she was silently weeping. As she entered, indicating to Maud that she should go downstairs again, she took in the sweet odour of sickness. The room was in shadow, just a candle on the washstand by the bed. The dark-haired child seemed almost lost in its depths.

'Mrs Rosa,' Tilly whispered, touching her arm gently, 'I've come to stay for just as long as you need me. We'll pull

19

Joe through this, I promise you.' But she could tell he was a very sick little boy.

Rosa unbent, turning to Tilly. 'He's asleep – has been most of the day. I don't know whether that's good or bad. He just burns up each night. That's why I moved him in here with me.'

Rosa's high-cheekboned face, accentuated by her severely drawn back black hair – not for her the softening fringe achieved by singing tongs, for Rosa was not vain although very proud – was ravaged by tears. Tilly rightly guessed that four-year-old Joe was her favoured child.

'What does the doctor say?' Tilly asked, keeping her voice low. Rosa wrung out a flannel in cold water and replaced it on Joe's forehead.

'Rheumatic fever. And on top of that measles, too . . . He told me the truth, Tilly. I asked him to. If he – if he recovers – he's likely to suffer some after effects – like a bad heart . . . Oh, Tilly, I'm *so* glad to see you!' Tears trickled unheeded down her face.

'I know that you're not too strong yourself at the moment, Mrs Rosa. I'm sure that's why Mrs Augusta thought I should come straightaway.'

'You know then, about my losing the baby?' Rosa looked at Tilly.

'Yes, Mrs Rosa. I felt so much for you. It must have been terrible, with your husband going away just after and all.'

They sat on the edge of Rosa's bed and talked.

Tilly saw the way Rosa clasped her hands across her flat stomach. 'I haven't had time to mourn her yet, Tilly, what with all this. My husband was so loving and understanding, but of course he had to go. I wanted to say: "You never knew her, Joe, you never even saw her. You never even held her in your arms." But that was so unfair because he got leave and came as quickly as he could; she'd already been baptised, Elizabeth Rosa, and was buried . . . It's so cruel, Tilly, to lose a baby – but it would be so much worse,' her voice broke, 'to lose little Joe.'

'I know, I know,' Tilly said simply. Then: 'Has Mrs Augusta ever told you my story, Mrs Rosa?' It might help Rosa, Tilly thought, if she had.

'I do know something,' she answered slowly. 'But it needn't concern us, Tilly. You see, we have more in common than you might imagine. I was in service as a cook myself, you know, before I married. Another reason for Augusta to protest that I am not good enough for her brother,' she added resentfully.

'I'm sure she doesn't think that,' Tilly said loyally. 'Look, here's Maud and Nandy with tea and muffins. You must eat and get your strength up.'

When they had eaten, Tilly coaxed Rosa downstairs for an hour.

'The other children need you too, you know, Mrs Rosa,' she reminded her quietly. 'I'll nip up and down, looking in on Joe.'

Rosa read Augusta's letter aloud to them:

I am devastated to hear the bad news of young Joe. Gussie and I are praying for his recovery. Why did you not tell me sooner? We are about to leave for Norfolk, for our Christmas visit to my family, and could not cancel our arrangements at such short notice – you might have realised that. However, it seems to me that you might be glad of Tilly to help, and also for the adult company, knowing your other two children only too well . . . Tilly is a competent nurse, as I know from experience. Her wages are naturally taken care of, and she is to stay as long as is necessary. The enclosed is to cover medical expenses and to purchase nourishing food for the invalid. (I shall be most offended if you refuse this.) You will be receiving shortly, I trust, a Christmas package from me.

I hardly dare to wish you all a Happy Christmas, but I sincerely hope to have better news from you soon. You know where to write. Have you heard from my brother yet? Gussie joins with me in sending our fondest love to you all.

Your affectionate sister-in-law,

Augusta

(It is a pity you did not take me up on my suggestion, to leave Joe with me over the winter.)

Wrapped in a square of felt were five gleaming sovereigns.

'Oh my!' Maud breathed reverently. It was a fortune in her eyes.

'Always a sting in the tail!' Rosa remarked wryly, wrapping the coins once more as she re-read the last sentence to herself.

'Joe loves the Island, like we do. He wouldn't want to stay with disapproving old Aunt A in Brixton any more than I would,' Maud said.

'She wouldn't ask *you*,' Nandy jibed.

'Or *you*!' Maud flashed back.

Tilly said: 'She might seem cross, but she really cares for you all. Time for bed, I think. Don't you, Mrs Rosa?'

It was soon decided that Tilly should share with Maud, and sleep in Nandy's bed – he was relegated to the sofa in the parlour, which suited him fine. Tilly suspected he would read by the firelight until the fire died down. Piles of books spilled over in every corner of the room.

Tilly supervised Maud's ablutions. The girl, clad in her chemise, teeth chattering ostentatiously, dipped her flannel perfunctorily in the rose-patterned bowl on the washstand. Then she sat on the edge of her bed to brush out her hair, muttering as she counted the strokes. The brass bedknobs sparkled, the feather mattress was irresistible – Tilly saw her swing her legs up in a sudden excess of fatigue. She covered her over as Maud sank down into the plump softness, her feet wriggling towards the comfort of the flannel-wrapped brick Tilly had placed there. She felt a wave of tenderness for young Maud.

'Go to sleep now, Maud, school in the morning.'

'Oh, I can't go while Joe's so ill – you won't make me, will you, Tilly?' Maud was struggling up again, anxious.

'I won't *make* you do anything, I promise,' Tilly told her. 'But we'll think about it, eh? Goodnight. I'm just going to help your mother now, to settle little Joe for the night.'

'Goodnight, Tilly – I'm glad you came.'

'So am I, Maud. And just turn over if you hear me moving about around midnight, won't you? I'm going to take over from your mother then, so she can get some sleep. She badly needs her rest.'

There would be little rest for Tilly during her first night under the sea wall.

THREE

Tilly was wondering what on earth she could cook up for supper. The doctor was upstairs with Joe and Rosa. Maud had had to be coaxed downstairs from the bedside, and Nandy was due back from school shortly.

There was a knock at the door. Maud flew to open it as usual.

'Tilly, here's Grandma Isabella!' she called.

Tilly had not met Rosa's mother before. She had heard, of course, that Rosa's parents lived not far away; that they worked in one of the big houses at Cheyney. They had a tied cottage. Grandpa William was a retired ship's carpenter. Now he was employed in a maintenance capacity in the house. Grandma was a fine seamstress and was kept busy not only with repairs but with sewing clothes for her mistress. Such was her skill; she cut without a pattern, and could follow the styles in the London magazines.

'This is Tilly, Grandma Isabella,' Maud said breathlessly before Nandy could make the introductions, for he had followed his grandmother in. 'She usually works for Aunt

A, you know, but our need is greater so she's come to help us and nurse Joe.'

'I see the doctor's here,' said Nandy. Dr Box's gig and pony were parked outside the cottage.

'I am glad you have come.' Isabella held out her hand to Tilly. Her accent was scarcely noticeable but she would never have been taken for an Englishwoman, not with those glossy black braids wound elegantly round her head; those sloe eyes and translucent, almost unlined skin. She must be seventy years old, Tilly conjectured, for Rosa at thirty-two was the youngest of seven, the only one still on Sheppey. But to Tilly's admiring eyes Isabella appeared a good ten years younger. What a bright, colourful Spanish shawl she wore round her shoulders against the cold air outside.

'I bring the beef tea for Joe. Mr Arthur gives me the meat to make it for the invalid. It is easy to digest, builds up the strength.'

Tilly knew just how many hours were expended in extracting the juices from beef. 'Thank you, it's just what he needs,' she told Isabella. 'You will stay to see Mrs Rosa and Joe after the doctor has gone, won't you? I am just about to make a pot of tea,' she added, pulling out a chair for Rosa's mother.

Nandy said: 'Anything to eat, Tilly? I'm starving.'

'I also have brought some stew – just to warm up, you know, Tilly.' Isabella brought out the pot from her basket, well wrapped in a cloth. 'I did not know you would be here. I hope you don't mind?'

'Mrs Rosa hasn't been able to go shopping for days. Apart from bacon, potatoes and onions, the cupboard is getting bare,' Tilly answered honestly. 'We'll be very glad of your stew.' She wondered how things were going upstairs.

Now and again Joe's eyes would focus on something, the fuzziness would clear and he would become sharply aware. He stared at a pair of hands with hairy wrists emerging from starched, white cuffs. The long, tapering forefinger of one hand touched lightly on his wrist; the other hand was cupped around a splendid gold watch, steadily ticking, its chain stretched tautly from a checked waistcoat. However, he did not focus on the compassionate, bushy-bearded face of a concerned Dr Box gazing down on him through twinkling gold pince-nez.

Each day of his illness seemed to merge one into the other for Joe. Yet there had been something different about the past hours. Sometimes the dark-haired figure, always beside him, had seemed to change into someone taller with fair hair, but the tender ministrations were the same. Feeling the chink of a spoon against his teeth, he struggled feebly as his head was lifted from his damp pillow. His mouth invariably slackened so that the liquid ran down his neck. Sighing, Rosa or Tilly – how could it possibly be Tilly, for she was at Aunt A's, he thought – would wipe him dry and try again. When the pain in his swollen joints became acute, he was jerked cruelly into consciousness.

Too often he was gently rolled, moaning, right across the bed to the very edge, trying to resist the pull of the under-sheet as it was removed; then he was returned, trembling and exhausted, to the centre of his mother's bed. The clean sheet and blankets were smoothed and tucked in lightly.

'You have some help now, I understand, Mrs Searle?' Dr Box asked. He had been with Rosa when the baby lost its brief struggle for life, and was concerned for Joe's mother too.

'Yes, Miss Reeder. So kind and thoughtful, she is, Doctor. I was almost at the end of my tether.'

Rosa had told Tilly last night of her great faith in her doctor. He was there when typhoid struck, working closely with the volunteer nurses, endeavouring against all odds to save the sickly, undernourished Island children, ask-ing no fee from those who could not pay. Indeed, he often dipped into his own meagre resources to help treat them. Dr Box attended meetings of the Sheppey Board of Guard-ians, pleading eloquently for those of his patients who were applying for relief. He passed no judgement on those men who seemed unwilling to work, or on inadequate young mothers. He believed that a child was a precious gift, whether or not it was born in wedlock. He was perhaps forty years old, but looked sixty, and his patients were una-ware that he was a sick man himself. Dr Box had accepted the fact that he had perhaps five more years to carry on his work, though he did not intend to share this burden with others until it became unbearable. He had never married for as he had said once to Rosa: 'I regard all the children I care for as my family, and my happiness and reward is when one of them recovers against all the odds.'

Downstairs, Dr Box tried to buoy up the spirits of Joe's anxious family. 'A little improvement, I'm sure of it.' He took a gulp of hot, strong tea, passed to him by Tilly in the outsize cup reserved for Rosa's husband when he was at home. There was that gripping pain in his stomach again. The act of swallowing seemed to ease the spasm. 'You make a good cup, my dear,' he said to Tilly. He saw by the look in her eyes that she had guessed his own pain.

Rosa went out to see him off. 'That is a very special young lady you have there,' he said thoughtfully.

'I know,' Rosa told him.

'Maud should go to school again, my dear. She is too wrapped up in her brother's illness – she needs to forget it for a few hours, enjoy being a child again. Could your friend persuade her, do you think?'

'Maud is so stubborn!' Rosa exclaimed. 'But Tilly has such a way with children; I can safely leave it to her.'

FOUR

Five evenings later, Tilly and Rosa sat together by Joe. The candle was burning low in a puddle of wax on a plain white saucer with a handle. The wind insinuated itself through the loose window frames and the sea seemed awesomely close to Tilly.

'It won't come over the sea wall, will it?' she asked anxiously. She suddenly missed, for the first time since she'd come to Sheppey, the familiar noises of Brixton at night: the late omnibuses; the friendly footsteps and callings out in the road outside Augusta's house; the reassuring light from the street lamp, its ornate bracket casting a shadow on her bedroom wall. The attic window was always open because servants were supposed to benefit from fresh air, she thought wryly. More likely to ensure they got up early to get the fires burning and warm the place up in winter! Tilly missed, after all, her narrow iron bedstead and the patchwork quilt which it had taken so long to sew, for she must keep her hands busy in her brief periods of rest. This contained many pretty materials, pieces from Augusta's ragbag.

'It never has yet,' Rosa told her. 'Or not in my time here. Don't worry about it, Tilly! Is that Nandy snoring downstairs? He's taking the opportunity to read until all hours, I believe – he'll addle his brain, let alone ruin his eyes. Goodness knows what he gets up to down there alone in the evenings . . . '

Tilly had discovered crumbs and a rind of cheese down the back of the sofa this morning, but she wouldn't give Nandy away. 'Shall I go and see, Mrs Rosa? I really think you should get into bed tonight, you know. Joe seems so peaceful, not feverish a bit. I'm sure you won't wake him up.'

Rosa appreciated her solicitude. 'I think I will, Tilly. I do feel I *could* sleep tonight, all being well. It's made such a difference, you know, your being here. Even Maud goes off to bed without arguing. And Tilly – how awful of me – I've only just realised that Christmas is almost upon us, and I haven't even given it a thought. My poor children – normally they are so excited but, bless them, there's not been a single reminder.'

Tilly turned at the door. 'Don't you worry, Mrs Rosa, we'll start planning something tomorrow. I'll tell Maud she *must* go back to school and I'll walk her there – Nandy, too, if he'll let me, though he's so independent, isn't he, going on his own since you've been tied at home with Joe – and they can show me all the shops.'

In the morning, when Tilly went to see why Rosa hadn't stirred, she found her still sound asleep, with Joe lying there awake, smiling at her. She knew instantly that the crisis had passed and the fever had left him, and felt choked with tenderness and joy.

'There are four towns in Sheerness, Tilly,' Nandy informed her importantly as they marched smartly along towards the school.

'Not so fast, Nandy, I want to remember my way back,' she told him.

'Marine Town, Banks Town, Mile Town, Blue Town,' Maud chimed in, skipping to keep up with Tilly's long stride. Her new boots were wearing in now, thank goodness, and Tilly had proved a dab hand with the button hook, giving that special little twist which impatient Maud could not master. 'I can't wait to get to school and show Miss Rayner my new navy serge dress. Don't you just love the *huge* sailor collar, Tilly? Isn't it clever of Grandma Isabella to think of that, Petty being a sailor and all?'

'Why do you call your father 'Petty'?' Tilly asked curiously. 'And I've always wondered why your mother permits you to use her christian name?'

'I expect Aunt A has told you how much she disapproves of that, eh?' Maud asked. Tilly nodded, grinning back. 'Well, Nandy started that one off, when he was little, and Rosa says she likes it, especially when Petty is away, 'cause it's nice to hear her own name. As for Petty, that was *my* idea – well, he's not very tall, is he? And Miss Rayner says 'petit' means 'little' in French. Petit homme, you see?'

'Little Man,' Nandy interpreted. 'And he's also a Petty Officer, so it fits.'

Tilly was enjoying the light-hearted banter after the worry over Joe which had clouded all their spirits. 'You said, *Blue* Town, Maud? That's a strange name, isn't it?'

'She's not supposed to talk about Blue Town.' Nandy was peeved with his sister. 'Anyway, I was telling Tilly – not you.'

'Rosa says it's a bit 'unmentionable'.' Maud *would* have the last word.

'That's odd,' Tilly mused, 'four towns within a town – I wonder why?'

'Petty says it's – um – ludicrous to call them towns,' Nandy informed her. 'You can walk round the lot in half an hour. The town's sort of divided according to ranks, that kind of thing.'

They had arrived at Miss Rayner's house, an imposing three-storeyed residence situated on a corner site, surrounded by a small paved courtyard. Tilly immediately recognised the privy, although it was primly shrouded in ivy.

She read the brass plate which seemed to her to need a good old rub: 'Miss Mildred Rayner, High Class School, Music Teacher'. A grey striped cat surveyed them balefully from his place on the front wall.

'He gets put outside while school's on. He doesn't care for children,' said Maud, giving him a sly caress as she passed him which caused his fur to rise.

Nandy let the heavy knocker fall with a bang.

A young maid answered the door. 'Not surprised you came back today, Miss Maud – what with its being the end of term party 'n all,' she said, winking.

Tilly made a quick exit as all the children sat down and began banging their desk lids. Miss Rayner soon had the pointer tapping, and as she opened the front door to leave Tilly heard the old familiar chanting. So they learned the same way in these posh schools, did they? It brought back memories of the board school she had attended, in made-over hand-me-downs. She had not been so much older than Nandy, she thought, when she'd left.

Having left Rosa's orders at the grocer's and butcher's, Tilly made her way to the draper's and spent an enjoyable few minutes staring into the window at the display of stylish clothes.

A haggard woman with wisps of hair escaping an old-fashioned bonnet and a holey shawl knitted in coarse wool dragged an unwilling child along, scolding all the while. Tilly, asking the way to the bookshop, noted with mingled pity and distaste the greenish discharge from the child's nostrils.

However, compassion rose to the fore when she saw the infant's thin legs, mottled with cold. The child was coatless, and it was a raw morning. She merely wore an ancient matted scarf wound inadequately round her narrow chest and tied at her back over a ragged dress. Tilly's own family had been hard up, but they had never looked as poverty-stricken as this pair, she thought, for they were a proud lot.

'Back up that way, love. You from London?'

Tilly nodded reluctantly.

'Thought so. Me, too! Real 'ole this is, I can tell yer. Don't stay any longer than yer 'ave ter!'

Thanking her, Tilly was walking away when she heard the woman call stridently after her: 'Watch aht fer the Navy, love!'

Startled, she cannoned straight into a sailor. A real jolly Jack Tar with bold laughing blue eyes, looking her saucily up and down. To her alarm, she felt a restraining hand on her arm.

'I do beg your pardon, ma'am, I wasn't looking where I was going.'

'That's quite all right,' she answered frostily, pulling free.

She was thankful to find that the bookshop was immediately in front of her for she was only too aware that the sailor was standing staring at her with an amused grin on his handsome face.

And here was the letterbox, too, so she had to pause for a moment to post the letters to Augusta – one from Rosa, thanking Augusta for her thoughtfulness in sending Tilly to her, but saying Joe was not out of the woods yet and she would be grateful if she could stay on a while, and the other from Tilly, hoping that they had arrived in Norfolk safely, and would have a very happy Christmas, promising she'd see them soon. Perhaps Mother could help out when they returned to Brixton?

'You dropped this,' the sailor said, scooping up a little card which had fluttered to the ground when she pulled the letters from her bag.

Tilly accepted it with some confusion. 'Thank you.' Another smile and he turned and walked away.

Tilly glanced at the card. It was the one the man on the train had given her. She had quite forgotten it. 'Heinz Rossel, Sheerness. Family Portraits by Established Photographer,' she read, and put it in her bag again.

A notice in the bow window of the shop proclaimed: 'Special attention given to the selection of books for boys and girls. Also beautiful books for the little ones – for Christmas'. Clutching Rosa's Christmas list, she ventured inside.

Not only were there hundreds of books on display, she saw, but there was a dazzling fancy goods department at the back of the shop containing all sorts, from bookmarks and enamelled boxes, to baubles and beads. A veritable Aladdin's cave.

The proprietress, Mrs Wiggins, was busy with a theatre booking. She looked up with a courteous, 'Good morning, madam,' and motioned the superior-looking male assistant to attend to Tilly's needs.

The chosen books mounted up on the counter. Mrs Wiggins had them all in stock: the latest Wells and Conrad, and fat annuals like *Chatterbox* for the children.

'Delivery this afternoon,' said the assistant, who was really very helpful, Tilly found, and tactful regarding her ignorance of some of the titles. 'Mrs Joseph Searle, did you say? Cheyney? Madam may settle the bill then or later, naturally.'

Tilly felt that she had earned a look at fancy goods. She would be reckless and spend her hoarded wages, all six shillings and threepence. She must buy presents for her new family – she already thought of them as that.

FIVE

On Christmas Eve Tilly carried Joe downstairs, still in his little red flannel nightshirt, and deposited him gently on the sofa in the parlour. Rosa wrapped him round with a puffy eiderdown, Nandy poked the fire to a blaze and Maud flung up the lid of the piano and struck up 'For He's a Jolly Good Fellow!' which they all sang with gusto.

'What's all this?' asked Grandpa William, appearing from the kitchen where he and Grandma Isabella were helping with the preparations for Christmas dinner, for the goose must go in the oven overnight. 'The best bird I've seen in years,' he added, 'and ready dressed, too.'

'Thanks to Augusta,' Rosa said, hovering anxiously near Joe. 'The most *enormous* box was delivered to us this morning, with everything you could possibly want for Christmas – the pudding, cake, mincemeat, fruit and nuts, crackers – and another big parcel, not to be opened until tomorrow.'

'Or else,' Maud put in. But she'd had a good feel round it, naturally.

Tilly thought, pleased: My name was on that parcel, too. 'Rosa, Tilly & Children', the label read.

'Tilly,' Joe whispered, as she bent to put another cushion behind his back, 'don't you just love Grandpa William's bald pate, and the way his beard is like grains of sea salt? Maud thought of that! And his eyes all screwed up from looking out to sea all those years?'

Tilly thought that, indeed, he looked the perfect grandfather, and father, too, the way he fetched in the coal and water every day for Rosa. She remembered ruefully her own grandfather who'd been an old tyrant and drunk away the money her grandmother earned scrubbing.

The mention of the bald head made her eyes prickle. Poor child! Joe's hair was coming out in tufts. She prayed he would not look in the mirror. Both she and Rosa had warned Nandy not to mention his bald patches, or the fact that Joe's face was red and peeling.

Nandy and Maud were now sprawled on the rug, playing with their homemade Happy Family cards.

'Not too much noise, you two,' she cautioned.

'Can I play?' Joe asked. Tilly looked at Rosa.

'If you don't get too excited,' she said.

Tilly went off into the kitchen to join William and Isabella. There were all the vegetables to peel for the morrow. She left the door open so that they could enjoy listening in to the children at play.

'Glad you've decided to talk again,' Maud said to Joe, dealing out the cards casually. 'D'you know, Tilly,' she called, seeing her watching as she sorted the potatoes from the sack, 'Joe didn't talk for *ages* when he had measles – we thought he'd forgotten how to! Then one day he shouted out, ever so loud: 'Rosa, Nandy's pinched my bread and butter!' 'Oh, you've got your tongue back,' she said, 'but you didn't need to yell like that. Nandy, just you give it back.' 'Can't,' said Nandy, 'I've eaten it!' Right, sort your cards out, Joe – can Grandpa come and help him?'

To William's amusement, the local tradesmen were easily recognised, even though they had been renamed. The butcher's wife, with her necklace of 'our world-renowned pork sausages' for instance. 'Silly,' as Maud remarked. 'They'd be 'off' long before they got right round the world, wouldn't they?'

'Shush, Grandpa! Now they'll know I've got *her*!' Joe turned his cards so that William wouldn't see them.

From the kitchen Rosa remarked drily: 'You'd better hide 'Dr Dose', Maud, before Dr Box arrives – I don't think he'd be very flattered at *that* portrait, after all he's done for Joe.'

Tilly loved the way the children were encouraged to express themselves – so different from Augusta's method of bringing up Gussie, she thought – and smiled at Maud's blithe reply: 'Oh, he wouldn't mind, Rosa, I told him I'm useless at drawing.'

Tilly opened the door to Dr Box. He had called to see Joe, to wish them all a Happy Christmas, and to collect the basket of things Rosa had told Tilly they always had ready for him. For, as he had said diffidently on his last visit, when he had pronounced Joe fit enough to come downstairs for a while today: 'I know a poor family who would be very glad of anything you can spare.'

'You are still here then?' He smiled at Tilly.

'Yes. They still need me, don't they?' she asked anxiously, thinking of Gussie in the Norfolk house, with her glum relations.

'They still need you,' he assured her. 'Mrs Searle as much as the children, for she was exhausted when you arrived. She has been through a bad time.'

Rosa had hastily removed her apron, and was wiping floury hands.

'Oh, Doctor, how can we thank you for all you've done for Joe? He's so very much brighter, as you can see.'

'I shan't take all the credit, you know, a loving mother can do more than any doctor – particularly when she has such good parents, and a loyal friend to help. You have a way to go yet, Joe, but the future is looking very hopeful.' Grandpa William made way for Dr Box to sit beside Joe and to take his pulse. 'Now don't sit up too long and get over-tired, young Joe. But you'll feel like eating some supper this evening, eh?'

They all watched as Joe nodded gravely. He was wondering if he would have a watch like Dr Box's when he was old. He thought you would probably have to be rich, too.

'Hello, Ferdinand, I haven't seen much of you – what are you planning to do in the future?' the doctor asked.

'I might become a naval cadet, like my father,' he said.

'I want to go to sea and be a sailor, too,' Joe said. Both Rosa and Tilly felt tears well in their eyes.

'Ah, perhaps not the best thing for you, young fellow. Perhaps you should aim to follow a scholastic bent,' Dr Box advised.

'Well, then, I shall be a doctor like you,' Joe decided out of the blue.

'Why not, indeed? Well, I wish you the best and happiest of days tomorrow, and I will see you, Joe, when the excitement is all over.'

Isabella had surpassed herself, Tilly thought, when the golden-crusted giblet pie was brought to the supper table, gently steaming through the funnel. They anticipated its tasty goodness when further delicious aromas were released as William sliced through the pastry. Even Joe managed some rich gravy with a few mashed vegetables.

'Do sit down, Tilly,' Rosa told her cheerfully, as she rose to collect the scraped clean plates. 'It's Christmas. Think of yourself as one of us – well, you are, after all you've done for us. For Joe. We all lend a hand here. And I think you should call me just Rosa, like my irreverent children do, eh?'

Tilly could only nod in reply. It was enough just to watch them, the family under the sea wall, all happy and pulling together.

After an hour at the table even Nandy rubbed his stomach ruefully and was told briskly by his mother: 'Right! You can wash up. Maud, you can wipe. Dad, please could you make the fires up? Mother, you sit with Joe on the sofa and have a rest. Tilly, *now* you can help me clear the table!'

Nandy dabbled his hands resignedly in the bowl of hot water on the kitchen table, swishing round the knob of soda; Maud flipped the red-bordered linen cloth at him impatiently. 'Don't dawdle, Nandy. The quicker you do it, the quicker we get back to our game.'

'It's cold enough to take your breath away,' William coughed, struggling in from the yard with a huge clanking bucket of shiny coal.

'What time will you need to leave, Dad?' Rosa asked, closing the door behind him. 'I do hope you can stay long enough to see the children hang their stockings up – and to have a bit of a sing-song, first?'

'Mr and Mrs Arthur are calling for us about quarter past eleven to take us to our midnight services. We don't need to go home between times. Mother's brought her best hat!'

Tilly thought that she would like to go to church, but didn't like to say.

Maud told her as she added to a precarious pile of plates: 'They all go to different churches, Tilly. Mr and Mrs Arthur are Anglican, so it's Holy Trinity for them. Grandpa is a Methodist so they'll take him to the chapel first. Grandma is a Catholic so—'

'She goes to the Catholic church, that's obvious, Maud. Look, you've all these spoons to dry up,' Nandy interrupted impatiently.

'I'll put the dishes away,' Tilly offered.

Maud ignored Nandy. 'D'you know, Tilly, *we* go to the nearest church to wherever we're living at the time – Rosa says it really doesn't matter where we go, so long as we *do* go sometimes. We've been to some really old churches, to some new ones and once to a hut in the middle of a field with a tin roof – you couldn't hear the sermon for the rain rattling on it.'

'That was a blessing in disguise,' Rosa said, as she took away the wet teacloth and found Maud a fresh one from the table drawer.

'Is Holy Trinity an old church?' Tilly asked.

Grandpa William had the answer. 'About sixty years, I reckon. You see, Tilly, Sheerness itself only dates from Charles II's time. He planned the naval dockyard and the fortifications. You should go to the Abbey for the feel of something really ancient.'

'Finished!' Nandy announced. He snatched at the end of Maud's cloth, and to her indignation, dried his hands on it.

'Grandma says she'll play for us,' Rosa told the children. 'There's all that new sheet music we had from Glaysher's last Christmas and never got around to playing – Maud, tell her to look in the piano stool.'

Maud went with alacrity.

'D'you think I should put Joe back up to bed now, Tilly?' Rosa asked.

'Well, Rosa, it does seem a shame for him to miss all the company, doesn't it, and the singing? If he falls asleep, we can just carry him up and ease him into bed.'

'You don't suppose all this excitement will harm him?' It seemed natural somehow to Rosa to ask Tilly's advice.

Tilly was pleased and flattered. 'No, I'm sure it can only do him good, Rosa. He's got some colour back in his cheeks – I noticed when they were playing cards. Just so long as he's not running around . . . '

They divested themselves of their aprons and joined the family gathering in the parlour.

'My Bonnie Lies Over the Ocean!' Maud always shouted, Tilly noticed, when she was excited. ''Specially for you, Rosa – to remind you of Petty.'

It occurred to Tilly then how much Rosa must be missing her husband now it was Christmas.

After the first verse, she said abruptly: 'Let's sing something more cheerful. And some carols, of course.'

Isabella struck up 'Home, Sweet Home'. Her touch was soft and true. Perhaps Tilly should have been reminded of Brixton, but right now *this* seemed the perfect family home, despite its drawbacks. She didn't even think of the sea, so close at hand.

Later, Tilly and Rosa lay awake until they were positive that the children were sleeping soundly then together crept, shivering in their night attire, round the stockings with the oranges to poke into the toes, the gleaming new pennies and the small gifts. They had already piled up the larger Christmas parcels on top of the piano for after-breakfast distribution.

Tilly's stocking, of course, remained empty. It was midnight.

Rosa said: 'I like to say a little prayer now, Tilly. Will you join me?' They knelt by the big bed. In turn they said a few, whispered words. Thanks for young Joe's being spared, and being able to enjoy this Christmas; blessings for Isabella and William; Rosa made a fleeting, sad reference to that little baby who would never be a part of the family; Tilly prayed for her own family, and for Augusta and Gussie; Rosa said thank you for Augusta's generosity, and wished she might be able to feel more fondly towards her, and a blessing for her fatherless niece. She ended with a request that her husband might be safely returned to her. Tilly said 'Amen' to that. Then they wished one another a Happy Christmas.

Between them, they lifted Nandy into Rosa's bed. 'It's not fair he should sleep downstairs alone tonight,' they said.

Tilly had felt lonely enough reclining on the settee until Rosa had softly called that it was time to make the rounds. Nandy had fallen asleep on his own bed earlier while chatting to Maud. Tilly felt strongly that families should be close at night.

She was soon asleep. Rosa made the effort to keep awake for who else would fill the stocking which Maud had insisted Tilly must hang on her bedpost?

SIX

Christmas morning, 1894. Maud, naturally, was the first one awake. She was curled so snugly in the hollow of her mattress that for a moment she was actually reluctant to make the scrambling dive to the end of the bed to feel for her stocking. Reaching out to Tilly in the adjoining bed, she inadvertently struck her on her nose.

Tilly was surprisingly indignant. 'Oh, do go back to sleep, Maud, it's still pitch black.' She rubbed at the sore place. For a moment she had believed herself to be back in her old home, sharing a bed with her two sisters, where a dig in the ribs from an elbow, as one or other tried to turn, or a scrape from overgrown toenails on a tender shin, was a constant irritation. Only the little-sister-in-the-middle was guaranteed her share of the meagre bedclothes, supplemented by dear Father's shabby overcoat in the freezing weather. There was always a surly struggle between the flanking sisters to grab a little warmth, Tilly remembered all too well.

'Sorry about your nose, I didn't mean to do it, honestly, but don't you remember what day it is?' Maud whispered plaintively. 'What you're *supposed* to say . . . '

'Merry Christmas, Maud!' came the muffled reply, Tilly having buried her head under the eiderdown.

'Merry Christmas, Tilly – that's better! *Please* will you light the candle?' Maud wheedled.

Resigned, Tilly groped for the matches, sighing: 'Satisfied? Now don't you *dare* make much noise. Joe must sleep on, you know, for as long as he can.'

Something landed on her chest as she slid down into her cosy bed again. 'There's *your* stocking, Tilly!'

How could she resist that? Soon the bedroom was odorous with peeled oranges and the stocking fillers were exclaimed over and enjoyed. Tilly was as pleased with the contents of Maud's stocking as with her own. Maud had a jerking monkey-on-a-stick and a tiny Dutch dolly with jointed arms and legs. Tilly thought that the painted face, the black eyes, red cheeks and black hair cut with a square fringe, was a perfect match for the glowing little face of Maud in the next bed.

Tilly stroked her red velvet pin cushion, and unrolled, much to her pleasure, the Christmas edition of her favourite magazine, *Forget-Me-Not*. Like Maud, she slipped her new penny under her pillow, and took a surreptitious bite of her sticky sugar mouse. Tilly wound the string tail round her finger into a curl.

In the other bedroom she heard Nandy nipping out of bed to use the chamber pot. 'Nandy's up,' Tilly told Maud. 'Put on your wrapper, and your slippers. Rosa said we could go in to see them when we heard moving about!'

They saw Nandy over at the window: the glass was iced over and he scratched at it ineffectually, but still couldn't see out. Tilly motioned Maud to wait while Nandy too lit the candle on the washstand and carried it over to the cane bedside table. 'Better be sure the others are awake,' she whispered to Maud.

Then she saw Joe's eyes, which seemed even darker since his illness, regarding them curiously. He wore a red night-cap, hastily concocted by Isabella yesterday evening to prevent the distribution of his remaining hair over the pillow. Rosa stirred uneasily. The boys had been restless bedfellows.

Nandy broke the spell. 'Happy Christmas, Joe and Rosa,' he sang out exuberantly. 'And here's old Maud and Tilly come to see what *we've* got!'

'Come under the quilt, at the bottom of the bed,' Rosa yawned, doubling her pillow behind her head. Tilly did so, but Maud pushed in next to Joe.

Nandy doled out the knobbly stockings – he had hidden one under his pillow, for his mother, which accounted for some of the restlessness.

Tilly watched, entranced and smiling, as the family squealed with excitement over the familiar trivia. Joe, she saw, had a stick monkey too, and a spinning top with a whip . . .

'You'll have to try that out on the kitchen floor, as you're not allowed outside,' Nandy told him bossily.

Joe licked his mouse and sent his monkey tumbling into a somersault.

Nandy was puzzled by a small thick square shape. Unwrapping it, he discovered a minute leather-covered dictionary with gold-edged pages. The next gift proved the means of deciphering same: a magnifying glass. Nandy promptly applied this to the back of Rosa's neck.

'That's strange. When I look at Rosa's mole through here, I can see a long stiff black hair protruding – sticking out, to ignoramuses like you, Joe. Yet when I look normally –'

Like Maud and Joe, Tilly shook with laughter. This had the desired effect. Rosa shot out of bed, reaching for her old flannel robe.

'I might have known it would be a mistake to give you *that*, Nandy.' But she really didn't sound *too* cross. She padded over to the door.

Tilly hurried after her. While Rosa opened up the damper on the range and basted the goose, she raked out the parlour fire, laid and relit it.

By half-past seven, breakfast was ready, the children had washed after a fashion, Nandy had filled the water jars and Tilly had emptied the slops. At least she didn't have to do that at Augusta's – ah, well, never mind.

'Tide's out!' she reported, having mounted the steps in the wall for a fearful look at the sea. The beach had been utterly deserted.

The porridge, mixed by Tilly last night, thick and slippery, had been standing on the stove for hours in its big, double pot. Tilly gave it a vigorous stir and brought it up to the boil once more. Porridge bubbling in the pot: was there anything more satisfying first thing, she thought? But on such a special day there were soft-yolked eggs, too, brought out from the isinglass bucket where they had been preserved when William's hens were laying well. Tilly packed the china rack with crisp golden toast and put Isabella's tangy coarse-cut marmalade and a dish of pale yellow butter, hard as a rock, on the table.

Sitting down with them all, Tilly really did feel just like one of the family. In Brixton, she usually ate her breakfast in the kitchen after serving Augusta and Gussie in the dining room. They had a more elaborate breakfast, of course, starting with grilled kippers, then scrambled eggs and bacon, toast and honey. Sometimes Augusta had cheese between the courses, and there was always fruit on the table. But this simple cottage breakfast tasted like nectar to Tilly on Christmas morning.

Hearing a clatter on the front doorstep, Rosa exclaimed: 'Oh, that'll be the milk. Tilly, would you be kind enough to take that other jug out to Mr Relf? We'll need extra today.'

Opening the door still in her robc, not realising it revealed the cleft of her bosom, hair tumbling untidily around her shoulders, Tilly came face to face with a young man. Despite the muffler wound round his lower jaw against the bitter cold, she recognised him immediately. This was the sailor she had bumped into on her shopping expedition. To her exasperation, he had often been in her thoughts since.

Disarmingly, he came straight to the point: 'You saved me the trouble of knocking and making some excuse! I *thought* you must be staying here, so I volunteered to help with the Christmas milk round. Oh, and . . . ' he felt in his pocket ' . . . I am not the only one making enquiries about your whereabouts, it seems. I was given this for you.' He handed an envelope to Tilly. 'For the Young Lady on the Train', was written in a bold, flowing hand.

In turn, she presented him with the jugs. 'One extra today, please,' she said.

'Oh, is that you, Oswald?' Rosa called from the parlour. 'How nice to see you again.'

'It is, Mrs Searle. Nice to see you, too. Happy Christmas!'

Rosa came up beside Tilly who was still standing there, the envelope in her hand. She glanced quizzically at Tilly's flaming cheeks.

'Happy Christmas, Oswald! Do come in to warm-up. Would you like a quick cup of tea? Your father's not ill, I hope?'

'Oh, no.' Oswald replaced the small churn and dipper on the handcart. 'I'd love the cup that cheers, I must say.'

He followed them indoors, skilfully balancing the brimming jugs.

'Where would you like these, Mrs Searle – on the table?'

Tilly was rather surprised that Rosa had asked this young man in when they were not properly dressed. She did not realise that the Relfs were the Searles' oldest friends in Cheyney, and that Rosa had known Oswald since he was Nandy's age. Anyway, she was not one to stand on ceremony.

'What's that, a Christmas card, Tilly?' Maud asked curiously. All eyes were on her when she opened it shyly. It was a colourful card with an embossed Christmas tree, bright with candles and coloured glass balls. Inside was a brief message: 'Wishing You a Happy Christmas on London clay. Heinz Rossel'.

'Tilly's got a suitor!' Maud chortled. 'Old Mr Lozenge, the German photographer! We call him that, Tilly, because he always offers us sweets, and Rosa doesn't mind us taking lozenges from *him* 'cause he's most respectable, you see, and we always have our portraits taken each year in his studio – but what does London clay mean?'

'Tilly doesn't have to explain to you,' Rosa reproved her daughter. But naturally she was intrigued, too.

'I met him on the train. I didn't think it was important enough to tell you,' Tilly said, and put the card up on the mantelpiece with all the others Rosa had received.

Oswald pulled up a chair and hardly needed persuading to have a slice of toast and marmalade with his tea. 'I had some bread and dripping, but that seems rather a long time ago!' He took a large, hungry bite.

Tilly concentrated on her egg. It was difficult, with him beside her.

'Christmas leave, Oswald? You're very fortunate. Mr Searle hasn't been home for Christmas in four years,' Rosa told him ruefully.

'I am indeed, Mrs Searle,' Oswald beamed. He needed a shave, Tilly thought. He was disturbingly close to her, and had hardly shifted his gaze from her face.

'Petty got Oswald into the Navy,' Maud informed her. 'He didn't want to be a farmer like his father, you see. You know those cows in the fields opposite here? The ones you were afraid of when they poked their heads over the gate at you? Well, they all belong to Oswald's father.'

'I did suppose that was where our milk came from,' Tilly replied.

'I'm still out in all weathers, slaving away, slipping in the water on the decks instead of the mud in the fields, so it's not as different as I thought it would be.' Oswald had an engaging laugh, unconsciously lifting his chin so that his Adam's apple seemed to bob up and down like the stick monkey, much to Joe's dreamy fascination. Tilly couldn't help looking, too.

Rosa exclaimed: 'D'you know, Oswald, I haven't introduced you to Tilly properly – that was remiss of me.'

'Tilly – that's all I need to know!' he put in quickly. 'Sorry to hear the little lad's been so poorly,' he added, winking at Joe, who tried in vain to return the signal.

'Had enough breakfast, Joe?' Tilly asked, in an excuse to move from Oswald's proximity. 'Don't you think he ought to go on the sofa now, Rosa?'

She caught the beseeching glance. 'That's a good idea, Tilly.'

'Let me carry you, eh, Joe?' offered Oswald. He pretended to stagger as he lifted Joe. The little boy's giggles were a tonic for all to hear. He's good with children, Tilly thought, as she followed them.

'There! Drink plenty of our milk, *that'll* see you right. Well, I'd best get on, it looks as if we might have some snow later on.'

Tilly found herself seeing him out. 'Goodbye, Tilly, I hope to see you again soon – I'm sure our paths will cross, like they did in town, and I mustn't let the grass grow under my feet or old Mr Lozenge will beat me to it, eh?'

Despite herself, she smiled at him. He put out a finger and lightly touched her warm cheek. 'Keep the fires burning, Tilly . . . '

And he went off, pushing his cart and whistling cheerfully whistling.

The children were excited at the prospect of snow, but Rosa and Tilly exchanged apprehensive glances.

Isabella and William had indeed encountered the first flurries of snow when they arrived around ten o'clock. 'I don't reckon it'll lay,' William said comfortingly, wiping his bare head. 'More likely it'll turn to rain.'

'Oh, Grandma, I just love the dress you made me – tartan's all the fashion! You are clever!' Maud flung her arms round Isabella and they hugged each other.

Tilly watched discreetly in the background as Rosa unwrapped her parcel from her parents. 'Gloves! Oh, and what fine, soft leather ones too – and they're long, all the way to the elbow, and with these pretty pearl buttons.' She couldn't wait to show off the peacock-blue silk kimono which had been her husband's gift to her. Tilly thought, as Rosa slipped it over her dress, that she looked quite oriental with that sleek hair and her hands tucked demurely into the wide sleeves. How wonderful it must be to receive such a gift, expressing love.

Joe looked hopefully at the bulge in William's pocket, and was not disappointed. 'I wondered where your present was, Grandpa!' he said candidly.

He was handed a lively little kitten which had been snuggled sleepily in the poacher's pouch, but had woken immediately on arrival. It still possessed baby-blue eyes, was black with a white bib and splodges on its nose and paws, and had a thin, kinked tail.

Joe could hardly believe his luck, even though the kitten sprang, claws unsheathed, straight from his arms to skitter in a panic on the floor and then hide under the piano stool.

'Let him make friends with you in his own good time,' William counselled Joe.

'I'll call him Tid,' Joe decided. The name just came to him out of the blue. 'You can share him, Maud – and Nandy – but he's *my* cat, remember!'

'I hope I've done the right thing, Father, letting you persuade me into this. You know I'm not over enamoured of animals. He'd better be house-trained. If not, it's bucket and mop for you today, my old dad – Christmas or no Christmas!' joked Rosa.

Tilly was pleased for Joe. She'd often thought how nice it would be for Gussie to have a pet of her own, but Augusta said no, because she was prone to asthma like her late father.

They hadn't forgotten Tilly either, and she was thrilled to find the length of mauve silk in her parcel. All her small gifts were warmly appreciated, too.

'And just look what Aunt A sent for Joe.' Maud had to be officious and show them. The minute violin was duly admired. But it was obvious to Tilly that right now Joe was more interested in his kitten. Time enough to become a musician, she thought. Augusta always bought the children presents with a purpose.

The table was laid with Rosa's wedding silver, cleaned with a will by Tilly and Nandy. Tilly had smoothed with pleasure, as if it were her own, the fine damask tablecloth with napkins to match.

William ceremoniously carved the goose: white meat for the ladies, extra for the 'men', a leg for William and a wing for Nandy. Tilly had only ever had the stronger meat served up to her by Augusta's brother Harold at the Norfolk Christmas dinner, not being considered a lady there. Vegetables were piled on the plates. They drank Stone's ginger wine in deference to William's staunch tee-totalism. But to the children and Tilly the pudding was the high spot. Each generous dark fruity portion had a silver threepenny piece, craftily palmed by William (this being a bought pudding, courtesy of Augusta). Rosa normally boiled the coins in her own puddings. They all topped their pudding with custard and cream. Only Nandy could manage a second helping.

'That boy will need a good dose of Mother Seigal's syrup!' Rosa said with feeling. This was a remedy to be feared, indeed – enough to scour your insides out.

The washing up was not tackled with much enthusiasm. The adults then settled down and closed their eyes, Tilly included (which had never been her privilege before, she thought). 'Just for a minute or two, don't worry, we'll *know* if you get up to any mischief.' Joe was taken, not protesting overmuch, to bed for an afternoon rest.

Maud and Nandy happily turned the pages of their new books with their stockinged feet stretched out towards the fire. Sheer bliss, even if the penalty was the inevitable itching chilblains that would follow.

Earlier, Tid had crept out from his hiding place, tentatively tasted a saucerful of rich scraps, arched his back as Tilly approached him, jug in hand, then dipped his whiskery face into some milk. Now, daringly, he insinuated himself between those twitching toes and the glowing coals.

And Tilly dreamed of a hand lightly caressing her cheek, and eyes as blue as that patch of sky on a cloudy day which is said to be big enough to make a pair of bell-bottoms for a sailor boy.

SEVEN

Despite the threat of a white Christmas, the following weeks were more dispiriting than cold. 'Wet, wild and windy,' as Maud wrote to Petty. Just when spring seemed set to burgeon, and Tilly was feeling guilty about staying on because Joe was so much stronger, a letter arrived for her from Augusta, asking 'when she would deign to return?' Then, the weather worsened dramatically. Perhaps it was just as well that they did not realise that there were many hard, ice-bound days ahead of them.

Rosa had received a missive from Augusta too: reading between the lines, she was on the point of reluctantly parting from Tilly. She had no real excuse for keeping her now, and it wasn't really fair as Augusta was meticulous about sending Tilly her money. Thank goodness a fine fuzz of new hair was sprouting on Joe's head, and the 'organ grinder's monkey' look, which Nandy had thoughtlessly mentioned – especially apt when Joe wore his little cap at a rakish angle – was diminishing rapidly. Joe was well, and Tilly must go back to Brixton.

'We'll see you in the summer, Tilly, when Augusta says she'll bring Gussie for a month here by the sea. She's considering coming by steamer as a treat and a new experience for Gussie,' Rosa said by way of compensation.

'Things won't be the same, Rosa,' Tilly said flatly. There was no answer to give to that. Tilly was more than contented with her new family, and the affection was reciprocated.

After her initial suspicions of his intentions, she had begun to look forward to Oswald's calls, and to long innocent walks with him, along the sea wall, or to the shops for window gazing. She had even permitted him to hold her hand occasionally. To her embarrassment, the first time this happened they had met up with Mr Lozenge, who had expressed his delight at seeing her again, and suggested that she might like to have her picture taken in his studio: 'For your young man, to take back with him to sea.' Tilly couldn't bring herself to say: 'We are just friends – he's not really my young man,' for Oswald had given her hand a delighted squeeze.

Soon this would all be over, she thought. For Oswald would be sailing away in a few days' time, and it could be three years before they met again.

They stood, shadows in the dusk, on the sea wall above the cottage. 'You'll write to me?' he asked, his breath warming her cold face as she held on to her hat, wishing she'd stuck her new pin in it and gazing apprehensively at the boisterous waves bouncing off the wall.

'Oh, Oswald, I'm *so* afraid of the sea,' she cried impulsively. 'I do wish you didn't have to go. Yes, I'll write, but I warn you, my spelling is not good – but I read just as much here as I did at Mrs Augusta's. Both she and Rosa want me to complete my education.' She was determined to emulate Rosa, who was also self-taught, but Tilly didn't think she was nearly as bright as her friend.

'Then I'll write long letters to you, Tilly. It'll keep me out of mischief!' He slipped his arm daringly round her waist and drew her close. For once she did not stiffen and pull away. He wondered why she was so nervous. Perhaps some rough lad had overstepped the mark. Oswald had never even kissed her, and soon it would be too late. Tilly looked at him, breathing fast. She saw, even in the gloom, that his face was full of longing and love. 'Oh, Tilly, it'll seem like a lifetime!' She pressed her face against the warmth of his chest, avoiding his lips. He kissed instead the golden knot of hair at the nape of her neck. How she was trembling! Their parting would seem like a lifetime to Tilly, too.

Tilly attempted to open the back door, but it refused to budge. 'Rosa!' she shouted in a panic.

The sea had leapt in a frenzy clean over the wall in the night and had frozen right up to the top of the door. It was impossible to clear the window to see out – not that she wanted to do so, really. It was still snowing relentlessly, as it had the entire night, and there was an eerie silence.

The water pipe, she suspected, would refuse to yield a solitary drip of water. She checked the contents of the water jars. Only one was full. Some sixth sense, however, must have made her decide to venture out into the freezing yard last night, despite Rosa telling her not to bother or she'd catch her death of cold, when she'd hauled in several sacks of coal. They didn't expect William to carry on with this task now that things were back to normal with Joe. The big scuttle by the parlour fire was full too she noted, thank goodness. Nandy had seen to that.

During the night they had all ended up in the big bed together, terrified that the sea would swamp the house, but at some unearthly hour its raging had finally died down and the snow had begun to fall in earnest. Now, at six o'clock or thereabouts, the others still lay in an exhausted sleep and Tilly felt that she must try to get a grip on herself, count her blessings. After all, they had survived the night.

Rosa appeared, yawning widely. 'What's up, Tilly?' Then she realised. Seeing the fear in Tilly's eyes, she told her: 'Don't worry, Dad will be along later if it's humanly possible. What a pity that Oswald isn't around, but thank goodness *you* are, Tilly!'

'I was going home tomorrow ... ' she said helplessly. Now Augusta would be really incensed. She had delayed her departure still further, to be with Oswald to the end of his leave. Rosa had covered for her by writing to Augusta to say Tilly had a bad cold and didn't want to pass it on to Gussie. Augusta had a fear of infection.

'We've come to rely on you so much,' Rosa said soothingly. 'Come on, let's make a pot of tea then check the larder in case this freeze lasts a day or two.'

'We're well stocked up,' Tilly told her. 'Surely this weather can't last long, as it has come so late in the winter?'

She bent over the small wooden barrel to check the level of the flour. 'Oh dear, it's less than half-full!' she exclaimed. 'But water's going to be the biggest problem. We'll all have to share a bowl this morning.'

She and Rosa had to lean heavily on the front door before they could shove it open, for the snow had obliterated the steps. Without thinking, Tilly grasped the door jamb, and to her shocked surprise her fingers seemed glued to it. She hastily pulled her hand free of the ice, sucking at it until she felt her fingers tingling. She bit her lip. She could easily have lost some skin!

It was strangely light outside, dazzling in fact: a cover of untrodden white stretched endlessly over the road and fields beyond. The cottages further along, some distance away, wore thick caps of snow; bluish smoke from a chimney drifted lazily in their direction. Myriad icicles hung down from their own roof, dangerously sharp and pointed. Tilly whacked at them furiously with her broom, whilst resolutely cleaning the top step. Her breath was coming in painful, searing gulps; the cold seemed to pierce her lungs. She closed the door firmly and leaned, panting, on the broom. She gave herself a mental shake. There were the children to think of, particularly impressionable Maud. She mustn't show fear to them.

Tilly held a sheet of paper to draw up the parlour fire. She felt so chilled that she was wearing Maud's tam o'shanter and woolly gloves. She just caught the paper before it scorched, crumpling it and adding it to the sudden blaze. The leaping flames cheered her up.

'Careful, Tilly,' Rosa cautioned. 'We can't cope with a chimney fire as well.'

'What about the kitten, Rosa? He ought to go out.'

'Well, he obviously can't today. One step out, and he'd disappear!'

'Let's put the ash box in the corner of the kitchen and show him that.'

Tilly knew just where the kitten was hiding – under the covers – for the children had been told to stay warm in bed.

Tid was most indignant at being plucked from his cosy hideaway and refused to utilise the ash box. Tilly was scratched as she firmly deposited him again. She admonished him: 'You just dare to make a puddle – or worse! – and you *will* be put outside, snow or no snow!'

Nandy, when Tilly informed him of the necessity for sharing washing water, said cheerfully: 'I won't bother to wash at all.'

'Good,' Maud approved. 'I wouldn't fancy washing after you, anyway.'

'You are *all* going to wash – youngest first,' Tilly said firmly. 'Take that blanket off your face, Joe. Maud, kindly come to the surface immediately!'

'You've more patience than I have.' Rosa sighed. 'You'd make a wonderful mother, Tilly, and I can think of some-one who'd make you a good husband – and *he's* got a way with children, too.'

Tilly said abruptly: 'I don't imagine I'll ever marry, Rosa. I'm happy as I am.' There was something she would never forget. After all these years, the pain was still buried deep within her.

It was two days before the soldiers appeared with their stout shovels, and a sergeant pounded on their door: 'Everyone alive and kickin' in 'ere?'

Tilly opened the door to him thankfully. It was a heart-warming sight: at least a dozen burly men digging vigor-ously, and a long stretch of cleared road behind them.

The sergeant, she noted, was in need of a good wash and shave, with eyes reddened from lack of sleep, but he was cheerful and reassuring.

'The water cart will be round soon; the train tank's arrived from Sittingbourne. We cleared the line last night, but rations will be strictly limited. Are you in urgent need of any commodity, ma'am?'

'I'll ask Mrs Searle,' Tilly said, and sent Joe, who was hanging onto her skirts, to fetch Rosa from the kitchen.

'Grub? Coal?' the sergeant asked Rosa.

'We can't get at the coal, can we, Tilly?' Rosa said. 'It's frozen solid in the yard. We can't open the back door, either. But we had some coal in, and we've been very careful with it – we've wood and rubbish we can burn, too.'

'Food's not too bad,' Tilly added, 'and the milk came today. We've been drinking that instead of tea. Mr Relf's been melting down chunks of ice for the cows . . .'

'How long d'you think it will last – this weather?' Rosa asked anxiously.

'The sea's like a great stretch of glass,' Maud butted in.

'Yes, lass,' the sergeant agreed. 'Some folks were daft enough to venture across it this morning as far as the Nore light, despite the warnings. I can trust you ladies not to follow their example, can't I?' He grinned. 'Well, we'll be along again tomorrow. Now don't you get cold standing on the doorstep – good day to you all!' he said, and gave a smart salute.

'Goodbye, Sergeant, and thank you!' they chorused.

William arrived at last, at the same time as the water cart. They were allowed just one jarful. 'Sorry – fair shares for all! We'll be around in a couple of days, if you're lucky,' William said as he carried it in.

Grandpa had a rabbit in one capacious pocket, half-a-dozen eggs carefully wrapped in torn layers of newspaper in the other. Maud and Nandy rushed to greet him with hugs as he stood by the door stamping his feet – which were clothed in short, stout leather boots – to remove the snow and warm his toes.

'Your nose has a drip coming off it, Grandpa,' Joe observed, from his cocoon on the sofa. He was having his rest by the fire. Rosa shook her head at her cheeky son.

'I'm not surprised.' William smiled. 'Rabbit stew for dinner today, I reckon – poor little blighter died of the cold right by my shed. Trying to get some shelter, I suppose. Here you are, Tilly, you know how to deal with it, I reckon?'

'Ugh!' Maud was squeamish. Tilly had no such qualms.

'I do,' she said firmly, taking up the offering. She laid it on the kitchen table on newspaper and took up a sharp knife.

'I shan't eat any. I couldn't!' Maud gulped, but watched round the door all the same. Nandy watched too, scoffing at his sister.

'Grandpa?'

'Yes, young Joe?' Like the rest of them, Grandpa William always looked indulgently on Joe.

'When I take my trousers off at night, Tid jumps straight into them to keep warm.' Hearing his name, Tid's ruffled head appeared through the vee-neck of Joe's pullover.

'Clever cat, that,' William approved. He tickled Tid under the chin.

'Rosa won't let me have him in bed with me.'

'Just like her mother,' William twinkled back at Joe. 'Isabella thinks of all the fleas. Now, *my* mother used to turn a blind eye to my little Jack Russell when I was a boy in Cornwall. That was before I joined the Queen's Navee, brought a bride back from sunny Spain and settled here on the Island. My little dog slept with me every night, his head on the pillow alongside mine.'

'Did you have more hair then, Grandpa?'

'Well, more on my head, lad. Not a whisker on my chin. Talking of rabbits, my old Jack was a champion catcher – rats, too. That's how he met his end – one turned on him, bit him and he died of blood poisoning. Filthy things, rats!'

'Oh, Grandpa, do stop it, you're making me feel really ill – Tilly, too, with what *she's* doing . . .'

'Stop looking then,' Tilly told Maud.

'I can't!'

'Don't stop, Grandpa, I like your stories!' Joe said.

'Better get back, I think. It'll take me some time; the road's like iron.'

The family under the sea wall looked forward to his next visit. He was a great one for cheering them all up.

'You have to agree, Maud, that rabbit stew smells good?' said Tilly later, ladling it out on to their plates.

They were hemmed in now between two walls: the sea wall and the promenade at the rear, awash with frozen waves, receiving a meringue topping of pure white from further heavy snowfalls. If they had been able to force open the bow bedroom window to see out, they would have had the uncanny impression that they could step straight out and walk across this deceptive crust towards the blinking lights of the Nore.

The second wall was man-made. Opposite the cottage was a great, uneven heap of grubby clods of snow, perhaps ten feet high in places, added to spasmodically after each fresh fall of snow by the military stalwarts who kept the narrow track to town cleared.

'D'you think there could be an avalanche?' Nandy enquired nonchalantly.

More likely a flood when the thaw finally comes, Tilly thought inwardly.

Rosa said merely: 'Don't be so silly.'

It was still impossible to gain access to the backyard. Not only was the coal tantalisingly near yet unobtainable, but the privy, not usually a favourite haunt, was also out of bounds. The box was ritually scrubbed weekly with the hot copper water after washday, and its three holes, varying in size – choose the right one or you'll fall in, as Maud always imagined – with strong-smelling pink carbolic powder. Now it seemed an inaccessible haven. They couldn't reach the wash-house, either. The emptying of the slops was not now limited to early morning. There was the added necessity of using a covered pail in a corner of the kitchen during the day.

Tilly found a practical solution: taking up a spade, she cleared a space alongside the outside chimney wall and placed the big tin tub there, liberally doused with Lysol. Slops were emptied as necessary, and a rough cover improvised from a plank of wood. Despite the faint warmth from the house wall, the contents continually iced over, which Tilly thought just as well.

'I'll *never, ever* have a bath in that tub again, Tilly!' Maud said vehemently.

Sittingbourne was experiencing a water shortage of its own, in common with the rest of the county – the country even. The water cart came rarely as the weeks went by with no sign of a thaw. The jar water was strictly for drinking. Tilly and Nandy collected fresh snow in buckets, melting it down on the range. The kettles were filled from this supply, and Tilly hoped that the boiling of this murky water would annihilate germs. Augusta's teaching had certainly rubbed off on Tilly.

Only essential clothes were washed and these items became very grey. Beds remained unchanged. At night they removed top garments only, retaining layers of underwear and stockings. Nightclothes were unwrapped hastily from the bed bricks and they added mittens and scarves on top.

'We should have greased ourselves with the goose fat, instead of making pastry with it,' was Tilly's feeble joke.

There was no flour left for baking bread. They were more than grateful for the side of smoked streaky bacon which hung, diminishing daily, from the hook in the kitchen, and for the sacks of potatoes and strings of onions which were the basis of every meal.

'I hardly tasted meat when I was a child,' Tilly said to Maud. 'Some bones from the butcher, if you were lucky, with a bit of flesh left on, boiled up with vegetables we children fetched from the market at the end of the day. They often gave them away, then. Mum used to bring home stale bread from work and other scraps.'

The milk delivery ceased. Supplies would have to be fetched from the farm gates.

'That's something I can do,' Tilly volunteered. 'Nandy'll help me, won't you?'

He had been quarrelling with his sister since first thing, Maud was sulking and poor Joe was reduced to talking to the kitten. 'I suppose so,' he said ungraciously.

'Shall we go on down to see why Mr Barry hasn't been, Rosa? We could collect the milk on the way back.'

'Perhaps you'd better not,' Rosa said, 'the road may be blocked further along. I'm sure that's the reason we haven't seen him since he brought the rabbit. You don't want to end up in a drift now, do you?'

So it was Grandpa William's employer, riding over on his hunter the next day, who imparted the bad news that William had fallen on the path to his cottage, had a suspected broken collar bone and dislocated shoulder, which the old groom, a bit of a horse doctor, had managed to put back in its socket.

'I'm going to town now; I'll ask Dr Box to look in on him as soon as possible. Don't worry, we'll look after him,' Mr Arthur said kindly.

Across his saddle was a bulky sack, stuffed with chopped firewood. Also a huge wad of old newspapers, tied with string.

'To keep the home fires burning, eh? The sergeant brought us our backlog of newspapers from the station on his last visit. There'll be more later in the week. Are you in dire need of anything?'

'Candles,' Tilly reminded Rosa.

'Sugar. And flour most of all,' Rosa added.

As he left, Mr Arthur gave her a letter from her mother. They watched as the big horse picked its way carefully along the icy ruts.

Dear Daughter,

Mr Arthur will tell you about Father. He is not in too much pain. He sends his love. As do I. It is good you have Tilly to uphold you all. The roots in the shed have been eaten by rats.

Kisses for the children.

My love,

Mother

Tilly gave Rosa's arm a comforting squeeze as she saw her friend compressing her lips and blinking rapidly.

The children sat down to write to their grandparents. Maud's script was abysmal. 'Maud!' Miss Rayner would often sigh reproachfully. 'You really mustn't allow your pen to run away with you!' She couldn't explain to her teacher just why she couldn't keep up with her thoughts. Joe hoped that Tid would sit still long enough to enable him to draw him, but as if reading his mind, the cat began his cleaning-behind-the-ears routine.

With such unexpected quiet, Tilly requested paper and ink from Rosa and began a letter to Oswald. She wouldn't be able to post it yet, she thought, but she could tell him all about the Big Freeze, how she was still here, in the cottage under the sea wall, and that she missed him.

It was the middle of March, and Joe's fifth birthday. Conditions were still severe, but not deteriorating. There was only one scattered snow shower and the daily diversion on the Island was the excitement of skating as parties of youngsters, supremely confident that the ice would not crack, glided across to the Nore light, and later skated boisterously back.

Mr Arthur's generous gift of flour enabled Tilly to bake a birthday cake for Joe, albeit a rather flat, leaden sponge because the temperature of the range fluctuated so, now that she was unable to stoke it regularly.

'Oh, Tilly, let me ice it – *please!*' Maud begged. She coloured the topping a virulent blue.

'Hope it's edible,' Nandy said, sidestepping a pinch. Tilly parted them firmly.

'It's *navy* blue,' she said, suddenly inspired.

There was fresh bread, if no butter, to spread with delicious bramble jelly.

'You'll have a proper tea, Joe, with Grandma and Grandpa, and more presents later,' Rosa assured him fondly.

Letters had arrived at last. The postman had abandoned his bicycle and trudged to them. 'This is as far as I'll go today. May I leave the farm post with you? Should be a thaw very soon, so they say.'

'Please,' Tilly said quickly, 'would you be kind enough to take this one and post it for me?' It was the letter she had written to Oswald.

There were four letters to Rosa from her husband, and three from Augusta, including a note for Tilly, to remind her that she expected her to return as soon as possible.

I understand that the weather has been most severe, as in Brixton – but this is a civilised *place! Gussie caught a bad cold in Norfolk and she has been coughing ever since. I caught her, one night, with the bedroom window open, drawing a fox with a chicken in its jaws by moonlight. Bare feet on bare floorboards, in her nightgown – no sense at all! Tilly, come back and keep my child in order.*

Tilly smiled wryly. If only Mrs Augusta could see what the children here got up to!

There was a proper letter for Tilly, too. Not from Oswald, to her disappointment, but from her younger sister Lil.

I went with my new young man, Tilly, to see the Thames frozen over. They were roasting an ox! I did have a lovely time, but I got back late to my lady's and my boots were wet through. Cook kindly let me in and said nothing!

Tilly was feeling rather homesick after all, being a Londoner born and bred. She missed the big house with its comforts, even if these didn't extend to her own domain, and thought wistfully that she would love to have witnessed the roasting of that ox with Lil.

Tilly shook the cloth into place on the table for the birthday tea. Joe had the first slice of cake, of course. He caught the oozing jam with the tip of his tongue.

'Mmm. I like Tilly's chewy old cake,' he beamed.

'Good, I rather thought it might taste like cardboard!' Tilly smiled back.

'It does,' Nandy said tactlessly, 'and Maud's icing is – *disgusting!*'

They made their own birthday entertainment: Maud, on the piano, thumping out the favourite nursery rhymes and simple tunes in which they all joined with gusto. Tid retired disdainfully to the kitchen, and his share of the cake.

Nandy recited, improvising quite a bit because learning poetry was not his favourite pursuit; Tilly sang a somewhat embarrassed solo, gaining or losing an aitch or two, 'Cherry ripe! Ripe I cry – full and fair ones, come and buy . . . '

She was relieved not to be asked for an encore.

Rosa then read from *Dombey and Son*, while Tilly had the pleasure of cuddling Joe on her lap, with Maud's arm linked through hers, and her dark head leaning against her shoulder. They had become good pals while sharing a bedroom, Tilly thought.

Of course, they had a full set of Dickens here; well used, unlike the beautifully bound books which had to be handled with such care at Augusta's, although he was a favourite author with her, too.

Rosa read: 'This house ain't so exactly ringing with merrymaking,' said Miss Nipper, 'that one need be lonelier than one must be. Your Toxes and your Chickses may draw out my two front double teeth, Mrs Richards, but that's no reason why I need to offer 'em the whole set . . . '

Joe gave an excited shriek, startling Tilly. His first milk tooth had fallen out.

'Use my handkerchief,' Tilly said. He wrapped it up. After all, it might be replaced with a silver threepenny piece . . .

Nandy read Rosa's expression accurately. Joe was rather young to be losing a tooth – supposing all the rest were to fall out, like his hair?

'Don't worry, Rosa,' he said brightly, 'I knew that cake was lethal. Sorry, Tilly – but it was enough to loosen any-one's teeth!'

'Oh, you!' she said, but really she felt like one of them.

They had endured almost six weeks of the Big Freeze when a sudden thaw set in. Most of the country had been brought to a virtual stand-still. Now everywhere, including the Island, there was feverish activity.

In the cottage, the kitchen was awash when the ice dis-persed with a thunderous crack. The water left fresh mis-eries in its wake. From a lack of water, there was now too much of it. The sea, released from imprisonment, tossed ugly, jagged lumps of ice onto the beaches, and ships sailed once more in and out of port.

Spring, calm and kind, really was just around the corner.

'I must get back to Mrs Augusta.' Tilly wrung out her floor cloth for hopefully the final time, and sank back on her haunches. She eyed the damp, flagged floor with weary satisfaction. 'I shan't want you all coming to see me off, mind,' she added fiercely, so that they looked at her in surprise. 'Or I shan't be able to force myself to go . . .'

But to her delight, when she arrived at Victoria, there waiting for her with a cab to transport her home to Brixton were Augusta and Gussie. The old loyalties resurfaced and Tilly received as convulsive a hug from Gussie as she had from Maud and Joe when she'd left the family under the sea wall that morning.

'I've got *such* a lot of adventures to tell you about,' she whispered into Gussie's ear.

EIGHT

Maud was over the moon. It was May and her father
– dear Petty to his children – was home. She loved his
round, ruddy face and his mop of irrepressible sandy
hair, but she shied away from the full naval beard, which
was blond and bristling, when he lifted her up in his arms
to kiss her.

She couldn't see why she had to knock on her parents'
bedroom door, and why it was firmly closed. There was so
much she wanted to tell her father, and she was, of course,
usually one for bursting in without ceremony.

Petty decided to enlist Maud's aid, suspecting that Rosa
would coddle Joe and be too protective unless he did something about it now.

'Boy needs a dose of fresh air. Why don't you and Nandy
take him to the old Ship on Shore to fetch me some beer,
Maud?'

'Oh, that's much too far for him,' Rosa worried. 'He's
only been up onto the beach once since the weather
improved, and then he sat on the sand.'

'I can always carry him on my back, if he gets tired,' Maud offered.

Nandy scoffed: 'You couldn't carry a baby on your back, let alone Joe!'

'He can take his time, rest when he feels like it. Wouldn't you like to go, lad?' Petty asked Joe.

He was already trying to lace up his boots, his face eloquent.

''Course he would!' Maud said for him.

'Oh, you won't need those.' Petty pulled the boots off again. 'You can walk along the sands all the way – tide's nicely out, isn't it, Maud? Dip your feet in and out of the water. Nothing like salt water and sea breezes for strengthening you – don't let him paddle out to sea, mind, Maud,' he joked with that rumbling laugh deep within his barrel chest.

'Don't know why you trust *her*.' Nandy made a face at Maud. She giggled happily in return.

Rosa fretted uneasily. 'Maud, just you bring him back if he finds it too much. Nandy, here's the jug for the beer, and sixpence. Don't lose it!'

They climbed the steps in the wall and dropped down on to the soft, sunwarmed sand. Further along it was shingly, where the old oyster catchers had toiled.

Maud discarded her stockings joyfully, and once out of sight of home, hitched her cotton skirts and petticoats above her knees, unwittingly revealing the buttoned back-flap of her frilly drawers. She rolled up Joe's knickerbockers for him. 'Your legs are like spindly white sticks,' she told him. 'Dig your toes in the sand, Joe. Don't you just love that cool dampness? And run the warm top sand through your fingers – doesn't that feel nice, too?'

Nandy also rolled up the legs of his flannels and threw his jacket behind a convenient rock, to collect on his way back, together with the loathed stiff detachable collar. He unbuttoned his shirt and strode ahead of them in a lordly fashion, swinging the pewter jug carelessly from its handle.

'Good, he's gone,' Maud said to Joe. They dawdled along behind him for a while and then sat by the water's edge to skim the waves with small pebbles, letting the sea lap over their gritty feet, scanning the horizon for sails. Nandy soon disappeared from sight.

The soft breeze stirring his fuzz of hair, the rushing and receding of the sea and the beneficial spring sunshine would often be recalled by Joe in years to come. It was a day of self-discovery, a strengthening time, as Petty had said.

'Why is the pub called The Ship on Shore?' Joe asked Maud as they watched a cormorant dive for a fish, strong wings beating against the swell of the sea which was deeper in colour, almost green, further out.

Maud loved to tell a story, to embellish what she had heard.

'Well,' she began, tracing her name with a sharp-edged pebble in the sand: MAUD AUGUSTA SEARLE. 'Whatever did they want to name me after Aunt A for, Joe? D'you suppose she *made* them? Bet she thinks it's a mistake now – don't you?'

'Um, what did you want to know? Oh, yes: there was a ship laden with barrels of cement, and it was wrecked. Oh, my, Joe, there was a *terrible* storm, the like of which we'll probably never see! (She quoted Grandpa William here, who had told her the story when she was Joe's age.) And some of these barrels were washed ashore, here on Sheppey, but they couldn't use the cement, 'cause all set solid, but then they had a good idea, and built the pub a grotto out of 'em, and gave it that name. But I always think it should be *Cement*-on-Shore – what d'you think, Joe?'

'Dunno,' he murmured, and screwed up his eyes. 'Look, someone's coming, Maud.'

'Oh, it's Mr Lozenge – you *know*, the German photographer. Don't stare, Joe, that's rude. Remember, we had those portraits done in his studio before we went to Southampton – for Petty to take with him to sea, in case he forgot what we looked like while he was away?'

'Mr Lozenge? He sent Tilly that Christmas card, didn't he?' Joe said innocently, just as the photographer came up to them.

'Good morning to you, young Searles.' Mr Lozenge wore an old-fashioned frock coat, yellow gloves and a tall collar. His only concession to the milder weather was an obviously new straw hat which he was unable to raise, being laden with photographic equipment. He seemed only too pleased to pause for a rest and chat to the children.

'Maud – and young Joe, isn't it? You would like a lozenge, eh? I always keep some in my pocket. You need them by the sea. Here you are.' He lowered his bulk on to the hummock near Maud. Belatedly, she remembered to pull down her skirts. Mr Lozenge pretended not to see. He was a gentleman. He continued: 'You shall come to my studio this summer, eh, for new portraits? To show your dear ones how much you have grown. And you will, perhaps, bring along your lady friend, the one I had the great pleasure of meeting on the train?'

'Tilly's gone back to Brixton – we wish she hadn't!' Maud said. 'I expect we will come to your studio again, when Joe's filled out a bit more. He's been very ill, you know, and we wouldn't want to frighten anyone with the way he looks now.'

Joe gave her a playful push. 'How long have you lived on the Island?' he asked Mr Lozenge curiously.

'Twenty years now,' Mr Lozenge supplied obligingly. 'I leave Germany in 1875, I think. I never go back, I like it here. My property, I own it, and it is a nice place. I like to watch the ships. I like it all.' He made a sweeping gesture. 'Your friend will come again, I hope? She has a beautiful face: the strong profile, a straight nose, such blue eyes . . . '

'Not like me,' Maud sighed. 'Boot-button eyes and a nose which turns up. Rosa, my mother, said she really doesn't know where it comes from – not from her side, anyway.'

'Your face tells your character. Your colouring also is delightful,' Mr Lozenge said gallantly.

'Here's Nandy!' Joe exclaimed as his brother came loping towards them, slopping the contents of the jug.

Having greeted him: 'And how are you, Ferdinand?' Mr Lozenge observed, 'I must go. I have an appointment for a family portrait at Minster.' He rose, shook the sand from his coat tails and picked up his equipment. He bowed slightly. 'I look forward to our next meeting, dear children.'

'Goodbye,' they chorused. 'Mr Lozenge,' Maud said under her breath.

'You two didn't get far,' Nandy said in his superior way.

'Nandy – what's that mark all round your mouth?' Maud accused him, knowing very well what it was.

'Well,' he said defensively, 'I was hot – and dry as a bone! Go on, Maud, you have a try!'

So first Maud then Joe quenched their thirst by supping the froth from the jug. Nandy was satisfied. Now Maud wouldn't be telling any tales.

In their absence, Petty had been down to the quay to purchase freshly caught cod. Maud was just in time to see her mother chopping off the fish heads, and to make a fuss.

Petty poured himself a tankard of beer. He cocked his head enquiringly at Rosa.

'Certainly not,' she said primly, gutting the fish with firm, clean strokes of her knife.

Maud motioned to Nandy that the tidemark round his mouth still showed. He licked his lips. The bitter taste was still there, and on the whole he rather liked it. Maud and Joe were not so sure.

'Tilly buys Aunt A's fish off a barrow in Brixton Market,' Maud said.

'Not as fresh as this,' her father said firmly. 'It was still squirming when I got it.'

That decided Maud. 'I won't have any then! How *could* you, Petty?' She stamped out into the yard, but hovered by the door, listening in.

'Talking of my sister, when may we expect her to descend on us?' she heard Petty say.

'Now, Joe,' Rosa answered, 'you know she won't be staying here. It's not nearly grand enough. She's booked at The Royal Hotel.'

Maud thought: Oh, good, surely Tilly will be coming, too?

Her father teased: 'No billiards in The Royal or sitting in the fug of the smoking room for me while Augusta's in residence, eh?'

'You should have recommended The Welcome instead,' Nandy said, tongue in cheek.

'Good idea!' Maud interrupted, coming back into the kitchen because Rosa was wrapping up the nasty bits of fish.

'Now, Nandy, I hardly think the Soldiers' and Seamen's Home, in Blue Town at that, is a lodging house that would suit your Aunt Augusta.' Rosa couldn't resist a smile at the very thought.

'Well, as advertised in the *Gazette* – move your hand, Nandy, so I can read it out.' Maud snatched at the spare sheet of paper spread on the table. 'She could have a hot bath, bed *and* a locker – and we could all visit her, 'cause it's open to the public 'til ten pm.'

Rosa waggled her scaley knife at the disrespectful pair. 'Out of my kitchen, *all* of you. Yes, you too, Petty Officer Joe.' And with a parting shot at Petty's broad back: 'If you don't just watch out, *you* can go to The Welcome. After all, you *are* a sailor! And *Augusta* can come here . . . '

'Only if Tilly and Gussie come as well!' Maud said.

NINE

Maud, unlike her mother, enjoyed these jaunts to the seamier side of Sheerness. Gazing out on Blue Town, slightly dazzled from staring into sun and sea, she found it immensely attractive. When she was older, she would say that it had the blurred beauty of an impressionist painting. All those tumbledown, haphazardly positioned wooden houses; the rakish, ruffianly charm which made the area so popular with sailors. Of course, there were a disproportionate number of jolly, bawdy public houses. There were various and varied entertainments, ranging from Missions to Music Halls.

Besides those relatives and friends waiting to go on to the pier to greet passengers from the steamer, there was the usual crowd of curious dockyard children. Maud endured the determined clutching of her mother's hand. There had been a recent outbreak of diphtheria in the area, and Rosa was taking no chances. Most of those poor youngsters were doomed if they contracted diphtheria or worse, typhoid, and there were still outbreaks of smallpox, despite the campaign for vaccination. Maud and her brothers all bore the deep whorl imprinted on their upper arms, a scarring which gave them immunity. Maud knew that was why they lived outside the town, despite the inconvenience of the lengthy walks to shops and school.

These youngsters in their baggy, crumpled dresses with tattered pinafores, torn shirts, cut-down trousers and battered straw hats or bonnets, with their filthy, calloused bare feet, were in stark contrast to those more affluent: to Maud, fidgeting in her navy serge because she had torn a great rent in her best summer muslin before they even set off to meet Aunt Augusta, Tilly and Gussie – itching in the heat, scratching at her neck and the backs of her knees, feeling and looking stifled.

'Keep still, Maud, will you?' Rosa muttered.

As they made their way slowly along the pier, Maud edged towards the rail and encountered a squeaky plank. This provided a few moments' entertainment until she felt Rosa grip her arm to pull her into line.

'It's not fair, Rosa, you didn't make Nandy come,' Maud muttered crossly.

'He's not exactly Aunt A's blue-eyed boy, now is he? When he said he'd rather go and help Grandpa, I thought that was not such a bad idea. You know how disappointed Tilly would be – Gussie, too – if *you* weren't here. You are looking forward to seeing them again, aren't you?'

'Yes, but . . . ' Maud gave up. She knew that Rosa had been praying for their safe arrival, for she had said that *she* would certainly never travel by steamer. When Maud asked her why – because to her it sounded like a much more exciting way of reaching London than by train – Rosa had reminded her of the tragedy of the *Princess Alice*. Of course, Miss Rayner had told them of this at school. In 1878 the pleasure boat left Sheerness crowded with around 800 passengers, over 600 of whom perished when she became involved in a terrible collision with *The Bywell Castle* in Woolwich Reach. Aunt A, naturally, Maud thought, always followed her own inclination. Which was jolly good luck for Tilly and Gussie!

However, the steamer was now visible on the horizon, and an excited cheer went up from the crowd. 'It's *The Royal Sovereign*!' Smoke billowed copiously from her funnels and her decks were swarming with wildly waving passengers, like so many milling ants. Maud was disappointed she couldn't make out Augusta's party. The steamer's flag streamed proudly and her horn boomed a greeting in reply.

The disembarkation took some time, and they scanned the passengers anxiously. Gussie came upon them unexpectedly. The salty air had tossed and teased her hair into a frizzy red mass, her hat had been knocked awry, and she had a sooty smear on her chin. She gave Maud an enormous hug.

''Lo, Aunt Rosa, Maud, Joe – Mama and Tilly are close behind me, I think! Oh, Maud, it was great fun, but all those silly rules. No smoking, which upset the gentlemen and

Mama, no standing on the paddleboxes, no one allowed on the Bridge ... Mama complained about all the crying children and the fighting dogs. Half of London seems to have decided to come to Sheerness for their summer holidays! And she refused to buy any refreshments 'cause she said the charges were scandalous, and Tilly felt sick even though it wasn't choppy, and –'

'You talk too much!' Augusta told her grimly, catching up with her daughter at last. Tilly, weighed down under most of the luggage, looked thoroughly fed up, although she soon cheered up at the sight of her friends.

Welcome and not so welcome embraces over, they moved slowly behind the crowd leaving the pier.

Maud said to Tilly in a piercing whisper: 'Look who's beside us, Tilly. He's been asking after you!'

'Ah, good afternoon, Mrs Searle, children.' It was Mr Lozenge who gave his usual courteous bow before introducing his companion, whom he had obviously met from the steamer. She was a stout young lady, bulging in unbecoming beige, with a thick braid of almost colourless hair wound round her head. She carried her hat in her hand.

'May I present my niece, Miss Anna Hoffman, here from Germany? She is staying in London at present and decided to pay me a visit.'

'My sister-in-law, Mrs Quayle, and her daughter Augusta. Miss Tilly Reeder,' Rosa returned. 'Mr – Rossel.'

Mr Lozenge bowed again. 'I am pleased to meet you, ladies.'

'*Now* you know her name!' Maud said wickedly, indicating the blushing Tilly.

'Indeed,' he returned, beaming. 'What a very striking young lady, if you will pardon my impertinence, Mrs Quayle. Please, you will permit me to make a study of her during your stay?'

'He is a photographer. Very reputable,' Rosa murmured to Augusta, who was looking somewhat alarmed at Mr Lozenge's suggestion.

'We'll see,' she replied shortly.

When Mr Lozenge and his niece had gone ahead, she remarked sourly: 'Never trust a German.'

'Mama doesn't trust any foreigners if she's truthful!' Gussie always became more daring with Maud to back her up. Now she linked arms with Maud and Joe.

'D'you know, Gussie, Petty said the Germans buy wild snakes and birds from India, like pythons and cobras – and sell 'em for big profits to the Berlin Zoological Gardens,' Maud reported with relish.

'Yes,' Joe added. 'He says all the officers on the Hamburg liners can't wait to get to Calcutta, doesn't he, Maud?'

'Little pitchers . . . ' Rosa said feelingly to Augusta. But, in unison for once, they both silently thanked goodness for innocence!

'How beastly.' Gussie shuddered, still thinking about the snakes. She was an innocent, too.

Tilly went thankfully to her own room, on an upper floor, after unpacking for Augusta and Gussie in record time. Augusta had insisted on Rosa and the children taking tea with her in the hotel.

'Don't forget to lay out our things for dinner, Tilly,' she said. Tilly guessed that she was being reminded of her place – she had seen Augusta's compressed lips when Rosa had relieved her of one of the heavy bags. She knew that Augusta considered they were too familiar.

She fervently hoped, however, that Augusta had not noticed when Rosa slipped those two letters into Tilly's pocket, giving her arm a sly squeeze. She had raised her eyebrows questioningly, and Rosa gave a little nod.

Now she sank down into the chair and withdrew the letters from their hiding place.

You must think I have forgotten you, but perhaps the untidy writing will give you a clue. The ship was in an awful storm – two poor devils lost overboard. I was bowled over myself and injured. My right arm is badly broken and I have also fractured my right hip. I am completely lopsided! They put me ashore at the nearest port and I was taken to hospital. I am to be brought home very soon – at the beginning of June – to convalesce.

If you are back in Brixton (you forgot to give me your address) I am sure Mrs Searle will post this on to you – for, dear Tilly, I know you will come to see me, wherever you are.

I just found a letter I wrote before all this, which never got posted. I'll send it with this one, so you have a more cheerful one to read! Tilly, there is always a bright side, for won't I be seeing you much sooner? And then, I might dare to tell you what I feel for you!

Your affectionate friend,
Oswald

Tilly sat sniffing and weeping like a child. And she had been thinking dolefully that he didn't care. And best of all, it was already June!

TEN

Feeling both excited and apprehensive, Tilly knocked diffidently on the farmhouse door. It was ajar, but she would not presume to just push it open and walk in. A sheepdog lying on the warm stones of the yard regarded her quizzically from wall-eyes but did not bother to bark.

Tilly stretched out a tentative hand and the dog rose and came over to sniff at her skirts, and finally to give her a damp, warm lick of approval.

'Come in, my dear – of course, you must be Tilly. Don't stand on ceremony!' Oswald's mother was short and as round as the butterballs she shaped so expertly in her dairy, with a weather-beaten, smiling face. She wiped floury, pudgy hands on her coarse apron.

'Oswald will be so pleased to see you. Rosa sent Nandy with your message. He's resting in the parlour. He gets such a lot of pain in that leg, poor boy, but his arm's mending well, though Dr Box wonders if it will straighten out properly as it was some time before it could be set. This way, my dear. You'd like some tea in a while I'm sure? I've just put some sconcs in the oven. Mr Relf will be in quite soon – just finishing off the afternoon's milking. Didn't he say hello to you when you were at Rosa's, back in the Freeze?'

Tilly nodded shyly. She knew intuitively that Mrs Relf approved of her.

The parlour was dim, the heavy curtains half-drawn across to keep the sun from fading the furnishings. Obviously not a room much used, Tilly thought, unlike the big, light kitchen they had passed through, with the good smell of baking pervading every corner. She had noticed the bunches of herbs on the marble slab ready for chopping, hanging clusters of vegetables, Windsor chairs with patchwork cushions grouped round a family-sized table, and a cluster of cats curled up asleep in a battered rocker by the stove.

'I'll leave you together . . . ' Oswald's mother departed unobtrusively.

'Tilly!' He struggled to set his bad leg to the ground, wincing with pain. Tilly unthinkingly put a restraining hand on his shoulder and instantly his own warm hand was clamped over hers and he was pulling her, unresisting, towards him.

'Sit down, Tilly, do. Next to me.'

She gently freed her hands and sat down carefully, leaving a little space between them. He looked at her searchingly and she was glad that she had put on the dress Augusta had given her for her afternoons off, even though it had taken much altering to fit her own slender shape. It was Augusta's favourite blue, such a fine, soft lawn that she wondered if it was too revealing – fitting so snugly over her breasts that he must be able to see how fast she was breathing, she thought.

Oswald was actually looking at the soft pink and white of her face, and at her beautiful hair, as blonde as a child's. Her cheeks had a delightful fullness too. Then his gaze lingered on her trembling mouth and he sensed her vulnerability.

'It's so good to see you again, Oswald, I never thought it would be so soon. Are you in very much pain?' To her chagrin, her voice was shaky, breathless, and she tried in vain to control the involuntary quivering of her knees. They were much too close for Oswald had shifted, closing the gap between them.

The hurried, tinny ticking of the clock on the mantelpiece, between the rather ugly china fairings, kept pace with her racing heart. Tilly could not bring herself yet to look directly into his eyes. That first glimpse of his drawn, sunken face, unexpectedly bearded, had disturbed her too much. She stared instead at the ornaments, concentrating with her slightly short-sighted eyes in order to decipher the crude patterns.

The unexpected happened but she was powerless to resist. Caught against his chest, against the warm, clean cotton of his shirt, encircled by his good arm, she felt his beard brushing harshly against her face. He kissed her hungrily, at length, until her lips felt bee-stung, then released his hold abruptly. Tilly covered her tingling cheeks and her tell-tale mouth with her hands.

'I'm sorry.' Oswald was contrite. Then: 'No, I'm not, Tilly! I wanted this to happen – I'm even glad about the accident. Three years away from you would have seemed like forever! Tilly darling, we needn't wait. It must have been meant, your being here again right now. You see, I shan't be able to go back to sea. I won't be that able-bodied, I'm afraid. The Navy won't have me, but there's plenty of room for us here on the farm . . .'

'Are you asking – me – to marry you?' Tilly's voice faded. His face was disturbingly close again; he was removing her defences, prising her hands from her face.

'I am, and you will,' he whispered.

She pushed him gently away. 'Oswald, I must tell you, I *can't* keep it from you. I'm – you see, I'm not the girl you think I am.'

He smiled at her tenderly. 'Of course you are, don't be silly.'

'I'm not; you won't want to marry me when you know. You *won't*!' She groped in her bag for her handkerchief.

'Nothing could be that bad!' he joked, but anxiously.

'It could. It *could*!' Slowly, while Oswald held her hand tightly, the story came out.

When she was almost fourteen Tilly's first post had been found for her. Her mother was pleased because she would not yet have to leave home where she was still much needed to help cope with the family. One of Mrs Reeder's ladies had informed her that she knew of a local couple who needed a girl to help out generally. So began Tilly's career as a maid-of-all-work. The hours were incredibly long and there was no one else to help, although a cook was engaged upon occasion.

Tilly's master, a jovial man of around fifty, worked from home. She was not sure what he did, but there were account books piled up on the desk in his study. To Tilly, at first sight, he seemed much more pleasant and approachable than his wife, who was short-tempered and stingy. There were no children, and there appeared to be no love lost between the couple. It was rumoured locally that she had been attractive to him only because of inherited money. Tilly's mistress considered herself to be a pillar of the church, spending most of her days visiting the poor and urging them to abandon their slothful ways and to send their many children to her Sunday School to learn their catechism.

Almost from the beginning Tilly had to endure, with suppressed terror, the unwelcome 'fatherly' attentions of the master when his wife was out. It was not something she could talk about at home, though she cried bitterly about it at night. Despite her large family, she was incredibly ignorant of the basic facts of life. She knew that babies were inevitable, that they caused suffering when they were born and hardship afterwards, but, in her experience, they were always loved and welcomed, if sighed over. It seemed to her that a father was not always necessary, for didn't a girl alone sometimes produce a baby which surprised even her own mother? Babies like these were usually accepted into the girl's own family, and very often came to think of their mother as an elder sister.

Tilly could not speak in detail of the terrible day when her master had had, as she could only now whisper to a shocked and dazed Oswald, 'his way'. She had run home in sheer terror, despite his threats to tell his wife, if this should get back to her, that Tilly had deliberately led him on. She had hidden her soiled, ripped clothes and resolutely refused to go back to that house.

For several days her mother had questioned her fearfully, gently, suspecting but not wanting to believe what must have occurred, until the painful truth was told. She promised that Tilly would be allowed to leave these dreadful employers, comforting the sobbing, distraught girl as best she could. Mother knew that trouble was inevitable, and she was right.

Tilly cowered, crying in her bed, while downstairs she heard the mistress railing harshly at her mother, calling Tilly's behaviour both disgraceful and unreasonable – thoroughly ungrateful. She would spread the word, she spat out, and Tilly would find it impossible to find further employment, and she would most certainly not be given a reference.

After three months, parents and daughter were despairing, deeply ashamed and worried because it was now all too obvious that Tilly was pregnant. She had looked down at her swelling young body and thought she might end her misery, but could not do so after all.

Bravely, Tilly's mother tackled her daughter's erstwhile employers again, and boldly stated the facts. The master did not deny the accusations, but insisted that Tilly had welcomed – encouraged – her own seduction. The mistress, enraged, but accepting her husband's version of events, refused to pay the wages still due to Tilly, but put forward her own 'Christian' solution. 'We will take the child,' she'd stated. 'Only if healthy, mind! Bring it here immediately after the birth. We will cover any medical attention, if necessary, and will undertake to bring this child up as our own. That is our Christian duty. But no further contact must ever be made between us, and I can assure you that no money will ever be paid to you or your daughter. Is that clearly understood? Tilly is a very fortunate girl. We do not wish to hear from you again until the birth is imminent.'

Tilly sobbed her heart out as she whispered to Oswald of the sheer agony as her son, a large baby, was finally torn from her immature body. 'Oh, Oswald, I held him just the once, wrapped in a bit of sheet, and then the nurse they'd sent, because Mother could not manage on her own, took him away. The nurse tried to be kind, said it was all for the best and that I'd come to see that. I'd get married when I was older, and I'd have other babies and forget this first-born child.'

Concealed in a rush basket, the baby was conveyed by carriage to his new nursery. The nurse, hoping to comfort them, had told them that the baby would be bathed and dressed in flannel petticoats and the finest, longest, embroidered gowns, and that he would be handed over immediately to his wet nurse: 'A motherly, clean woman, with a baby of her own.' So even this link was denied Tilly. She suffered fever and acute distress when the milk rushed forcefully into her swollen breasts. Now, Oswald saw, she pressed them unconsciously, as if the pain were still there.

The proud parents named their baby Edward, after the jolly Prince of Wales. This news came to Tilly's family in a roundabout way through the cleaning fraternity.

Tilly's wet face rested against Oswald's comforting shoulder as he stroked her hair soothingly, like she were a distraught little girl. Tilly realised that this was a very different young man from the rather cocksure young sailor she had rather surprisingly fallen in love with after so short a courtship. This was someone she could trust and lean on always.

'Then you went to Mrs Quayle's?' he prompted quietly after a while.

'Yes . . . Mother told her everything. I know she seems a funny old thing – she's all for women having rights and a *vote*, you know. But Mrs Augusta said I'd been wronged, and it was wicked; said I deserved much better and she was willing to give me my chance. And she has, Oswald. I know

I have to work hard, but she's been really good to me. Oh, you won't want me now I've told you all this, will you?'

'Oh, my dear girl, of course I want you! Your Mrs Augusta was right; you were sinned against and treated abominably. It makes no difference to the way I feel about you. And, Tilly, I promise I'll never, ever bring it up against you, whatever happens . . . '

She turned to him then, and returned his kiss.

When his mother came in with a loaded tea tray, she smiled happily to see them so close and contented.

'Mother, good news! Put the tray down. Tilly's promised to marry me. Within the month, if we can arrange it. Do tell us you're pleased?'

'Oh, I am! You're surely not crying with joy are you, my dear?' Oswald's mother embraced her warmly. 'Welcome to our family, Tilly. We've been saying it's time our boy settled down. And his dad needs him on the farm now, for last winter was nearly the end of him and I can't help more'n I do.'

Oswald's finger gently brushed away the last traces of tears from Tilly's face.

'Try another of Mother's scones, Tilly – and mind, I shall expect you to bake 'em just the same!' he teased.

Tilly waited to impart her news until after Gussie had retired to bed. She went down to the lounge where Augusta sat, reading the evening paper and drinking her coffee. Augusta looked up, surprised to see her. Tilly usually kept

to her room in the evenings. You could not relax stand-
ards in a hotel as you could in your own home. It was not
quite the thing to treat one's maid as a fellow guest, but
she invited Tilly to sit beside her and called for another
cup of coffee.

Sipping and trying not to make a face, for she had not
acquired a taste for coffee, Tilly wondered where to begin.

'Have you enjoyed your afternoon off?' Augusta enquired.

Tilly nodded, and decided to make a bold statement.

'Mrs Augusta, I'm – getting married. To Oswald, the
young man I told you I was going to see today.'

The expected explosion did not materialise.

'I suppose congratulations are in order, Tilly? I imagine
you consider yourself engaged?'

'More than that, Mrs Augusta. We're getting married.
Soon.' She gulped down the rest of the coffee in one go.

She could hardly believe her ears. 'Gussie will be a bridesmaid, of course, and perhaps Maud?' Mrs Augusta replied.
'We might even trust Nandy to hand out the hymn books.
The wedding will be here, I presume? I shall naturally pay
for everything.'

Tilly faltered, 'I thought – no fuss, really. I'm sorry to be
letting you down—'

'Nonsense! You must have a day to remember.'

Before she could stop herself, Tilly leaned over and
kissed her employer's cheek. 'Thank you! I'll work right up
to my wedding day . . . '

'Really!' Augusta dabbed at her cheek. 'You must have a couple of days off.'

Tilly knew she must give in gracefully. After all, Oswald's parents, who had no daughters, were eager to play their part, too. She couldn't disappoint *them*.

'I'll never forget how kind you've been,' she said, and meant it. She added softly: 'I *told* him, Mrs Augusta. He said it makes no difference. He really loves me, as I am.'

'Then he sounds a thoroughly nice young man, Tilly.'

She rose. It didn't do to take advantage, sitting here like this with her employer. 'Goodnight. I'll turn your bed down, shall I?'

'Yes, please. Goodnight, Tilly.'

Augusta watched her go. Tilly would never have guessed that her employer was thinking how very much she would miss her.

ELEVEN

'There! They won't see us now,' Maud exclaimed to Gussie in breathless satisfaction. 'Let's take our shoes and stockings off, Gus, I'm *gasping* hot. Oh, my! Aren't you?' She plummeted down onto the short, springy grass, ignoring the prolific rabbit droppings, kicked off her shoes, then wriggled out of her stockings in a most unladylike manner. She bundled them up and aimed them into a patch of thistles.

Gussie giggled, following suit. She hauled up her cream tussore silk skirts and froth of starched petticoats, which Tilly had ironed so carefully, and recklessly exposed her elegant lace-trimmed underwear. In the company of her cousin Maud, Gussie always seemed a different girl.

'Ta-ra-ra-boom-de-ay!' she sang loudly, pirouetting. 'Come on, Maud, see how high you can kick!'

'I haven't got nice long legs like you,' she said ruefully. 'But I s'pose you can't expect too much with a little mother and a *petit homme* for a father.'

They sang the rude street version which Gussie had heard rendered by cheeky youths to passing young ladies when she walked to Brixton Market with Tilly.

'Lottie Collins has no drawers,
Will you kindly lend her yours?
She is going far away,
To sing – Ta-ra-ra-boom-de-ay!'

They collapsed in a perspiring heap, helpless with laughter.

They had run far ahead of the others along the cliff edge, blithely ignoring the anxious, warning calls directed after them by Rosa and Augusta, in accord for once: 'Keep well away from the edge – remember the cliffs are crumbling – oh, do *take care*!'

The cliffs towards Warden Point were notorious for land-slips, but famous for their wonderful, breathtaking views and for the profuse wild, almost tropical, flowers which flourished there.

The sun blazed down from a cloudless sky and a butter-fly settled briefly on Maud's outflung hand. She kept very still, which Rosa would have said was impossible for her to do, feeling the tickling on her wrist, and quite enchanted by it. In a sudden flit, the velvet-winged tortoiseshell left her to land on a swaying flower.

'Why does Aunt A *always* ask Rosa about babies?' Maud nibbled on the white juicy end of a long grass. ''Specially when Petty's home for a bit,' she added.

Gussie propped herself up on her elbows. 'I don't really know – does she?'

'Mmm, she does. Petty says she's obsessed with the subject – d'you know what that means?'

'I think it means she's *too* interested . . .'

'If my little sister Elizabeth had lived – did you know she had red hair, like you and Aunt A, Gus? – I should have wanted her to grow up to be *just* like you, 'cause you're sort of a sister to me, you know. Am I to you?'

''Course you are! I just wish Mama would be nicer to Aunt Rosa. I think she's jealous because she wanted me to be a boy. I reckon she'd change me for Joe if she got half a chance.' Gussie sounded a trifle wistful.

'Well, Rosa would never agree – and nor would I! Joe's all right, you see. Now that terrible Nandy . . . but Aunt A would throw a fit at the very thought, wouldn't she? Not that I wouldn't love *you* to be part of our family,' Maud added quickly.

'Tilly's been mooning about ever since she got engaged, hasn't she, Maud? I'm going to miss her so much. She's always on my side – even if she can't say so – when Mama is going on at me for being so lazy with my school work. I wish she wouldn't teach me at home, I'd far rather go to school like you do.'

Now she hasn't got a class to boss about, I suppose she has to make do with you, Maud thought.

'Where's my bag? Trust you, Maud, you're lying on it. Lift up a bit, let me pull. That's right. I'm going to do some sketching. I've got some spare pencils or charcoal, only I know how messy you are, and plenty of paper, if you want to have a go too?' Gussie offered.

'I might as well, thanks.'

Maud rested the sketch pad on her hunched bare knees. Rosa, hurrying towards them, felt the familiar exasperation rising within her as she saw that her daughter was letting the side down as usual. Augusta's scandalised voice transfixed Gussie.

'What on earth do you think you girls are playing at? Bare feet, like guttersnipes! Just you put on those stockings and shoes, this instant!'

Maud, of course, could not resist answering back: 'Petty – your beloved brother, Aunt A, remember? – says it does you nothing but good to let the sea air get to your legs and feet. Anyway, who needs shoes along here?'

For answer, her wrinkled stockings and shoes flew towards her, aimed by her irate mother. Maud actually thought it prudent to put them on quickly and say no more.

'Tidy yourselves immediately, you girls.' Rosa sounded agitated. 'Can't you see who's coming?'

In the distance, strolling gently arm in arm, were to be seen Mr Lozenge and his niece, Anna.

Maud exclaimed before she could prevent herself: 'Oh, my, I do believe, Rosa, that he's wearing spats!'

Tilly, who had been bringing up the rear deliberately, so that she could daydream happily about her coming wedding to Oswald and the sweetness of last night's kisses snatched during their evening stroll, loosened Joe's grip from around her neck and set him down thankfully. Nandy, who had been forced to carry the picnic basket 'like a gentleman – for once', at Aunt A's command, and who had not been permitted to discard his reefer jacket, glared balefully and proceeded to unfasten the basket straps. 'I reckon it's time for a drink and something to eat,' he stated firmly.

'Oh, wait 'til they've gone past, or we'll have to invite them to join us.'

They were sitting in a prim semi-circle, gazing reflectively out to sea, when they were greeted jovially: 'Good afternoon. What a very beautiful day this is. I am telling my niece about the antiquity of this place – the many extinct species of birds, animals and reptiles their remains, that is, along these very cliffs, preserved in this heavy clay.'

'I told you the Germans liked that sort of thing,' Maud murmured wickedly in Gussie's ear. They bent their heads quickly over their drawings, to mask their mirth.

'However,' he continued, with a sidelong glance at Tilly, 'my passion is for the ships. I watch them each evening and mark their names – like the *Kaiser Wilhelm* and *The Prince Albert*. It reflects their pride in their country, so?'

Another whisper from Maud to her cousin: 'D'you suppose he's a *spy*?'

'Well, good afternoon, ladies, children,' he said.

Tilly let the talking buzz comfortably around her as she sat a little apart, enjoying the relaxing sea air and staring out across the iridescent water. She was unaware of the effect of the sunlight on her blonde coronet of braids that was shimmering like a crown.

Turning to a new page of her block Gussie, with a soft, freshly sharpened pencil, captured this illusion and entitled it: 'Princess, looking out to sea'. Then she slipped the picture into her bag before her mother could see and comment on it. Perhaps she would paint a picture later from this sketch, she thought. Tilly had been with her since she was a baby, knew so much more about her dreams for the future than Gussie could ever confide in her mother. Gussie *needed* Tilly still.

Maud had dashed off a bold sketch, too – by a fluke she had managed a fair likeness of Tilly. Maud didn't see her as a princess but as a blushing bride, for she had added a veil and a bouquet and scribbled the title: 'My Friend Tilly on her Wedding Eve'.

Tilly would indeed prove the staunchest of friends to both girls through the ups and downs of life in the years to come.

TWELVE

Tilly lay in the bath on her wedding morning, steam rising from the deliciously hot water, glad that Augusta could not see through the walls of the hotel bathroom because she had warned: 'Not too hot, Tilly – it'll make you feel faint.'

She had chosen the bath, rather than the bride's traditional lie-in and breakfast in bed, and had soaped herself all over with *Regina Violet*, supplied by the hotel. It was sheer bliss, looking shyly down at her firm young body, wondering . . .

She had washed her hair the evening before. Rosa had brought Maud over, for Augusta had agreed that she might share Gussie's room as a special treat. Rosa had brushed Tilly's waist-length hair, which smelt fragrantly of the rosemary shampoo that, together with a new tin of toothpowder, was a gift from Augusta. Like the little girls, Tilly had resembled a hedgehog when Rosa's nimble fingers had completed their task: they all bristled with tightly tied rag curlers.

She hadn't slept much, but didn't feel tired. She stepped out of the bath reluctantly, reaching for the large, soft towel. She rubbed herself slowly, until she was completely dry, appreciating its luxuriousness.

A little later Tilly stood almost in a trance, barely aware of little tugs at the pale blue silk of her wedding dress. ('Oh, Mrs Augusta, I couldn't possibly wear white,' she had insisted.) Isabella, who had made the dress at such short notice, crawled around on the thick pile of the carpet, skilfully adjusting the hem, her mouth bristling with pins.

Tilly heard Maud murmur to Gussie: 'I wonder if Grandma Isabella has ever swallowed any?' Tilly smiled absently at them as they sat decorously side by side on the edge of Augusta's bed. Like a pair of snowy goslings, she thought, in their starched white dresses, fine stockings and dainty kid boots. At Tilly's suggestion, their sashes and wide satin hair ribbons complemented her blue. She saw Maud tentatively touching the unfamiliar curls clustering on her shoulders. She agreed with Maud's candid comment first thing that sleeping on the rags had been sheer torture: 'Gus didn't need them anyway, but I suppose it's worth it, isn't it, Tilly?'

'Doesn't she look just beautiful?' Gussie breathed now in admiration.

'Don't move your head, Tilly,' Rosa told her, stretching up gently to coax and smooth each unwound tress into a perfect ringlet. The final touch, Tilly thought, would be the tortoiseshell combs that were Oswald's gift to his bride, sweeping her hair into the nape of her neck, with just a tendril or two teased out around the hairline and ears.

Tilly submitted to Augusta tilting her face imperiously with her slender bony fingers, dipping into her pots of cream and then deciding on rose *papier poudré*. She pressed the paper leaves onto Tilly's skin and then dusted off the surplus with a swansdown powder puff.

'There, Tilly, how do you like yourself?' Augusta removed her gold wire spectacles and slipped them back into the chatelaine case dangling from her belt.

'Oh, Mrs Augusta . . . ' Tilly breathed in rapture at her reflection.

'Isn't it strange?' Rosa mused, sliding the combs experimentally into position, now that Augusta had ceased interfering. 'Who would have believed, when you came to help us out when Joe was so ill, that you would be my neighbour in a matter of months? Where *is* Joe, by the way?'

'Petty took him and Nandy out for a ride round town with Grandpa. Wasn't it kind of Mr Arthur to lend Tilly and Oswald his carriage? I know we could have walked to the church – well, Tilly couldn't – but it's really special to arrive in style, isn't it?' Maud answered.

'You're only included, Maud, because you are a bridesmaid. I do hope they bring the carriage back in time to collect the bride!'

Augusta stood back to admire the effect of Tilly's completed toilette. Tilly herself was allowed to sit only with caution, because of her bustle, now that her hemline was secure.

'Thank you, Mrs Barry – Mrs Augusta – Rosa,' she told them all gratefully, hoping that Augusta and Rosa would not take offence at being thanked first or last. They were so touchy when they were together, she thought.

'Allow me to cream your hands, Tilly,' Isabella offered. 'Hold them well clear of your dress then we shall ease on the gloves.'

Tilly thought wonderingly that Isabella had created a beautiful wedding dress for one so ordinary – for young Tilly Reeder, Mrs Augusta's maid. Still, Mrs Augusta had insisted: 'No expense is to be spared.' Tilly might have been her own daughter in that respect.

She gazed at the enormous puffed sleeves, the tight bodice with its inserts of fine creamy lace that matched the long gloves. She herself might have preferred a higher neckline, less revealing than the gown's low neck. She curled her toes in her satin shoes, aware of the ruched blue garter just above her knee, with the half-sovereign from her family sewn securely into one of the ruffles, and the tiny borrowed cambric hanky, scented with Mitcham Lavender, tucked into the hollow of her bosom. All would be well, she thought happily, for she had the required 'borrowed and blue'. If only her family could be with her on her great day. But she knew that the half-sovereign was their sacrifice and the reason they could not come.

That coin meant more to her than the ten sovereigns Augusta had presented to her in a leather pouch this morning: 'So that you will have money of your *own*, Tilly. Just in case.' But she was grateful, of course, for her employer's generosity.

The interior of the church was dim and cool; the brasses sparkled in the shafts of sunlight, the pews smelled of polish, and as Tilly made her regal way down the aisle to a joyous pealing from the organ, her train held firmly by the children, she felt the comforting pressure of the arm supporting hers, and suddenly the quaking ceased and she gave Petty a quick half-smile in return. She was so thankful that he had returned in time from Portland, where he had been these past three weeks, to give her away.

Oswald, managing with a silver-knobbed stick, was resplendent in his dress uniform. When Tilly slipped her hand into his she shed the illusion of dreaming and became aware that reality was even sweeter.

* * *

As they drove back in style to the wedding breakfast, which, somewhat to Augusta's chagrin, was being held at the farm, the Town Crier patrolled slowly before the carriage, almost like a wedding herald, but bellowing the usual warning that guns were about to be fired in practice, and the townsfolk should leave their windows open because the War Department would not be liable for the breaking of glass.

'Hurry up, Albert, we want to get to the wedding feast!' Maud shouted back. But the Crier was impervious to the insults of saucy little girls.

The big barn had been cleared by Oswald's family the day before with gusto. The wide-open doors welcomed the guests inside to the long trestle tables covered with crackling cotton sheets and groaning under a veritable feast.

Cold meats were heaped upon enormous trenchers. There was a vast crenellated pie bursting with various succulent game meats and rich jellied gravy. There were covered dishes crammed with steaming potatoes and vegetables, and great loaves of crusty home-baked bread just awaiting slicing and generous spreading with unsalted farm butter. The centrepiece was the wedding cake, made by Oswald's mother, silver-frilled and thickly iced.

Thwarted in her intention to pay for the wedding breakfast, Augusta had hired a local band to play while the guests made inroads into the food and drink. Two fiddles, a flute and a squeezebox was not Augusta's idea of a quartet, but the brothers in the band were surprisingly tuneful and toes were soon tapping.

Later, Tilly could not recall eating a single thing, nor could she remember the impromptu speeches. Like the day she had sat on the cliff top, she was aware, yet unaware, languidly allowing the laughter and cheerful raised voices to wash over her and recede like the tide.

Maud asked Augusta: 'What are your yellow beads made of, Aunt A?' Her aunt wore a necklace of heavy shining gold globes.

'Amber,' Augusta said sharply, touching them proudly.

Tilly knew how much Augusta prized her amber so she was amazed when her employer unclasped the necklace, running the warm beads through her fingers, then slowly held it out to her.

'I would like you to have this as a small token of my thanks for all you have done for us. I meant to give it to you before – I hope you will treasure it as I have done,' she added.

Oswald fastened the necklace round Tilly's throat.

'Oh, Mrs Augusta, I will always think of you – and Gussie – when I wear it!'

'It will bring you good luck,' Maud said admiringly. 'And look, Gus, doesn't it just match Tilly's hair?'

Suddenly it was all over. Augusta was unexpectedly kissing Tilly's cheek and Gussie's arms were oh so tight around her, with her face buried in the folds of sensuous silk, and she was shedding tears, Tilly knew, because she could feel the dampness.

'Oh, Tilly, who will look after me when I'm ill?'

Rosa, in rose to match her name, with a sleepy Joe drooping his head over her shoulder and Petty's arm tight around her waist, whispered: 'See you soon! It's been such a lovely day, Tilly . . . '

'You're so slim, it seems impossible you're the mother of three, Rosa. Thank you for everything!'

Grandpa William roguishly asked if he might be allowed to kiss the bride, and was given permission to do so by a smiling Oswald. Then Grandma Isabella, so happy because the dress was so admired. And finally Maud rushing up to report that: 'Nandy has just been as sick as a dog outside!'

'You go up, Tilly,' Oswald's mother said. 'No dishes for you tonight!'

She lay in the big bed which had known many births and deaths, suddenly weary. Oswald had vanished discreetly to his old room while she undressed and slipped swiftly into a full cotton nightdress, a last-minute gift from Rosa.

'Shall I tell you a secret?' She had smiled. 'I made it for *my* wedding night – but I never wore it . . . '

'Oh!' Tilly said, blushing all over.

She looked at the billowing sleeves with their tiny bows at the cuff, as she folded her arms outside the covers as if hugging them to her for protection. She still wore the heavy amber beads.

Oswald limped painfully into the room and the crossed arms were the first thing he saw. Then he looked down at Tilly's face, drained of the excited pink of the afternoon, framed by flaxen hair so thoroughly brushed that only a faint frizz remained. He smelled the fresh lavender she had sprinkled on her pillow.

'You've forgotten to take off your beads,' he said gently. She did not move.

Not quite sure how to approach her, he sat down slowly on the edge of the bed, to the side of her.

Tilly reached out her hands then and began to rub gently at his bent arm. They sat without speaking for five minutes or so, she not looking at him, but he regarding her gravely.

'Come to bed, Oswald,' Tilly whispered at last. 'I'll ease your leg for you.' She leaned over, her warm body brushing his, nipped out the candle, then threw back the covers. She shifted to make room for him, but not too much.

There was nothing to be afraid of after all.

THIRTEEN

They shared their honeymoon with the children before Augusta and Gussie departed for Brixton. In Minster Abbey Oswald caught Nandy looking reflectively at a recumbent stone effigy which had been much scratched over the years with the names of all those small boys who, like Nandy, carried a penknife in their pocket.

'Sailors know it as the Horse Church,' Oswald told Tilly. 'Did you notice the horse's head on the weather vane? And, of course, there is the legend of poor old Grey Dolphin.'

'Whoever was that?' Tilly asked him.

Oswald was pleased to air his local knowledge, as one born and bred on Sheppey. 'He was the favourite horse of Sir Robert de Shurland. Over five hundred years ago, Tilly, he, Sir Robert, killed a priest during a furious argument. He repented, and decided to ask the King's pardon for his crime. As the King's ship was anchored in the estuary, old Sir Robert swam out there on his horse—'

Nandy interrupted here, to quote solemnly the prophetic words of the old witch he had met on the shore on his return:

"This horse, which today your life doth save, will one day bring you to the grave."

'And then,' added Oswald, as patient as his Tilly with children, 'in another rage, Sir Robert killed his horse, to make sure *this* wouldn't happen. Much later, he was walking along the beach one day and found the horse's skull. He kicked it away, making fun of the prediction. His toe was pierced by one of the bones, infection set in, and he died.'

With a yelp of horror, Joe dashed outside into the sunlight, closely pursued by Gussie and Tilly. Maud said to Nandy hotly: 'It's your fault – you grisly beast!'

'Don't you dare frighten *our* children like that!' Tilly rebuked Oswald in bed that night, nestling comfortably against him so that he would know she wasn't really cross.

'I won't,' he promised. Our children, Tilly had said. They both hoped for a baby soon, but neither had said so.

Tilly and Oswald sat in Rosa's kitchen. William and Isabella arrived presently with a basket of homegrown runner beans.

'You two really ought to enjoy a jaunt by yourselves,' Rosa told them.

William, who had been put to slicing the beans, remarked: 'Look at this, in the paper you spread on the table – an excursion to the Crystal Palace.'

Tilly and Oswald thought that would be very exciting.

'Mrs Augusta has taken Gussie there several times, but I've never been,' Tilly said.

But first there was the appointment at Mr Lozenge's studio. He had sent the happy couple a wedding card with the suggestion that they might like to avail themselves of his highly professional services. 'A wedding photograph is a treasure forever,' he added.

The farm wagon received a brisk cleaning from Oswald and his father, straw bales provided prickly seating and there was some tiresome jostling for places as the farm folk climbed aboard, with reminders from Oswald to: 'Leave some room for Rosa, Petty and the children, mind.' Other guests made their own way, mostly on foot, grumbling at the dust from the road clinging to boots and shoes. There would need to be much mutual brushing down before they would venture into the studio.

Sheeting covered the bales for bride and groom, Tilly was grateful to see. She would have hated to spoil her beautiful wedding dress.

All was ready for the group photograph: fragile gilt chairs stood before a raised platform where some of the minor guests would have to stand – the ornate columns and drapes had been moved aside so that the backdrop would not be too distracting.

They were ushered to their allotted places by a joking Mr Lozenge, endeavouring to lighten the atmosphere and provoke a smile or two. As usual on such occasions he failed. His clients sat grim-faced, praying that they would manage to remain immobile during the ordeal ahead.

'Now this I cannot understand, you see – at the dentist's, well, yes, where your teeth are pulled. Ow!' he demonstrated, but the stony expressions did not waver. 'With the *agony* . . . Here, all I ask is a moment's sit still!'

'Tilly doesn't look the same. She wouldn't do the rags, said she couldn't have Oswald seeing her like that – although Mama said she must.' Augusta, behind her daughter, administered a warning pinch.

'Ouch!' exclaimed Gussie.

'That is better,' beamed Mr Lozenge. 'Now I see your teeth. A nice smile, everyone, please . . .'

Tilly knew that Oswald's leg was troubling him. They had followed Dr Box's advice – to exercise through gentle walking – all week, but the pain was often bad. She dared to move her hands from their limp clasp in her lap, as artistically placed by Mr Lozenge, 'Ah! Such a lovely bride! My old eyes mist,' and to slip her right hand into the crook of Oswald's arm. This caused a blur on the first plate, and some tutting from Mr Lozenge.

Finally, the flashing and minor explosions over, the majority of the company relaxed visibly and departed as speedily as possible, hardly waiting for Mr Lozenge to emerge, perspiring, from under the stifling cloth, and to raise his hands in a benevolent gesture to indicate that the sitting was at an end.

Then Gussie was posed by a Grecian column, her hair released from the confining bow, and Mr Lozenge was granted his 'great desire' to make a portrait of 'such young beauty, such innocence'.

Maud whispered to Tilly that *she* was only too glad to escape the crick in the neck and the pins and needles which were inevitable when Mr Lozenge was feeling artistic.

Meanwhile, Tilly and Oswald went to book their excursion tickets. 'Penge – including admission to the Crystal Palace, third class three shillings. Leaving Sheerness at 9 a.m., returning the same day from Victoria Station at 11.50 p.m., or by ordinary train at 7 p.m.,' the clerk in Wiggins's told them.

'I'd love to see the fireworks. Can we come back by the late train?' Tilly asked Oswald.

He smiled. 'Of course, my Cinderella!' he teased.

They met up with the others in the street. Augusta and Gussie were about to step into their cab. The wagon waited further along.

'We'll tell you all about it on Saturday, Mrs Augusta, Gussie – we're coming to see you off on the steamer!' Tilly called over her shoulder as she and Oswald set off in front of the wagon party, arm in arm, just like an old married couple.

Standing in the entrance to the vast empty concert hall, they gazed in awe at the colossal organ. Tilly had that spine-tingling sensation that is always prevalent in such immense auditoriums.

'I'm not at all musical, of course, but I wouldn't mind coming to a concert here, would you, Oswald?' she asked. 'Maud would be in her element,' she added.

'So long as I'm with you, I'd listen to anything,' Oswald replied fondly.

Tilly felt claustrophobic as they moved through the tropical greenhouses: the sun beat mercilessly down through the dust-streaked panes; the atmosphere was damp and pungent. She was uncomfortably aware of the dark wet patches under the arms of her beige satin blouse. She really should have made time to sew in dress preservers, she thought.

Passing along the displays, they cautiously touched the somewhat chipped and flaking plaster reproduction of a huge Egyptian sphinx, inscrutable and aloof, Tilly thought, despite the dents and scratches. Ahead, she was relieved to see, was an exit to the gardens. The sideshows were becoming more tawdry, souvenir stalls with sharp-eyed owners calling out persuasively in strident voices, even clawing and clutching at the sleeves of passers-by. They halted by the fortune-telling booth.

'Dare I?' Tilly wondered, with a delicious shiver, tightening her hold on Oswald.

He felt in his pocket, eager to indulge and spoil her. 'Oh, go on, Tilly, here's sixpence. You must cross her palm with silver, you know.' He sank thankfully onto an adjacent bench. The throbbing in his thigh was insistent today.

Tilly sat opposite the fortune teller, her heart thumping. There was a powerful smell of unwashed flesh, she couldn't help noticing, overlaid with cheap perfume. Between them, on the round table, stood the crystal ball, gleaming mysteriously in the darkened space. The woman wore a crimson silk shawl, marred by caught threads, a headband encrusted with beads, and huge golden loops dangled from her earlobes. Her plump uncovered arms, grained in the creases with dirt, rested either side of the crystal, palms uppermost.

She pressed her sixpence into the woman's hand. Fingers curled swiftly round it. The words, delivered in a singsong way, as if often repeated, were trite: 'Some past unhappiness, I see, dearie – was there someone you feared? But there's much joy from a new lover, from over the sea, and more good fortune in the years far ahead. *Except* . . . ' She gazed into the depths of the shimmering ball. 'This happiness you have now will be short-lived,' she said abruptly. 'There will be a sad loss for you – great walls of water, I see – is it the sea? But those you care for will help you through, and there *will* be better times ahead.'

The woman bowed her head and let her hands drop from the crystal. The telling was over. Tilly barged through the curtain and hurried Oswald out into the fresh air.

'Nothing much – silly, really,' she answered his enquiring look.

They found the prehistoric monsters fascinating: Tilly thought they were a bit too realistic on close inspection.

She enjoyed watching the lovely dresses swish by. 'No balloon going up today.' Tilly was disappointed.

'Never mind – there's a bicycle race anyway.' Oswald steered her towards the start.

As dusk descended the Palace quivered alive with thousands of the new electric lights and Tilly and Oswald retired to the restaurant to eat their very first meal on their own together, and to marvel as Brock's glorious fireworks sparkled above and lit up the fountains and gardens. They had an uninterrupted view through the glass walls, Tilly constantly exclaiming at the sizzling silver, purple, green and gold stars which seemed to travel ever upwards to join the real ones in the darkening heavens.

Their food cooled as they gazed on these wonders, and then lovingly, still shyly, at each other.

'We must bring our children to see this,' Oswald said.

Tilly blushed. She really longed to have his baby. She would always miss that first little son, she knew, but a baby with Oswald would be a joyful experience, a seal on their love, so sweet, so unexpectedly passionate.

'I'd like at least half-a-dozen,' he added, 'the first one as soon as you like!'

There! Tilly thought. Oswald can put it into words. 'So would I. Oswald . . . ' she had to know ' . . . you really aren't going back to sea, are you? I couldn't bear it!'

He looked searchingly into her troubled eyes. 'Now, Tilly dear, you know I won't. I would have been sad about that once, but I really don't care now – I couldn't leave *you*, either!'

Relief washed over Tilly. There was no need to fear, she thought, or believe what the fortune teller had told her. She was probably just gaining some vicarious satisfaction from making up an imaginary misfortune. Oswald was not going back to the sea, so how could she possibly lose him to great walls of water? But she touched her amber beads superstitiously.

'Oswald,' she whispered, unaware of the amused smiles of the other diners who could see they were newly-weds, 'I love you. I love you so much! I'll never forget this happy day. Just us, by ourselves.'

FOURTEEN

They scuttled along the beach, a strong wind at their backs, but really this new year was proving much milder than the last. Maud pulled her tam o'shanter over her ears and glanced at Joe, to make sure he was still wound around with his scarves. They had been allowed out for a breath of air, she suspected, because Tilly had come down to have a chat with Rosa this afternoon. They seemed to be having lots of private talks recently, the kind where 'little pitchers' were mentioned meaningfully by her mother.

Nandy had gone on his bicycle to meet Petty at the docks. Maud was very envious of Nandy's new acquisition: she had been only partly mollified by the magic lantern she had received for Christmas. The family had already sat several times through the flickering adventures of Miss Grace Darling, the lighthouse keeper's heroic daughter. 'It isn't fair!' Maud had moaned. 'Gussie's got a bicycle.'

'Now, Maud,' Rosa reminded her. 'You know Nandy will need one when he goes to his new school. Your turn will come.'

'Even Aunt A's got one . . . ' Maud grumbled.

The warships were gathering, so Petty had told Rosa. But all Maud could see on the horizon was a solitary ship, hardly visible, as grey as the January ocean. 'Look, Joe, see the ship?' she called to her young brother, as he paused to pick up yet another treasure. His pockets were bulging with odd-shaped stones, glittering green glass, which he imagined to be emeralds, a dead, smelly crab and countless broken shells. Joe turned and stared curiously out to sea. 'Is it a warship, Maud?'

''Course it is.' Maud was the fount of all knowledge to Joe. 'It might even be a *German*,' she imagined. 'Spying on *our* ships.'

'Why?' Joe wanted to know.

Maud, despite the little pitchers label, had been listening in to her parents' conversations to some effect.

'Petty says matters are becoming grave between England and Germany.'

'Why?'

'Well, I *think* it's something to do with England's rights in the Transvaal.'

'Where's that?'

'Not sure. Africa, I think.'

They had ventured much further than Rosa had suggested.

'Look!' Joe pointed. Someone stood at the water's edge, training binoculars on the ship. It was Mr Lozenge.

'He's spying, he *must* be – he's a German, you know!' Maud breathed to Joe excitedly. 'Stand still, we don't want him to see us.'

But someone else had arrived unexpectedly, quietly, behind them. A heavy hand descended on Maud's shoulder, and a gruff voice advised: 'I should go home, young 'uns, if I were you. It'll be dark before you know it.'

It was a policeman, cape whipped up by the wind, breath curling like smoke. They watched as he walked on towards Mr Lozenge. They saw the photographer turn, lower the binoculars, raise his hat politely – but they were too far away, to Maud's disappointment, to catch what was being said.

'Come on, Maud,' Joe said, pulling at her sleeve. 'Let's go.'

'Wait 'til I tell Petty and Rosa that it looks as if Mr Lozenge has been arrested! I bet Nandy didn't see anything half as exciting on his old bicycle ride! Empty some of that out of your pockets, Joe, you're all weighed down!'

Tilly came over to the cottage under the sea wall nearly every afternoon for, much as she liked Oswald's mother, she had soon learned that her husband would be absent from her side for many hours. He was busy with what he could manage on the farm, for he must earn their keep, and the older woman had a very comfortable routine which Tilly would not have dreamed of disturbing. Little was expected of her except helping with the cooking. A baby would have kept her happy and contentedly busy.

'D'you think it's a judgement, Rosa? You know, for what happened years ago?' Tilly asked her friend. 'Oswald wants us to have a family just as much as I do.'

Rosa poured out tea, the universal comforter. 'Why not ask Dr Box, Tilly? He might be able to help—'

'Oh, Rosa, I *couldn't*!' Tilly's distress was evident. 'I'd have to tell him – everything. Whatever would he think of me?'

'He'd think the same as those of us who know already,' Rosa said stoutly. 'He's a good, compassionate man, Tilly.'

'Well, maybe I will, but I'll give it another month.' There was a pause, then: 'I saw him once, my little boy, you know,' she said very quietly. 'I used to wait for the nursemaid to wheel him out in the perambulator. I went there on my afternoons off. I never told Mrs Augusta. I daren't get close, in case *they* saw me. When he was about two, the nurse had him by the hand one day. She walked him to the gate, to talk to a friend. Rosa – oh, he had fair hair like mine, and my blue eyes – I wanted to rush up and snatch him away . . . Soon after, they moved away, I don't know where, and I had to try and forget him. But I never will. And now I'm being punished for it.'

'I lost a baby too, remember,' Rosa said softly. 'I understand. You can always talk to me, Tilly, you know that.'

Then the family arrived back in a state of great excitement. Nandy spiked Maud's guns. He and Petty had witnessed Mr Lozenge being escorted to the police station in town, and it was obvious it wasn't just for staring out to sea through his binoculars, like Maud thought.

'I must go,' Tilly said to Rosa. 'I'll – I'll think about what you said . . .'

As she went out, she heard Petty remonstrating with Nandy.

'Nothing's certain, lad . . .'

Then Maud saying with conviction: 'He *must* be a spy!'

He's just a nice old man, Tilly thought, who came to the Island a stranger, like me. *He* told me my feet would still be on London clay . . .

'Poor old Rossel,' Petty said. 'It's not the first time. He'll have to watch his step.'

Dr Box thought he had seen his last patient for the morning. He rose, with difficulty, from behind his desk, and crossed to the drugs cabinet. He would have to take a dose of morphine, it had come to that. His nurse watched with concern but said nothing. How much longer could he carry on? His clothes hung on him, for he was unable to eat much now. He sat down again, waiting for the agony to subside, or at least become bearable.

There was a tap on the surgery door. The nurse opened it, about to say that the doctor had finished and would be going out on his rounds. But Dr Box could see who was standing there.

'Come in, Mrs Relf,' he called. 'Is it about your husband?' He had not treated Tilly as a patient, but of course he had known her since she'd stayed with the family under the sea wall, and helped to care for Joe during his illness. And Oswald had visited him regularly for treatment, sometimes with his wife, when he'd first returned home.

'No,' Tilly faltered. 'I just wanted to ask you something, Doctor . . . '

The nurse busied herself discreetly at the sink. Dr Box saw a young woman who appeared to be in the best of health. Tilly saw a shadow of the kind man she had first seen caring for Joe, not much more than a year ago. She suddenly knew that she could not burden him with her troubles, tell him that story which must have been all too familiar to his ears. She said merely: 'I have been married some months now, Doctor, and we are anxious to start a family. Is – is there anything we can do to – help matters?'

The pain was blurring at the edges. Dr Box's grip on the edge of his desk slackened.

'Patience, my dear Mrs Relf – and don't worry. Things are bound to happen in due course.' It wasn't the answer she was hoping for, he was sure of that. He added: 'And make the most of the happiness you share right now with your husband, before you have to cope with the demands of little ones.'

Tilly's face cleared. He seemed to have said the right thing after all. They were so happy; they could wait a little longer.

'Thank you, Doctor.' She smiled.

'I look forward to seeing you again, Mrs Relf, when you wish me to confirm good news.'

As the nurse ushered Tilly out, he rested his head in his hands. That good news would need to be soon, he thought dully, for surely he would be unable to carry on much longer?

When the nurse returned, he asked: 'Would you write out an advertisement for me, Nurse, and send it to the *Journal*? I think it is time for me to have an assistant.'

'Oh, Doctor, you're right – we'll get it in the afternoon post,' she replied, and turned so that he would not see her tears.

FIFTEEN

'That would be wonderful!' Tilly said. 'But of course we don't want you to go. That little house under the sea wall, your family, meeting Oswald – well, it changed my whole life, coming here.'

Rosa had just told her that Petty was leaving on *The Revenge* for Delagoa Bay – war seemed imminent. Rosa and the children were returning to London. It seemed the sensible thing to do, with the older children's schooling in mind. They had offered the cottage to Tilly and Oswald – so convenient for the farm – and now Rosa added:

'Just the two of you together. It might help, Tilly, to give you your heart's desire . . . '

But first there was the visit to the pantomime – Petty's treat, he insisted. There were two to choose from. The mention of the Demon Rat in *Dick Whittington* made Maud blanch, so it was *Ali Baba and the Forty Thieves*.

They formed a large and merry party, strolling along to town with a swinging lantern to light the ruts in the road.

When they reached the built-up area this could be doused as the lamplighter would have set the gas globes flaring, illuminating the shuttered shops.

It was quite mild but they were all wrapped up, especially Joe. Rosa pulled his cap down and muffled his mouth with a thick scarf.

Tilly and Oswald brought up the rear, because then Oswald could put his arm round her waist, which was not really the thing to do in a family party. Every time he turned to talk to her, she felt his warm breath on her cold cheek, and knew she looked pretty wearing Augusta's boa, because he'd said so. To please him, which was so easy, she had plaited her hair into a crown, but she knew Oswald liked it best when she let it fall in a golden cloud each night round her shoulders, before she slipped into his arms in bed. Her heart still thumped alarmingly when they were close, but now she thoroughly enjoyed the sensation.

She watched the others, walking briskly ahead, with pleasure. What good friends they were. Joe and Maud, one either side of Petty, literally skipped to keep up with their father, she noted with a fond smile. They were adamant that they were not tired, despite their failure to take an afternoon nap as Rosa had required. She linked arms with Isabella and William. Nandy, of course, loped at the front of the party with the lamp.

Now and again Oswald would break into a tuneful whistle. Recognising 'She Was a Dear Little Dicky Bird', Petty,

Maud and Joe sang snatches of the chorus. Oswald winked at Tilly as they observed Rosa giving Petty a reproving poke in the back.

'Rosa thinks it's what Mrs Augusta calls infra dig,' Tilly whispered to Oswald. 'It's your fault, whistling.' But she gave him a daring little kiss – fancy, in public, she surprised herself – just to let him know that *she* liked his cheeky ways.

Petty had booked the second-best seats, in the stalls, and had also wisely paid the extra sixpence for 'early doors' to avoid the crush. Maud would have loved to have gone up in the gallery, and Petty had thought, Why not? remarking that: 'The atmosphere up aloft is much more colourful.' But Rosa had refused. 'Think what we might catch up there, Joe, we'd all soon be scratching. And as for colourful . . . the air is quite *blue* with ribaldry! And the *smell*! When they're not shouting coarse remarks, they're eating or, worse, drinking – no, it's well worth the extra to sit in comfort. Much more suitable for Mother, Tilly and me, and the children will have a better view of the stage.'

'Not fair!' Maud had moaned resentfully.

Petty wondered aloud slyly how Rosa knew so much about what went on in the heights. 'So that's what you and your friend Tilly get up to, eh, Rosa, when I'm away?'

The foyer walls were completely covered in huge posters, which enchanted Tilly. She gave Oswald a meaningful nudge, and he purchased a couple of penny programmes for them to share, while Petty produced their tickets with a flourish. 'Early doors, if you please!' They were ushered with due deference to their seats.

There were other family parties already ensconced. Jolly young clerks with cigars taking the place of the more familiar pencil tucked behind one ear; portly shopkeepers with their wives and offspring; pretty young ladies in hats adorned with sweeping feather wings, glancing coyly at escorts sporting the newly fashionable handlebar mustachios, which marked the bicycle enthusiast.

Refreshments were evident, even in the hallowed stalls, for there were already freshly cut ham sandwiches for sale.

'We'll get those,' Tilly told Rosa, proud that Oswald could provide as well as Petty.

She watched Maud, knowing that she was eagerly breathing in the smell of the place: hair pomade, powerful cheap scent, oranges being peeled, cigar smoke. Tilly smiled to herself as she saw Maud wriggling blissfully on the soft plush seat and staring up at the fat gilded plaster cherubs. Maud echoed Tilly's thoughts by saying aloud: 'I wonder how they got up there?'

Tilly passed the programmes along, and even the numerous advertisements were appreciated: Maud, naturally, was the most voluble. 'Ooh, look, Tilly – Rosa – Glaysher's is selling songs at one-third off – and banjoes. Wouldn't you rather have one of those than your old violin, Joe? And I don't believe this – it says Hood's sarsaparilla cured this woman's son of pimples. Ugh! Just look at this ghastly illustration, Nandy.'

'You'd best send for some, son,' joked Petty. Nandy, who was at a spotty stage, bridled.

Tilly and Rosa were more interested in the potted biographies of the main performers. Tilly observed of the leading lady: 'Must be forty at least – I wonder what she'll look like in tights?' Both being slim, they giggled, for the actress was extremely well upholstered.

Isabella gazed openly at the gorgeous hats and critically at the ominous split under each arm of the costume worn by the plump lady immediately in front.

Oswald, sitting at the end of the row, turned to contemplate with pleasure their varying expressions. Maud, much too excited to keep still, sat whispering in young Joe's ear, while Rosa and Petty held hands.

Oswald reached for Tilly's hand. She allowed his fingers to curl round her wrist, to insinuate themselves under her cuff: the delicious tingling caused her to turn from perusing the programme and smile at him. 'I love you,' was the message conveyed by the pressure of his fingertips.

How lucky I am, Tilly thought, to be able to keep my husband with me at home. Poor Rosa . . .

'I hope we have lively children like these, Tilly,' Oswald whispered.

'So do I,' she whispered back. 'Oswald – look how alike Maud and her grandmother are this evening. The way they cock their heads to one side when they're chattering – those black eyes –' Perhaps Maud was so special to her because she was of an age with Tilly's lost son.

None of them, in the years to come, would remember much of the pantomime story, but various individual impressions would remain. Joe would recall evil catapulting onto stage from the hidden trapdoor in a blinding flash of magnesium; Maud would remember the throaty singing of the Principal Boy, then the chorus coming through the audience, dispelling illusion with their tawdry costumes which had seemed so splendid under the bright lights. There had been the sudden shock of a youthful face with sores encrusting painted lips. Nandy stared longingly at the Gods where the exuberant occupants jostled on the wooden benches, and would recall the gnawed drumsticks flying through the air to strike unfortunates in the orchestra pit. The musicians bravely played on. Tilly would remember laughing, and clutching at her husband in the more frightening parts of the pantomime.

They left the hall with its litter of curling orange peel, its fascinating odours and deafening noise, and stepped outside into the deserted street. The magic remained during the brisk walk home.

Tilly and Oswald provided the necessary transport for the family and their luggage to the station. The larger stuff had been sent ahead by carrier. The cottage was empty but not for long, for Tilly and Oswald would be moving in there tomorrow.

Isabella clutched her daughter and the children in turn, her ready tears spilling onto them. 'I wish you did not go!' she sobbed. William cleared his throat noisily.

Tilly said softly: 'I will keep an eye on them, Rosa.' She gave her friend a brief hug, whispering for her ears alone: 'I'll write the minute I *know*, and I'll come and see you in a month or two – Mrs Augusta and Gussie, too, of course. And if you ever need me . . . '

'Oh, Tilly, thank you, but *he* must come first, remember that.'

'Train's coming!' Maud announced.

'We'll keep the home fires burning for you,' Tilly said, just as Oswald had said to *her* last Christmas.

SIXTEEN

Sunday 28 November 1897 was a blustery, breezy day: the swirling, bruise-dark clouds formed a wild kaleidoscope of changing patterns, yet the wind was south-westerly and the people of Sheerness were not unduly perturbed. Released from morning church, the young, 'with the wind in their tails', raced energetically up and down the beach, revelling in the tumult of the sea, spray smacking against their backs as they retreated from the waves. Dogs barked, skidding after pebbles; fires, fanned by the draught, roared up the chimneys of the cottages near the sea wall and loose window frames banged.

In Brixton, Augusta and Gussie dismounted from their bicycles after their morning spin. Augusta groaned: 'Honestly, Gussie, I must be off my head, going all that way to Hyde Park to bicycle round and round like the aristocracy.'

'The toffs don't have as many spills as you do, Mama!' Gussie grinned.

To their surprise, it was Tilly who opened the door to them, having been let in by Rosie, her sister, who was now taking her place. Augusta's genuine smile of pleasure faded when Tilly told her truthfully that she had been staying with Rosa and her family overnight. 'But I couldn't go back without seeing you both, Mrs Augusta.'

'Oh, well,' she said grudgingly.

'You can rub Mama with that awful embrocation, Tilly,' Gussie suggested. 'The whole house pongs of it!'

'Would you, Tilly?' Augusta groaned again. 'My lower back – you *know* – that hard saddle – and my calves . . . '

'Of course I will, Mrs Augusta. And I can stay here tonight if you'd like me to?' Tilly said brightly. Augusta was duly mollified.

In the bedroom, Tilly soon got to work with her soothing touch, tactfully massaging Augusta under cover of a towel while she lay face down on her bed.

'We miss you, Tilly.' Augusta's voice was muffled. 'How is married life? Still blissful, I hope?'

'Oh, yes, Mrs Augusta.' She'd answer the next question before it came, Tilly thought. 'A baby would make things perfect, but we'll be lucky eventually.'

'I understand how you feel.' Augusta's tone was wistful, for she was remembering those long years of waiting and hoping with George. 'Rosa and the children are well, I hope?' she continued more briskly, as Tilly's capable hands smoothed in a little more of the embrocation, which did, indeed, as Gussie inelegantly put it, pong. 'That's the spot – thank you, Tilly . . . Rosa hasn't bothered to come over for a week or two.'

Loyal as ever to both sides, Tilly replied: 'She'll be coming shortly, I'm sure. Joe has another cold, and she didn't want him to pass it on to Gussie, as she seems to go down with chills so easily.'

Augusta considered it very liberal of her to invite Tilly to share lunch with them instead of partaking of this in the kitchen with Rosie, which, naturally, Tilly would have preferred.

Gussie prattled happily: 'We saw the Diamond Jubilee Celebration, Tilly. The Queen looked so little – and, oh, so *old*!'

'She is old,' Augusta said. 'And I feel about the same age sometimes, particularly after a spin on that bicycle. But everyone who is anyone pedals these days, so I suppose I must.'

'How's Joe's Tid? Any more kittens?' Gussie asked. Joe had been persuaded that it was in the tom cat's best interests to stay on with Tilly and Oswald rather than risk being flattened on the streets of Tooting.

'He's very spry, Gussie. All the new kittens on the farm have bibs and paws just like his!' Tilly smiled.

Rosie came in with the dessert. She gave Tilly a wink. They'd catch up on the family gossip later.

Augusta, who never missed a trick, said surprisingly: 'Take the afternoon off, Rosie, you'll want to see something of your sister. You can amuse Gussie at the same time. I'll take a nap, to ease my aches and pains.' She could be kind and perceptive when she chose.

Back on the Isle of Sheppey, in the early hours of the next morning, the wind veered towards the north, increasing in force until it became a hurricane: more than twelve hours of terror lay ahead for the unfortunate inhabitants of the Island – their fortress was in the grip of an unstoppable force.

Chimney pots sheered off and crashed down, slates were hurled from roofs, and in the Broadway there was an ominous cracking as the wooden supports gave way in a tent which had been erected by a luckless Mr Cartlage to display his household wares. As the canvas collapsed, there was a thunderous crashing of all the crockery therein.

There were some narrow escapes, but mercifully no fatalities. A guest in the Britannia Hotel lay in bed smothered with plaster, staring, stunned, at a gaping hole in the ceiling. The party wall between her room and the next had received the impact of the tumbling chimney stack. The adjoining room's furniture was splintered like matchsticks. Thankfully, the room was unoccupied.

All over Sheppey people huddled fearfully together in downstairs rooms, some descending into damp, dark cellars. Mothers swathed their children in hastily snatched blankets, hugging them close. Each dwelling seemed an island in itself, terror creating isolation.

There were those who had been caught unawares, out and about at their daily work: a sailor unloading stores in the dockyard camber escaped death by mere inches when a metal plate came hurtling towards him. He swore before belatedly thanking God.

Battling towards their destroyer in a small boat, a crew who had been ashore celebrating the evening before were unable to embark and were forced to return to the pier where they moored up, taking what gear they could carry with them to the naval barracks. The shock had sobered them up. Their boat was badly damaged, and the vessels in the harbour were buffeted and battered ceaselessly.

The receding morning tide was forced back to the harbour by the gale and to the locals there were the unmistakable signs of an abnormal tide to come.

Oswald and his father, sensing this danger, began the task of driving their cattle and sheep onto higher ground. William and Isabella hurried to the big house, at the behest of Mr Arthur, where the attic rooms were hastily being made ready in case of flooding.

Soon after one o'clock the sea roared over the wall between the Toll House and West Minster. An hour later the tide rolled inevitably over the embankment. The pier was overwhelmed by furious white-crested waves, 'the wall of water' the gipsy had predicted to Tilly, and the ships in the harbour rocked like toy boats.

Blue Town was absolutely inundated. The flood water approached so rapidly, the teachers in the board schools had scarcely time to evacuate their pupils who had been dutifully sent to school despite the obvious danger. The small fry had to be carried away in the arms of their teachers, or on the backs of bigger children.

The station master's residence at Sheerness was flooded to a depth of three feet, likewise the police station. The good old Metropolitan Police firemen were quick to action, pumping out.

A couple of ducks swam serenely nearby, causing a little light relief. However, Blue Town did not suffer to the extent of other parts of Sheerness. By Tuesday morning most of the thoroughfares would be clear of water and the cellars pumped out. The flood in Mile Town was inevitable once the marshes and ditches were swamped – water invaded hundreds of homes there.

From Neptune Terrace to Cheyney Rock the waves rolled relentlessly. The terrace, which had suffered much from the invasion of the sea in the past, had been considered impregnable since its defences had been considerably strengthened. Yet as early as noon the waves cascaded over the stout breakwater and the wall was breached with devastating effect.

There was discordant music from the deep as a piano bumped monotonously against a ceiling in a house where furniture drifted downstairs.

Sections of the wall between Cheyney and The Ship on Shore were partially demolished, but from the pub to the Point, the War Department wall stood firm. Beyond the Point the damage was horrific, and the gunners filled the gaps with over 20,000 sandbags.

As the floods swept on, Oswald rode his horse recklessly through the surging water in an attempt to save a pitifully bleating ewe which had escaped his herding earlier. As he bent to grasp its fleece, it was swept away and the raging water almost took him, too. He felt the horse stumble, then it began desperately to swim. He clung on for dear life, his arms tight round the pulsating neck, with the coarse mane whipping back to sting his face. He suddenly thought of Sir Robert de Shurland, and Tilly's dear alarmed face when he'd related the story to her, for wasn't his own valiant steed a grey? Somehow, the horse scrambled on to safe ground and Oswald slipped off, crawling and scrabbling towards the farmhouse. His bad leg had completely given way. His mother came running towards him, shouting for help.

When at last she was able to peel off her son's sodden clothing, she heard him mumble: 'Thank goodness Tilly isn't here! She'd be so frightened . . . '

By Tuesday morning, when Sheerness resembled Venice, with small boats ferrying to and fro, tradesmen delivering what they could from their small stocks of undamaged goods to customers leaning dangerously from their bedroom windows, Oswald was burning and shaking with fever.

His mother needed no doctor to tell her that her son was suffering from pneumonia. He was gasping for breath, struggling to raise his head from pillows soaked with sweat. He constantly called, in his delirium, for Tilly. But she, although she had left Brixton on the Monday afternoon, was not yet home.

Dr Box was dying. He needed no other physician to confirm that. His nurse administered morphine, the ultimate dose, praying that he would not realise what was happening in the world outside. He slept fitfully and his young assistant looked in from time to time. He was newly qualified, not at all sure, poor chap, that he would be up to what lay ahead. Mercifully, the list of casualties was small.

When the message came from the farm, handed on from house to house, it was the young man who was rowed out there to do what he could for Oswald. When he returned from that struggle for life it was to find that Dr Box had passed peacefully away. The young doctor was saddened: in the short time he had been privileged to know the older man, he had learned something of what being one of the Island's doctors was about. He only hoped he could eventually live up to the ideals of Dr Box.

'We all loved him,' wept his nurse, who had been with him to the end. 'He was one of us, a Sheppey man.'

SEVENTEEN

The first intimation that Tilly had that the Island had been badly hit by the hurricane was when she was at Victoria station. The early evening papers reported damage from high winds over much of the country, the Medway area of Kent being particularly badly affected. She fretted throughout the journey from London, which was halted more than once whilst fallen trees were cleared from the line.

The last train to pass over the line to the Island on the Monday afternoon was the 2.20 p.m. from Sittingbourne. Tilly, arriving later, was told that there would be no further trains that day. The kindly porter at Sittingbourne, who had stirred the fire to cheer her on another winter's day, now staggered in with brimming buckets of coal to see the travellers who were stranded through the night. 'Got to keep warm, folks, you know!'

The stationmaster's wife bustled after him with cups of steaming tea. Tilly accepted one gratefully, warming her hands on the thick white china, sipping continuously, putting an invisible barrier between herself and the other passengers who were discoursing loudly.

'They reckon the pier is gone.' She heard this from one who had ventured out into town, seeking information. 'And the dockyard is badly hit . . . gas still on, believe it or not . . . unlike most of the Medway . . . Wonder how the wedding party is faring?' These people, their celebratory mood undampened, had decided to hire a carriage. For answer, a cheerful chap poked his head round the waiting room door:

'Room for one more! Anyone in a hurry to get home?'

Instantly Tilly was on her feet, spilling her tea.

'You go, missus,' the others urged her. 'You're on your own – got a young man waiting for you back home, we daresay? Us old 'uns don't mind the wait.'

'Oh, thank you, thank you!' she said fervently. She was soon hoisted up into the carriage and squeezed between an ample-figured grandmother and a reserved young man, absently fingering the faint down on his upper lip.

Tilly watched as the driver chivalrously spread a blanket over the laps of the bridal pair. She was reminded of the time they had journeyed in the wagon to Mr Lozenge's studio when Oswald's dad had spread a sheet for the two of them to sit on, to protect their wedding finery from the coarseness of the straw bales. A lump came into her throat. If only, she thought, she had not chosen this particular weekend to visit Augusta, and Rosa and her family.

'You can hold hands now!' the driver joked to the bride and groom. 'And the rest of you, hold tight, it may be a bumpy ride!' He shook the reins and they were off, to the rousing cheers of the ones left behind at the station, who had added a drop of something stronger to their tea.

It was a hair-raising journey. The terrified horses were soon struggling gamely through treacherous flood water, often over four feet deep. The carriage swayed and jolted alarmingly, and Tilly found herself clutched at from either side, almost crushed once as the heavy lady slipped sideways, causing Tilly in turn to be pressed against the young man's chest. He, in an agony of embarrassment, pushed them both upright once more. There were shrill screams from the bride and her mother, and soothing rumbles from their menfolk. The brandy flask passed from hand to hand. Tilly declined politely. She wanted to keep her wits about her, in case of catastrophe.

Several times they were in grave danger of overturning. It was impossible to see out of the carriage windows, which were blurred by their agitated breath, but they were aware of overhanging branches being wrenched free as they blundered along, and all too infrequently of dazzling lights.

Just before the King's Ferry Bridge, they were trundling through deep water when the front wheels struck a drowned sheep, and then everyone was shouting and panicking as the vehicle finally overturned. They all ended up in an undignified heap, Tilly cushioned by the plump woman's ample stomach. Rescue came swiftly. Strong men materialised from somewhere, righted their carriage and assisted the occupants in descending, one by one. They stood knee-deep in swirling, icy water. The blowing horses were released from the shafts, calmed and led away.

Tilly, hoisted unceremoniously over the shoulder of an unknown benefactor, was carried along with the rest of the party to a nearby house where they joined the family in an upstairs bedroom. Backs were turned whilst they divested themselves of saturated, torn outer garments, then they were urged to sit over the fire, decently shrouded in blankets, while minor cuts were seen to and they were plied with tea laced with alcohol, for the shock. The hiccupping sobs of the bride continued for some time.

Poor girl, Tilly thought, remembering her own wedding night, when she had cast off, at last, the painful memories of the past, together with Rosa's nightgown. She glowed at the very thought.

None of them slept at all that night.

The ballast train, hauling sixteen loaded trucks, steamed slowly and cautiously over the Swale Bridge the next morning. Thus tested, it was mercifully found to be safe. The damage to the line was extensive. The gang made the necessary repairs, yard by slow painful yard, as much of the track was still under filthy water.

Tilly, like her companions, was ferried home by rowing boat. The farmhouse, being well set back and on a rise, had escaped most of flooding, though the dairy had been awash.

Oswald's mother met her at the door and held her tightly in her welcoming arms. Tilly was shaking violently, as if she, too, were feverish, teeth chattering uncontrollably.

Gently, the older woman freed herself, took Tilly's hands firmly in her clasp, and told her what had happened.

'Now, Tilly dear, you must be very brave – the doctor hasn't been able to reach us again yet but I nursed his father through the same some years back.'

'How can I help Oswald?' she asked despairingly.

'All you can do until the crisis comes is to be with him, and pray for him. Come on up now. Dry your face, my love, that won't help.'

Tilly touched Oswald's cheek, adjusted the cooling pad across his forehead. She was all too aware of the fetid, warm smell of sickness. Oswald appeared to be staring back, but his gaze was blank. Desperately Tilly began to pray aloud, falling down heavily on her knees beside the bed, resting her hands on her clenched fists: 'Oh Lord, help us, I am unworthy, but Oswald, my dear Oswald . . . ' The rest was incoherent, a jumble of words. Oswald's mother retreated to the door, waited for a brief moment, then sadly left them together.

On the Thursday morning Tilly, curled up stiffly beside her husband on top of the covers and still wearing her travelling costume, for she had refused to leave Oswald's side, awoke sharply, suddenly, knowing that it was all over. His laboured breathing had ceased. And she knew that she was not even to have the solace of carrying his baby. They had to prise her away from him.

As the Island struggled back to normality, two funeral processions made their way to the church. The dedicated Dr Box and Oswald were laid to rest in adjacent plots.

EIGHTEEN

Clutching her basket case, the tall, thin girl in black walked along the seemingly endless street of mean houses. She turned in at Rosa's gate. Tilly placed her burden on the top step, and pulled the bell. Snow, for there had been a brief January fall, still lingered on the flower beds in the tiny front garden, but the road outside had been cleared by the roadmen with their shovels.

It seemed some time before the door opened, and Rosa stood there looking dishevelled. She was swaying slightly from fatigue, her face as pale and drawn as Tilly's own.

'Oh, Tilly – thank goodness you've come! I thought – I shouldn't have sent a telegram, you know, for you've had so much to bear, but—'

'I'm glad you did.' The ironic words, the sailor's term for Sheerness, followed unbidden: 'It was sheer necessity. You needed me, didn't you? All of you.' Tilly closed the door. She could immediately smell the Lysol-soaked sheets which must shroud the upstairs doors.

'Yes. Diphtheria,' Rosa told her. 'Joe first, although he's pulling through, thank God, then Nandy – the doctor's with him now. And Maud ... Tilly, it's so unfair of me, my dear, but the doctor insisted I must send for someone. I shouldn't have brought you here, *you* might ... '

'I had *two* telegrams,' Tilly told her. 'Mrs Augusta sent one too. She said, 'They need you, Tilly, please go to them.' Can I go straight up?' she asked.

Once more, Joe wore his little monkey cap. Maud's long tresses had been shorn, and she vowed to keep them so, revelling in the freedom once she was on the mend. She would learn, when she was older, that it had been Tilly who had saved her life by breaking the foul membrane which had closed up her throat and would surely have suffocated her. Nandy, fortunately, had suffered no hair loss due to his fever.

Tilly watched them fondly. She thought she loved her children from under the sea wall equally, but even Rosa and Augusta could tell that Tilly now had a special place in her warm and loving heart for Maud.

Rosa watched out for Augusta and Gussie on their first visit since the quarantine had been declared over.

'Catching up on your schoolwork?' Tilly asked Nandy approvingly as he opened his exercise book on the table.

'There'll be a few awkward moments, I guess. Tilly, don't you?' Rosa asked. 'Oh, here they come, will you let them in?'

She was right.

'Won't you come back to me now, Tilly?' Augusta asked her directly. 'I would still keep Rosie on – there's plenty for you both to do.'

'She's not going to leave *us*,' Rosa said firmly.

'Let's go upstairs, Gus, Joe . . . ' Maud sensed an argument ahead, and she wasn't up to joining in. Nandy kept his head down over his books. He intended to hear all.

Tilly sighed, looking from one to the other. She was so fond of them both, she thought. If only they could unbend towards each other. She didn't relish being pulled between them. But her mind was made up.

Rosa flashed her a grateful glance as she said, 'I think Rosa needs me the most at the moment, Mrs Augusta. But I don't actually *need* to work for my living now, you know. Oswald's parents are going to sell up and retire. When everything is settled, they have promised me Oswald's share so that I can be fairly independent.'

'You are very fortunate,' Augusta observed. Yet she was relieved to see how resolute Tilly could be. So her training of the girl had not been wasted. Still, it rankled that Tilly had chosen Rosa on this occasion. She added her usual last word: 'If you two ever fall out, you know where to come.' She would spring her surprise after tea, she thought.

'Of course,' Tilly added, 'if you ever need me in an emergency, you only have to say, Mrs Augusta.' And she really meant it.

'I brought some things – cakes and biscuits. Your sister's baking is improving by the day, Tilly,' Augusta told her, handing her a basket. Augusta was definitely licking Rosie into shape.

'I'll make the tea,' Tilly told them, glad to escape to the kitchen. Old habits died hard, she thought.

'I'm hoping to come to your school in September,' Maud told Gussie.

'Oh, good.' She grinned. 'Then you'll probably be in my class. Mama gave up on me, you see, says I'm a real duffer. She couldn't do any more for me, and says perhaps it's worth paying for me to go to school after all.'

'You've a got a *real* gift, Gus – just look at your art,' Maud enthused.

'Mama thinks that's all by the way. She says it's not fair you three have got all the brains in this family,' Gussie confided. 'Maud, isn't it exciting that you're going to move nearer us, too!'

Joe butted in, puzzled, 'Are we, Maud? Rosa hasn't said anything to us.'

'Better keep quiet about it, then,' she said wisely, for once.

Tilly could see Rosa massing her defences as she served tea. Augusta obviously had something more to say.

'I have bought another house,' she announced at last. 'Not too far from our home. I have written to my brother to say that I intend to offer it to you. You will need more space, especially if Tilly is staying on with you indefinitely – where on earth you imagine my brother can go when he comes home on leave next, with you all so cramped up . . . and you may pay me rent, Rosa, so that you need not gripe at my offering you charity. This new house will be far more suitable for your needs, nearer the children's schools and in a much more salubrious area. No wonder they were so ill. This is the sort of place where germs are rife.'

Actually, Tilly knew, Rosa had been thinking along the same lines. But she also knew that Rosa would not appreciate Augusta's interference.

'I'd love to be nearer Gussie,' Maud put in.

Oh, let Rosa accept graciously! Tilly thought. I wouldn't feel I was deserting Mrs Augusta and Gussie then. I could easily pop between the two of them.

'I suppose we can look at it and see if it's suitable,' Rosa agreed reluctantly. 'But it would only be a temporary arrangement,' she added.

'When I – when I am better off,' Tilly said, trying hard not to remember why this was, 'we, Rosa and I, have a few ideas for going into business together. Just in a very small way, you understand,' she floundered, aware of Rosa's reproachful look. Augusta would no doubt begin her usual probing now. Had she said too much?

But Rosa's capitulation over the house made Augusta magnanimous. 'You can move in as soon as you like,' she said. And asked no more.

It was to be several years before Tilly and Rosa could fulfil their ambition to begin buying a property of their own, in joint partnership, to show Augusta that they were capable of running their own lives, in their own way. In Brixton, not in Sheerness.

They went back to the cottage under the sea wall several times each year, but now it was Tilly who paid the rent, for she knew she could never part with that precious reminder of those last few happy months with Oswald. One day, she promised herself, she would return for good.

Tilly didn't think she would ever marry again, for where would she ever find his match?

PART TWO

1904–1907

ONE

Brixton, September, 1904: where the electric trams whined and jolted along their allotted lines yet the Tilling horse-buses still reigned supreme. The busy main thoroughfare was crowded with bustling, thriving shops, everyone's favourite store, the Bon Marché, being the most packed of all. On the other side of the road was the raucous, sprawling, hotly odorous market, with the lemonade sellers squeezed in between the fresh-fish stalls and fruit and vegetable merchants, dispensing glasses of their iced drink. They were having a field day in what was truly a glorious Edwardian summer. Likewise, the short dark smiling Italians, mopping their brows with their brilliantly patterned kerchieves, turning the handles of their ice buckets until the ice cream was thoroughly chilled. Shaded by the striped awnings over their handcarts, they called: 'Hokey pokey, penny a lump – that's the stuff to make you jump!'

Maud was much too inclined to loiter, entranced by the sales spiel. Tilly had just led her firmly away from the winkle stall where the challenge had been issued directly to her young friend: 'Winkles h'as eaten by Miss Marie Lloyd – aphro – dissi – ac. Now, can *you* resist 'em, young lidy?'

Maud could actually. Now she said: 'D'you fancy an icecream, Tilly?' She added, in a fair imitation of Augusta: 'Mind, you'll have to finish it before we leave the market – and don't you dare walk about licking it!'

They were both laden with heavy baskets. When Tilly said: 'I'd love something to cool me down, and an ice cream will do very nicely, thank you,' Maud plumped her burden down at her feet in relief. She ignored the skinny little terrier with the prominent rib-cage wriggling out from a nearby stall, eager to investigate her shopping. Tilly shooed him away.

Maud fanned her rosy face with a theatrical gesture, which owed more to Aunt A than she would care to think. Just seventeen, she topped her petite mother Rosa by a mere inch. To her chagrin, she was not as slender as her willowy cousin Gussie, but to the young Italian scooping deep into the ice cream, she appeared delightfully rounded. She wore a pretty blouse of soft nun's veiling, with a broad belt nipping in her neat waist and emphasising the fullness of her pale green cotton skirt. As a concession to Rosa and Tilly, for she hated hats, she wore her old school panama at a jaunty angle.

Noting the shining fall of black hair tucked behind her ears, and her merry, almost almond-shaped dark eyes, the vendor dared to ask, with a sidelong glance at her companion whose good looks he also appreciated: 'Are you one of us, miss?'

Smiling, Maud shook her head. 'I'm afraid not. There's just a touch of Spanish in my blood – my grandmother, you know!' She observed, from the corner of her eye, that Tilly was wearing her mock-disapproving look – she could always get away with things when she was with Tilly, she thought, unlike Rosa who, as her mother, considered she needed pulling up now and again, even though she had now left the Girls' High School and was enrolled at the Typewriting College.

The young man spread his hands in mock disappointment.

'Come on, Maud,' Tilly whispered in her ear. But she couldn't be cross, for the girl was completely natural and friendly.

'My treat,' Maud said. She paid the older seller for the ices. 'Let's stand back here a minute,' she said. The ices were blissfully cooling. Maud rolled her tongue right round hers. 'Mmm. Now, who else can make ice cream like the Italians, Tilly?' The younger seller gave her a saucy wink.

They had chosen an unfortunate place, right by the tooth-pulling booth. There came an agonised bellow and a large man staggered back, his mouth still agape, blood pouring from an empty socket.

Maud paled at the sight of this, clutching at Tilly's arm. The perpetrator of the pulling held aloft in triumph the offending molar, still clenched in the pincers. He had made sure of payment before he lunged, and expected no gratitude. The injured party stumbled away, clutching his grubby handkerchief to his face.

'You'll thank me tomorrer!' the pincer man called after his victim. Another customer edged forward nervously. The previous patient's bad tooth was dropped into the waiting bucket. 'Got yer money ready?' the 'dentist' asked.

A small crowd was gathering to watch the fun. Maud lifted her basket. She had a smear of ice cream on her lip. 'How disgusting!' she exclaimed loudly. 'I feel quite sick, Tilly, don't you? Can't we go home now? We must have got everything on Rosa's list – and more, eh?'

Tilly nodded. Home was the new house she and Rosa had just taken on. At long last they were going to be free of any obligation to Augusta. And Petty, Rosa's husband, was coming home – for good this time! He was retiring from the Navy, and was shortly to take up a post with a shipping company in Fenchurch Street, so they would be very conveniently placed in that respect.

As they walked towards their turning, they paused at the corner of a cul-de-sac to watch as the billstickers dipped their long-handled brooms into the paste buckets, unfurling then smoothing with such consummate skill the posters displaying the forthcoming attractions of The Empress. Top of the bill was Fred Karno's Company with *The Mumming Birds* and . . .

'Ooh, look, Tilly!' cried Maud in excitement. 'The *Bioscope*! D'you suppose Rosa'll let us go?'

'I'll put in a good word.' Tilly smiled. 'I reckon you deserve a reward for passing your Matric.' She was very proud of Maud's scholastic achievements. 'I'll even take you, if Rosa says she's too busy.'

The billstickers' rival, the boardman, paraded ponderously with his boards, one to the front, one to the back.

'We must tell Rosa about *this*!' Maud exclaimed. 'Furniture auction. Not far, Tilly, just down the road in fact, at two o'clock. We can't miss that; we need more stuff to fill that great house, don't we?'

Tilly reminded her: 'I thought Rosa said we'd keep those beds the landlord left behind? Joe and I enjoyed making a bonfire of the mattresses before you were up, I must say.'

Maud wrinkled her nose. 'I couldn't come downstairs because it was all smoky everywhere. I'm jolly glad Rosa decided to order new feather tickings. She keeps on saying she wants the rooms to look homely for the lodgers, so I know she'll want to go to the auction.'

'*If* we get any lodgers . . . ' Tilly told her.

'Rosa says you won't be able to pay the mortgage between you if you don't!' Maud grinned, which was all too true. 'Rosa's recklessness seems to have rubbed off on you, Tilly, you know – Aunt A thoroughly disapproves.'

The local bobby, sweltering in his thick uniform, gave them a friendly greeting as he, too, paused to peruse The

Empress's poster while unobtrusively easing his tight collar. The weight of his helmet caused a perpetual headache, resulting in an unintentionally stern expression, enough to scare off the scruffiest urchin. Also, he was suffering from the raw, red patch which the strap had rubbed under his chin.

The other onlookers melted away as if by magic. Street traders lurking near the Town Hall steps crossed the road in peril from the ceaseless traffic; a gaunt man, with greasy side-locks curling on his threadbare collar, shoulders bowed under the weight of a row of stiff rabbits hanging from their toes from his pole, was followed by a young shoeshine boy in sacking apron, incongruously bare-footed, clutching his dirty rags, brushes and blacking. Maud blenched at the sight and stench of the rabbits. She suddenly recalled the one Grandpa William had produced from his pocket during the Big Freeze on the Island. Her eyes filled with tears and Tilly, intuitive as always, gave her a tender little smile.

Grandpa had died quite unexpectedly only two weeks after the old Queen. He had sat down to lace his boots, had given a tiny sigh, and his life was at an end. Although he had been seventy-four, quite an age, to the family he had seemed indestructible. Isabella had come to them in Brixton for a week or two, but had soon returned to the Island, to busy herself once more with her endless sewing, content with her memories once the first shock and pain of losing her William had eased.

The flower girl, middle aged and motherly, beshawled despite the heat, remained comfortably in her favourite shop doorway, where her flowers would not fade. She smiled at Maud and Tilly, proffering a bunch of mixed blooms from her basket. 'Sniff these, my luvs, breeve yer cares away.'

'Got sixpence, Tilly?' Maud asked. 'I spent my all on the ice cream. You know how Rosa loves a vase of flowers in the hall.'

Their latest abode was situated at the not quite so desirable end of a solemn street crowded with solid three-storey middle-class residences. Down their terrace, several of the front windows displayed discreet cards which merely said: 'VACANCIES'. Tilly and Rosa had already agreed that they would be more specific, which Maud joyfully anticipated would cause ructions when Aunt A found out.

The coal-cart outside the house was a very welcome sight. The coalman had just levered up the cast-iron cover, with the elaborate patterning which Maud was looking forward to making a rubbing from, and was preparing to shoot the first load down into the cellar. They sidestepped the cloud of choking dust as the huge, glistening coals poured forth.

There was just a minute front garden, sparsely grassed and enclosed by high, ornate railings. Hazy smoke still drifted lazily round from the back garden beyond the conservatory which Rosa longed to fill with plants, fondly remembering the great glasshouses at Mr Arthur's house on Sheppey. The smell of the burnt mattresses caused Maud's sensitive nose to twitch again.

'Still, I suppose the bugs won't bite now, eh, Tilly?' she said.

Tilly fumbled for her key. 'They must be out the back still. Well, Maud, we can soon have the fires lit to air the bedrooms – d'you know, the sweep said he'd never seen so much soot? The last people must have been really careless. We were cleaning up all yesterday. You were well out of it at College.'

They crossed the lofty hall, with the galleried landing above, treading in the reflected rainbow patterns from the stained-glass window over the front door. Down the short flight of steps into the kitchen to put down their baskets on the familiar table – the one from the cottage – with a sigh of relief.

'Maud, behave herself?' Rosa asked.

'Of course,' Tilly replied demurely. She filled the kettle and lit the gas with that satisfying plop. 'Luxury – a gas stove at last!'

Maud said sharply: 'Rosa, I'm *seventeen*, you know – not seven. Tilly doesn't have to be my keeper.'

'I'm not so sure . . . ' Rosa flashed back.

Maud began to unload the shopping. She wished she could remember to keep her mouth shut on occasion. She wouldn't hurt Tilly for the world – she was like a second mother to her, she thought, someone she could confide in much more readily than her mother who sometimes flew off the handle. Not that Tilly *looked* like her mother, more an older sister, she supposed, even though nowadays she wore her glorious flaxen hair coiled in a thick knot in the nape of her neck. Tilly was still so pretty, it was a wonder she hadn't had proposals, especially being an independent widow.

Maud had done well at school, duly winning a scholarship, delighted to have Gussie, despite her seniority, as a classmate. Nandy, following technical school, had recently left home to become a naval cadet. Clever Joe was now a pupil at the grammar school. Now the family were off her hands, it was time for Rosa and Tilly to put their plan into action.

'There's an auction this afternoon,' Maud informed Rosa. 'We can all go, can't we? It begins at two o'clock.'

'Don't see why not,' she said. 'If you make the sandwiches for lunch, Maud.'

'What with?'

'Oh, use your initiative.'

'I forgot to say,' Tilly remembered belatedly, 'a parcel came from Dartmouth . . .'

'Must be Nandy's laundry. It'll have to wait to be done with ours on Monday, eh, Tilly?'

'Initiative sandwiches,' Maud moaned. 'What d'you reckon, Tilly? Cheese?' Tilly passed the block they had bought in the market. 'Don't you think,' Maud continued, 'that Rosa's hard on old Nandy – she says he makes far too much of the terrors of the lower deck.'

Tilly said: 'He's just growing up, like you.'

Maud cut great lumps off the cheese. There was no arguing with that.

Joe appeared from the garden, and grabbed a sandwich with his filthy hands. Maud whacked the back of his hand with the bone handle of the butter knife, and said: 'I know you've got to eat a peck of dirt before you die, Joe, but – well, I hope you get *indigestion*.'

TWO

The auction room was already crowded, mostly with men. Tilly felt excited for she'd never been to a sale before. She took their advice and stuck close behind Rosa and Maud. Being small, and determined, they managed to slip and wriggle their way through, here and there, hanging grimly on to each other's belts. Finally, with hats knocked awry, and the odd bruise or two delivered from a protesting elbow, they found themselves on the extreme edge of the front row, forced to stand as all the seats were firmly occupied. They couldn't resist exchanging smug grins.

'You two . . .' Tilly grinned at them. They were so alike, and didn't know it.

The items to be auctioned were brought through, one by one, from the store room, carried by muscular men wearing long white aprons, sleeves rolled up, collarless, but with bowler hats clamped firmly on their heads.

Tilly was fascinated by the auctioneer, with that tram-line centre parting in his well-oiled hair, grizzled side whiskers and neat chin beard, for he possessed a rich, resounding fruity voice and some amusing sales patter. Each piece was shown with a little anecdote, mostly invented, Tilly suspected, on the spur of the moment, but she was at one with the thoroughly appreciative audience, mostly there for the entertainment.

'This musical instrument, may I inform you, is wholly holy – reluctantly cast forth like many a sinner from the Primitive Methodist Chapel – but that's not to say that it should be touched by the paws of a primitive performer. Oh, no, indeed. Just note the quality of the casing of this harmonium, the gleaming of the keys – not a single one missing! This, may I say, cries out for harmonious hands. Now, what am I bid for this handsome h'article? Did I hear *five shillings*? Who is having me on? Come, gents, we can do better than that. We'll start at fifteen, twenty, twenty-two and six – was that twenty-five? Twenty-seven and six? Yes, Madam, the little dark lady at the front – thirty? Any more bids? *Sold!* To Madam on my left.' The hammer crashed down.

Rosa's face was flushed. 'Should I have?' After all, it was Tilly's money too.

''Course,' Maud returned, while Tilly was still thinking about it. 'It's for Joe, isn't it? He'll be over the moon,' she added generously.

As the afternoon wore on, Tilly failed to stem Rosa's recklessness. Maud, naturally, egged her mother on.

'It's a prayer chair, girls, a prie-dieu. Oh, I've always wanted one!'

'For praying?' Tilly asked wryly.

'No, for *sewing*!' There was brisk bidding, but it was knocked down to them for twenty-five shillings.

Their most expensive purchase was a chaise-longue. It was definitely the auctioneer's story which won Tilly over this time. Such a romantic tale!

'This marvellous piece of furniture has been out to India and back – note how it hinges in the middle for easy transportation. Belonged to a general – got himself garrotted, he did.' A ghastly grimace. 'His widow returns home, quickly ties the knot again and decides to dispose of a few quality pieces of furniture. Now, you may not want to ship it back to India, but if it's Islington you have in mind, you can take it to pieces just the same. Quality horse-hair stuffing, fine black leather. Gild the lily – gild the carving – and you'll be able to repose regally and ruminate. Fifty shillings? Not a bad start. Sixty, seventy, eighty – thank *you*, Madam, shall we say four whole guineas? *Sold!*'

'Did you really intend to nod, Tilly?' Maud was impressed. 'Fortunately, the roll didn't roll overboard, eh?' She was irrepressible.

'Did I *really* buy it?' Tilly asked faintly.

To their surprise they were the sole bidders for a banquette seat which would be ideal for the lodgers.

'Surplus to requirements at The Old Swan – just a few beer stains on the old red plush!' The auctioneer looked directly at them.

Maud was despatched to fetch Joe. They watched as their goods were piled on to the handcart.

'You're welcome to borrer the barrer. Tell your lad to bring it back smart, though. Two bob suit?'

'Got a florin, Tilly?' Rosa whispered.

'That leaves me with – nothing.' Tilly obliged with the coin, thinking thank goodness they had paid this month's mortgage in advance.

Joe gripped the handles, Maud pulled from the front, and Tilly and Rosa rushed alongside, anxiously pushing back anything which appeared precarious.

'Push, Joe!' Maud shouted. 'When you go slow, it wobbles.'

'You're impeding progress, Maud,' Joe called back. Tilly thought fondly what a fine boy he had grown into, shooting up rapidly since his fourteenth birthday.

They steered dangerously round the corner into their street.

Tilly spotted her first; that familiar figure, some distance ahead.

'Mrs Augusta! Heading for our house . . . '

'The Brixton Empress!' Joe sang out saucily.

The rumbling of the wheels caused Augusta to turn, then stare, aghast, hand on hip. The four of them kept pushing, hopeful smiles frozen on their faces, because there was no escape.

'Whatever will your new ncighbours think?' Augusta was outraged.

'They'll think how enterprising we are, Aunt A,' Maud retorted.

Augusta's lips compressed. There was an indignant rustling of her silk skirts. She wore a hat in matching blue secured by a massive hat pin which she would obviously have dearly liked to use on them in turn.

'Tilly, I'm really surprised at *you*,' Augusta told her. 'All that good sense I instilled in you, gone right out of your head!'

She rushed to open the gate, propelling Mrs Augusta through.

'We won't get the cart past the posts,' Joe said. 'We'll have to unload on the pavement and carry the stuff through!'

Tilly babbled: 'Come into the drawing room.' Why was it, she wondered, that one look from Mrs Augusta and she slipped back into her serving role?

There were fierce whispers from the hall. Tilly was sure that Mrs Augusta could hear, too.

'Go and entertain her, Maud.'

'You know she can't stand me . . . '

'Well, I can't put up with her – not 'til I've washed my face and hands and powdered my nose . . . '

Tilly was acutely embarrassed. 'They don't—' she began.

'Don't mean it? Don't be ridiculous, Tilly, of course they do. To tell the truth,' Augusta was actually smiling, 'I enjoy stirring 'em up!'

'Oh!' As Tilly turned to rush to the kitchen, she almost collided with Joe, who was struggling in with a large section of the chaise-longue.

'Make way for the worker!' he sang out cheerily. 'Maud and I will put it together for you to lounge on. Then you'll have to forgo the pleasure of my company while I take the handcart back.'

'I'd much rather wait until it's been cleaned,' Augusta returned tartly. 'You mentioned tea, Tilly? I don't approve of females doing furniture removals.'

After all, it was Maud who brought in the tray of tea for her aunt. 'I brushed the straw off the plates. I poured the tea in the kitchen, hope you don't mind, only the spout got chipped in the move, and it drips.' She plonked down a shop cake on the table. 'How's Gussie? Tilly and I swapped places,' she explained. 'She's stronger than me.'

'My daughter has a nasty cough, poor child. I didn't feel she should come with me.'

'Nice of you, though I don't suppose we'd have caught it.' Maud passed her a slice of cake.

'That was not the reason.' Augusta was riled. 'I thought there might be too much dust about here, and I was right.

Maud!' she expostulated, as her niece bent over the table. 'I do believe you're not wearing stays!'

'Right first time, Aunt A. I can't abide 'em. They torture your insides.'

Even though Augusta was constricted by her own corset, she wasn't having that. 'It's not decent. Whatever is your mother thinking of?'

'I don't think she's noticed, to tell you the truth.'

'And what's all this Gussie tells me, about *lodgers* . . . Surely my brother doesn't approve?'

'Yes, he does. Shall I refill your cup, Aunt A?' And she added, under her breath, 'I won't forget to put in plenty of sugar for the shock.'

As Maud dodged out of the room, Tilly looked round the door.

'Leave this madhouse, Tilly, come back to me,' Augusta entreated.

'Just off with the cart,' Joe called from the hallway.

'I'm going,' Augusta said abruptly.

'I'll see you out,' Tilly said quickly.

Rosa reappeared at last, and thanked her sister-in-law for calling.

Augusta turned at the door. 'Come to lunch tomorrow,' she suggested gruffly. 'I've a few things you might be glad of, if you *must* have paying guests. Have you treated the bedsteads, Tilly? Spirits of Naptha, that's the stuff.'

'Nothing hopped out when we burned the old mattresses,' Tilly reassured her. Augusta shuddered. Bugs were such disgusting things.

'I shall, of course, send *my* things by *proper* means,' she emphasised. 'Come promptly at one o'clock.'

THREE

The copper was bubbling, the washboard leaned soapily in the sink, and Tilly was already turning the mangle on the first batch of rinsed washing when she noticed Nandy's untidy parcel on the shelf in the scullery. 'We've overlooked our young sailor's washing!' she exclaimed. 'Never mind, there's plenty of room in the copper. Can you give the clothes a poke, please, Maud? You've got a spare moment before you go to College, haven't you?' she asked.

Monday morning was always so hectic. They rose about 5 a.m. – Tilly's mum had been unable to oblige this week either. Over the years their roles had become defined: Tilly, in return for her keep, was still, in a way, maid-of-all-work, only there were plenty of hands to help. Rosa, whose profession it had been after all, did most of the cooking. But the nice thing about this unofficial arrangement, Tilly thought, was that she felt independent, an equal member of the family. When Petty had come on leave in the past, she could unobtrusively vanish to the cottage for a while, visiting Oswald's parents and Isabella, or go to stay with

Mrs Augusta from time to time, especially when Gussie was unwell. Lately, despite the impulsive acquisition of this house by herself and Rosa, and their involvement in taking in lodgers, she had begun to wonder if she should really have committed herself to all this. How would Petty take to the notion that she would always be around? Also, she had to admit to herself that her funds were getting low.

Tilly unravelled the knot on the parcel and put the string in her apron pocket: Rosa would have thrown it away, but she would add it to the big ball in the table drawer later. She still practised the little economies she had learned in service. She extracted the letter from the parcel, handed it to Maud to pass on to Rosa, just coming in, with another load of linen in her arms, and tossed the whites into the copper.

'I must put on the hated hat and be off in a moment – what does Nandy say?' Maud asked.

Seeing Rosa's grim expression, Tilly enquired anxiously: 'Not bad news, I hope?'

'He's got *married*, girls, that's what – under age, too. Never said a word. Some young girl just your age, Maud! Not that he *had* to, or so he says, but maybe he had reason to think that he *did* . . . D'you know, all this happened six months ago, can you believe it? They've kept it secret all this time. The girl is still living at home and they haven't even told her parents yet. Tilly, why ever didn't you wait before you threw those whites in the copper?'

'Sorry . . . ' poor Tilly murmured.

Rosa scribbled hastily on the back of the letter with a stub of pencil, snapping the point with her final full-stop. 'There – that should let him know what we think about it: 'YOUR WIFE CAN DO YOUR WASHING IN FUTURE.'

'Maud, tie it up and take it away!' She wiped away the angry, scalding tears on the hem of her apron.

Tilly at once made up her mind to write to Nandy, proffering the advice that the girl should tell her parents immediately. As she tried to soothe Rosa, it was Maud who heard the banging on the front door.

Then she saw who was standing on the doorstep: 'Petty, you've timed it just right! Come and see what's up, Rosa's bawling her eyes out!'

Tilly went quietly to put the kettle on. She did not want to witness the bear hug in which Rosa then Maud were enveloped – despite Rosa's protests that she was all damp and soapy and that Petty might have given warning of his arrival so that she could have combed her hair, and that they wouldn't have started the washing if they'd known . . .

Tilly wanted to cry too. It was seven years since she had lost Oswald, yet still she stretched out her arms in longing when she woke in the night. Would she ever get over it?

'Cup of tea when you're ready,' she called. She knew that Rosa would forget the washing, that she had a hard slog ahead of her, but it was best to keep out of the way for a while, she thought.

Thanks to Tilly's intervention, another letter arrived shortly from Nandy, revealing that the girl's irate parents were pressing for an annulment. Nandy begged forgiveness from his mother for a 'foolish mistake'.

'Write back soon, won't you, Rosa?' Tilly asked. She and Joe had moved another bed into Joe's room, for she had said firmly that Nandy must have a home to return to.

She usually made some excuse to leave Rosa and Petty on their own in the evenings. Once, Petty discovered her sitting alone in the scullery, and said: 'Oh, come on, Tilly, why the long face? We wondered where you were. Come and talk to us.'

She replied: 'I was just going up to bed. Goodnight.' And left him standing there.

She broached the subject first. 'I don't think it's right after all, Rosa, that I should stay on here. You don't need me like you did. I can always go back to Mrs Augusta.' They were peeling potatoes for supper.

'Tilly!' Rosa was reproachful. 'How can you say that? After all we've planned! Did you think I'd abandoned our idea for the lodgers and all?'

'Well – it's not just that. I've been dipping into my capital – and – I should have realised you and Petty ought to be on your own. You don't need me hanging around all the time . . .'

'But he thinks it's a wonderful idea, Tilly, he'd hate to lose you as much as I would. You're part of our family – you kept us all going while he was away. You never said your funds were getting low. But that's not a problem, is it? We'll be working women shortly!'

Tilly put down the paring knife. 'I must say, I wasn't sure I could go back to what I was—'

'That's settled then!' Rosa told her. 'We'll all sit down tonight and work things out properly this time. Happy again?'

'Oh, yes!' Tilly smiled. 'I am!' This way she could keep her status, and her independence, and still be part of this happy household.

They were all prepared for the lodgers: Tilly and Joe had the two attic bedrooms and Maud the room next to the upstairs bathroom. Rosa and Petty slept in the front room opposite the drawing room which had folding doors leading to the family breakfast room. This left the big double room on the first floor, and an adjoining single room, free to let. The dining room would be exclusively for the lodgers' use and sharing the drawing room was no problem for weren't 'theatricals' out in the evenings?

It was a wonderful idea, Tilly mused, for there were all those theatres and music halls, all within a tuppeny ride of Brixton, and the late-night trams were so convenient. And, oh, what fun! as Maud enthused. *Their* lodgers wouldn't be boring old dodderers who'd expect their shoes to be cleaned and it to be quiet at all times . . .

Tilly leaned to look over Joe's shoulder as he penned a card for the front window. 'Such lovely copperplate, Joe,' she marvelled. Then she whispered: 'I saw you, shaking your pen – put your foot over the ink splatters for now, I should, and I'll try a drop of milk on 'em later . . .'

Maud and Rosa were unpacking the last box of books to stack in the large oak bookcase Augusta had given them. They had all worked like blazes this past week to make ready for the lodgers.

'Ah, the old *Quiver*!' Rosa exclaimed. 'All moral stories. Poor little orphans – abandoned babies—'

Stories about girls like me, Tilly thought, wincing, as Maud banged the old Sunday reading books together to dispel the dust.

'Just look at Joe's notice,' she said to Maud and Rosa.

ROOMS TO LET. THEATRICAL BOARDING HOUSE.

BED, BREAKFAST AND EVENING MEAL. £1 PER PERSON, WEEKLY.

APPLY WITHIN. TELEPHONE INSTALLED.

As Joe went to display the card prominently in the front window, there was the unaccustomed shrilling of the telephone. They were all still highly nervous of using this.

'Are you there, Rosa?' crackled Petty's voice in one ear while she stuck her finger in the other. She nodded, both Maud and Tilly nudged her, and she managed: 'Yes, dear, I am – is that you?'

''Course it is!' Maud put in impatiently, eavesdropping.

It was Tilly who answered the knock on the door. She poked her head round the drawing-room door and almost squeaked: 'The card's worked already – a lady, Rosa! What shall I do?'

'Show her in, please, Tilly.' Rosa composed herself hastily as she replaced the receiver with shaking hands. She had cut her husband off without a farewell.

'Miss Kitty Moriarti,' Tilly announced. Her eyes widened at the sight of Miss Moriarti's elegant backview as the lady swept past her, making her entrance. Oh, the nipped in waist of that lovely turquoise jacket, the slightly flared skirt just skimming the tops of exquisite little boots, dyed to match. Tilly had never seen anything like it.

'Don't go, Tilly,' Rosa said. Her eyes beseeched her friend: You're in this too, remember.

They all took in the glowing face, skilfully enamelled, the halo of rich brown curls visible under the brim of her hat. Joe blinked at her incredible bosom, Maud at the sparkling paste jewellery. Miss Moriarti held out her hand. Dangling from her wrist was a dorothy bag.

She had a breathless voice, with just the hint of an Irish brogue.

'We were cruising in the cab, getting rather desperate, you see, because we are appearing at the Surrey Theatre, Lambeth, this very evening. I *knew* we should have travelled down yesterday! We've been up and down most roads in this vicinity, hoping against hope, and yours is the first saying THEATRICALS on the card. Oh, what luck!'

The others all seemingly struck dumb with excitement, Tilly spoke up: 'I am Mrs Relf, the housekeeper. This is Mrs Searle. We shall be pleased to accommodate you, Miss Moriarti. We have a very nice single room, newly decorated and close to the bathroom, if that would suit?'

'Tilly,' Maud breathed, 'you sound as if you've been taking in theatricals for years!'

FOUR

Miss Moriarti, it transpired, was not alone.

'I have two gentlemen companions, fellow players, Mr Senacre and Mr Aris. They are anxiously awaiting the verdict.'

Tilly really had taken up her new appointment in earnest. In for a penny, in for a pound, she decided. And that was apt, at £1 per person, per week. 'We also have a double room vacant, would they object to sharing?'

'I don't imagine so, they usually do! I'll go and tell them the good news.'

'Well done, Tilly!' Rosa applauded. 'All the lodgings taken in one fell swoop – I quite thought we'd need to be putting an advertisement in *The Stage*, too, didn't you? But what more could we ask? Maud, run upstairs and open the windows as the rooms still smell of paint – then, Tilly, you can show them up!'

Maud executed a little jig of sheer bliss. 'Did you smell that *scent*!'

'Nearly knocked me for six!' Joe said.

'Shush,' Tilly told them. 'Here they come. Maud, go on.'

'What, and miss all the fun? I'll go in a minute, I promise.' And she stayed put.

Mr Senacre, middle-aged, with a haughty expression and a curiously elongated neck, carried in the heaviest luggage, a hamper containing stage costumes. Behind him trotted a person who, at first glance, Tilly supposed to be a boy. Close to, however, his face was the somewhat pouchy one of nearer forty than twelve years old. He clutched Miss Moriarti's valises. She was delayed for surprisingly, as Tilly glimpsed through the window, it was she who counted the fare into the cabby's outstretched hand.

Mr Aris gave Tilly an approving smile. She smiled uncertainly back.

'This is most kind,' stated the older man.

'Most kind,' echoed the treble voice of Mr Aris. He winked playfully at Maud and Joe. 'Who plays the harmonium, then?'

'I do.'

'And you are—?'

'I'm Joe and this is my sister Maud.'

'And I'm 'Arry – 'Arry Aris – not much point in sounding the 'h' on Harry, with a surname as 'as dropped it, eh?'

'This way, gentlemen, if you will,' Tilly requested primly, leading the way to the big room upstairs. It was fortunate that she was unaware that Mr Senacre was watching her neat ankles appreciatively as she ascended ahead of them.

However, she certainly did notice the way he purposely brushed against her in passing, although his expression was inscrutable as befitted a portrayer of psychic powers, the legend emblazoned on his bag. Tilly would definitely warn Maud to turn her key in her door at nights, she thought.

'Very nice,' Mr Senacre observed, looking at Tilly.

'Bathroom along there,' she indicated. 'Please come down when you're ready.'

Downstairs she found Kitty talking to the others. 'You'll call me Kitty, I hope? They all do! Now, would you like a week's rent in advance?'

Rosa looked at Tilly who gave a slight nod. Your turn, she indicated.

Rosa said primly: 'I believe that's usual – Kitty – thank you.'

She loosened the top of the little bag and dug down in the depths. 'I'm the holder of the purse strings, as you see,' she confided. 'I'm afraid Mr Senacre has a small problem. Likes a bottle or two, you understand, that's why I keep him short and sober. And 'Arry – well, he'll spend his wages all in one go, on the silliest things, just like a boy. Don't be persuaded to lend either of 'em a penny! Here, three guineas. Please keep the extra towards the telephone, which is very necessary in our line of work.'

'How long will you be staying?' Tilly asked.

'A while, if convenient to you. And if you approve of us, of course.'

Kitty gave Joe a special little smile, and he blushed furiously.

Tilly thought: Dear Joe is an innocent, and we want him to remain so. No following in Nandy's footsteps if we can manage it!

Kitty continued: 'We'll do a week here, a week there, sometimes two theatres in one night, so this will be the ideal resting place. Shall I follow my friends up?'

'I'll take you,' Maud offered eagerly. She was dying to see what Kitty had in her luggage.

'And I'll carry your bags!' Joe was not to be outdone.

Watching Kitty as she sprang lightly up the stairs, Rosa sighed: 'Oh, my! What have we done, Tilly?'

'I'm not quite sure,' she replied, 'except we aren't dreaming!'

Tilly remained wary of Mr Senacre – Old Sennapod, as Maud and Joe soon irreverently labelled him. 'Arry she had taken to unreservedly, for he posed no threat. Like her other boys, he soon became the recipient of little treats, like cocoa made with milk and served with thick slices of Rosa's sultana bread, when the theatricals arrived home in the early hours. She had volunteered to come down to let them in each night. Rosa and Petty, she thought, needed that precious time together behind closed bedroom doors now the children stayed up later. She would never disturb them once they'd said goodnight. She hoped fervently she was not envious of their closeness, but could not be sure.

Kitty would lean her head back thankfully in her chair, slip her feet out of their constricting boots and sigh: 'Sheer luxury, being waited on – anyone ever tell you you're an angel, Till?'

She took this with a pinch of salt.

Theatricals, it appeared, did not surface for breakfast until mid-morning – it seemed to Tilly that she had just about finished serving them when Rosa was cooking lunch. Also their rooms could not be tidied until they were settled in the drawing room for the afternoon, for they seldom went out.

Mr Senacre rustled *The Times* and puffed thoughtfully on fat cigars; Kitty relaxed on the chaise-longue, neglecting to pull together the sides of the diaphanous robe she wore, her bare feet tucked under the filmy folds, flicking over the pages of *The Stage*. She wore a silk scarf round her hair, revealed as fine and mousy without its false fringe. She's older than I thought she was at first, Tilly considered, determinedly dusting round them. Despite Kitty's charm, she didn't really trust her.

At five o'clock the lodgers required their evening meal, which was rather early for the family, with Petty yet to come home, so once again this meant a double stint of cooking and washing up by Tilly and Rosa. Still, once the theatricals had departed, and they themselves had eaten, they were able to settle down to their various interests undisturbed.

Joe and Maud remained in the breakfast room; Joe busy with endless homework, Maud scratching away impatiently at her shorthand outlines. Her *Stenographic Soundhand* book was propped against the cruet set. A sound fourpennyworth for her future, as her mother too often reminded her. It would be so much more romantic to go to Art School like Gussie, Maud had sighed.

Rosa and Petty retired to the drawing room; Rosa to her prayer chair and her sewing basket, Petty to tussle over figures in the books he brought home from work. No pay for overtime!

Tilly would go into the kitchen where she ironed busily, dampening the linen so that the flat irons, heating alternately on the gas ring, sizzled smooth the creases. She was still trying to come to terms with the changes. Petty was kindness itself, and included her in everything, but she knew that the evenings when she and Rosa had sat putting the world to rights were a thing of the past. Something else was needed in her life, but right now she had no idea what that might be.

FIVE

One chilly, damp Friday evening, young Joe escorted two pretty ladies to The Empress. He linked arms with Tilly and Maud. They were all greatly excited, for weren't their very own theatricals on the bill tonight? After the interval it was true, and early on, because their names were in the small print.

'Let's hope they actually get there in time,' Tilly remarked, for they knew that the trio were appearing in the first half at another hall. Nellie Wallace, Little Tich, Bransby Williams ... Tilly gave a little sigh of anticipation, for these were top of the bill here tonight.

There was already quite a queue, jostling and jolly, stamping chilly feet in leaky boots, breath curling like smoke, with steaming newspaper bundles full of sustenance tucked under shawls or bulging out of threadbare jackets. 'Warming yer cockles,' as one of the crowd said. Tilly could see that there were bottles in baskets or trouser pockets, too.

Joe indicated to the girls that they should skirt the gallery lot warily, for *they* had complimentary tickets for the stalls, courtesy of Kitty.

The Hallelujah lasses, busy and beaming, called out earnestly: 'Who will be saved?' directing those in obvious need to the nearest soup kitchen. Some abuse was directed at them by a couple of foul-mouthed fellows, already swigging their porter, but most of the onlookers viewed them tolerantly, intent on their own form of salvation and release, anticipating eagerly the warmth and light that would greet them when they clattered at last up the stone steps, their boots striking sparks, to the world of magic and escapism.

Tilly slipped a threepenny bit into the tin one of the Sally Army girls was rattling.

'God bless you, my dear. That will help to buy the Bread of Heaven!'

'Hallelujah!' fervently echoed her companion.

Tilly thought that they were good, and brave, venturing among the crowd.

Joe urged them forward, for he was their guardian tonight.

'Hang on a minute, Joe,' Maud exclaimed, 'do let's watch the buskers.'

The mournful scraping of the fiddle, and the appearance of the fiddler, clad in a ragged kilt, with a flowing white beard almost down to his waist, brought tears to a few sentimental eyes. The small person beside him – was it a boy or a girl? Tilly wondered – was ready to whip off a battered cap to catch the coppers. The Scotsman addressed his audience.

'It's no' so long, ye ken, since I stopped the traffic in the West End – a family tragedy caused me to pawn my Stradivarius. Now, my grandchild and I walk the streets. Thank ye, kind friends . . .'

'Hallelujah!' echoed the Sally Army lasses.

A grubby hand tugged at Tilly's sleeve. 'Got a penny, miss?' wheedled the fiddler's companion. Tilly hastily obliged.

'Lucky we came early,' she said, as Joe gallantly showed her into her seat.

'Lucky Rosa doesn't realise that The Empress ain't really for the likes of us!' Maud smoothed her skirts under her. 'And if the *real* Brixton Empress knew how we were spending the evening . . . well! I wanted to ask Gussie to come, too, but I daren't.'

The smells set her sensitive nose twitching. Oranges in the gallery; below, hair pomade and cheap scent too lavishly applied to conceal the sour smell of smart clothes fetched forth from cupboards where all too often they had been hung away unwashed. Maud fanned herself vigorously with her programme.

'You'd never survive up there, would she, Tilly?' Joe observed, craning his neck to look up at the packed gallery. Tilly, smiling at him, knew just how much Joe would have loved to have been part of all that was going on up aloft, for he wasn't as naive, since the lodgers arrival, she thought. Like her, Joe could probably make a good guess as to what was causing all that ribald laughter.

Within ten minutes the place was packed out, the audience swivelling in their seats to see who was who, boots tapping to the music.

'What does psychic mean, Joe?' Tilly wondered, having found their friends' names at last on the programme.

'I reckon it means seeing into the future – the unknown – that's why Old Sennapod looks so disdainful, I expect.'

'More like he's got a bad smell under his nose!' Maud butted in.

Tilly was secretly disappointed that there was no red-faced chairman with tankard of ale to whet his whistle and facilitate his bellowing. The numbers of the acts were illuminated instead on the sides of the proscenium, thanks to the wonders of electricity.

The galleryites almost drowned the music as The Girls in Blue danced. Joe and Tilly grinned to see their mouths opening and shutting, but the words of the song were completely lost. 'Never heard a word!' moaned Maud.

There was a rousing cheer from above for the ventriloquist who had no need to pretend inebriation through the medium of his dummy for he'd obviously imbibed the Mother's Ruin he made much play of. The dummy's head rose well above its shoulders, revealing the inner workings, then jerked back to front, quite unintentionally – but how they all loved it! A screwed up ball of greasy news-paper hit the ventriloquist smack in the face and other missiles followed. Dodging the fusillade, he bundled the dummy back in its case and hastily backed off stage.

'Arry arrived, breathless, just after the end of the first half, when the male members of the stalls were rapidly making tracks for the bar at the back. 'Don't yer forget me glass o' porter!' their young ladies called boldly to their retreating backs.

'Wait for it, we're next,' he told them.

The curtains rose on a touching scene. A young girl – was it really Kitty, Tilly marvelled? – dressed in white, a red rose tucked demurely in her bosom, sat at the piano. Old Sennapod – now he seemed to have aged! – stood waiting for her to begin playing. The noise in the audience died down. Kitty played a tinkling little tune, supplying the cadence with her voice. It was such a sad lament that Tilly felt unexpected tears well in her eyes.

'Now you, dear Father,' Kitty trilled in her sweet Irish voice, 'it's your turn to entertain.'

The spotlight moved slowly, illuminating eager faces, wavering on Joe, so that he caught his breath in excitement, then stopping at 'Arry sitting in the audience with them.

'Come up, young fellow, we need your assistance!' Old Sennapod called.

The audience whistled, stamped and clapped as 'Arry was helped up on to the stage by Kitty.

Blindfolded, the Professor proceeded to reveal the contents of 'Arry's pockets. The usual collection belonging to a boy, eliciting much laughter as Kitty held it up for all to see: a catapult, a filthy hanky with a hole in the middle through which she waggled her finger, a mouldy apple core, a poke of sticky bullseyes, cigarette cards, a penknife, a halfpenny, and finally, to 'Arry's shame and much tutting from the watchers, a crumpled Woodbine packet, shaken upside down by Kitty to prove that it was empty.

The spotlight shifted round once more and a lady was invited on stage. Kitty slipped a friendly arm around her waist while 'Arry hovered attentively on the lady's other side.

This really was magic, Tilly thought, for the Professor knew the initial of the lady's name and that of her maid, and the contents of her purse, two florins, even their dates, and that the purse was silver in colour with a broken clasp. The smooth patter continued, a florin disappeared from the purse much to the lady's dismay, then reappeared, to friendly booing, in a discomfited 'Arry's pocket.

Blindfolded still, the Professor then proceeded to call out at speed items held aloft by the audience, picked out at random by Kitty. He was correct every time. Finally he freed himself from the scarf with a flourish.

The three bowed to amazed applause. 'Arry returned to his seat.

'However does he do it?' Joe asked as he squeezed past.

'I can't say, he'd shoot me!'

Bransby Williams held them all spellbound with his rich voice, his elegance and eloquence. Tonight he *was* Bill Sikes, the murderer of poor doomed Nancy. Maud buried her head against Joe's shoulder.

Nellie Wallace, with her cheeky songs and outrageous style of dressing (Tilly whispered to 'Arry that she looked like a *man* dressed up as a woman!) brought the house down when she advised the audience to 'Always Look Under the Bed'.

Too soon, the entire cast was assembled on stage, singing their hearts out in the finale.

There was yet another treat for Tilly and Maud. Whilst Joe went along with 'Arry to wait for Mr Senacre and daringly to request the great Bransby Williams's autograph on their programme, the girls were shown to the ladies' communal dressing room where Kitty sat among the other artistes, including the wonderful Nellie, at a long mirror, removing her gaudy makeup.

Tilly gasped and Maud breathed, 'Oh my!' when Kitty stepped out of the demure white dress to reveal silk knickers, lavishly trimmed with torchon lace. Within five minutes she was wearing her elegant costume and had buttoned up her boots. She folded the dress expertly into her tapestry bag.

'With looks like yours and that beautiful hair,' Nellie Wallace said to Tilly, '*you* ought to be on the stage, too, my dear!'

'Oh!' she gasped.

It was difficult to quieten down when they reached home. Tilly hurried out into the kitchen to find Rosa already filling the teapot and a plate heaped with potted meat sandwiches. Petty came yawning out of the bedroom, all rumpled, in his dressing gown, enquiring what all the hilarity was about. Joe and Maud enlightened him.

'I'll take my cup up, I think,' Mr Senacre said frostily. He had had quite enough of entertaining for one night.

'I'll fetch your hot water,' Tilly offered, running upstairs ahead of him to fill the brass can at the bathroom geyser. She rightly guessed that the others would be glad to see the back of him. Only Kitty, of the lodgers, used the bathroom for her ablutions; the men used the washstand in their room.

Mr Senacre closed the door firmly, and Tilly turned to see him eyeing her speculatively.

'Please excuse me,' she stated firmly, but her heart was thumping. He caught her wrist cruelly between finger and thumb. She could see the excitement in his hooded eyes, hear his heavy breathing.

'Let me go!' she spat fiercely. His finger nails were biting into her skin. She could see little beads of sweat on his domed forehead, smell the bay rum on his hair. She had no idea how desirable she looked with her hair in its smooth coronet, as Maud had wheedled her to arrange it, with her slimness accentuated by the clinging purple satin of her dress – one of Gussie's cast-offs, which Augusta had tossed their way.

His breath was hot and sour in her face. 'Lead me on, eh, then get cold feet?'

'I never – I didn't!' she cried, wrenching her arm free and making for the door. He shrugged and turned to the wardrobe. Dismissal, thank God.

Outside the door, Tilly clutched at her heaving bosom as if to quell the pounding within. She took several deep breaths then went quickly downstairs.

Joe, she saw, was about to play the harmonium. 'Pull out all the stops!' Maud cried.

The music swelled and reverberated around the lofty hall where the instrument was situated, the drawing room being considered too constricting when Joe was 'inspired'.

Soon they were all singing lustily as he improvised all the latest tunes: Maud was backstepping valiantly, trying to avoid her father's heavy tread, Kitty was dancing with 'Arry, with his face firmly pressed against her front and even Rosa was swaying irresistibly to the swing of the music. Tilly's toes were soon tapping too.

They gave a rousing rendition of 'My Old Man Said Foller the Van', ending in giggles when they recalled the manoeuvring of their handcart.

Then there was a furious yelling from above and, startled, they all looked up to see Mr Senacre, on the galleried landing, clad in a short flannel nightshirt, scarlet with rage and practically dancing himself.

The harmonium squealed to a stop and their voices faded out: 'She is the Lily of Laguna—'

'Why am I allowed no rest?' came his bellow.

'No rest for the wicked!' Maud whispered slyly to Tilly.

'For a man who 'sees' he seems singularly unaware of what *we* can see . . .' Petty's infectious laughter rumbled up from his rounded stomach, causing them all to collapse in hysterics as they stared at Old Sennapod in his all-too-revealing garment. They clung helplessly to one another, only calming down when they became aware of the invective directed at them.

'He's dribbling – like the teapot!' Maud gasped, wiping her eyes on Tilly's sleeve.

'He's *drunk*,' Tilly realised.

'Where did he get it from?' Kitty asked, looking accusingly at poor 'Arry.

'Don't ask me, but I reckon it was in the wardrobe. He locked it up before we went out this evening.'

'I'll get him back to bed,' Petty declared. He had had plenty of experience with inebriated sailors in the past. ''Arry can go in with Joe tonight,' he decided. 'Fun's over. Off you go, the lot of you.'

They bade each other a subdued goodnight. Joe closed the lid of the harmonium and wisely escorted Maud and Tilly to their rooms.

Tilly suffered a sudden agonising cramp in her left leg after kneeling to pray as usual. She hopped around on the cold oil cloth, grimacing, and felt the rush of tears as she often did when she had been carefree.

Am I always to be paid out for my sins? she wondered sadly. Why should that horrible man think I am no better than I should be? Was that why I had to lose my dear Oswald so soon? She clutched at the warm amber round her neck, drawing comfort from the smooth beads. As she drifted at last into an exhausted sleep, she had a sudden vision of the bright-eyed Hallelujah lass in her black straw bonnet.

SIX

Tilly saw the girl again next time she visited the market. The Salvationists were holding an open-air meeting. Just three bandsmen, the Bread of Heaven lass, squeezing her concertina, and several others rattling their tambourines. There was quite a crowd singing lustily along with them and as Tilly hesitated on the fringe there was the exhortation to: 'Come to Jesus now! Give up your sins! Accept Salvation now!'

Some walked away, but somehow Tilly found herself edging into the gap. The bright-eyed girl with the squeeze box came over to greet her. 'I thought I'd see *you*!' she exclaimed, and pointed upwards with her index finger. Tilly was nonplussed.

'Our salute,' her new friend confided cheerfully. 'Means we've recognised a fellow traveller to Heaven. And it's a pledge – to do all we can to get you there!'

Tilly clutched at her basket. She had merely dashed out for kippers. You got the choicest ones in the market.

The stirring music resumed and Tilly's friend joined in as the Salvationists marched away in the direction of their hall. Various hangers-on followed sheepishly, and to her surprise Tilly felt compelled to join them.

The hall was already packed when the open-air soldiers, as they were known, arrived. Tilly's eyes widened as she saw the down-and-outs, hungry not for religion but for the warmth and friendship offered, expecting a hand-out and a bowl of good, thick soup later. There were those more respectable, but desperately poor, sitting with a semblance of dignity on the wooden benches. Then there were the ladies of ill-repute, as Mrs Augusta called them, some too old and weary to carry on with this way of life, with raddled, rouged faces, and there were those who smelled objectionable, clad in filthy rags, with drink-sodden countenances.

At the far end of the hall, there was a raised platform on which stood the Salvation Army captain and his wife, both in their distinctive uniform. The captain's wife was stoutly encased in a navy-blue Princess robe, falling to the ankles. The bright light struck the silver shield brooch pinned at her neck, bearing the legend SALVATION ARMY, and the metal 'S' on either side of her collar. Round her shoulders was slung a long cape, an essential garment for the Army was often out in the chill early hours. The captain wore a red military-style jacket with his narrow navy trousers, and a peaked cap. Both possessed such happy, rosy faces. Standing respectfully to one side was the corps sergeant major.

The singing swelled once more and Tilly stumbled through the words, aware of her new friend beside her, encouraging and supporting her with a firm hand under her elbow. They had taken a place near the front.

The first song – 'We don't call them hymns!' Tilly's companion whispered – consisted of short verses with rousing choruses, which were repeated several times as fervour mounted:

'O, my heart is full of music and of gladness
As on wings of love and faith I upward fly
Not a shadow-cloud my Saviour's face obscuring
While I'm climbing to my homestead in the sky.'

The chorus was easier. With the rest, Tilly 'climbed the golden stairs to glory' at least four times.

The invitation was given to sinners to come to the Mercy Seat. Tilly felt the emotional response of the motley crowd on their knees with her: there were those who sobbed loudly, those whose silent tears dripped on to their clasped hands, and then there were those who rose abruptly and almost ran towards the Seat.

Tilly's companion looked at her searchingly. Tilly nodded. Then her elbow was gripped once more and her friend gently assisted her to rise. The basket of kippers was pushed aside, and together they followed the others.

When their turn came, they knelt side by side and prayed together while the songsters began to sing, very softly, unaccompanied by music:

'I am coming Lord,
Coming Lord to thee,
Wash me, cleanse me in the blood,
That flowed from Calvary.'

When the service was over, and a bemused Tilly was walking home, she wondered just what she had promised. All she could remember was that her friend had told her she was a 'convert', and that she would never regret her decision. Her step was light, and so was her spirit. But what would Rosa and the family – particularly Mrs Augusta who pronounced herself an agnostic – make of all this? She decided to hug her secret to herself for the time being. At least, she thought, Old Sennapod would be unlikely to spoil her newfound peace of mind for Petty had given him a sound ticking off the morning after his exhibition. He had warned him that he would not tolerate drunkenness and swearing in his house, or any other undesirable behaviour – which Tilly fervently hoped would cover *that*. It was good, she mused, to have such a solid, male presence with the family once again.

Rosa had said: 'None of us is blameless. All that noise! Goodness knows what the neighbours thought!'

Tilly smiled to herself as she recalled Maud's instant response: 'You sound just like Aunt A, Rosa!'

Her mother had quelled her with an oblique glance, and added: 'No more pulling out all the stops, Joe.'

'Aw, Rosa, it was only a bit of fun. You must admit you enjoyed yourself as much as anyone else.' Joe was silenced with a look, too.

Then poor 'Arry had said, on behalf of them all, 'Sorry!' so that Tilly had wanted to give him a hug.

Shame, she mused now, quickening her step, that they'd gone and spoiled it all by upsetting Mrs Augusta so soon afterwards.

Rosa was waiting anxiously for Tilly on the doorstep. 'Where on earth have you been?' she fumed. 'I sent Joe out to look for you – they were packing up in the market, and he said you were nowhere to be seen. Can't you just guess what went through my mind when he reported back? White slavers and all that.' She saw that Tilly was flushed with excitement. Whatever had happened?

'I had to go . . . somewhere.' Tilly was still in a dream. Surely one wasn't converted so quickly? Had she made a fool of herself? But she didn't really care.

'I know it's not late, Tilly, but how often have we warned Maud and Gussie, even young Joe, that it's not safe to walk the streets after dark, alone and unescorted?' Rosa's voice was rising uncontrollably.

Petty appeared behind them. It was the first time Tilly had seen him looking really cross.

'Tilly, Rosa, don't stand on the step, come inside!' His voice was unaccustomedly sharp. He had been worried about Tilly, too, and besides he was hungry. There had been no mention of his dinner since he'd arrived home from the office.

Rosa began saying, 'It's our first quarrel,' as Tilly shouted, 'I don't have to account for *my* movements!' Then she pushed past and stomped upstairs. Almost immediately she returned to dump the basket at Rosa's feet.

Rosa gave Petty a little push, indicating that he should take Maud and Joe away. 'Leave it to us two to sort out,' she said. Then, snatching up the basket, she cried childishly: 'The kippers smell 'off' already – they can go straight in the dustbin!' She made for the kitchen, and Tilly, feeling thoroughly upset now, the euphoria vanishing, came after her.

'I'll tell you where I was, if you really want to know . . . ' She stopped because Rosa wore that tight expression which Tilly had last seen when she was reading Nandy's unfortunate letter.

'You needn't bother, Tilly,' Rosa said fiercely. 'As you so rightly remarked, you don't need to account for your movements to *me*. But I thought we were such friends . . . oh, I entrust secrets to you all the time yet you're being really evasive with me. I was only cross because I was worried you'd been abducted – or worse.'

'But, Rosa, it wasn't worse – it couldn't have been better! I've joined the Salvation Army, that's why I was late. I just didn't think; I lost track of time. I'm sorry, it seemed the right thing to do at that moment . . . ' She put out her hands appealingly. 'We can't fall out over that, now can we?'

'Salvation Army?' said Rosa in utter disbelief. 'Tilly, d'you want to be persecuted, laughed at? How *can* you join like that – out of the blue? You've never even mentioned to me you were interested in them, have you? Oh, I know they do an immense amount of good, but—'

'They're much more accepted these days, Rosa, really they are. And it did happen, just this very afternoon – I can hardly take it all in myself. But when I get into it, learn all about it, I'll have something to fill my life with now that Oswald's gone. I'll be helping those less fortunate. Girls who have been abused as I was. Drunks like Old Sennapod.

Oh, it's wonderful! Please, please, dear Rosa, don't be cross with me. I want your friendship just as much as ever, but you've got Petty home with you now, and you *don't* need me like you did, even though we're enjoying running our little business together. Now that's the truth, isn't it?'

Tilly looked so distressed that Rosa reached out and gave her a sudden convulsive hug. She said contritely: 'It's I who should apologise, Tilly. You won't ever leave us, will you? We *all* think so much of you. But I will just say this: don't jump into it with both feet at first. Tread a little cautiously, be sure it's what you really want, and if it is, we'll back you all the way, I promise.'

Tilly hugged her back. She didn't say what she thought: Maud's right, sometimes you do sound just like Mrs

Augusta – for who could be more impetuous than *you*, at times, Rosa?

Being practical, she unwrapped the kippers and washed them vigorously under the tap. 'They'd sweated a bit in the warm hall, that's all it was. They won't finish 'Arry off if he has 'em for breakfast!'

She didn't notice that Rosa, watching her, was trying to control the trembling of her lips. Tilly was right, she knew. They didn't need each other as they had in the past – in those days at Sheerness, in the cottage under the sea wall in particular.

SEVEN

'Tilly's seen the light, Gus; she's joined the Salvation Army! She hasn't got a tambourine yet, but she hums hymns all round the house!'

Maud and Gussie were having a girls' get-together in Maud's room. Gussie had come round to impart the exciting news that not only was she going to Art College in September, but to the illustrious Slade, no less.

'Perhaps Tilly's seeking salvation, Maud? Because, I believe, there was some mystery about why she came to us originally. You know, before the Sheerness days with you, and before she was married to Oswald. Her sister let it slip once, when she was talking to her young man. I was banished to the kitchen with them 'cause Mama was entertaining in the drawing room and she said my hands were disgraceful, all paint stains, and I smelled of turps.' She lowered her voice dramatically: 'Rosie said something about a *baby*.'

'If Tilly had had a baby, even if she wasn't married, then she'd never have parted with it, so that can't be right,' Maud said stoutly. 'We'd all love to see her married again, but if she prefers religion, well, as Rosa says, that's fine by us.'

In the New Year, Tilly was sworn in as a soldier while she and the other converts stood nervously, yet full of exultation, facing the assembly. The colour sergeant held the flag aloft. Tilly promised to serve God and the Army and to do all in her power to bring others to Christ. Wearing her uniform, every stitch sewn by hand, she learned that she had been 'Saved to Serve', to love the unlovable, to care for those rejected by society. And she knew that she had found that new purpose to her life.

A few days later she stood outside the music hall once more, but 'on the other side'. She put from her mind the memory of how much she had enjoyed those other times – here, and so long ago with Oswald on the Island.

Kitty shot her an irritated glance as she and Mr Senacre jostled through the crowd. 'Arry, however, paused for a moment, listening to the joyful singing which competed with the one-man band clashing discordantly nearby:

'Is there a heart that is waiting,
Longing for pardon today?
Hear the glad message proclaiming,
Jesus is passing this way . . . '

The light from the street lamp seemed to halo Tilly's golden hair, framed so attractively by her bonnet.

'Come with me, 'Arry, come to our meeting.'

'I daren't,' he replied. 'I owe it to Kitty, Tilly; she's worrying that he's getting the drink from somewhere again. He *makes* the act. We might get the push – singers are two a penny, you see.'

The music struck up again and Tilly rejoined the Hallelujah lasses. As 'Arry slipped away, a pale-faced girl with a thin shawl covering her head and a squirming, grizzling baby clutched to her thin body, approached Tilly, plucking at her sleeve.

'Can I help?' she asked softly.

'I dunno.' The girl's voice was despairing. 'Me 'usband's gorn, I can't pay me rent and the old crone's arter me for it. Says she'll frow us aht. Where'll we go?' Her breath literally reeked of gin.

Tilly held out her arms impulsively for the baby. He was sopping wet, and the smell of ammonia was overpowering.

She said confidently: 'My friends and I will come with you, sort things out. Show us the way. Have you got a family to go to?'

'Me muvver frew us aht, too.' The girl's voice was a whine.

The bright-eyed girl who had converted Tilly – whose name was Sarianna – and Tom, a burly, older Salvationist, accompanied Tilly and the girl. Tom had been a boxer in his youth, a talent which proved a positive asset at the lodging house where the girl had been staying. Of course, he didn't use his fists nowadays, but the sight of him was a deterrent.

Later, their ears still ringing from the shrill abuse directed after them by the landlady, they took the girl and her baby, and the few miserable possessions which were thrown after them, back to the soup kitchen.

The girl almost dipped her face into the bowl, like a hungry animal. 'I ain't 'ad no proper food fer days.' They would not reproach her that pennies spent on drink could have bought food, for that was not their way.

'Try and give him a little feed,' Tilly suggested tentatively. She cradled the smelly baby close, brushing her lips over the top of his scurvy head. She felt a strange reluctance to pass him over, but this tiny soul was ravenous, too, she knew. As the girl casually opened her bodice, Tilly added: 'We'll go to your mum's when he's satisfied. You've got to come out of this, for him. Don't you *ever* part with him – he's the one good thing that'll save you from yourself.'

The girl's maternal home was no improvement on the hovel they had already visited. The mother, with a baby not much older than the little boy Tilly once again held so tenderly, was not at all pleased to see her daughter.

'Two more, in this place? You don't know what yer bloody well askin'! I told 'er to go when she was expectin', din't she tell yer? I told 'er 'e was no good, but they never listen, do they?'

'She could get a job, bring some money in, help you all, if you'd take the baby on with yours,' Tilly suggested bravely.

Sarianna added her piece. 'We'll keep in touch; bring you round bits of food. Pray for you . . . '

'It'll take more'n prayers,' the mother said hopelessly. But she opened the door wider, and let the girl and her baby pass inside. Then she slammed the door in their faces. They were left standing in the fetid air on the steep stairs.

'Blood's thicker than water,' Tilly said confidently.

'You'll learn life's full of disappointments, but maybe, just maybe . . . ' Sarianna's voice trailed off into a vast yawn.

After midnight, exhausted, but well pleased with the outcome of her night, Tilly said goodbye to Tom who had seen her safely home. They had left a light burning in the hall for her. She felt a pang of compunction. She hadn't given Rosa a second thought – she would have had to stay up to see to the lodgers' supper, thought Tilly.

Joe's door, alongside hers, opened cautiously. 'You're late, Tilly – I couldn't go to sleep 'til I knew you were home.'

'You're a good kind boy, Joe,' she said fondly.

'Goodnight, Tilly, sleep well!'

She ruffled his hair affectionately. He would always be young Joe to her.

Despite the late hour, Tilly knew that she had a deal of praying to do before she closed her eyes.

She still seemed to feel the fragile weight of that sodden little bundle in her arms, the way the baby had nuzzled round her neck, and finally slept against her breast as she carried him along.

EIGHT

Tilly was out in the garden, pegging out her uniform to air. Maud and Rosa watched her from the kitchen window.

'She hasn't washed her new clothes already, has she?' Maud asked, surprised.

'No, she's just hoping to freshen 'em up, Maud. She was holding a poor little baby last night, all sopping wet, you see. She was out 'til very late trying to help its mother and her family. She got her share of the chores done early on because she wants to go round to see how they're doing today. She's taking her Salvation work very seriously, as you can see.'

'Well, I can help today, it being a day off, can't I? Oh, by the way, I found this note on the mat, addressed to Tilly.'

'Go and give it to her then. I'm just going upstairs to sort out a few things,' said Rosa.

Tilly came in, wearing an old brown holland dress dating back to her days at Augusta's. 'Thought if I was out of uniform, not too smart, Maud, the people I'm off to see might let me in. Always someone worse off than you, isn't there? How lucky we are, to be living *here*.'

'A sick baby, Rosa said?' Maud enquired.

'Well, I think he's sick, poor little mite. But the best I can do is to try and persuade them to clean the place up a bit.'

'This came for you.' Maud handed her the note.

'It's from Tom. The big chap I told you about, Maud – he's a good old sort to have around . . . Oh, he's written to tell me about a Jewish doctor – Dr Mann – who treats those who can't pay for *nothing*, Tom says.

'Listen: You have to gird your loins to go in his waiting room, Tilly; some of his patients are really filthy! But he listens to all your troubles, even mixes the medicines himself. You could take the baby to him – if they'd allow you to.'

She didn't show the note to Maud, because Tom couldn't spell and it wouldn't be fair to him.

Rosa pulled the rush basket out from under her bed. It had been brought along to each new house, and now and again she opened it to check that all was well. When Petty first came home, she had thought: perhaps I'm not too old to have another baby . . . Then she had smiled at her foolishness, because there was her eldest son, already sporting a beard. Nowadays, as Petty told her, airing his medical knowledge, there were ways and means of *not* having a baby, and he rather thought they should take advantage of this. They were so fortunate, he said seriously, to have three grown children when Tilly had been so cruelly parted from her one and only, and no chance of another baby. In a few years, Rosa thought wistfully, there could be grandchildren and that would be wonderful.

She took out an armful of baby clothes and went back to the others. Without a word, she folded the things and placed them in a bag, which she handed to Tilly.

'Rosa dear, you don't want to part with these, I know,' Tilly said helplessly.

'I was silly to hang on to them all this time. I'm not going to start all over again now, am I? I've kept a few things back. They say it's unlucky to get rid of everything, don't they?'

Tilly kissed her warmly. 'Thank you, Rosa. Cheerio, you two!'

'Good luck!' they called as she hurried off, with a chill wind blowing leaves and scraps of paper underfoot.

'Please let me in, Mrs Worrell,' Tilly pleaded. The door opened a mere crack.

'Miss Sally, ain't it? Lorst yer bonnet?' came the surly reply. Tilly was obviously not welcome.

'I have a few things for your daughter, Flo – for the baby. I want to help her. Perhaps I can help you, too?' Tilly persisted.

The stairway smelled horribly of cabbages and tom cats. Suddenly the door was opened and Tilly was pulled rudely inside. 'Don't want *them* dahnstairs to know all our business,' was the explanation.

One room was all this family had, Tilly saw. Rubbish overflowed from the rickety table, there were only two chairs, and the remains of a third had obviously been fed to the fire on which a blackened kettle hissed and spat. A mattress had been shoved against the far wall on which lay Flo, the girl, trying to suckle her baby. The mother's infant crawled, bare-bottomed, among the debris on the floor. An older child with matted hair squatted listlessly by the unguarded blaze.

'She's laid there ever since you brought 'er back.' The girl's mother's tone was defensive. 'It's a mess, ain't it? I've three bigger 'uns, but they clear aht first thing.'

'What about your husband?' Tilly asked.

''E's gorn, Miss Sally, not that we legally tied the knot – just like 'er,' came the terse reply.

Tilly swept the things on the table to one side, putting down her bags. 'Have you a bowl? May I wash and change the baby – babies?' she amended. She hoped that Rosa had included some clothes big enough for poor little bare-bottom.

The older child was despatched with a cracked jug to fetch cold water from the communal tap on the ground floor, to replenish the kettle and to cool hot water in the basin. Tilly spread a towel on the table, took the mewling baby from the girl and carefully peeled off the layers of soiled clothing. Stirring herself at last, the older woman provided a handleless bucket.

Tenderly, Tilly cleaned the little body from top to toe with soft yellow tow, blessing Rosa for thinking of that. She indicated to the girl's mother that there was food for them in the other bag, averting her eyes from the toddler's grubby hands as he grabbed at the oatcake and began to gobble it.

Flo's baby, Bobby, was painfully skinny and obviously undernourished. Tilly gave instructions in a firm voice as she dressed him in the soft white woollens which Rosa had knitted so hopefully for the little daughter she had lost.

'Wash your daughter's face and hands to freshen her up, Mrs Worrell, then make her some bread and milk. Oh, good, here's a pilch for your little one, but please let me clean his backside first.'

Bare-bottom's brother came sidling up shyly, eyeing the oatcakes, the loaf of bread, the margarine, the slipper of gammon and the newspaper bundle of root vegetables intended for soup. The milk she had decanted into a large washed medicine bottle, firmly corked. It was similar to the parcels Tilly's proud mum had been forced to accept when her father was out of work during Tilly's childhood. Food, yes, but not *this*, she thought, with a lump in her throat.

She wrapped Bobby in a square of flannelette and laid him back beside his young mother. 'What's your name?' she asked the half-naked child. His turn, poor soul. That bottom was almost raw. She winced for him as she sponged him off, but the child did not even flinch.

'Here you are,' Tilly said, sawing at the bread with the blunt knife provided. She thought wryly that perhaps it was just as well there wasn't anything sharper – people did terrible things when possessed by what the Army called the 'demon drink'. She spread the slice thickly with margarine. 'Your mum's going to make you all a good square meal with that lot. Now you eat that up,' she said to the older boy, 'then go and scrounge some more kindling for the fire, eh?'

At last, Mrs Worrell was galvanised into action. A pot was filled with vegetables, unpared but washed, the ham added, then put in the place of the steaming kettle.

The hot water was used to clean the room as best they could, Tilly wishing fervently that she had remembered to include some yellow soap. The rubbish was added to the fire, together with a discarded orange box brought back in triumph by the child. As Tilly leaned over him, to prevent him getting too close to the blaze as he thrust his offering in the flames, she saw that his head was literally alive with lice. No wonder he had scratched his hair into such a state. She forced herself not to recoil.

'I'd like to take the baby along to the doctor's, Mrs Worrell, if you'll let me?' she suggested daringly. 'Don't worry, it won't cost anything, and even if it did, I'd pay it somehow. That abcess in his groin wants attending to. While I'm there, I'll try and get something for you to treat the children's hair with. They're bound to be all running alive with the little beggars. Look at your own, too, while you're about it.' It was no good mincing words. She was more than glad that she had tied her own hair up in a scarf, but she'd get Rosa to have a search through when she got home, she thought. Her own mother had always been over their heads regularly with a toothcomb; she would have been horrified to see that poor child's head.

Tilly gave a precious sixpence to the lad to fetch more milk – she daren't trust his mother. It would probably go on another sort of liquid she deduced. The empty bottles were testimony to that.

'I must go. I expect the doctor's only there in the morning.' The women offered no resistance to this idea.

The waiting room was as Tom had said. Children with coughs and runny noses; an old woman cradling her massively swollen stomach with her crabbed hands, her face seamed with pain; an old man rambling incoherently; and another young mother with a new baby, its face as yellow with jaundice as the tow Tilly had used. Her own small charge nestled against her shoulder as she waited her turn. They were the last to be seen.

The surgery was dark and dingy, the blind drawn across the small window. But Tilly could smell carbolic, which was reassuring. The doctor worked from a terraced house down a short alleyway.

He was young, perhaps younger than herself, she thought in surprise. It made her realise that she had just turned thirty. He leaned his cheek in one hand, elbow resting on the desk, gazing at her thoughtfully as she told him about the baby.

'This is not your baby then, Mrs—?' he asked. He must have seen her wedding ring, she thought.

'Mrs Relf. I am a widow.' She would wonder later why she had said that. 'No, you see, I am a Salvationist, and am trying to help the baby's mother and her family. They are very poor.' She must make it plain. 'I understand that you don't charge a fee, in such cases?'

'That is so, Mrs Relf. I must introduce myself – David Mann.' His voice was quiet, deep, slightly accented. For a moment, she was puzzled as to where she had heard that intonation before – then it came to her. He sounded like Mr Lozenge – as they still called him – the German photographer in Sheerness. They exchanged cards every Christmas, though whenever 'war clouds gathered' he would always be under suspicion of spying.

She saw that the doctor was exceptionally tall as he rose and came round the desk to examine the baby on her lap.

He smelled of disinfectant, too; his hands, long and slender, were incredibly gentle. His dark head was very near Tilly's face, and for a moment she held her breath. No man had been as close to her since Oswald's death.

'The baby's diet is deficient – not enough goodness in his mother's milk, that is obvious, Mrs Relf.' He straightened, and Tilly's breath was expelled in a soft sigh. 'I shall prescribe some drops. Perhaps you will supervise their taking? The boil must be painted with gentian violet – it would be best for you to keep this, if there are other children around.' He handed her a ribbed bottle. 'You would like a tonic for his mother, too?'

'Yes please, Doctor – and, if it's not too much trouble, something to rub in their scalps. They're smothered with lice.' She felt again the urge to scratch her own head.

Dr Mann opened the cupboard on the wall and took out the requisite lotion. 'This will be more effective than paraffin. But the whole family will need to be treated, or it will recur.'

'Thank you,' Tilly said gratefully, as he placed the bottles in her bag. She lifted the baby back on her shoulder so that he felt secure, his pale eyelids flickering shut once more.

'Now, if you will just tell me their address, I will call in to see this family just as soon as I have the time,' the doctor offered.

Later he ushered her out, locking the surgery door. They walked along together.

He made Tilly feel short, which was ridiculous, she thought, for she was five feet six inches tall, quite a height for a woman, particularly one who had come from the less privileged section of society. She looked up into his nice face – very Jewish – like the lively, extrovert market traders who were always ready to drive a shrewd bargain with those who had money jingling in their pockets, but warm and generous to those who had nothing at all. David Mann was unlike those jolly fellows in that he reflected before he spoke, and then said very little. He was aware of her gaze, and seemed to read her thoughts for he smiled: 'Yes, I am a Jew, a German Jew to be exact. My background is of no importance. I will treat anyone who is need of medical care; it is as simple as that. We will meet again for the Army makes much use of me!' He raised his hat to her as they came to the parting of their ways, as if she was a real lady. 'Good afternoon, Mrs Relf.'

Tilly was warm inside despite the chill wind with the underlying threat of snow on the way. What a pity, she thought as she hurried the baby back to his mother, that she had not worn her smart uniform. Still, Dr Mann was obviously indifferent to outward appearances. He, as she was learning to do since her conversion, looked beyond that.

Today she had met a wonderful man. She said aloud to herself: 'Another Dr Box, I believe.'

She would not have believed it had anyone told her that Dr Mann was thinking, too, at that very moment, that he had just met someone very special.

NINE

Tilly had completely overlooked the fact that it was Sunday, and that it was unlikely Dr Mann would have a surgery, even though she knew the Jewish Sabbath was celebrated on a Saturday. As she hurried along, another thought struck her: how could she have forgotten the open air service in the park this morning? She felt better when she remembered what the good General William Booth always said: 'People come before prayers.'

She was not even sure if the doctor lived on the premises. In fact he did not, but she was in luck: he was just unlocking the door as she arrived.

'Dr Mann!' she called out breathlessly, as if he would go inside and leave her standing there. 'Are you too busy, or could you come with me to Flo's?'

He turned. 'Something wrong, Mrs Relf? Please come into the surgery while I fetch some medicine. A child with croup, and her mother up all night. She sent for me first thing.'

He listened to Tilly as he made up a prescription, shaking and then labelling the bottle. 'We shall leave this on our way. This mother is most competent and caring, she knows what to do.'

They walked swiftly along the litter-strewn street. Children were already out; some kicking a ball made of newspaper stuffed in roughly sewn material; some squatting over marbles in the gutter. One or two lucky ones were clutching their breakfast: bread with a scraping of jam. They looked up curiously at the tall doctor and at the young woman whom they knew to be a Sally Army lass, almost running to keep up with his lengthy stride.

The croupy child's mother was watching out anxiously for the doctor's arrival. She flung the door wide, standing there with the tired child drooping in her arms, gently massaging her back with a circular, soothing movement of the palm of her hand.

'Oh, Doctor, thank you! How much do I owe you?' she enquired anxiously. This was a mother with a husband in steady employment, with just this one surviving child, although still very poor. Dr Mann accepted the coppers with a smile. 'I trust Harriet will be better directly. Do call me if you have need.' He touched the child's head gently. The wan little face turned towards him and the child gave him a tremulous smile. Tilly was instantly reminded again of dear Dr Box, who had had a similar affinity with sick children, and had helped Joe to recover against the odds.

'The children love you,' she remarked impulsively as they walked away, then, as always, her fair skin betrayed her embarrassment.

Flo's mother took her time answering their knocking. 'Oh, it's you is it? My lad did give you the message then, Miss Sally – found yer 'ouse awright? Bobby's real bad. *She* can't stop bawling. I told 'er ter snap aht o' it, but she says it's 'er fault. Leavin' last night, and then comin' back in such a state. I give 'im some milk on a rag, but 'e jest choked, like, couldn't seem ter swaller, 'e wouldn't 'ave it.'

Bobby, being rocked in a distraught Flo's arms, was burning up with fever. Dr Mann took him and laid him on a towel on Tilly's lap so he could examine him. His expression became very grave. He opened his bag and extracted a swab.

'Tilly,' he requested, using her Christian name for the first time, 'you must help me by holding Bobby's jaw, please – I need to swab his throat. It could be diphtheria.' Flo's wailing intensified.

'Kids dahn below 'ad it – one died larst week,' her mother said woodenly. 'Our lot's 'ad it, couple of years back, 'cept for the little 'uns. But he looks awright, don't 'e?'

'Would you agree to my giving him the anti-toxin?' Dr Mann asked. 'It is proving most effective.' Flo's mother nodded, though unsure what he meant.

'Good. Then I shall administer this to them both. It is not too late for Bobby.'

'Will the baby have to go to the Isolation?' Tilly asked on poor Flo's behalf. They would have no chance at home if the disease struck, she thought – not like the times she and Rosa had nursed Nandy, Maud and Joe at home.

'We shall see. I must go back to fetch the serum. You will stay here to help? You are not afraid of this?' he asked Tilly.

'I had it as a child, Doctor. I will stay.'

Tilly turned to Flo's mum when the doctor had gone. 'You'd best keep the others in.' She indicated the older children, cowering and subdued on the mattress in the corner. 'Don't worry; they don't reckon you get it more'n once. The prick in the arm that the doctor will give your little 'uns will have the same effect.' Tilly was being kind, but it was an effort, for they never did a thing for themselves unless they were chivvied. Mind you, with frequent visiting, she had kept them up to cleaning the room regularly, even if she, with much help from Rosa, did have to provide the means to do this. That reminded her: 'That bundle of sheeting my friend sent – have you a piece, a long bit, left? Then soak it in the Lysol and hang it over the door, just in case.'

They were at last persuaded to do something. While they saw to this, Tilly undressed Bobby and sponged him with tepid water. It was something Rosa always did, to bring down a high temperature, as advised by Dr Box when the children were tiny. Bobby's limbs were jerking feebly. Pray God, Tilly worried, he doesn't have a fit.

She was still steadily trickling water over the baby's body when David Mann returned. She saw that he approved.

The injections were given to some affronted screaming from the toddler and a mere whimper from the babies.

'Don't wrap him too tightly, let the air circulate around. Sponge the head until cool. I think we shall have been in time. You will remain here, Tilly, until the symptoms ease?' he asked her.

'I will, Doctor,' she agreed.

Rosa received quite a shock when she opened the door to an unexpected caller: she did not realise that the tall bushy-bearded stranger, holding his hat in his hand and dressed sombrely in black from head to foot, was Tilly's wonderful Dr Mann.

'Mrs Searle?' he asked politely. Rosa warmed to the timbre of his voice immediately. His dark eyes regarded her gravely. A handsome man, she thought, but definitely a stranger.

'Yes?' Rosa still had not comprehended.

'I am David Mann. I come to warn you that Tilly, Mrs Relf, may be delayed for some time. You see, she is helping with the sick baby she was called to first thing.'

Rosa saw that his smile transformed that serious face. She decided immediately that she liked him. Hearing Tilly enthuse about him had already made her hope that perhaps her friend might, in good time, be prepared to share her life once more with the right man. But she kept these thoughts to herself. Now, she knew, was not the time to divulge them. It was too soon.

'Thank you, Doctor. I do appreciate your coming to tell me this,' Rosa said. She smiled back, with her brown eyes as well as her lips. She, like Tilly, had been powerfully reminded of Dr Box. Not that there was any similarity in looks, it was more a *presence*, she would tell herself when he had gone.

'I shall escort your friend home,' he assured her. 'If it should be late, don't worry.'

'I won't. Do tell Tilly I hope things will turn out better very shortly. And not to worry about things here. Being Sunday, I shall not be coping with the theatricals on my own.'

David looked puzzled. 'I'm afraid I do not understand?'

'Didn't Tilly tell you? She and I run a theatrical boarding house here. We began this before Tilly joined the Salvation Army. She is a recent convert, you see.'

'She told me you are her great friends, you and all your family. The rest I had not yet learned. We meet in a professional capacity.'

An impersonal phrase, Rosa thought, but he is attracted to Tilly, I just know he is.

David Mann gave a little bow, turned to go, and almost collided with Augusta and Gussie who were wheeling their bicycles up the path.

'Good morning, Mrs Searle,' he said. Then: 'Good morning, ladies.'

'Good morning, I am sure we shall see you again. Thank you very much for coming.' Rosa was flustered. Trust Augusta to come along at the wrong moment!

Augusta stared after Dr Mann as he departed. 'Whoever was that, Rosa – really you have the most peculiar friends!' Rosa hoped fervently that he had not heard.

'Is this just a passing call, because I can see you are out for one of your spins, or are you coming in, Augusta?' Rosa asked tartly.

She wouldn't enlighten her as to the stranger's identity, she thought.

Tilly was dozing by candlelight, the baby still in her lap with his family huddled together on the mattress, top to toe, when she awoke, startled by the tapping on the door.

'Tilly! It is only me.' David's voice, low but urgent.

Before she answered, she felt the baby's brow fearfully. The heat had subsided, and there was just a spasmodic rattling of the tiny chest as Bobby breathed in and out. Tilly hoisted him gently in her arms, then tiptoed to the door.

'Doctor Mann! He's so much better, praise be,' she whispered. The exhausted family stirred, one of the children muttered, then there was a concerted heaving under the thin blankets as they instinctively turned in unison.

'David. Call me David,' he said. His face was as drawn and tired as her own. He did not tell her, there, that he had been called to other homes where diphtheria had been proved positive. It had been a terrible day. A child had died before he reached him.

'We must make mothers aware that immunisation can save their children from all this.' His tone was fierce, and Tilly realised that there was an intense, passionate side to the quiet doctor.

Flo's mum sat up, startled aware by his voice, her eyes fixed anxiously upon them.

'Young Bobby will recover. I am sorry to wake you,' David Mann told her. 'I must take Tilly home now. Put the baby in his cradle, Tilly. We shall be back in the morning. Or, at any rate, I shall. Tilly may have other duties.'

'Oh, thank you!' Flo's mum rubbed at her eyes with her rough knuckles. So she does care, Tilly thought.

Tilly tucked Bobby up in the makeshift crib she had made him, an oval-shaped fruit basket she had begged from the greengrocer and lined with soft flannel, with an underlay for comfort. It was surprising how ingenious you could be when needs must, she said to herself, giving Bobby a fleeting kiss on his damp head – still scurvied despite all her efforts.

Then she followed David out of the room and down the stairs. The old building seemed full of creaks and sighs. It should have been condemned years ago. A shaft of moonlight through the filthy, uncurtained windows lit their hesitant steps.

The street was deserted, the road sweepers not yet bent to their task along the main road. The last tram had gone long ago. Tilly faltered. Her companion turned to her, concerned. Then his arm went firmly round her sagging shoulders, supporting her. He slowed his pace to match hers. They walked on in silence.

This support was so comforting, Tilly drew strength from it. She had no fears it might lead to unwanted attentions. How good it was to have a strong man to lean against once more – she could not quell that thought.

He waited at the gate until she found her key. 'Straight to bed, Tilly. You can sleep now all is well.' He did not say that *he* would have no rest that night; he would be returning to another patient to whom he had given the anti-toxin.

Tilly said: 'Goodnight, David. Thank you for helping me home. I would never have got here on my own.'

'You must always call on me when you are in trouble,' he told her. His handclasp was warm and firm.

She watched him as he closed the gate. 'I will,' she whispered, not intending him to hear. 'I will, David.'

TEN

Maud covered her Remington Standard thankfully. In a final overenthusiastic burst of speed, not guaranteed to impress the tutor who was just collecting her metronome from the beginners' table, Maud had seen most of the keys fly upwards to become tiresomely entangled. In prising them apart she had smothered her hands in ink and had subsequently smudged her copy considerably. 'Yours fatifully', she noted, unsurprised, before she quickly stuffed the foolscap sheet in her bag. 'Oh, A, S, D, F, G, *thump*!' she muttered explosively.

'I haven't as yet called a halt to proceedings, Miss Searle,' came the teacher's dry reminder. Then, as Maud reached out for the metal cover: 'Oh, go on, there are but two minutes to go, and it's obvious there'll be no decent work from you this afternoon. I suppose you *did* surpass yourself in the short-hand test first thing, I grant you that. Have a good weekend!' Maud had that sort of softening effect on the dourest of folk.

'Thank you – same to you!' Maud beamed and hummed the catchy little tune which Kitty had been singing around the house lately as she made her way to the washroom.

Gussie too, she thought happily, would soon be on her way from the Slade – they were meeting for tea at Lockhart's shop.

Gussie had arrived first, and she was not alone.

'I see that Dr Williams's pink pills are working!' Maud said wickedly as she kissed her cousin's flushed cheek. Gussie's hair hung in a tawny mane down her back, secured with a wide green velvet ribbon. She was so incredibly slender, to Maud's everlasting envy, that she certainly had no need of the Fitu corset Augusta insisted that she wear. Gussie had fine soft skin without a single adolescent eruption, very pale except for the surprising pinkness of her cheeks. There were a few faint freckles sprinkled over the bridge of her small straight nose. How Maud yearned for a nose like that. 'Mine,' as she often remarked ruefully to Gussie, 'is more of a blob!'

The green velvet costume Gussie wore today was a trifle heavy for the late-spring afternoon, but it made Maud feel positively dowdy in her college attire – long, straight serge skirt and bone-necked white blouse.

Gussie's companion looked at Maud with frank interest, seeing what she was quite unaware of: the glossy hair, eyes narrowed as she smiled in friendly greeting, her little hand, so hastily washed that it was still stained with ink, thrust forward impulsively. He liked very much what he saw: he had heard a great deal about this small, lively – 'Oh, she's much cleverer than me!' – cousin of Gussie's, of whom she spoke with such affection.

'This is Maud, Pino – Maud, this is Pino, my friend from the Slade. Remember I told you we met on my very first day? He aims to be a sculptor, not a water colourist like me! Watch out or his grip will crush your hand. He's getting stronger by the day, chipping away with his chisel!' Gussie wanted so much for these two to approve of each other. She was not to be disappointed.

'Pay no attention to her,' Pino said, squeezing Maud's hand all the same. 'I haven't chipped much yet – I'm still labouring in the anatomy classes. Let's go inside, shall we? It's getting crowded.'

He was tall for an Italian, not as dark-skinned as Maud had imagined, for she, naturally, had already heard much about Gussie's beau. His eyes were as liquid and dark as Maud's own, and he played the part of artist to perfection, she thought, with his floppy bow tie and long hair curling on his collar. He had full red lips and a ready smile, revealing large, perfect teeth. But it was his voice Maud found fascinating: deep, husky, tinged with cockney, despite the fact that he had born in Clerkenwell's Little Italy. He was the middle son in a family of Italian musicians, Gussie had already told Maud. Great had been the sacrifices made by the parents and elder brothers to send this talented family member to the Slade.

Pino and Gussie sat side by side, unselfconsciously close, facing Maud across the table. Tea and buns arrived for three:

fat buns, full of currants, soft and fresh, glazed with sugar, and a pot of tea out of which you could squeeze 'another half cup apiece' as Gussie said.

The young waitress smiled. There wouldn't be much of a tip, she thought, unashamedly eavesdropping, for it was obvious these three were students. They looked so happy to be taking tea and talking together that she felt happy, too, despite her swelling ankles, inevitable with the long hours she spent on her feet. She considered that she was very lucky to have such a pleasant job and to meet such interesting people, and didn't she get her own food half-price? Paid holidays, too! The ten shillings she earned weekly, plus tips, made her feel quite independent.

'Poor little girl,' Pino observed, as the waitress went reluctantly towards another table. 'She looks worn out.'

He's compassionate, Maud thought. She liked that in a man; it was the thing she admired most about Petty. She took an unladylike bite of her bun, nearly choking herself. Pino rushed round to thump her on her back.

'Watch out, you're spilling the tea!' Gussie cried, steadying the teapot in mid-flow.

'Now, Maud,' Gussie said, handing her the cup, 'I expect you wondered why I telephoned you yesterday evening and suggested we meet here when you were coming to spend the weekend with Mama and me anyway. It's just that, well,

I knew I wouldn't get the chance to talk to you without Mama listening in, and I need your moral support! You see, Pino has asked me to Saturday tea at his house, and Mama's bound to disapprove, and even when I wheedle round her (which I will), she'll say I need a chaperone, and that's where *you* come in . . . '

'Not exactly, Gussie,' Pino interjected. 'We shall be honoured to have Maud at our table in any case. So, now I issue an invitation – will you come, please, Maud?'

''Course!' she agreed cheerfully. 'I'm absolutely dying to see Little Italy, you know, it sounds so colourful.'

'Oh, we're quite conventional, I promise.' Pino kept a straight face. He, Maud thought, didn't look conventional, not one bit. Oh, she did like him!

'Don't you believe him, Maud. I can't wait to visit it either,' Gussie told her. 'Oh, you're a real sport, you are. We ought to dash, Pino,' she added reluctantly. 'Mama will be expecting us.'

'I feel most nervous, Gussie, you make your dear mama sound formidable.' His tone, however, was bantering. 'Let us just finish the buns, eh?'

'My hands!' Maud exclaimed ruefully, noting their state belatedly. She took her share of the last bun, which Pino divided exactly between the three of them. He scooped the crumbs into a tiny heap on the marble tabletop.

'And mine, just look,' he put in gallantly, 'for they also bear the marks of great industry: charcoal under the nails.'

Not to be outdone, Gussie stretched forward *her* hands for inspection. Maud saw that they trembled slightly as Pino, taking his time over his scrutiny, held them between his own square ones. 'Spotless, I'm afraid, not even a smudge of your favourite Prussian blue!'

'In fact, Gus, you look rather grand altogether for an art student,' Maud remarked candidly, not meaning to give offence.

'The costume, you mean? Ah, well, Mama refused to allow me to leave home or arrive back in my smock, so I change when I reach the Slade. She says it's high time I put my hair up, too, but you know what difficult stuff it is – far too curly. Just like hers really, it will go its own way.'

'It is beautiful,' Pino said softly. It was Maud who coloured up now as she intercepted the look between the two of them. She felt de trop, as Aunt A would surely have tartly remarked.

Pino invited them both to take an arm as they departed. The young waitress collected their crocks and slipped into her pocket the three-penny piece which she had discovered under Pino's plate, for he had settled the bill. Then, to her delight, she discovered a florin, discreetly folded into Gussie's discarded napkin. She hoped she would see them again. But which pair, she wondered, were the lovers?

'I will call for you tomorrow, just after two, then I will have time to show you The Hill, which *we* call Little Italy, you know. Do please assure your mama, Gussie, that I will naturally escort you home again also. Goodbye, Gussie. Goodbye, little Maud.' To her surprise he bent solemnly to kiss each burning cheek in turn. Gussie merely held out her hand for him to brush briefly with his mouth.

'I don't understand.' Maud was flustered as they hurried for their tram. 'Why would he kiss *me*, and not *you*?'

'Well, you see, my dear cousin, you are a mere baby in his eyes ... ' Gussie teased, as they hitched their skirts, stepped aboard, and then clattered up the winding stairs to sit on top of the bus.

'I'm jolly well not!' she protested. That made her cross, but why?

'Well, you like him, Maud, don't you? I just knew you would! But can't you just guess Mama's reaction when she meets him tomorrow?'

Maud certainly could. But she wondered at her own reaction, too.

'A foreigner!' Augusta was aghast. 'From that part, too – I might have known you'd meet a lot of bohemians!'

'At least they're not *barbarians* – oh, don't be such a snob, Mama.' Gussie was quite heated. Augusta thought grimly that Maud was a bad influence.

'I'll have Maud with me for support,' Gussie continued determinedly, 'and you know what a strong character *she* is, just like Rosa. If she doesn't approve of Pino's family she'll have me on the first bus home, I promise you! Anyway, you'll meet Pino before he sweeps us off to Bohemia. You see, he won't allow us to go there unescorted. That proves he's a gentleman, doesn't it, Maud? And he'll bring us home, too – oh, go on, Mama, do say we can go.'

'I'll reserve my judgement for the moment. Take Maud to your room – show her your paintings or something. Exchange all those girlish confidences you keep from me, why don't you? You've given me a real headache, Gussie, with your demands . . . '

The girls sat on Gussie's bed while she opened up her folders and leafed through her collection. Maud gave a little whistle. 'Bet you daren't show Aunt A *that* one, Gus . . . '

'Just a drawing from life,' she said demurely. 'No different from a still life really, neither moves.' It was a powerfully muscled male torso.

'Just as well.' Maud grinned. 'Don't you feel embarrassed, Gus?'

'Not at all. I love every minute of it – the days aren't long enough. I hated school,' Gussie added, with unexpected passion. 'And now that I've met Pino—'

'You look all dreamy and daft, Gus,' Maud teased her.

'You'll enjoy the feeling when it comes over you!' she retorted before her irritating cough caught her in a sudden spasm. 'Oh, I can't shift the wretched thing!' she gasped, falling limply back on the pillows. Maud scurried to fetch her a glass of water from the flask on the bedside table.

'Hope it's fresh.'

'Thanks. Mama says it's just a silly habit, and the doctor seems to agree . . . ' Gussie drank water greedily, then coughed convulsively once more, holding her handkerchief to her mouth to stifle it. She was not quite quick enough. Maud caught sight of a bright stain before Gussie stuffed it back into her pocket. Apart from the hectic spots on her cheekbones, she had gone extremely pale.

'Gussie, wasn't that – *blood*?' Maud, too, had a white face now.

'Only a speck, honestly, Maud. It's nothing to worry about. Sometimes, if I cough too hard, I break a tiny blood vessel in my throat. That's how the doctor explained it to me.'

'Have you told Aunt A?' Maud was both concerned and afraid for Gussie.

'No, and you're not to either. You *know* how she fusses. I'm not ill, Maud, honestly. In fact, I feel really fine.' She coughed again, smothering it with her handkerchief.

'Well, if you're sure . . . ' Maud said doubtfully.

''Course I'm sure. Let's go and see if Mama has recovered and challenge her to a game of Old Maid, shall we?' Gussie seemed intent on changing the subject.

'Well, I shall win that,' Maud said ruefully. 'I'm the only likely candidate. Aunt A's been married, and *you* obviously will be. You know, your mama once said what a pity it was I was as plain as a picked chicken, and didn't even have a nice disposition to compensate.'

'Whenever did she say that?' Gussie sounded really cross.

'Years ago, Gus, when I was about two, before I grew much hair and was subject to terrible tantrums. Rosa can testify to that! Don't worry about it, I don't.'

'It's just not true, Maud. D'you know, when you came towards us, outside the teashop, Pino asked me: 'Is that Maud? That pretty little dark girl?''

'Did he really? Then I shall love him forever!' Maud said solemnly. And they both burst out laughing.

During the night, from her adjoining bedroom, Maud heard muffled coughing, as if Gussie was attempting to hold her breath, or covering her face with her pillow. Later she woke again to hear footsteps padding across the floor and the sound of the window sash being thrown up. Maud slid out of bed, fumbling her feet into her slippers, and went as stealthily as she could in order not to disturb Aunt A, who was sleeping in the room opposite. She must see what Gussie was about, she thought.

In the moonlight, with the curtains pulled aside, she saw the frail figure silhouetted. Gussie was gulping deep lungfuls of cold night air to try to quell the tickling in her throat. Maud slipped a steadying arm around her. To her horror, she realised just how little flesh Gussie had on her bones, as she felt her body through the silk of her nightdress. Her breasts were mere buds compared to Maud's often-lamented proud young bosom.

Maud guided her back carefully to bed, helped her in and smoothed the covers. She was aware that there was sheer terror in Gussie's eyes, which was surely mirrored in her own.

'Please,' Gussie pleaded, in a tiny, strange, hoarse voice, 'don't fetch Mama. Just give me some of that linctus on the washstand, that's a good girl.'

Maud complied. Gussie struggled up, smiling. 'There! That's much better. It's just that this room gets so stuffy. Go back to your bed, Maud, sweet dreams of tomorrow . . . '

Back in her own bed, she fought with her conscience. She really ought to tell Aunt A what she had just witnessed, she knew that, but instead she'd ask Tilly's advice when she got home. Suppose – just suppose – she shivered fearfully, it was the *galloping consumption*? She fell at last, around dawn, into an exhausted, nightmarish sleep.

ELEVEN

Augusta, despite her prejudices, was charmed by Pino and his good manners, and actually found herself telling him that he must soon visit them for tea, in turn. 'Don't be late back!' she warned, but waved them off affably at the door. She must speak to Rosa about Maud, she thought. The girl had risen late and looked wan today. Perhaps she was outgrowing her strength.

Going into the drawing room, she took up the photograph of Gussie's father, whom she had sadly never known. Her daughter might have inherited her own good looks, she acknowledged with her usual vanity, but Gussie was a dreamer like poor George. She dusted the glass with her sleeve. Really, the new girl Rosie was training up – she was only coming in the mornings at present – wasn't a patch on her, and no girl was ever going to live up to Tilly. It was always going to rankle with her that Tilly preferred that other household, though she rightly suspected that her former maid was really fond of her. She hadn't been able to find the words to express her sorrow for the girl when she was widowed so tragically young.

There was something she intended to do for Tilly very soon, which Rosa couldn't do, she thought. Tilly had let slip recently that she would have to give up the cottage under the sea wall: 'Silly to carry on renting a place, leaving it empty most of the time, when I can't afford it anymore. And now I don't get the time to go there very often, what with my work for the Army, Mrs Augusta. But . . . '

Augusta had known intuitively, what Tilly left unsaid. That place, inconvenient as it was, meant so much because of Oswald. Augusta was going to write to Mr Arthur, who had originally rented the cottage out to Rosa and Petty and offer to buy it. She would offer to pay over the odds so he couldn't refuse.

She studied the sepia likeness of George for a few moments with unexpected tears, for after all her husband had been gone so long. Despite her often overbearing manner, she genuinely adored her only daughter, although she could never bring herself to tell Gussie so.

Augusta thought that she would have to talk to her brother, confide in him her fears concerning Gussie's continued ill health. She replaced the picture. Their elderly doctor still insisted that the cause was asthma, inherited from her father, but Augusta was becoming increasingly concerned. Yet Gussie was so happy now that she was involved with her artistic studies, and seemed to have a breathless, nervous energy which kept her on the go.

Today Augusta had been all too aware, although they had not been remotely physically close in her presence, of a vibrancy between Gussie and Pino: of pent-up feelings which, inevitably, would sooner or later burst forth gloriously. She had observed that same quizzical, reflective look directed by Pino at her daughter – that intimate gaze she had known so well when George had first courted the younger, more impetuous Augusta. 'And I thought the Italians were so voluble and excitable,' she said aloud, to George's portrait. 'But I'm not ready, George, for Gussie to have a sweetheart just yet . . . ' A voice, not her own, seemed to intrude into her thoughts, saying: 'Time is precious, it may not be on their side. Allow Gussie to be happy while she can.' She shook her head violently. 'Leave me alone,' she chided her conscience.

'You two young ladies look most charming,' Pino approved, as once out of Augusta's view he linked arms with them both and they walked jauntily to the bus stop.

Gussie wore another shade of green, in crêpe today, with a little bolero. She shook her hair loose so that it almost obscured the little pearl studs in her earlobes.

Maud had been forced to wear her serviceable skirt, but had on a new blouse in soft, snowy voile, with a silvery thread running through the material in a delicate stripe. Isabella kept her well supplied. She had borrowed a clean pair of gloves from Gussie. 'Look, I have a whole drawerful!' her cousin had said.

It was another softly sunlit afternoon and the main street was crowded. On the corner, a barrel organ played. An appealing little monkey, dressed in a blue jacket and pillbox hat, sat hunched on his master's shoulder, holding out beseechingly in one almost human hand a tin cup for the pennies of passers-by. Pino recognised an old friend from The Hill and they chatted briefly in Italian then bade each other 'Ciao.' They were followed by the strains of 'The Lost Chord' from the somewhat discordant, old-fashioned organ.

The bus being packed, they climbed the stairs. 'Hold on to your hats!' Maud sang out blithely as the horses lurched forward and began their lumbering passage through the Saturday afternoon traffic. The girls sat either side of Pino and he shared his attention scrupulously between them.

They clung precariously to each other, the bus being open-topped, as their vehicle suddenly swerved, clashing wheels with a hansom alongside which, in its turn, caused the rider of a bicycle to wobble dangerously and miraculously escape being crushed by a fire engine. Brass bell clanging furiously, steel-helmeted firemen yelling indignantly, whips were flailed and cracked viciously, horses reared and snorted, and the traffic ground to a halt. The cause of the chaos was a gleaming Packard motorcar which had shot forward rashly from a side street.

The passenger, a lady, sat staring impassively straight ahead. Her hat, secured beneath a flowing chiffon scarf tied under her chin, was framed by the folded back hood. A young buck wearing a curly-brimmed bowler and seated next to the chauffeur in the front of the car glared furiously around. They were subjected to much invective from the other drivers: the smartly uniformed chauffeur, Maud saw, kept his gloved hands poised on the wheel, biting his lower lip nervously.

The fire engine, on urgent business, was the first to move off again, the turncock giving the parting yell: 'Watch yerselves!'

Those pedestrians who had seized the opportunity to dodge from one side of the dangerous road to the other, now fled for their lives.

Maud became aware of Pino's restraining hand on her shoulder, of the warmth of his fingers through the thin stuff of her blouse as she craned in excitement over the rail. Suddenly the lady in the motorcar looked upwards and caught her eye. Maud was flabbergasted when she interpreted the exceedingly rude expression mouthed by one who appeared to be a member of the aristocracy. She sat back on her seat.

'Well!' she said ruefully. Pino released his grip, grinning at her. He'd noted the vulgarity, too.

'Probably not all she seems, eh?' he teased.

Gussie still clung to his other arm. 'Oh, what a shock – I imagined we were going to *fly* out!' she confided tremulously.

The Packard moved ahead, and then they too were on their way to Victoria. From there, they took another bus to Vine Street.

Down the street steps they went, into another world. Maud drank in the fascination of it all. Narrow streets, tall shabby houses, and everywhere she looked, people. They were clad in brilliant, eye-catching colours, the women with their thick gleaming blue-black hair just visible beneath knotted cotton kerchieves. The men were mostly moustachioed, swarthy, sporting cheerful neckties. Maud caught the glint of gold earrings as one tiny child peeped, shyly smiling, from behind her mother's full skirts at the strange ladies passing by.

'Early each morning,' Pino informed them, giving them the guided tour, 'the ice cream churning begins, then the barrows are set up. Here, see, the organ grinders store their instruments, in this big place. They change the tunes every few months, but some of the old favourites are always kept on the barrel.'

There were many barbers, cobblers, cafés and – 'Ugh!' shuddered Maud, avoiding the sight of the pig's heads, trotters and offal in one butcher's window.

'We call that the Piggy-Wiggy pork shop!' Pino said wickedly. He'd soon discovered Maud's weakness, and he was used to slyly teasing his young sisters.

Other tradesmen worked at benches along the pavements, puffing contentedly at their pipes. There were the 'mend your boots while you hop about and wait men', knife grinders, then Pino pointed out a special window. 'This is where they make the most marvellous mosaics. Here they fashion religious statuettes, see? I have an uncle in this line of business. You shall meet him today, I believe. Perhaps that's where I first had the great idea of becoming a sculptor, eh?'

'D'you mean they *all* work locally?' asked Gussie. It seemed to her that they surely must.

'Some go off to wait in the big London hotels, of course, all the best waiters are Italians,' Pion told them proudly, 'but you don't need to venture beyond the Quarter for any-thing you need – should you want a dressmaker or tailor, well, they are here, too.'

'Do your hot chestnut men come from here?' Maud loved to buy a bag of these, roasted in a fiery brazier, when there was an autumnal nip in the air.

'Ah, they do indeed, little Maud.'

She tried to stretch up another inch. 'Rosa, my mother, says that Saffron Hill and Leather Lane are known as 'the seats of the Italians',' she remarked artlessly.

'Then she is right.' Pino smiled. Towards them now came an ice cart, horse-drawn. The girls exclaimed over the beautiful hand-painted designs embellishing its sides.

'You are right in the heart of the community here – Back Hill,' Pino informed them. 'This is St Peters – *our* church – built in true Neopolitan style. You must come again in

July, both of you, on Procession Sunday, in honour of Our Lady of Mount Carmel. It is such a joyous occasion, and the celebrations! Well, they go on for days . . . '

Pino was greeted affectionately on all sides. Gussie and Maud were introduced over and over again. Their hands were grasped with enthusiasm and once they were even serenaded by a fine tenor voice belonging to a handsome man who leaned out through an upstairs window.

'And here we are; this is where we live.' Shyly they followed Pino into a house where the door had been left invitingly ajar.

They were greeted in the dim, narrow hallway by Pino's mother.

'My mother, Celestina Barbieri – Mamma, this is my dear friend Augusta whom you shall call Gussie, for that is also her mother's name, and this is little Maud, her cousin.'

Celestina took a strand of Gussie's hair and matched it against her own auburn locks as she embraced her. 'What a compliment he pays his mamma, eh?' She was plump, with a delightfully dimpled face and surprisingly blue eyes.

'Yes,' she said in halting English, reading Maud's expression, 'some of us are fair while you yourself might be Italian.' Then Maud was enveloped in a friendly hug, too. 'Come in, the family, they are all here.'

A long table was already laid for tea, covered cornerwise with a creamy lace cloth over a starched white one.

Pino's father, Carlo, was an older, thicker-set version of his son. The elder sons sported luxuriant moustaches like their father; the younger boys were still clean-shaven. Each gave a polite nod as he was introduced. The three little girls, demurely pig-tailed, were dark-eyed, but the middle daughter, Luisa, had inherited her mother's light complexion and titian hair. The girls made a little bob.

'And this,' Pino said, turning to a shortish man standing back politely from the family, 'is our friend. We – everyone – calls him Brother James. He does much good, kind work, among the poor in this place.'

Brother James now came forward diffidently, and with an involuntary catch of her breath, which she fervently hoped he was unaware of, Maud noted that he had a deformity, a hunched back.

'James Inkpen,' he introduced himself. 'I am delighted to meet you both,' he said in impeccable English. 'I am, as you can hear, as un-Italian as yourselves, and an Anglican to boot, but these good folk do not hold these misfortunes against me. It is a privilege, I insist, to be allowed to join with the community here and to help in small ways wherever I can.' He shook their hands.

'If you would like to wash your hands, Luisa will take you,' Celestina told them. 'Then shall we have our tea.'

'Tonight,' added Papa Carlo, 'we are to make concert at a private celebration. This is our work, you understand? Yet we still have time to entertain *you*!'

In the best bedroom, Maud and Gussie laid their hats and gloves on the pristine bedspread and washed their hands in the bowl on the corner stand. Opposite was a low narrow bed in which the youngest child obviously slept. Luisa stood by with a huckaback towel, waiting whilst they tidied their hair in turn before the mirror in its ornate frame of gilded plaster. Maud looked curiously at the religious pictures on the wall and the statuette of the Madonna and Child. Over the big bed hung a crucifix.

Carlo took his place at the top and Celestina hers at the bottom end of the table. Gussie was invited to sit on Carlo's right, Maud on his left. Pino was seated next to Gussie on her other side, and Brother James was ushered to a seat adjacent to Maud. A newcorner, introduced as Uncle Luigi, now put in an appearance. 'Uncle is invited to join us, otherwise we would be thirteen,' Brother James whispered to Maud. Carlo said grace in Latin.

Maud was unsure how she felt about sitting next to Brother James. She would have to confess to being no saint and a very irregular churchgoer these days, she thought ruefully, should he touch on religious matters.

However, she was soon reassured: Brother James was a delightful conversationalist, although on occasion Maud's attention wandered as she peeked round at Gussie, thoroughly relishing the attention she was receiving from both Pino and his father. Once or twice Carlo intercepted her

glance, smiled kindly and enquired if she had been provided with this or that from the ample spread before them.

'I have been so fortunate all my life,' Brother James
told Maud, completely dismissing that infirmity which
to most people would have seemed a cruel misfortune. 'I
was born to a family which has always been comfortably
off, who loved and encouraged their children to make
the most of any talents. I was sent to good schools, then
to university, and for a while I considered becoming a
lawyer like my father and grandfather. Then my younger
sister married a clergyman and they went to China as mis-
sionaries. I wanted to do the same but was turned down
by the Society on health grounds. Ridiculous, because I
am as fit as a flea! My wise mother told me I could still
help those less fortunate, and to look much nearer home
so – well, here I am.'

'So you are a sort of missionary after all?' Maud was
intrigued.

'Sort of. But I do not aim to 'convert' these good people. Their faith is so much stronger than mine, and I have
received, spiritually, far more from them than I have ever
been able to give. I can help fight their legal battles, be
their spokesman, advise, interpret and comfort – yes,
Maud, I do believe *this* may be my mission in life! But
I am talking too much about myself. So now tell me all
about Maud!'

They discovered a common interest in music and were soon chatting away like old friends. Maud completely forgot her original discomfiture at his misshapen spine.

Lean, spicy ham, coarsely minced sausages, salami and smoked cheese were eaten with Celestina's home-made bread. Maud had rarely tasted such good bread for there was an elusive nutty flavour to it. Yeasty fruit cake, almond-topped, was then sliced generously on to clean plates. Tea was served, hot and very strong, in large plain white cups.

The table was cleared swiftly, the family working to an easy routine, and the guests were invited to relax on an upright sofa set in the window recess.

The young people politely excused themselves to change into their costumes for the evening's entertainment. Celestina, Carlo, Brother James and Pino stayed to talk to Gussie and Maud. The questions came thick and fast. From Carlo: 'You are an artist, Maud, like Gussie and Pino? No? Then what is it you do?' Maud told him. Carlo again: 'Ah! but you, too, love to make the music, we learn? In our family we all do so.'

Papa, Mamma explained, was very proud of his musical family: 'We are called The Barbieri, you know. We play mandolin, piano accordion, triangle – and *how* we sing! And our little girls, such dancing!'

The brothers returned to display their finery shyly. Maud mentally made a note of it all, for the family at home would want to hear all the details, she knew. They wore tasselled caps, knee stockings criss-crossed by laces, breeches and braided boleros worn over white shirts with billowing sleeves. The sisters shortly joined them to show off their short patterned skirts with silk aprons, their white stockings and dainty shoes, the ribbons in their looped braids, blouses and boleros complementing those worn by the boys.

'You all look absolutely *beautiful!*' Maud cried impulsively, then blushed fierily at her awful cheek. Everyone smiled at her. Mamma and Papa went to change now.

'Oh, please, may we have a song from you before we all have to go?' Gussie enquired eagerly. The young Barbieris were happy to oblige.

The strains of '*O Sole Mio*' seemed to fill every corner of that small overfurnished room, and the listeners on the sofa sat spellbound. Gussie leaned towards Pino and his arm stole round her waist. Maud actually found herself gripping Brother James's hand, then apologising when the song ended. 'No need,' he said.

'There!' Luisa, the most extrovert of the daughters, dispelled the magic. 'See, Mamma and Papa come to make goodbyes.'

There were kisses and hugs all round, for the visitors had been accepted completely by this warm-hearted family.

'You will come back soon,' Carlo said firmly. His middle son had picked a beauty, reminiscent of the young Celestina in Carlo's view. Not of their faith but that could be remedied, couldn't it?

'We will,' they assured him. 'Thank you for the splendid tea.'

'I can hardly move,' added Maud. The family crowded together at the door, holding the smaller fry aloft to wave them an exuberant farewell.

'I would like to walk with you to your bus,' Brother James suggested. He offered an arm to Maud, whilst Gussie and Pino led the way.

'May I call you something else? Brother James sounds so – monastic!' Maud remarked, candid as always.

'Of course, Maud. Why not just James?'

'No, I've got it. B.J.?'

He nodded his acceptance with an amused smile.

'It was all over much too soon, I really loved them all,' she sighed.

'They are good people – good friends,' B.J. agreed. As he turned to leave them, he said, 'I do hope we will meet again, Maud – Gussie?'

'Oh, I'm sure we shall,' Maud answered for both of them. She eagerly caught hold of Pino's other arm. B.J. was soon forgotten. As they walked on, she was unaware that Brother James had paused to watch them until they were out of sight.

'You're a fool,' he chided himself with a wry chuckle. 'A girl like Maud would never look at you . . . ' He pulled at the concealing folds of his coat, comforted by its loose cut. Then he went back down the street to be greeted affectionately by a group which readily split ranks to absorb him.

Yet B.J. was destined to play an unexpected part in Maud's future. And she? Maud was falling in love, but didn't know it.

TWELVE

Joe was waiting at Augusta's to take Maud home. Bursting with news, too. 'Maud, Old Sennapod's done a bunk! He's pinched Kitty's savings to add to the aggravation – she's having hysterics! But she got on to her stepbrother, George, who was resting as they say, and he's rushed over from somewhere or other – they're going to have a quick practice, he's a singer, too, and when I get back I'll accompany them on the piano. You're to come home with me *now* . . . ' He ran out of breath.

'You *knew* I was going to stay here with Gussie overnight – now you've ruined everything!' Maud was thoroughly disgruntled. It was very rarely that she fell out with her brother, and Gussie looked really astounded. The cause of this reaction stood politely to one side. He had actually been invited in by Gussie's mother. He didn't know that Maud was loth to leave his company. Also, she would have to forgo the heart-to-heart chat she had been anticipating with Gussie at bedtime.

Joe took no offence. 'Oh, sorry, Madam Maud, I'm sure. But the *real* reason you're to come home is – Nandy's back! He's off to Malta on Monday, and we thought you wouldn't want to miss seeing *him* as he hasn't been home since before he got married – or has he? – and it might be ages before he gets leave again.'

'Naturally you must go, Maud,' Aunt A insisted.

'Oh, all right,' she conceded ungraciously. 'I s'pose we haven't seen him since he blotted his copybook, as you say, Joe. D'you need me there to jolly things up, is that it?'

'Joe,' Augusta ordered, 'go and help your sister with her bags.' She motioned Gussie and Pino to go into the drawing room.

'Anyone would think he was *your* young man—' Joe began, as he waited in the bedroom doorway, and really couldn't understand why Maud swung her bag into the small of his back.

As they arrived home the front door burst open and Kitty, false fringe dangling dangerously into her eyes, rushed out, followed by a lanky young fellow wearing a shiny suit and trodden-over boots. Behind them trailed 'Arry. 'Took your time, Joe, we had to practise without the piano! Can't stop, we've missed the first performance and it'll be curtains for us if we don't turn up for the second house . . . '

'He pinched me!' Maud was irate, rubbing her rear as they went inside.

'Who, 'Arry?' Joe laughed.

'No, you fool, he wouldn't dare – I mean that so-called brother of Kitty's.' Maud was nearer the mark than she imagined.

And here was Nandy, ill at ease, sitting opposite his mother. Maud noted Rosa's severe expression.

She thought Nandy looked very dashing in his uniform. He jumped up in relief at the sight of her and greeted her warmly – you would never have known they had been at loggerheads all through their childhood.

'Good to see you, old Maud!'

'I see you haven't got that many whiskers yet. Didn't that stuff you sent off for work then?'

Nandy exchanged a wry look with Joe. He fingered the wispy beard which adorned his chin. 'She hasn't changed.'

'I'll just run my things upstairs, then we'll have a good old chinwag,' she promised him.

Maud met Tilly on the stairs. 'Come and talk to me for a minute in my room,' she suggested.

'I was just going to my meeting,' Tilly said, but followed Maud in.

'I *must* tell you, Gus has met the most – the *nicest* young man – an Italian, called Pino – and I've been with Gussie to tea at his house, this very afternoon. We met his entire family. Even Aunt A seems to approve of him. Will wonders never cease? Oh, and Tilly,' Maud concluded breathlessly, dragging the comb through her locks without bothering to look in the mirror, 'how can you tell if someone has consumption?'

Tilly had to sit down abruptly. 'Whoever do you mean?' she asked Maud urgently.

'We-ell, Gus, if you must know. She has a horrible cough, and she's unbelievably thin, Tilly.'

She showed relief. 'I thought you must mean this young Italian. Oh, don't worry too much about Gussie, Maud. Mrs Augusta says the doctor considers she has inherited her father's weak chest – asthma's a wretched complaint, but it's not infectious.'

She sounded so positive that Maud quite forgot to mention the blood-stained handkerchief.

By the time Petty came home, they were all talking animatedly of old times, particularly of the days when they were the family under the sea wall.

'I never imagined you'd turn out so nice-looking,' Nandy told Maud. 'You were a dumpy little pudding when I left.'

'She can still blow up over the silliest things.' Joe spoke with feeling after the bash on his back. Maud batted him another one with Petty's rolled-up newspaper.

'Well, I like a girl with spirit. Just like her mother,' Petty put in, receiving a warning poke from Rosa's steel knitting pin, which merely elicited one of his rumbling guffaws.

'It's good to be home.' Nandy meant it. 'I wish Tilly had stayed.'

'Oh, she's too busy with the Salvation Army,' Maud said.

Rosa leaned forward and gave Nandy's hand a sudden pat. 'I'm sorry for what I said. Remember there's always a place here for you, Nandy. Tilly insisted I make that clear. She's always right! I know you've never lived in this house, but it's your home.'

'Thanks, Rosa. I was headstrong, foolish, I see that now. I understand how hurt you were at my marrying in secret. You needn't worry, we didn't, er—' Nandy cleared his throat.

'Consummate?' Maud put in helpfully, not really knowing what that meant in this respect but earning her mother's displeasure.

'Well, anyway, it was over before it began. I was forced to agree to the annulment. I won't get caught like that again – I promise!'

Maud, forgetting her disappointment over being summarily brought back from Gussie's, rightly guessed that it was the moment for reviving memories of childhood pleasures.

'I made a new set of Happy Family. Fancy a game?'

'All the local tradesmen, I suppose?' Nandy teased.

'Oh, these are *theatrical* cards, Nandy. Wait 'til you see my version of Old Sennapod-who-sees – pity you missed him!'

'Can't wait,' he replied. It was just like the old days in Cheyney. No sound of the sea, of course, and a few dear faces missing.

Maud felt really happy. How long was it since they'd all been together like this? It was so nice to see Rosa direct a special 'welcome home' smile at Nandy, she thought.

The young couple were standing, much too close, embracing. Pino's hands were entwined in her long red curls. A tender, possessive gesture. They had spent the evening together, and Gussie had been bold enough to say to her mother, when Augusta hinted that it was time they retired, that she would see him off. She struggled to suppress a cough as he brushed her closed eyes with his lips, then, daringly, sought her mouth.

Reluctantly, she pulled away. 'You'd better go . . . ' They looked at each other, smiling shyly, for a long minute.

There was a light in the kitchen. Gussie thought she might take a glass of milk upstairs.

The maid, Rosie, was in there, sniffling.

'What's wrong?' Gussie asked her.

'My young man's sister died this morning. Of consumption, Miss Gussie. Doctor says Bob might have it – he's to go away, to a sanatorium. We can't get married 'til his lungs are clear – he won't come again, 'cause he don't want to pass it on to me, he says . . . '

Gussie took a gulp of the milk. If she coughed now, it would upset Rosie, she thought. 'I'm sure your Bob will be all right,' she comforted Tilly's sister. She knew what she would feel like if she and Pino were parted now.

THIRTEEN

Tilly was still out and about. It had been a busy evening in the soup kitchen. Had Rosa and Nandy patched things up? Was Gussie really just asthmatic?

Flo's young brother was plucking at her sleeve. She smelt him before she saw him. Flo's mum was slipping again in the cleanliness stakes. But could she really be blamed, Tilly thought, living where and how she did?

'Miss Sally,' the boy was breathless, having run in sheer fright along the night streets, 'Mum says c'n you go and see if'n our Flo's still in the pub? She left little Bobby yellin' and runned orf wivaht a word. Mum wants you to give 'er a right tickin' orf if you see 'er an' ter tell 'er to mike 'er mind up wot she's at 'cos we ain't 'avin' the baby wivaht 'er ter look arter 'im. Will yer, Miss Sally?' he appealed. His peaked, dirty face went straight to Tilly's kind heart.

'I'll do my best, dearie. That's if she is there, of course. You wait in here in case of trouble. Sarianna'll find you some soup and bread.'

She went out and looked down the road, trying to see through the mass of people, most of whom were staggering home from The Prince of Wales. Tom was not yet in sight; they usually met up here at this time, for Tilly was not supposed to go by herself into the pub.

The jollity inside was still in full swing. Tilly gathered her courage together and marched determinedly through the doorway. She spotted Flo right away. The girl was awash with euphoria, her voice coarse and loud as she joined with the ribaldry of her companions. Beside her lounged a huge fellow, bellowing at the jokes with beer mug in one hand, the other fondling Flo, who looked very dishevelled.

At the sight of Tilly's uniform the noise abruptly ceased. Several of the regulars who knew her well and had reason to be grateful for her help, greeted her with a sheepish: 'Evenin', miss.' Flo, bouncing tipsily to her feet, her blouse unbuttoned, was not likewise pleased.

'You jest clear orf and leave me be, will yer?' she cried angrily. The big fellow lurched up beside her, banged his glass on the table so that it shattered and then advanced menacingly towards Tilly, his ham fists raised.

'You 'eard my girl – she don't want nuffin' ter do wiv your sort!' He belched rudely. There was an uneasy snigger, quickly suppressed, from an old woman in a corner; she knew the man of old, had been thumped by him on occasion for remarking sneeringly on his choice of female companion. He whipped round to stare at her balefully.

'An' you keep aht o' it, you old biddy!'

Tilly walked bravely towards Flo and attempted to grasp her arm. 'Bobby needs you, Flo. You love him, you know you do. Oh, come back to your mum's with me . . . '

The man's great fist caught her sharply under the chin, so that she bit her tongue and her teeth rattled. Tilly dropped like a stone to the sawdust-strewn floor. There was a piercing scream.

She knew nothing of the fight which ensued: Flo turning on and punching her new lover in the vulnerable area of his kidneys, so that he bellowed like a stuck pig; others seizing the chance of a free-for-all. Someone ran for the nearest policeman. The bartender hastily swept the bottles and glasses from the counter into his folded up canvas apron in one fell swoop, then ducked down low – and Tom and the constable arrived simultaneously.

Flo, sobbing noisily, minus a clump of her hair which had been pulled out viciously by the old biddy getting her own back, was yanked outside by her young brother who had given the slip to Sarianna and had been hovering nervously by the open door, despite Tilly's warning.

'Let's git 'ome, Flo. 'Ere comes the Law!'

Tom hoisted Tilly up over his shoulder and carried her straight to her home, declining offers of assistance. She was coming to, and mumbling, when Petty and Tom laid her gently on Rosa and Petty's bed, it being the nearest, while Rosa sent Joe and Nandy, who had come down to see what all the disturbance was about, for hot water and towels.

'If Maud shows her face, tell her not to come in here, but she can make poor Tilly a strong cup of tea for the shock,' Rosa told Joe.

Rosa untied the strings and eased Tilly's crushed straw bonnet away. Tilly stared up at her, barely comprehending. There was a raging pain in her jaw. She was attempting to open her mouth to speak, and a bruise was already appearing on her swollen chin.

'I ought to fetch the doctor,' Petty said to Rosa.

'No, no,' Tilly managed faintly, 'I'll be all right.'

Petty, with the expertise gained from feeling many a sailor's jaw after a fight in port, examined the damage carefully.

'Not broken, I'm sure. I'll fetch her a sedative from my bag. She should stay in here tonight, Rosa, with you, and I'll join the boys upstairs.'

'Thank you, Petty. Take my bed ... ' Tilly whispered, trying to smile. She didn't know she would sleep the next day away.

It was hard trying to prevent her from rising on Monday morning.

'Rosa,' she began, through a mouth which felt as if it had been sewn up, 'it's a busy day – the linen to change, the drawing room to have its good do, the shopping – and Nandy to see off.'

'Stay right where you are,' Rosa said firmly. 'There's someone to see you. Come in, David, and try and talk some sense into her, will you?'

Rosa hesitated for a brief moment in the doorway then decided that Tilly was in no state to need a chaperone. She went away quietly, leaving the door ajar.

'Tom called first thing,' David told her, 'asked me to pass on the good news that Flo got home safely. She's back with her mum and her baby, and very sorry to have caused you all this trouble.'

Tilly saw anger for the first time in his eyes as he examined her sore face.

'Try, Tilly, to open your jaw – just a little more. Bad bite on your tongue, but it's stopped bleeding. Mr Searle is right, I don't think your jaw is broken, but it might well have been . . . Who did this to you?' he asked explosively.

'I – don't know him. Doesn't matter—'

'Doesn't matter?' he almost shouted. 'Of course it does! I'd like to do the same to him.' His own fists were clenched. Quiet Dr Mann, Tilly saw, was extremely upset on her behalf.

'David – *no!*' Her distress was evident. Concerned, he bent over her once more, blotting the tears gathering in the corners of those blue eyes.

'Forgive me, Tilly, I cannot share your compassion on this occasion. It devastates me that this could happen to an angel like you . . . ' His breath was warm on her cheek, which he now humbly kissed.

'Tilly, you *must* know how I feel—'

She put her hand weakly to his mouth then drew his head slowly on to her shoulder, holding him close to her as he knelt by the bed. It was not too different from the way she had held dear Oswald on their wedding night. Yet it *was* different, she thought fleetingly, because that had been so joyful, so fulfilling. Oswald had not been intense like David; his light-heartedness had always lifted her spirits. Yet she was aware, despite her present pain, that feelings which she had thought buried with Oswald were stirring within her again.

They remained like this for a few moments, Tilly quietening him as if he was the one who was hurt and suffering. Then David disengaged himself as they heard the boys approaching the door.

'I've come to say goodbye, Tilly old girl,' said Nandy.

'Good luck, dear Nandy – you'll write, won't you?' she said.

'It was a knock-out, Tilly,' Joe said with awe, looking at her chin.

'You were out for more than the count,' Nandy grinned, and kissed her forehead. 'Of course I'll write.'

David stayed until the family had all left to see Nandy off at the station. The theatricals, of course, were around, and 'Arry was nobly washing up the breakfast things.

'Now, Rosa will be back within the hour,' David said.

'You're getting familiar, aren't you?' Tilly teased. She was propped up now, sucking the tea 'Arry had brought in from the spout of a little teapot.

'I must go; there will be a crowd at the surgery. You should stay here another day or two, I think, Tilly. I will call again tomorrow.'

'I can't pay you!' Her eyes were smiling even if her lips couldn't curl upwards at the corners.

'I am your friend, not your physician.' David smiled back. His emotions were under control now.

'Yes, you are my friend,' she told him.

By the end of the week she was working as usual, despite Rosa's protests. They couldn't prevent her from going to the Friday meeting.

They had left the light burning on the landing for her return. There was a note on the hall table from Rosa: 'Theatricals fed and watered! Go straight up, you bad girl, staying out so late. Goodnight! R.'

Tilly trod quietly halfway up the stairs, then paused. She saw George suddenly emerge from 'Arry's room, which they had agreed he might share on a temporary basis. She watched as he turned the handle of Kitty's door. As Tilly stood there, staring upwards, she saw them for a brief moment: Kitty in the revealing negligee, brazenly reaching out to George. Then he kicked backwards with a bare leg to close the door behind them. She heard Kitty's excited, throaty laugh, quickly suppressed.

After a long moment, Tilly continued cautiously up the further short flight of stairs to her own bedroom. She supposed she should be thankful that George had not tried to force his way into Maud's room. She and Rosa had been right to be suspicious of him, she thought. Then realised sharply that there had been no surprise on Kitty's face, just expectation.

Tilly knocked on Rosa and Petty's door, balancing the tea tray. Rosa came to the door wearing the old kimono; plenty of pulled threads now, and a darn or two, but she'd never part from it.

Tilly stood back, for she had glimpsed Petty in bed. He had to work Saturday mornings, of course. It might be tale-telling, but she *must* say.

'You were late, Tilly, I didn't hear you come in,' Rosa reproached her mildly. ''Arry was quite upset when you weren't here to give him his cocoa. And d'you think you should work so hard when you've hardly recovered from that horrible experience yet?'

'Rosa,' Tilly whispered, 'I'm over that honestly. But I've something to tell you . . .'

'Let me just give Joe his tea then I'll join you in the kitchen,' Rosa said, instantly catching on.

As they drank their tea, Tilly told her what she'd seen on her arrival home. They dispensed the rest of the tea automatically, hardly bothering to ensure that Joe and Maud were awake. Tilly knocked very firmly on Kitty's door. There was no reply. They hesitated, then turned to the other door. Rosa rapped on that.

There was a sleepy 'Come in!' from 'Arry. Tilly followed Rosa inside. 'Arry's small, round head was just visible over the cosy quilt. The other bed was just as they had made it up. Obviously, no one had slept in *there*.

''Morning, 'Arry, here's your tea. Stir yourself.' Tilly crossed the room to pull the curtains. 'Arry muttered his sleepy thanks.

Rosa marched downstairs with the tray still bearing two cups of cooling tea. Tilly poured it down the sink, as if trying to wash sin away.

'A relative, too, Tilly – oh, I don't believe for one minute he's her stepbrother, but we were meant to think so, and with our young people around, too. Maud—'

'That's why I told you,' Tilly said.

'They'll have to go, Tilly. Oh, I wish we'd never even thought of taking *theatricals*.'

'She might have been up to the same with the Sennapod.' Tilly shuddered involuntarily.

She had to poach the haddock for Petty's breakfast; Rosa was still raging.

He said: 'Try and get round her, Tilly, will you? I'm going to be late for work!'

'I'll smooth her down,' Tilly assured him. 'And I'm sorry I stirred it all up!'

FOURTEEN

It was rather an anti-climax. 'I'm sorry,' Kitty said pleasantly enough, coming into the kitchen where Tilly was washing up, 'but I've decided to leave with George – this morning – now. We're travelling up north; we have hopes of an engagement there. I've got to think along new lines now.'

'What about poor 'Arry?'

''Arry? Oh, he really wouldn't have a place with George and me. It was obvious at last night's performance, I'm afraid. Still, he usually finds someone to latch on to,' Kitty said candidly.

'Have you told him?' Tilly asked.

'Well, no, I wondered . . . ' She smiled appealingly.

Tilly thought crossly that Kitty had a self-satisfied air about her this morning, and she knew why!

'All right,' she agreed reluctantly, 'we'll tell him. But we don't approve of the way you're doing this.'

'Oh, thank you, Tilly. Look, I'm pretty broke, as you can imagine. I can just about manage our fare, but will you

286

let Mrs Searle know that I'll send what we owe in lieu of proper notice as soon as I can. I don't think I can face *her* this morning, either.'

George appeared now. He had the effrontery to ask, 'Any chance of a bite or two to take with us, Tilly? We missed breakfast.'

'I wasn't aware that *you* had paid for your board here,' she said primly, surprising herself. But she reached for a brown paper bag and filled it with swiftly made cheese sandwiches. 'Here you are.' She gave them to Kitty. He wasn't worth bothering with.

'Thanks!' Kitty repeated. 'I'll have to leave the big trunk, I'm afraid, but I'll send for it as soon as I can. Say goodbye to Mrs Searle for me.'

Sunshine and dappled shadows in the park, ducks floating, dipping and diving on the pond, children rolling down slopes, lovers flirting on the benches, family parties strolling along the paths to admire the immaculate flower beds, and the crowd gathering in anticipation of the Sally Army band.

Tilly always enjoyed these services in the park. She sang quite unselfconsciously these days, her voice soaring to the high notes. But today she needed to have her mind taken off what had transpired first thing. She had called in on Flo and her family, and Mrs Worrell had said wearily: 'Gorn.' When pressed, she admitted there had been another awful row. Flo had been carousing at The Prince of Wales again, and goodness knows where after the pub closed.

'Bobby?' Tilly enquired anxiously.

'I said, 'You're not leaving 'im, my girl,' so she bundled 'im up and 'orf they went. No, I dunno where they've gorn, and I can't say I care. She ain't worf the worry, Miss Sally. Find some other pore sod to do good by.' And the door was closed firmly in Tilly's face.

Now she sang the familiar chorus:

'Jesus is looking for thee
Jesus is looking for thee
Sweet is the message today
Jesus is looking for thee.'

As she hung on to the last lingering note, to the quivering of the tambourines and the final slow beat of the drum, Tilly looked round at the sea of faces with hope in her heart.

It was impossible to miss the tall woman, smartly but sombrely dressed in grey, her head well above those of the others standing there. She stared directly, disconcertingly, at Tilly.

Then she felt Sarianna nudging her, reminding her that she held the collecting tin. 'Dreaming, Tilly?' she joked. 'Time to come down to earth and raise others to heaven.'

When Tilly looked again, the woman had gone. She rattled her tin determinedly. 'Who will give the Bread of Heaven to feed those less fortunate?' she cried.

Then Tilly marched out of the park and along the street with her fellow Salvationists and didn't know that she was still being watched.

'Arry was upset when Tilly told him about Kitty's defection, but he had come to the same conclusion about the act last night and had made up his mind to join up with some old friends, if he could contact them.

'Stay here, dearie, 'til you get fixed up,' Tilly said.

Petty said to Rosa and Tilly: 'Why not forget about lodgers for a while?'

'Oh, we can't afford to do that, can we, Tilly?' Rosa cried. 'You all reap the benefits, you know, when things go well.'

'Let's reap the benefits of Joe being a master of the pianoforte and have a good old family sing-song?' Maud suggested.

Joe was happy to oblige. But was it necessary to strike up with 'What Shall We Do With a Drunken Sailor?' when Nandy was back on the high seas?

Tilly had been summoned to Augusta's as her sister was indirectly involved in a new worry about Gussie's health.

Augusta came straight to the point: 'I'm feeling frantic, Tilly. I felt I must get a second opinion on that chronic cough. I had to force her to go to the doctor's yesterday as she didn't want to miss her classes. More because of Pino Barbieri than her art, I suspect.'

'You don't approve of Gussie's . . . friend?' Tilly floundered.

'I can't say that. I *do* like him – don't look so surprised – despite his lack of prospects. I wouldn't even say no if they decided to marry, Tilly – oh, not yet, I hope – but I could help them get started.'

If they let you, Tilly thought.

'After all,' Augusta continued, 'she's my only daughter. No, this is my dilemma, Tilly. The new quack suggests that I take her away this winter, and knowing full well that I can afford it – seeing that I can afford *him*! – has suggested Australia, of all places. We would be away six months. When I mentioned it to Gussie, she almost threw a tantrum – just like Maud! – actually shouted at me, said she'd hate me forever if I forced her to leave Pino.'

'I'm sure she didn't really mean that,' Tilly told Augusta.

'To think,' she went on, 'that we used to worry that Joe was the delicate one in our family, and now my only one has been struck down with . . . ' at last she was forced to admit it . . . 'consumption.' That most chilling of words.

Consumption had claimed Bob's sister, Tilly thought, and Rosie was so afraid it would take him, too. Now she knew why Augusta was confiding in her, instead of Rosa and Petty.

She said a quick prayer for guidance. 'Then you must persuade her to go, Mrs Augusta. Tell her young man. You must, to be fair to him. He'll want what's best for her, I'm sure.' Tilly clasped Augusta's hands in hers. Had Gussie been told? she wondered.

'By the way,' Augusta pulled away, feeling for her hand-kerchief, 'the doctor doesn't consider Gussie to be infec-tious, but will you warn Maud and Joe to be careful? I had to tell Gussie *that*: that she must be careful – showing her feelings – until she is well again. For Pino's sake.'

'I'm sure that was wise,' Tilly said quietly. 'Mrs Augusta, why not let her enjoy the rest of the summer here, make her friend welcome, then perhaps she'll realise it's for her own good to go away next winter?'

'Thank you, Tilly.' Augusta cleared her throat and blew her nose noisily. 'Gussie is already testing the water, so to speak – goes to church with Pino now. I've never been reli-gious, as you know, but Tilly – I've been down on my knees quite a bit recently . . . '

'So have I, Mrs Augusta, for you both,' she told her. 'You wouldn't object then, if she joined their church? You were so good to me when I joined the Army.'

'D'you know, I don't think I would. Tilly, it's been a real relief, telling you about Gussie. I keep thinking the worst, then I have to get a grip on myself. I must treat her as I always have. If I show too much emotion, she'll guess things are more serious than I've said. You'd best go in the kitchen now, and have a heart to heart with your Rosie, but don't tell her anything of this. She's got enough to bear right now.'

When Tilly received an unexpected hug from Augusta, she said softly: 'May God bless you both, Augusta.'

FIFTEEN

The cage full of doves, symbolising peace, innocence and the Holy Ghost, and fragrant flower heads – soft petals which, when released, would shower down like snowflakes – was suspended high above the heads of the crowd who were seething with excitement, waiting all along the street. Flags were fluttering from many windows. Sills, lintels and lamp brackets were garlanded with more bunches of flowers. It was Procession Day, 1905.

All were dressed in honour of the occasion: the men in the dark suits reserved for weddings, funerals and festivals. Their neckties had been replaced by hard collars and ties; caps were worn by the majority, but others sported beribboned straw boaters more suited to the sunny day, for which all were grateful as this was proving an indifferent summer so far.

Wives' and daughters' clothes contrasted with the men's sober attire. Shiny silk or satin dresses were sleeked down over slim or generous hips, according to age or child-bearing. Babies were held high so that their rucked-up frocks revealed elaborately trimmed cotton petticoats, long white socks and soft white shoes. The young girls were also clad in virginal white, with floppy bows securing their rippling, raven tresses. They tossed their heads, revelling in their freedom from the usual tight braiding.

Music from several bands, either accompanying the procession itself or stationed at various points along the route, heralded its imminent approach. Maud shivered with pleasurable anticipation, squeezing Joe's arm. Most of Pino's family were involved with the procession, including Pino himself, but Brother James had steered them into the front ranks of the crowd, while himself keeping the promised eye on Gussie, Maud and Joe.

Towards them seemed to float a veritable sea of white as the school-children marched in unison with their teachers. Their demure expressions were often belied by sparkling, sidelong glances at familiar faces in the throng. Round their heads they wore floral wreaths.

There was a sudden, expectant hush. 'The statue of Our Lady of Mount Carmel,' whispered Brother James. 'Look, Pino is on the left, at the rear.'

He walked proudly with his three companions, sharing the burden. They stopped immediately below the giant cage. Restraints were loosed and the contents showered down upon the statue. All around doves fluttered. The onlookers gave a great happy cheer. Children rushed to retrieve a memento before the procession continued, trampling the petals underfoot, the participants singing fervently. Many followed behind, and Maud, clutching Gussie's hand, urged her companions to do the same. But they arrived at the church just as the gates were closed.

'Stay awhile,' Brother James suggested. 'They will open them again for the Benediction. Those who can cram inside will do so. The rest will eventually be blessed, too, for the priest will come out to them.'

'Oh, I do wish I could go inside!' Maud lamented.

'It's so beautiful,' Gussie said dreamily, caught up in it all. 'There is the most wonderful marble statue – *una bella statua bianca di marmo*. There, Pino taught me that, aren't you impressed?'

'Who does the statue represent?' Joe asked, enchanted.

'Saint Vincent Pallotti,' Gussie told him, 'the founder of this church.'

'And did you realise,' Brother James added, 'that this is the very first Italian church built anywhere in the world outside of Italy?'

Much later, after the blessing, they walked lazily back down the hill with some of Pino's family, pausing to buy sweet little cakes from a street vendor, cramming them into their mouths there and then, just like everyone else. They smilingly declined the voluble invitations in excited Italian to 'Come inside, make merry, eat and drink with us!' from those who knew and loved Brother James. He translated and replied in fluent idiom.

'He is with *us*!' Luisa replied in a jealous way, steering him past.

'Tonight,' Brother James told the visitors, 'there will be music played and everyone will dance in the streets. No flagging until dawn breaks.'

'Oh, I do wish we could stay on for the dancing.' Yet Maud knew that Joe would uphold Rosa's request that they be home by midnight, accompanied by Brother James, naturally, for safety's sake. 'You're so lucky, Gus,' she said enviously, 'being allowed actually to stay the night with the Barbieris. I really can't imagine what's come over Aunt A, you know. She's so tolerant lately.'

'I don't mind what's come over her!' Gussie rejoiced. 'Remember, Maud, Pino and I are engaged. That makes all the difference.' She proudly displayed the thin gold wire ring with its single pearl. 'I couldn't believe it when she said we had her blessing . . . Of course, she's still insisting that we go to Australia in November, but I really don't mind half as much now because . . . ' she bent to whisper in Maud's ear, as Brother James, Luisa and Joe walked just ahead ' . . . because, Maud, she's agreed we can marry once we return, although she insists we must both finish our studies. The snag is she expects us to live with her! Not that we could afford to do otherwise, eh? Oh, duckie, aren't you thrilled for us? It'll be worth going all that way away if I can get myself really fit once more, don't you agree?' It was a long speech, and Maud was aware that

Gussie's hoarseness had increased dramatically. They paused while she hung on to Maud and suffered a bout of coughing.

'I do,' Maud said. 'And I'm *so* happy for you both.' She had to suppress her real feelings: the unworthy pangs of envy, her instinctive reaction to this totally unexpected news of an early marriage. She stretched up to dab a quick kiss on her cousin's flushed cheek. Belatedly, she remembered that this was taboo. Oh, what rubbish! she thought. For Gussie and Pino must surely have kissed – properly – when he proposed. How could this little peck possibly count?

During the course of the evening there was much imbibing of wine.

Brother James watched as Maud and Joe joined the dancers. It was obvious, he thought, that they were good friends as well as brother and sister. What a lissom girl she was, despite her lack of height, which was just right when she tucked her arm under his and coaxed him outside, too. He could even rest his chin gently on her dark head as she took the lead in showing him the steps. He wondered if he suspected the cause of Gussie's frailty. If not, he guessed that she would be devastated, for she and Gussie were so close, more like sisters than cousins.

The music was vibrant, thrilling. Maud looked into the kind face smiling at her excitement and was suddenly sharply aware of what must be the marks of past suffering, the shadows under Brother James's brown eyes, lighter than her own which were almost black and sparkling.

'You really love music, don't you, Maud? I'm sure that as a musical aficionado you have heard of Henry Wood and the LSO? There is to be a concert soon in the Queen's Hall. The conductor will be the great Hans Richter. Would you and Joe like to accompany me to this?' His tone was diffident. Maud would have been surprised if she had realised that B.J. had never asked a young lady out before.

'I'd love to – and I'm sure Joe will want to come, too,' she said immediately. 'Oh, that's made me really thirsty. Let's go back in and have a drink, eh?'

'Two glasses, that's your limit, and I believe you've had those already,' B.J. told her.

'Water will do!' said Maud pertly.

The only ones left in the house were Gussie and Pino. Maud saw Gussie resting against Pino's broad shoulder, shutting her eyes in sheer contentment at their closeness. Maud bit her lip and turned to Brother James. 'I'll drink it in the kitchen, then we must do some more dancing. You're enjoying it, aren't you?'

'I've never danced before,' he told her truthfully. 'But with you to encourage me, anything is possible.'

Nearly an hour later, Brother James thought it was time to remind Maud and Joe that they must hurry if they didn't wish to walk all the way home.

'Goodnight, Gus, goodnight, Pino,' Maud sang out from the doorway. Gussie opened her eyes and blew a kiss.

'Goodnight, darling Maud – see you soon. Oh, it's been a wonderful day, hasn't it? A day to remember forever.'

'Forever,' Maud echoed. She looked at Pino. He looked near to tears, she thought in surprise.

'The wine ... it has that effect, sorry,' he murmured, blinking. 'Thank you for coming, Maud and Joe. I, too, hope to see you both soon.'

Celestina enveloped them in turn in her warm embrace. There was so much more of her to cuddle up to compared with her own mother, Maud thought.

'You will come again, Maud, with this nice brother Joe?'

Despite his sheepish sidestepping, Joe was pounced on too.

More hugs and kisses when the rest of the family were called from the dancing.

'I hope you don't all develop blisters!' Maud said.

'Ah, Maud, Joe, dear Brother James ... you like our Procession Day?'

There were more embraces from complete strangers among those still milling in the streets as they made their reluctant exit from the magic of Little Italy.

Maud linked arms between Joe and B.J. 'I'm a bit shivery, you two. Keep close!'

B.J. asked perceptively, 'Anything wrong, Maud?'

'The silliest thing, B.J., I just suddenly felt, you know, that today had been, well, *too* perfect . . . '

'Too much fresh air, Maud, on top of the wine,' he said, as lightly as he could.

'Here's the bus!' Joe said. 'Run!'

SIXTEEN

Tilly was just placing the bundle of carrots in her basket in the market when her ears were assailed by shouted expletives and the sound of pounding feet. Those in the path of the ragged boy, swerving and ducking to avoid his pursuer, jumped smartly out of the way. The boy skidded on a cabbage leaf, which had been cast aside first thing and so trodden underfoot since that it had become slimy and slippery. As he stretched out his arms in a vain attempt to stop himself falling, his head connected with the sharp corner of the stall and the fruit and vegetables went flying. As Tilly went to help the dazed boy to his feet there was more shouting, from the greengrocer this time. The stallholder who had been chasing the boy stuck a rough hand down the lad's shirt front and came up in triumph with a whole wet cod. Satisfied, he went back smartly to his fresh fish, intent on seeing what else had been pinched while he'd left his stall unattended.

'Leave him alone, you bully!' Tilly cried hotly to the greengrocer. Amused customers were busy retrieving the rolling apples, onions, cabbages and lettuces. He was not an unkind man. Once the first shock was past, he had been concerned to see the gash on the boy's forehead pouring blood.

'Git the lad away from 'ere then, missus, 'e's contaminatin' the goods.'

Tilly obliged, holding the boy firmly by his arm, and went in search of Rosa.

'I'll have to rush him round to David, Rosa – he should still be at the surgery, I hope. I'm sure this'll need stitching up. Got a spare hanky? Mine's already sopping.'

They removed themselves to one side to bind the wound as best they could. The boy had a sullen, suspicious face and was obviously unsure of their intentions. His were to make a break for it when the dizziness had passed.

'I'll see you later. Well, I'll be back home just as soon as I can,' Tilly said to Rosa, passing her the basket of vegetables to add to her own.

'Don't worry, do the best you can. I don't need to buy much more and I can manage the baskets, they're not so heavy. It's so much better now we're going to let the new theatricals do their own catering, isn't it? Though I do wish they didn't have onions with everything! The whole house smells of stew.' Rosa felt impulsively in her purse. 'Here, lad, you don't need to steal – you can buy what you were after later.'

He snatched at the shilling without a word of thanks. With a wry smile at Rosa, Tilly took him away.

David was still at the surgery, although the waiting room was empty. It was the first time Tilly had seen him since she had recovered from the attack in The Prince of Wales, for Flo had not returned and she'd had no urgent need of his medical services for a while.

He was not alone. As Tilly entered the surgery to his: 'Come in!' she immediately saw the tall woman standing by the window. There was instant recognition on both sides. This was the woman who had stared at her so intently in the park. The memory still niggled at Tilly.

David's first concern was for the patient. After the wound had been cleaned, Tilly had to hold the boy very firmly while it was stitched. He didn't yell out but they could hear him grinding his teeth. He refused to divulge where he lived, although he came out with a grudging, 'Orright – c'n I go nah?' when David asked him to return in a few days to have the stitches removed. Having come sharply to his senses while the needle was being plied, he was gone like a shot from a gun.

'You are Tilly, I presume?' the woman asked, as David washed and dried his hands. Her voice was slightly accented like his, clipped, her expression haughty. Somewhat in awe of her, Tilly managed to reply: 'Yes.'

'I should have introduced you, I'm sorry,' David said. 'Tilly – this is my sister Esta, with whom I live.'

Tilly thought that David had not mentioned his sister before. Nor had she ever told him about Oswald. She was not sure why.

'David has been with me since eight years old. My husband and I brought him to England when our mother died, in Germany,' Esta informed Tilly coldly. She knew intuitively that Esta resented her friendship with David.

'They were second parents to me. They put me through all my studies at great sacrifice to themselves,' he said, glancing fondly at his sister.

'My husband was also a doctor, an Englishman. We adopted David, having no children of our own,' Esta continued pointedly.

She is telling me all this, Tilly realised, to prove that she has a prior claim on David's affections.

'I am sad to say,' Esta said after a pause, 'that Bernard died last year.'

'He was just like a father to me, and inspired me to my vocation. He, too, worked in this practice until he retired.' David indicated the photograph on his desk. Tilly had noticed this before, and had guessed it to be his father. He had not told her he was adopted. The late Bernard had a nice face, she thought. Despite there being no blood-tie, they must have had much in common.

Esta moved towards the door. Tilly resisted the compulsion to follow, though she guessed it was expected. 'Bernard was an idealist, as is David.' Esta turned again to face Tilly directly. 'I came only to bring David a message. My delaying him meant he could see to your boy.' She waited, issuing a silent challenge.

'I am very grateful,' Tilly answered in a subdued manner. Then an angry thought crossed her mind. She was, of course, grateful to David, not his sister.

He seemed unaware of the tension. 'Tilly also is an idealist, Esta – a Salvationist, as I have said to you. She could equally well have been – well, she *is* – a splendid nurse.' Now his fond smile was directed at Tilly.

'You are obviously most capable,' Esta informed her. She was not unlike her brother in appearance, but not nearly so dark, apart from beetling brows over deep-set eyes.

As he showed his sister out with his customary courtesy, she added unexpectedly: 'David must bring you to our house. Tomorrow is convenient. We should get to know one another better.'

Whatever for, wondered a bemused Tilly. She and David, when he had packed his bag, left the surgery together.

Esta's out-of-the-blue remark – she hadn't even been given time to accept the invitation, Tilly realised – prompted her to ask David: 'Does your sister mind our being friends?'

He paused in his stride, looking down at her. 'I am so happy that you consider me your friend, Tilly,' he said sincerely. 'I called you an idealist. In fact we both have the same views on life, I believe. We both wish to help those

305

less fortunate, show compassion for others. I admire you for your beliefs, your Christianity. That should not be a barrier between us.' Tilly gave a delicious little shiver at this unexpected speech.

It was not the time or place to pursue it. She bade him goodbye as he went one way, she the other. 'Call for me tomorrow at seven, David,' she said shyly.

'I shall come,' he called after her. Tilly broke into a run. She had deserted Rosa for too long.

David and Esta lived in an eminently respectable street. Tilly was almost sure that the curtain was shifting behind the bay window on the left-hand side of the Georgian house as she and David walked down the path.

Then she was ushered into a depressing hallway, assailed by a musty odour. *Their* entrance hall was always flooded with light, she thought, and smelled of fresh polish and flowers. She could tell that this was a neglected place.

Esta came out of the room where the curtains had twitched. 'Good evening, Tilly. I'm afraid we have no maid to announce you or to take your things,' she stated. Tilly was acutely aware of the sarcasm. 'If you would like to follow me upstairs, you may leave your hat and gloves in my room. David will fetch us coffee in the meantime. I understand that you do not partake of alcohol?'

Tilly was given no chance to reply. She nervously ascended the stairs behind her hostess.

Esta's room obviously doubled as a study, for the bed was pushed under the window, the walls were fitted with shelves spilling over with books, and a huge desk was covered with paper, pens, pencils, bottles of ink, dictionaries and reference manuals.

'I make translations from the German. It is necessary for us to survive financially.'

Tilly removed her hat in silence and laid it on the bedspread, then waited. She was sure that Esta had brought her up here, away from David, to tell her something. She was right.

Esta launched straight into the attack. 'I am glad to have this chance to speak to you before we rejoin David. He tells me that he intends to ask you to marry him.' This bald statement came as a complete shock to Tilly.

'I – I told him—' Tilly must choose her words carefully, she knew, and refuse to be intimidated. Rosa had warned her of that, perhaps suspecting what Tilly had not. But it was easier said than done. After all, the only time David had betrayed his feelings for her was when he'd visited her after she was laid up from the pub attack. She thought that they had agreed to be good friends, but what had actually been said was hazy because of the circumstances.

'He has strong powers of persuasion,' Esta stated. 'He is single-minded.'

'I'm not ready to marry again. I might never be.' There, Tilly had said it. She was gathering her courage now.

'If you really mean that, I must confess it is a relief to me. You see,' Esta said chillingly, 'this is my house, Tilly, and I do not intend to share it with another woman. David will never leave me. I made him promise that when Bernard died.'

'And you don't want to share *him* either?' Tilly flashed.

Esta did not reply to this directly. 'David cannot afford to marry, though money is immaterial to him. And if you imagine it is a case of differing religions, then you are wrong. I myself was married to a gentile. No, David believes, as did Bernard before him, that you should not take from those who have nothing to give. I applaud this attitude, do not mistake me, but it is I who have to subsidise his work from what I can earn and from my savings. It is I who pay for the upkeep of this house, who must manage with no domestic help. It is I who pay for food and other necessities from my own pocket.'

'I am sure David is grateful to you, but he is entitled to marry if he wishes. The right woman could be just as much a support to him as you have been . . . ' Tilly hoped fervently that she was saying the right things.

'There you have it; *I* am the *right* woman, not *you*.'

Tilly flinched at the malevolence of this. Esta actually smiled at her. 'Come down now, David will wonder where we are.'

They sat, Esta facing Tilly, on dusty, tapestry-covered chairs, in an awkward silence. David sat between them.

'It will be a cold meal, I am sure you will not object?' Esta said finally. 'Cooking is not one of my interests and David, he keeps such erratic hours, I should have burned many a dinner had it been my passion.'

Afterwards Tilly wondered what on earth the meal had consisted of; every morsel she forced into her mouth tasted like chaff. Esta was even being amusing now that she considered she had put Tilly in her place. David constantly glanced at her to see how she was responding, but he did not say much.

They were finally left to themselves while Esta swept out to make more of the bitter coffee which Tilly had disliked at first taste.

'David,' Tilly said, leaning back in her chair so that her face was in shadow, 'I want to tell you something before Esta returns. When I was still a child, before I married my dear Oswald . . . ' She must not cry, she *would* not cry, she willed herself, as she had in that original confession.

'You had a baby, is that it?' he asked quietly.

'How did you know? I wasn't allowed to keep – him – but it wasn't my wish, you must believe me. It wasn't my fault but I've paid for it ever since. So you see, I would not be a proper wife for a doctor . . . '

He unclasped her hands, clenched in her lap. 'It made no difference to your Oswald, did it? Am *I* less of a man? It makes no difference to the way I feel either. Please don't shake like that, Tilly. I am sad for you that you had to part with your child, that is all. For you are a born mother. I knew that when I saw you so tender with that little baby, that first time we met.'

Tilly thought wonderingly that he had responded exactly as Oswald had all those years ago. But surely there was a difference? For a start, she had to admit to herself that she was fond of him, admired him greatly, yet . . . 'That is not the only barrier between us, David,' she said quietly.

'I know. You refer to my sister. To Esta. I can handle this.' He would have moved closer, to disarm her completely, but the spectre of Esta returning at just the wrong moment was a deterrent to them both.

'But, David, she dislikes me – I can feel it.' And I am not ready for this, even after eight years, she cried silently.

'She would dislike any woman I chose. But when she knows you well . . . why, everyone loves you, Tilly!'

'I am sorry to intrude but here is the coffee,' came Esta's dry tones from the open doorway. Tilly, with burning face, wondered just how much she had overheard.

Esta talked deliberately of the old days in Germany and the life they had led there: comfortable, upper-middle-class, a Jewish family. She talked of her own time at university, of meeting Bernard – her expression even softened as she spoke of him – she told of her love for her new country and of all the hopes, so happily realised, that she and Bernard had cherished for their adoptive son. 'He has paid us back richly. In return, it is my pleasure to look after him as I *always* have done, and shall continue to do.'

How could Tilly tell, in return, of her own poverty-stricken childhood, her lack of formal education, and her struggle to remedy this? She made the excuse that she would be needed at home: 'to get the lodgers' supper'. There, having lodgers would be a common thing to do in Esta's eyes, she thought.

Tilly and David walked home in the late-evening light. 'What is your reply to what I said?' he ventured at last.

She stopped and turned to him. 'David, I am *so* fond of you, I really am. But there seems too much against it just now . . . May we go on for a while as we are? You see, when I joined the Salvation Army, I thought I'd found all I would ever need to replace what I had lost.'

'If that is what you wish.' His voice was sad but resigned. They walked hand in hand, in silence, to her gate.

She would not ask him in, it would not be proper for it was obvious the family were abed. But she suddenly reached up to him, as they stood on the top step, and kissed him on the lips. His beard bristling against her cheeks felt strange. When he left the sea for good, Oswald had been clean-shaven. 'Don't be disappointed in me, David. I shall always be your friend – *always*, I promise!'

He did not attempt to hold her. 'And I yours,' he said gravely. Tilly waited as he walked away. She knew that she could never, ever live with Esta in that house.

SEVENTEEN

Augusta pulled the curtains together. Gussie had at last succumbed to the sleep of sheer exhaustion after a battling night when she had clung to her mother in terror, feverish and gasping for breath. The doctors, both of them, had returned first thing, but there had been more grave consultations and muted murmurings outside Gussie's room than the action for which Augusta begged.

This relapse had taken them by surprise: Gussie had been resting in bed, as advised, these past two weeks, and had been talking of returning to the Slade when the new term commenced. Pino had reluctantly stayed away, but he intended to be there for Gussie's birthday this coming Saturday. Gussie was determined to be better by then. She would be twenty, a turning point, she said optimistically.

Outside it was a mellow autumn day, but Augusta wanted to shut out the sunlight. She sat down, fingers tightly interlocked as if she were praying, watching over the still figure in the bed. She was alone now with her daughter, for Rosie had left her service just before all this happened. She had gone to another situation where she would be nearer her Bob, who was making splendid progress. The new girl had lasted only four days before she had told Augusta candidly: 'Me mum don't think it's right I should be workin' where there's lung sickness. She's found me another place to go to. Sorry, missus, but I'm to leave right away.' How could Augusta blame her? This disease was rightly feared, she knew that.

So she had written to Tilly, not saying too much, but merely asking if she could help out for a few days. Tilly would have received the letter this morning.

'Mama—' Gussie whispered, so faintly. Augusta was barely in time to lift her daughter's head before Gussie haemorrhaged. Somehow, she stemmed the massive flow with the towels she had ready, then she threw these to the floor, not wanting Gussie to see them. Shaking, chilled and clammy, Gussie indicated that the pain was in her back. Augusta rubbed her gently, then let her slip back on to her pillows. She sponged Gussie's face tenderly: the pale lips were still frothing. Although Gussie's eyes were closed, she was trying to say something. Augusta listened intently.

'Thank you, Mama – I love you . . . ' Gussie managed.

Augusta stroked her cheek. 'I love you too, Gussie.'

For a few more minutes she waited, but Gussie seemed to have drifted into sleep. Then she hurried downstairs. She must telephone and demand that the specialist return immediately. Replacing the receiver with violently shaking hands, she became aware that someone was at the front door. Thinking it might be the other doctor, she went quickly along the hall.

Tilly stood there. Before she could say anything, Augusta was pulling her inside and up the stairs, not giving her a chance to remove her hat and coat.

Tilly paled at the state of Gussie's room, then pulled herself swiftly together. 'Mrs Augusta – have you plenty of ice in the icebox?'

Augusta nodded mutely.

'Then I'll make an icepack for her chest. You stay here, leave it to me.'

The specialist arrived, and while he was with his patient Tilly humped up the soiled linen and took it to the bathroom. She ran the cold tap. She would leave all this to soak in the bath. She had to avert her eyes when, to her horror, the water became crimson.

A little barley water, that was all Gussie could take, into which they mixed the sedative the doctor had brought. He sat by the bed, feeling her pulse at regular intervals, his expression anxious. Augusta remained very still on her other side.

Tilly busied herself with mundane tasks. Downstairs, while she made more tea, she realised that it was late afternoon: Joe would already be home from school. She decided to telephone Petty and ask him to come to Augusta's as soon as he could, but would suggest that he went home from the office first to warn them, without going into details of how things were at Augusta's. 'Tell Rosa not to say much to Maud – we don't want *her* rushing round here, you know what she's like. Joe's so much more sensible.'

'I'll try to be in and out before she arrives back,' Petty said. 'I'll be with you within the hour, I hope.'

The doctor motioned to Augusta to come outside. His patient was sleeping peacefully again; she could be left for a few moments. It would make no difference.

Augusta knew what he was going to tell her.

'I'm very much afraid that you are going to lose your daughter, Mrs Quayle. There is nothing more to be done. I'm so sorry. I imagine she will just slip away within a few hours. By tomorrow . . . Would you like me to stay?'

His concern almost broke down her resolution. She was determined that Gussie should not hear her weeping.

'You may go, Mr Barnes. My friend is staying with us. My brother will be here shortly. I will call you again when I need you. Thank you for coming.' She put out her hand. He shook it gravely. Augusta's hand was as cold as her daughter's.

'If you are sure?' he queried. She was a very brave woman, he thought.

'I am sure,' she repeated. Then she left him to go down-stairs alone while she returned to her vigil with dear Tilly close beside her.

*

'Mrs Augusta,' Tilly said simply, 'let me see to things. Please.'

Augusta was unnaturally calm, both Tilly and Petty felt that.

'I must thank you, both of you, for staying with me – with Gussie – all these hours. You must be very tired. You should go home now, see Rosa. Tell her – it's all over. Gussie is at peace.'

Tilly went upstairs quietly. Oswald's mother had done what was necessary when he had died, to save Tilly the pain. Now she could do this service for Augusta.

When she came downstairs, after some long time, Augusta still sat on, in the drawing room, holding a long envelope in her hands.

'This is for you, Tilly. Gussie wanted to give it to you on Saturday; she wanted to see your face. I'm not sure if this is the right time, but – here you are.'

Tilly took the envelope from her. Inside was a card decorated with delicate flowers round the edges:

To Dear Tilly, in appreciation for all you have done for us over the years.
   With our love,
   Augusta and Gussie

There was a document, too. The cottage under the sea wall was Tilly's.

She was too choked to say anything: she carefully replaced the foolscap sheet and the pretty card.

'Gussie painted it,' Augusta told her. 'There is a great deal to do, so much to arrange, before the family comes. Will you help me, Tilly?'

'You know I will. And, Mrs Augusta, thank you for this. It means so much. Will you come up now?' She helped Augusta to her feet.

'Tilly, you will stay – for a while, won't you?'

'I'll stay. You need me, don't you?'

'Oh, Tilly, what would we all do without you?'

Tilly's strong arms went round her, held her close. 'What would *I* do without all of you to care for?' she asked.

EIGHTEEN

The family had all been delighted when Maud was sent, with a letter of recommendation from her typing college, to an interview at one of their favourite London stores.

'They actually liked me!' Maud had whirled Joe round in a dance of triumph. 'I'm to start the last Monday in September!'

She had come down to earth with a bump following a carefree week spent on the Island with her grandmother, who had been kept busy fitting her out with her office clothes.

Maud was employed in the Stationery Department; some of the work was routine, but a great deal was varied and interesting. As the newest typist, Maud was naturally given the more mundane tasks, but she was assured that, if she came up to scratch, she would in time be allowed to take and transcribe shorthand notes and to type highly confidential reports, for the store offered an efficient secretarial service to its customers. 'Maybe,' she told her family, 'I'll rise to the dizzy heights, and be allowed to type up manuscripts for famous writers!'

The senior typists, rather autocratic ladies, were often required, at short notice, to attend clients at home where their skills would be put to good use. A cab would arrive, a typewriter would be carried out by the office boy, whilst the fortunate one would sweep out after him, bestowing a self-satisfied smile on colleagues busy with boring balance sheets.

Maud was thrilled with her roll-top desk: she lovingly fingered its polished surface, and Rosa and Tilly would have been amused to know that she dusted it daily. Once the first trepidation was past, Maud found it a pleasure to thread that first sheet of paper into her Royal Barlock machine, to clatter away merrily, and hope that she would not fill her basket with too many screwed-up rejects.

Like her companions, she was soberly dressed. Her hair was still too short to put up properly, but she tied it back severely from her expressive face. Prim she may have appeared, but inside she was bubbling over with a lively interest in her fellow workers. Maud would never change. How the family enjoyed all her stories about her job, though as Joe said: 'You have to remember that she embellishes everything!'

The hours were long, yet the conditions were good. In Maud's office, the odd, whispered conversation and occasional giggle were not commented upon. She took a packed lunch and spent her precious lunch hour in pursuit of pleasure.

For she had soon discovered the music department. On her third day she visited her new friends among the younger members of the sales staff. She donned the special earpieces and was transported to another world as she listened to the latest recordings. Somehow, she thought, it was fitting to brush the crumbs from her serge whilst Adelina Patti sang the poignant 'Home Sweet Home'. Maud relished telling the others that she had actually seen and heard the great Patti at the Albert Hall recently, on one of her regular musical excursions with B.J. Of course, Patti was more or less retired, so that had certainly not been an occasion to miss. Joe did not always accompany them for he could see what Maud seemed oblivious to, that B.J. was keen on his sister, though Joe really couldn't think why!

'I shall buy this for Gussie's birthday,' Maud decided now, after listening to the record. She was unaware, because they had kept it from her at home, that Gussie was gravely ill again. 'We don't want to spoil Maud's first days at work, do we, Joe?' Rosa had said quietly.

The record, Maud thought, would remind Gussie of home when she was in Australia.

The supervisor had received a telephone call. She summoned Maud kindly to her desk. 'Miss Searle, your father will be coming for you in about a quarter of an hour – an urgent family matter, he says. You have my permission to leave your work. Perhaps you would be good enough to show me what needs to be finished today?'

Petty was waiting for her at the staff entrance. He looked awful, old and grey, Maud thought. She had to know: 'What's up, what's wrong, Petty?' she demanded urgently.

'I'll tell you in a minute.' His voice was scarcely audible. He took her bag from her, and hurried her along to the bus stop. They waited in silence. There were others there, too, so he could not tell her now.

'Maud, you must be very brave,' he told her at last as they took their seats inside the bus. 'I'm afraid I've got some terrible news . . . It's – it's Gussie. She's – dead, Maud. Dear God, that sweet child is dead!'

So that was why he'd been away last night. Rosa had been evasive as to the reason.

Now Petty turned to his daughter for comfort, pressing his face against her shoulder and sobbing soundlessly. Maud sat rigidly. They were both oblivious to curious glances.

Maud seemed to see blood, endless blood, as she had read about in romances when the heroine expired from consumption. 'I don't believe it . . . ' she said at last. But she did. She had shut the prospect out of her mind for too long.

Petty's voice was muffled. 'I know. Augusta said they'd been making all sorts of plans for the wedding. Gussie was trying to persuade her mama to bring it forward. It's so cruel – oh, why?'

'She died happy,' Maud stated, in a surprisingly calm voice. She felt absolutely numb inside. 'Pino . . . does he know?'

'I had to send him a telegram. He'll be there by now.'

'What good will it do?' Her voice was angry now, rising sharply. 'It's too late, isn't it? Someone should have fetched him last night.'

'You want to come – now? Rosa's there, of course, and Joe.' He straightened up, blowing his nose fiercely on his pocket handkerchief.

Maud nodded. 'I said it's too late, but I must see for myself, Petty, otherwise I won't believe it.'

Augusta, still tearless, took them upstairs and left them for a while. Still Maud, who usually cried so easily, did not break down.

Below there was the sound of weeping. Pino sat hunched, head in hands. Brother James stood beside him, quite unable to help for once.

'Excuse me, I must make more arrangements . . . ' Augusta said, as Petty and Maud came slowly down the stairs. She motioned him to follow her into the study where Rosa and Tilly waited. She had insisted that Joe be sent home again. 'He is too young for all this,' she'd said.

Oblivious to B.J., Maud fell heavily to her knees beside Pino. Then his arms went convulsively round her, almost squeezing the breath from her. Now they were crying inconsolably together, with his streaming face and lips against her silky hair. Pino! Oh, Pino! Maud mourned inwardly.

Brother James moved away slowly, as if in pain. These two were best left alone together.

After the funeral, Brother James came to break the news to Maud that Pino's family had sent him away, back to his grandfather in Italy where the country air would help to ensure that his lungs kept clear. He would work through his devastating sadness and resume his studies later.

'Celestina, Carlo, all the family,' Brother James said, 'send their love to you. They will come to see your aunt when they feel it is the right time. They judged it would be too much for her at present. They want so much to keep in touch with you, too, Maud. Oh, my dear, don't cry, please.' He looked so distressed she was surprised.

'I'm not crying for myself – it's Pino. I-I can't bear it. Oh, why did Gussie have to die, B.J.? She was such a lovely girl, and they were so happy together.' She couldn't under-stand why Pino hadn't come himself, to say goodbye.

'Everyone has a time to go, Maud. And none of us who has known her, even for a short time like myself, will ever forget her. When the hurting is over, you will remember all those good times you spent together. You were so close, you two!'

'Aunt A gave me all her drawings, boxes of them, all she'd ever done. I can't bear to look at them yet.'

'One day you will. It's good you have something of Gussie's to treasure.' He rubbed her chilled hands between his. 'Pino will be back, he will need us – you, in particular, Maud.'

'I love him, B.J.,' she said painfully.

'I know.' He continued his comforting massage of her small hands.

'No one else knows, only you,' she told him. Brother James was sure in his own mind that this was not so. Maud could not disguise her emotions, he thought, from Rosa, Petty or Tilly – even from quiet, thoughtful Joe, who had decided without prompting from the family that he would sleep at Augusta's house at nights until she felt the need to be by herself. Tilly was there every day, of course, and Rosa and Petty kept her company most evenings.

Maud was alone with Brother James in the house at this moment: for propriety's sake, she really shouldn't have invited him in, but she knew that, although Rosa on her return from Augusta's might reprove her, she and Petty trusted Brother James implicitly. Everyone did.

'I'd like to show you something,' Maud said suddenly, withdrawing her hands from his clasp. She fetched the heavy photograph album and they sat very close as she turned the pages. She would close the book before reaching the black-bordered cards, particularly the one recording the death of her baby sister in Sheerness.

Brother James was all too aware of their proximity. He smiled over the early photographs of Maud and her brothers, taken by Mr Lozenge in Sheerness, of course. He noted her protective arm round the little Joe's shoulders as she knelt beside him on the seat, crumpling his baby dress. Nandy, bored and unsmiling, stood behind them, arms folded. Brother James could see how like her mother as a young woman Maud was. Disturbingly, her hair brushed against his face.

'Mr Lozenge, B.J. – well, *he* was suspected of being a spy! Petty thought he was hounded just because he was a German. But Joe and I saw him once, training his binoculars on a warship! We even saw him apprehended! Yet he was always so nice to us when he took our portraits – a bit of an old fuss-pot, I suppose. And just look at this! These demure little girls, they're Gus and me – Tilly's wedding. Doesn't *she* look just beautiful?'

Brother James agreed. The next picture, of an enchanting child with cascading hair, was obviously of Gussie.

'She will always be young and lovely to you all,' Brother James told her wisely. As he knew Maud would be to him.

She embraced him impulsively. 'Oh, dear B.J. – you always say the right things! I do *like* you so much! Thank you for coming to cheer me up today.'

Those words, said earlier, still hung in the air. '*I love him, B.J*' '*I know*.' If only it had been: 'I love *you*.'

NINETEEN

Tilly's hands and feet were freezing, but as always her face was shining as she sang with the songsters. The hall was packed. Perhaps there were more bodies to be saved than souls at this time of year, she thought, but the two went together, of course.

She never ceased to be moved to tears when the motley crowd surged towards the Mercy Seat. With her head bowed in prayer, she sang quietly but beseechingly: "Humbly at Thy cross I bow, Jesus saves me, saves me now!"

The woman was there again, at the back of the hall. She clutched her shawl around the lower part of her face but her eyes, blackened by blows from a cruel fist, stared at Tilly as she talked to the homeless, the hopeless and the hungry. All would be fed. Some could be helped; some could only be despaired over. Yet because of these people, she had met her wonderful friend David.

The woman was still there as the hall slowly emptied. Some drifted back to the streets, others were taken to a temporary refuge. Tilly touched the woman's arm. There was something familiar about her. The shawl slipped and despite the grime, exhaustion and bruises discolouring that pale face, Tilly recognised Kitty.

'Oh, Kitty!' she exclaimed. A travesty of her old smile revealed two broken teeth.

Tilly sat down beside her on the bench, arms round her, rocking Kitty gently like a baby. This was a lost soul, someone who needed her protection and who had known that she was the one to come to.

The story came out slowly. George was a plausible ne'er-do-well, thrown out at an early age by Kitty's mother who had lived with his father. Kitty, despite being some ten years George's senior, had already become romantically involved – they had toured the northern halls, singing when he was sober, Kitty supporting him when he was drunk. Finally he had taken off with a younger girl and she had joined forces with Mr Senacre and 'Arry. But, from time to time, she and George met up for a short-lived, passionate fling. This time, as usual, George had tired of her company after a couple of months, particularly when he discovered that she was pregnant.

'He said, Tilly, that I should get rid of it – but I wanted to keep it. I thought he might change when we had something to share.' Her voice broke.

Trapped, George had stayed, but Kitty paid the price. She was thirty-nine and it was not an easy pregnancy. She had gone on stage nightly because they needed the money, until her condition became obvious, and her face was too swollen to conceal the cruel bruising beneath heavy makeup. Penniless, owing rent, deserted once more, she had done a moonlight flit, and had walked, or taken a chance with lifts, once in a dustcart, nearly two hundred miles back to London. Tilly looked down involuntarily at her feet in their rucked-over boots, then she saw with compassion that the shawl was to hide her still-swollen belly. From its position, low down, Kitty's baby must be about to be born. Poor girl, Tilly thought.

Tilly helped her to her feet, keeping a firm arm around her. Tom and Sarianna came over, sensing they were needed. They always worked as a team.

'I know this lady,' Tilly told them. 'She's coming home with me. Please help, she's hardly any strength left, poor soul.'

Between them, they half carried her along the streets, aware of curious glances from those loitering in doorways or staggering along drunkenly themselves.

Rosa, the only one still up, opened the door to them and took in the situation immediately. They managed to help Kitty up the stairs to the bathroom, hoping that they would not disturb the theatricals who had just retired for the night. Maud's door opened, and she stared in astonishment at the uniforms and the drooping figure the Salvationists were easing on to the seat by the bath. Rosa put her finger up to her lips then indicated that Maud should put on her robe and come to help. Tilly took Tom and Sarianna back down, then returned to the bathroom.

'I'll just take off my bonnet and change – I'll be as quick as I can,' she whispered. 'Light the geyser, and get the bath filled. She can sleep with me tonight, it's best she's up top, and the lodgers needn't even know she's here for the minute.'

'What about Joe?' Rosa asked.

'I'll try not to wake him. Don't worry. Is Petty asleep?'

'Yes, thank goodness,' Rosa replied.

The three of them rolled their sleeves up and slowly, carefully, divested Kitty of the layers of dirty clothes. Tilly observed that Maud's eyes widened as she saw Kitty's distended stomach, but she said nothing, bending over the bath to test the water.

Kitty was so weary she was almost asleep as they swiftly sponged her clean, exclaiming in pity at the sight of her raw feet with their broken blisters. Somehow, between them, they managed to haul her out, seat her once more, swathed in towels, and to rub her dry as gently as they could.

'Fetch a clean nightgown from the airing cupboard, Maud dear,' Tilly requested, 'and some bedsocks – those ones of Joe's will do, she needs them to be loose.'

Tilly spread zinc and castor oil on the bruises while Rosa bandaged Kitty's feet. Tilly could hardly bear to look at Kitty's face, once so pretty and vivacious, now barely recognisable. She gave the fine hair a brief brushing. It badly needed washing, but now was not the time.

They tucked her tenderly inside Tilly's bed. Tilly said she would sleep on the little truckle bed that used to be Joe's and was now kept as a spare. 'Are you hungry, Kitty, or thirsty?' she asked belatedly.

'Not hungry. Just – some milk?' Kitty mumbled. Maud was despatched to fetch this. She met Petty in the hall, coming out to see where on earth Rosa had got to. Maud explained quickly, and her father accompanied her to the kitchen. 'You take the milk up, and when you're all settled, I'll be along with a cheering cup for you all. What a business, eh?'

Kitty slept away four days. 'We ought to call the doctor,' Rosa said.

'I think we should wait.' Tilly thought: David will be back from his holiday in a couple of days – he'll come to see her, of course he will. Not that it's really been a holiday for him. His aunt had died and he had to take Esta to the funeral. Kitty just needs to rest up at the present, and she'd hate anyone else to see her in this state. David never asks questions.

'Augusta rang, you know, Tilly – she's back from Norfolk and wants Petty and me to stay with her over the weekend so that she can sort out the rest of Gussie's things. We had promised to. She feels she can face it now, and she's thinking of selling up. Too many memories in that house. Could you—?'

'Manage? 'Course we can, Rosa. Maud'll be here, and Joe.'

'You don't think, the baby . . . ' Rosa asked.

'Well, it can't be long to go, but you won't be far away, will you? And there's always the instrument, isn't there?' Tilly sounded quite nonchalant, having used the telephone at least twice.

'All being well, then, we'll go this evening, after supper. Joe's got a music lesson after school, and Maud's not working tomorrow – it's her Saturday morning off, so she can help with the dinner. I thought steak and kidney pudding—' Rosa mused.

'That's nice and easy. You can put it on and forget about it,' Tilly said.

'I don't think I can eat anything – no, really.' Kitty gave a grimace at the very thought of the meat pudding. Tilly was about to remonstrate, remind her that she ought to provide sustenance for the baby if not for herself, when Kitty, downstairs for the first time since her arrival, gave an involuntary gasp. Her hand went to her bump, now decently covered with a skirt which Rosa had hastily adapted for her.

'Did you have a pain?' Tilly queried anxiously.

'Not really – baby butting me with his head, I suppose.'

'You haven't told us exactly when the baby is due, you know,' Tilly reproved her.

'Well, I can't be sure, but I reckon the end of January – another fortnight at least. So don't worry, Tilly, you can eat your pud in peace!' There was something of the old, spirited Kitty in her retort.

Tilly said: 'I shouldn't really be telling you this, Kitty, because it's up to Mrs Searle, but you might feel a little easier about things if you know that Mrs Augusta said right away, when she heard about you, that she would pay for a nurse to come in—'

'*She* doesn't owe me anything. I can't accept that.' Kitty actually sounded cross.

'You'd rather Mr and Mrs Searle engaged a nurse, is that it? They can't afford that, you know. You should be grateful that Mrs Augusta is so generous when she's had so much to bear recently. She lost her only daughter at the end of September.' It was Tilly who was cross now. Well, cross for *her*.

'No, I didn't know – how could I?' Kitty sounded genuinely contrite. 'I'm sorry, Tilly, but it wasn't unexpected, was it? The poor girl was obviously consumptive, from what I saw of her. So thin, and those pink cheeks. My own mother died of it, it's a terrible thing. No cure.'

Maud came in with the pudding, setting it down with a flourish.

'Don't cut into it for a minute or two, Maud,' Tilly said. 'I'm just going to make Kitty some bread and milk.' She bustled off to make that panacea for all minor ills. You could manage that when all else was anathema.

After the lodgers had left for their matinee, they all sat down cosily by the drawing-room fire. Joe was finishing off an essay on Egypt, a task made easy because of the books Augusta had provided on the subject. Maud and Kitty were playing draughts.

When Joe had finished writing they sat on in the firelight, loath to turn on the electric light. At last Tilly went into the kitchen to make the cocoa. All this business with Kitty had made her very weary. Thank goodness the theatricals now had a key to let themselves in, so she needn't stay up.

Not that she anticipated much sleep on that narrow bed alongside Kitty, snoring away gently on Tilly's own soft mattress. Still, she *had* offered. 'Used to your comforts now, aren't you, Tilly Reeder?' she chided herself, reverting to her maiden name.

TWENTY

Tilly awoke suddenly to see the night light burning and Kitty's covers thrown back. Silly girl, Tilly thought, why hadn't she made use of the chamber pot instead of going down the flight of stairs to the bathroom and probably disturbing the lodgers and Maud en route?

She discovered Kitty crouching over the WC bowl, being noisily sick. When she had finished, Tilly helped her to the chair and washed her face with cold water. Kitty's teeth were chattering uncontrollably.

'What time is it?' she managed.

'I don't know – I didn't stop to look at the clock – but it's obviously some unearthly hour. D'you feel well enough for me to get you back to bed now, Kitty?' Tilly asked.

Maud followed them up the stairs. 'You know I'm a light sleeper! Is it the baby?' she asked in an excited whisper.

'No!' Tilly said. At the same time, Kitty gasped: 'Yes!' They stopped in their tracks, instinctively supporting her through a strong wave of pain. When she felt Kitty relax,

Tilly urged her forward. 'Come on, Kitty dearie, we've got to see what's what.'

Back in bed, she said weakly: 'Maud shouldn't . . . ' then her voice faded away abruptly. She turned her face to the pillow, gritting her teeth.

'Rubbish! I studied biology at school, you know,' Maud said robustly. She wasn't going to admit that she knew nothing whatsoever about the process of human birth; that she wasn't even sure exactly where babies came from. Rosa, in the obligatory talk when Maud became adolescent, had skirted gracefully around that area. When Maud had supplied the word 'consummate' for Nandy on his last visit, she really had no idea what it meant.

'You'll have to wake Joe up, but tiptoe past the lodgers,' Tilly decided. 'Ask him to find a big bundle of newspapers and some brown paper – we'll need that to cover the mattress, we mustn't spoil that – and we'll need jugs of hot water. He can fetch that from the bathroom and we'll use the jug and basin set in here. Then you can bring me plenty of bath towels from the airing cupboard, Maud.'

'Isn't it exciting?' She gave a little whistle.

'Not for me it isn't.' Kitty actually managed a wry grin, then groaned as the pain hit once more.

'Hang on to me!' Tilly urged her. She'd held on to her mum when her youngest sister was born, even though she was only twelve at the time. Her mum had sent her away when the actual birth was close. However, the memory of her own confinement was still vivid.

Maud turned at the door: 'Shouldn't I send Joe for the nurse or the doctor, Tilly?'

'We haven't got around to booking them yet, I'm afraid – and David's away. If it's coming in a rush like this, Maud, there wouldn't be time anyway. We'll have to manage between us!' She tried to sound confident.

Joe was shooed outside the door again as Tilly took the newspapers from him. 'Go and get that water. Leave it outside,' she ordered. 'Then back to bed. We'll call you if we need you again.'

'Now, Maud, what's about to happen is not a very pretty sight and you know how squeamish you are.' Tilly had to warn her. She hoped fervently, however, that Maud would not decide to leave her in the lurch.

'I wouldn't miss it for anything,' Maud assured her, and Tilly wondered briefly if Rosa would forgive her for teaching her daughter the hard facts of life so unexpectedly.

They lifted Kitty when the next bout of pain subsided, and spread out the newspapers and finally the brown paper.

'Stand back, Maud, I must just see how things are going. Turn your head, I should,' Tilly advised. Then she shouted in amazement: 'I can see the baby's head!'

The strangest, most animal noise issued from Kitty's open mouth. Tilly saw that her eyes were screwed up, her fists clenched into balls.

'Towel, Maud!' Tilly commanded, laying it ready. The unearthly groaning continued, tailed off, then began again. Kitty pushed herself up on her elbows and gave a tremendous heave. The baby shot forth: greasy, blood-streaked, not yet crying, for the cord was tightly knotted round its neck. Maud gulped. She'd witnessed it all.

'Help me, Maud!' Tilly yelled frantically, hanging on to the tiny, slippery form. Dashing forward, Maud somehow managed to loosen the strangling rope and ease it over the baby's head. Then she sank down abruptly on her haunches and put her head between her knees. Kitty's hand wavered over her in a grateful caress, then she slipped back on the bed, exhausted. Tilly held the baby upside down and banged its back. The child gave a sudden, wailing cry.

'Don't stay for the next bit. That'll make you feel really bad, Maud,' Tilly told her, as she wrapped the little scrap in the towel and laid it across Kitty's breast so she could see it. 'Just pass me that bowl before you go, please,' she added.

As Maud closed the door, Tilly neatly caught the afterbirth. Fortunately, her sewing things were to hand. She had cut the cord and tightly tied it within seconds, then pushed the bowl out of sight under the bed.

'You can come back again, Maud, and bring the jugs with you,' she called. Her own legs were almost buckling under her now, she realised.

Maud sat tenderly nursing the baby. Tilly had made sure its nostrils were unblocked and that the infant was breathing properly before she handed it over and concentrated on Kitty. The newspapers had saved the sheets and the mattress, she noted gratefully. She rolled them up and shoved them beneath the bed, too. She hoped that the fire was still alight downstairs, for there was a deal of burning to do.

Within ten minutes, Kitty was washed and comfortable, a clean soft old nightdress slipped over her head. Tilly padded her out with a thick piece of towel and took the baby from Maud. Giving birth was a messy business!

'Ask Joe to make that tea now, please, will you? And remind him to ginger up the fire.' They could all do with a cup to revive them.

'Thank you, Tilly,' Kitty said weakly, watching her as she sponged the mewling baby and wrapped it again in a flannel sheet. Tilly slipped the baby into the crook of her arm.

'Mind you don't roll on the baby, Kitty, this is the best we can do for now – we'll fix you up with a cot and clothes in the morning. I'll telephone Mrs Searle, first thing, and then we'll arrange for the nurse to have a look at you both, but I think everything is in order. David – Dr Mann – will come on Monday, I know.' Tilly had the feeling he would be proud of her night's work.

'Tilly, you haven't said yet – what is it?'

'Oh, my dear! It's a baby girl. Quite a big one, too, it seems, despite coming a bit early.' Tilly was glad she hadn't had to deliver a little boy; the memories were flooding back as it was.

'What are you going to call her?' Maud asked brightly as she perched on the end of Tilly's bed, together with a sheepish Joe, all drinking the welcome tea and trying to take it in. It was rather a nice celebration.

'I hadn't thought.' Kitty smiled. 'But – yes, Amy, after my mother.'

'I like that,' Maud decided. Then she added, quite shyly for her: 'And could you add Elizabeth? I know Rosa would be pleased.'

'Why not?' Kitty smiled. 'Amy Elizabeth. It goes well, doesn't it?'

They all agreed. Then Tilly reminded them, 'Off you all go, and no getting up early tomorrow morning, there's no need – Sunday, remember? Tomorrow, did I say? I mean today! I don't know how the lodgers slept through all this excitement, do you? But you'll hear me up and about, no doubt, because there'll be plenty for *me* to do.'

Amy Elizabeth slept in the little crib which Rosa had never been able to part from. She wore a warm flannel gown, knitted vest and socks, taken from the box of baby things and thoroughly aired by the fire. The elderly nurse, bustling around, eyed Kitty cynically, for she was playing the part of the proud mother to perfection. The nurse had dealt with these acting types before. They invariably demanded a bottle-fed baby and couldn't wait to get back to work. Nurse didn't approve of the constant stream of visitors either, though she could hardly reprimand the lady of the house, could she? Rosa sat nursing the baby now. One little cry and she'd said: 'Oh, may I?' and Kitty had replied: 'Of course.'

Rosa had even brought her little prayer chair upstairs for this very purpose.

'Amy Elizabeth, you're beautiful,' she told her, smiling.

Kitty smiled back. 'Well, she would be, Mrs Searle. The females in our family are always said to be good-looking.' To Nurse's disapproval, Kitty was all dolled up and really did look blooming.

'Motherhood suits you,' Rosa told her.

'I don't know about that,' she answered. It was all very well, lying back like royalty, being brought grapes and flowers and fussed over, but the reality was this attic room which she could see would probably be her lot from now on. 'I must thank you for all you've done,' she added.

'Well, it was mostly Tilly and Maud's doing, wasn't it?' Rosa replied. She had been really pleased with Maud's part in the baby's arrival. She wouldn't have believed her daughter had it in her. Maud had taken a list to the nursery department of her store this morning. Rosa, as always, was being rash and enjoying it. Blueing the housekeeping again.

Tilly, Rosa knew, was hovering downstairs, waiting for David to call. She wondered if anything would come of their close relationship. She did hope so! Of course they were of different faiths which might prove a barrier since Tilly had taken so to religion. But anyway, she was glad Tilly had a friend outside the family.

Hearing their voices, she rose and handed the baby to the nurse. 'I'll make you a nice milky drink, shall I, Kitty? I'll bring it up when the doctor's gone.' Kitty made a face. Milk! You could have too much of it.

David said hello to Rosa as she came out of the room. 'Are you not proud of Tilly, Mrs Searle? And your daughter, I learn, is also a born nurse!' What? Squeamish Maud? Rosa had to smile at that.

As she hurried downstairs, Rosa mused that Tilly too was blooming today. She hadn't seen her look so pretty since she'd lost Oswald. And that, Rosa realised, would be nine years ago in November.

Later, as he was about to go, David said softly to Tilly: 'Doesn't this make you think about marrying again? Having babies of your own?'

Tilly bit her lip. She had not told him of the problems she had had in conceiving during her marriage. That would not be proper, she thought. She recognised the longing in his eyes and said only: 'Goodbye, David, it was good of you to come. I am glad all is well with Kitty and the baby.'

What had he said to upset her? he wondered.

Augusta really had come up trumps: not only had she said that she would pay for the services of the nurse and David (which pleased Tilly), she had also ordered a perambulator with bouncy springs and reversible hood in that serviceable American cloth.

'It should arrive shortly,' she told Kitty on her first visit to mother and baby. Mind you, she reminded Kitty that she owed a great deal to her rescuers, particularly Tilly, 'who learned so much in my household', and even to Maud whom she grudgingly supposed was more of a Searle than she'd thought. And she mentioned the price of the perambulator, all of £3.5s. Kitty looked suitably impressed.

They were left together, for Rosa and Tilly had taken the opportunity to go shopping and Nurse was busy washing the baby's linen.

'Would you like to hold Amy Elizabeth, Mrs Quayle?' Kitty asked disarmingly. The baby was wide awake but not crying. Augusta had not intended to do any such thing, but found herself lifting the tiny warm bundle from the crib. She sat down awkwardly on Rosa's low chair.

Augusta looked down at the puckered little face, the lips making sucking motions, and at blue eyes which seemed to be staring back at her although she knew it was impossible at such a tender age. At last the scalding tears fell. She held the baby close, hoping that Kitty would not observe this. It was fortunate Rosa was not here to see her weakness, she thought.

The baby girl had fine hair, but what she possessed, Augusta saw, was a definite coppery shade. There had been tears shed like this when she'd first held to her breast another auburn-haired infant, twenty years ago. Here was another little girl without a father. Augusta was desolate for them both.

TWENTY-ONE

Amy Elizabeth was eleven days old when Kitty left her, believing it to be forever. She dressed rapidly by the night light, racing against time for Tilly was downstairs preparing the early feed. Kitty had firmly resisted the pressure to breast-feed. She touched her baby's soft cheek, put two folded pieces of paper on the pillow, then opened Tilly's bag and reluctantly took out a few coins. She would regret this more than deserting her baby for that was for the best, she genuinely believed. Stealthily, she crept downstairs, opened the door fearfully, then was swallowed up in the dark morning outside.

I'm sorry to let you down, all of you, especially you, Tilly, but I'm not cut out for motherhood and despite what he did, I want to find George. Don't be too bitter.

I really love the baby, but it's best that she is brought up by someone who can do more for her. She is to go to Mrs Quayle, whom I feel needs someone to love. I have

put my signature to a note for her, to this effect. Thank
you for everything. Sorry about the money, Tilly.
    Love, Kitty

The sheets of paper slipped to the side of the crib as Tilly
picked up the baby and settled her comfortably on her
lap for the feed. She tipped the milk expertly in the boat-
shaped bottle and the baby seized the teat easily and sucked
strongly, throat pulsing as she swallowed hungrily.

No movement from Kitty, Tilly thought, glancing over at
the bed. She supposed she really should have insisted that
she give the baby the bottle herself, she would have to learn.
But Tilly was already very attached to Amy Elizabeth: she
had been thinking wistfully that maybe she could offer to
take her on while Kitty went back to work. She had mentioned this tentatively to David. He had looked at her eloquently and advised against it. 'Tilly, no, my dear – where
would it all end? You know what *I* wish more than anything, don't you?'

Then the bottle jerked from the baby's mouth, causing
her to cry out in protest.

'Sorry, my sweetheart. We must see what your mummy
is up to.' Tilly placed the bottle on the washstand, covering
the teat with a piece of clean butter muslin. She took the
baby with her, loving the feel of her in her arms, in search
of Kitty.

She, naturally, was not in the bathroom. Joe stood at his door, rubbing his eyes. 'Joe!' Tilly cried. 'Run and wake the others, Kitty's disappeared!'

By the time they discovered the note, it was obviously too late, but Joe dressed in a rush and dashed up the road to see if she was waiting for an early bus or cab.

'What on earth will Mrs Augusta say?' Tilly said helplessly to Rosa and Maud, while Petty stirred the fire to life and then went to make tea.

'I'm too old,' Augusta said faintly, having been summoned to a family council. 'What mother could leave her baby like that? Hopefully I have a buyer for the house, too – I shall be busy viewing property for some time. I intend to stay in a hotel for the time being. Tilly would have been the obvious choice for a substitute mother, if Kitty *had* to abandon the child . . . '

Tilly winced. 'Think about it for a few days, Mrs Augusta. We can keep the baby here with us for the present, can't we, Rosa? I don't know what we can tell the nurse . . . '

'D'you think Kitty is all right?' Maud asked. 'She's hardly got over having the baby, has she?'

'If she could walk all that way before giving birth,' Tilly said, 'well, I don't think we need worry too much about that.' Yet she couldn't help recalling the battering and bruising Kitty had suffered.

'I just cannot understand,' Augusta said, 'how a woman can voluntarily return to a man who has treated her so shabbily. She can have no pride.'

Tilly held the baby as if she could not bear to part from her. 'She must love him, Mrs Augusta.' It really was as simple as that, she thought sadly.

'What, *me*?' Maud exclaimed. She could hardly believe what she was hearing. The hotel Aunt A had mentioned was in Scotland, the house was all but sold, and Aunt A was asking Maud, of all people, to accompany her, all expenses paid, to look after the baby for her.

'Perhaps the store would keep your position open for you, for a few months?'

'What d'you think, everyone?' Maud asked. She was actually beginning to like the idea, now that the first shock of actually being asked was subsiding.

Her parents were in agreement. 'It's up to Maud; she's over eighteen, old enough to decide for herself.'

Joe said: 'Aw, go on, Maud!' Though he knew he'd miss her a lot.

'Wouldn't you rather take Tilly? She knows so much more about babies,' Maud asked generously, although she intended to say 'Yes!'

Tilly butted in quickly: 'Oh, no, Maud, I couldn't leave Rosa in the lurch with the lodgers and all. (And I couldn't leave David, she thought.) You'd soon learn to look after Amy Elizabeth – oh, you mustn't miss this chance.'

Hearing her name, Amy Elizabeth gave a sudden crow of pleasure. She kicked busily on the hearthrug at their feet. Maud bent to tickle her tummy, making her laugh louder. 'Well, it seems Amy E wants me go go with her, so I'd love to, Aunt A.' Being Maud, she added, 'When are we off?'

Tilly and Rosa had scoured the house from top to bottom because they couldn't let Maud go without a bit of a do. It meant juggling with the housekeeping, Tilly mused ruefully, for just yesterday there had been a spot of unpleasantness with the lodgers doing a moonlight flit, leaving an ancient violin in lieu of a week's rent. Well, they hadn't actually stated that was their intention.

Tilly smiled to herself as she recalled Joe's opinion that the violin might fetch more if they pawned it rather than attempted to sell it, but she'd said reprovingly, 'Now, Joe, we haven't come down to that yet.'

Still, it was reasonable to blame Augusta for this exodus. She had come to Sunday tea, to discuss with Maud the travel arrangements, and commented rather too loudly on the male musicians' idiosyncrasies while they were within earshot.

Tilly had looked up the long word but it didn't exactly make sense. No one thought to ask Petty, who would have known, but would have replied tolerantly, 'It takes all sorts.'

'We'll have to search out Joe's card and hope it'll be spotted soon,' Rosa said, as she and Tilly tidied themselves before going to the market.

'I could manage without my money for a bit. You'll be missing Maud's contribution, too,' Tilly offered generously.

'I won't hear of it, Tilly! We'll get by, don't we always? Maud seemed a bit subdued this morning, didn't you think? I'm not sure if it is such a good idea her going to say goodbye to the Barbieris today, although it gives us a chance to prepare things here.'

'I managed to tip the wink to B.J.,' Tilly said as she closed the door behind them. 'It was nice he called for her.'

Rosa said: 'I'm grateful Augusta declined to join us this evening. We don't want any last-minute upsets.'

'She might rub you up the wrong way some – well, most of the time,' Tilly said wisely, 'but I know she really appreciates all you've done to help her cope with everything since dear Gussie passed away. She needs to argue with you, Rosa, because it keeps her going.'

'Where did you learn your tact, Tilly?' Rosa asked affectionately. 'Not from Augusta, and not from me, if I'm honest with myself.'

'I learned most of what I know from you two,' Tilly told her firmly, 'and I learned that if you don't get to the market before the rush, you miss all the bargains!'

TWENTY-TWO

Tilly and Rosa were busy dressing the crabs: they had sniffed them suspiciously but there was no hint of ammonia, the shells were bright and shiny – they were indeed fresh. Tilly skilfully removed the stomach bags and grey-brown fingers, then simmered the shellfish in salted, boiling water for a good half-hour.

For those who did not care for shellfish there was a huge pork pie, crammed with succulent belly meat and jelly. They had prepared platters of salad and Rosa had mixed her speciality, a wonderful mayonnaise, with several egg yolks, expensive olive oil and best vinegar – very rich, but a real treat. The Duchesse potatoes Tilly had mixed with yet more yolks and butter, then piped into large rosettes.

The table had been laid much earlier with a damask cloth, napkins and polished glasses, set with the wedding silver which Joe had painstakingly cleaned last evening as his contribution.

As they slipped out of the pinafores covering their good clothes, Tilly gasped, her hand going to her mouth.

'Tilly, you nearly sent that bowl flying!' Rosa remonstrated.

'Pork pie . . . ' Her voice was a strangled squeak.

'David? Oh, really, Tilly – this great cheese board, the fish . . . just don't offer him the pie, you cuckoo!' Then she added, before she could stop herself: 'Tilly, is this becoming serious at last? You and David, I mean?'

'I'm not sure,' she answered honestly, 'and remember, his sister has warned me off. But I've got my work with the Army, do I need anything else?'

Maud was lying face down on the counterpane, sobbing spasmodically. She had not responded to her father's knock on her door. He touched her heaving back gently, his face full of loving concern.

'Maud, old dear, we're waiting for you downstairs. A little surprise party.'

She rolled over and sat up, stretching her arms out to him, looking very woeful. 'Oh, Petty darling, I can't – not looking like this . . . '

He held her close, making what he supposed to be soothing noises.

'You'll be singing 'Lily White' before you know it,' Maud sniffed.

He had often entertained the children when they were young with this macabre rhyme which had first been chanted in the Great Plague.

'Lily White – Muffin-oh, when you die – h'up you go!' he murmured wickedly.

Maud grinned through her tears. 'I'm not sure I want to go to Scotland now. I always manage to rub Aunt A up the wrong way so that she spits like a scalded cat!'

'You'll handle her splendidly,' Petty told her soothingly. Then, because he understood her so well, he added: 'That wasn't what you were really crying about, was it?'

'Well, it was going to Little Italy today, thinking about Gussie and Pino – how I was looking forward to all this excitement. It's as if I was taking her place. Does that make sense, Petty?'

He nodded. She wiped her eyes on his shirt front.

'Here, before you wipe your nose as well.' He fished out his handkerchief. 'Gussie would have been the first to have said: 'Look after Mama for me, she needs you.''

'I opened one of her boxes and found this.' Maud showed him the pencilled sketch. The picture was entitled 'Ta-ra-ra-boom-de-ay!'

'Maud, what splendid memories you will treasure all your life. When you were together on old Sheer Necessity, eh? Come downstairs now.'

'My eyes are all swollen, look, like bloated currants! Oh – never mind. Lead on, MacDuff!'

The crisis was over, thanks to Petty – Maud was going to the party.

They rose with one accord as she came in on Petty's arm and was taken to her seat between her parents at the top of the table. She looked round at all the smiling faces: Brother James, next to her friend from the office, Ellie, Joe, Tilly, and – good gracious, she thought – David! I hope *that* means something.

Each course was exclaimed over and enjoyed, and to Tilly's relief David showed no embarrassment over the pork pie. Glasses were refilled frequently, and for once Rosa did not glance reprovingly at Petty. Tilly naturally drank lemonade, and David tactfully did the same. Maud, unused to anything stronger herself, smiled round at the company, feeling quite beatific.

Petty and Joe cleared the table and declared their intention of tackling all the washing up when the party was over. Maud exclaimed happily, 'Are there any witnesses to that?' and everyone laughed.

Then they all went into the drawing room where the evening sunlight flooded through the windows and the air was heavy with the scent of all the flowers the guests had brought for Maud.

'I must make the coffee, if you will excuse me for a while,' Tilly whispered to David.

Maud, flushed and sparkling, flung up the lid of the old piano. 'Joe, you can accompany me on the violin – or is it the other way around? The rest of you can sing. Let's have a jolly evening, shall we?'

Brother James came to stand by the piano to turn the pages of her music. Their heads were almost touching as they riffled through the song sheets. She said to him, 'D'you suppose this means that David is now officially Tilly's beau? He's really nice, despite all that fierce hair on his face.'

'He's a charming fellow,' B.J. said diplomatically. Maud's comments were not as discreet as she imagined: David, glancing their way, looked amused.

Joe tucked his violin under his chin and shyly invited Ellie, whom he thought was rather fetching if a little too old for him, to be at his side and to lead the singing. She was one of Maud's fellow lurkers in the music department at lunchtimes. They were fellow gigglers too.

The songs were sweet, unsophisticated and sentimental. Eyes were soon awash with tears. Rosa clutched at Petty's hand as they shared the sofa with Tilly and David, which actually had the effect of pushing the other couple into bodily contact.

Just before ten o'clock the telephone shrilled, frightening them all into silence. Maud eased her foot from the loud pedal and turned to watch as Rosa picked up the receiver. Maud could recognise the voice from right across the room.

'I'll tell her, Augusta,' Rosa said, trying to stem the flow of words and glancing helplessly over at her daughter.

'I know,' Maud said cheerfully, 'she thinks it's time the party was over and yours truly was tucked up in bed. I've got to go all the way to Scotland very soon, you know, folks. Tell her that goodnights are just being said, then she'll be satisfied and we can get on with having fun!'

Rosa relayed this message, listened again, then bade her sister-in-law goodnight. 'I really think perhaps Augusta is right . . . you need to rest Maud,' she began.

'Rubbish, Rosa! We've got at least four more old favourites to sing – one for all you bashful men, in parts, and a solo for the best lady singer present. Not me, I'm afraid.' Brother James touched her hot cheek lightly. 'You're on fire, Maud.'

'Fan me with the music, then!'

The telephone rang again. 'Shush!' she said to them all. 'Let it ring, she'll think we've all gone to bed.'

It might be someone important though, Rosa thought, watching the telephone uneasily.

'Shush!' Maud said again. Rosa gave Petty a push. 'You speak to whoever it is.'

The caller was, naturally, Augusta. They stifled their mirth as Petty assured her that the party had drawn to a close and that Maud would certainly be along, as arranged, early the next morning. As he replaced the receiver there was a concerted sigh of relief, though B.J. was prompted to remind Maud that he had promised to call a cab and see Ellie safely home before midnight.

Joe cleared his throat. 'Brixton won't be the same without you around, Maud,' he said for them all. 'Or without the Brixton Empress,' he added.

'I'll be back, don't worry,' Maud wept. She flung her arms round Brother James's neck. 'Darling B.J., keep an eye on them for me, won't you? Dear Tilly's the only one with her feet on the ground!'

'Perhaps this is a good point for me to take my leave, Tilly,' David said regretfully. 'I must make an early start tomorrow.'

When the goodbyes were said, she told him: 'I'll see you out,' and closed the door firmly behind them. The party seemed to have taken off again.

They stood in the hall. David glanced over at the painting on the easel which Maud had suggested Rosa put in the recess. The rainbow light from the street lamp filtering through the pretty window illuminated the canvas.

'That is you, Tilly, is it not?' he asked. She nodded shyly. He crossed to take a closer look at the picture, which had been Gussie's first attempt in oils.

'Mrs Augusta's daughter – dear Gussie, who died – painted that when I was working there. You see, David, I knew her from two years old. Rosa and Maud thought this one should be on show, but I said not in the drawing room. I wasn't quite sure—'

'It is lovely, Tilly. Such a likeness.' He bent over it, tracing gently with his finger the shape of the glowing face, the fall of golden hair, now so primly braided, and too often concealed beneath her Army bonnet. It was almost, Tilly thought, as if he were touching her actual face and hair. She began to tremble.

He turned towards her. As the music swelled from the drawing room and the singing began once more, he moved to draw her close to him. Tilly stood stock still. His arms went round her. Then his lips sought hers, urgently, passionately.

Tilly couldn't help responding. His beard had pricked her face and as he released her she put both hands to her hot cheeks. She was actually shaking now.

'Ah, Tilly.' He was upset by her reaction. He was so perceptive, she thought, as Oswald had been. 'I should not – please, you are not afraid of me? I should hate that. Or is it old memories that hurt?'

Impulsively she reached up and kissed him briefly again. He was right of course – she was so drawn to him, but could anyone replace her first great love? There was Esta, too, with her irrational jealousy, and above all, there was her commitment to her faith.

'Be patient, dear David, that's all I ask,' Tilly said simply.

When he had gone, she went towards the kitchen to busy herself and collect her thoughts. When Maud had left, when things had settled down, she decided, before they took on new lodgers, she would go to the cottage under the sea wall and be alone there, except for all the memories. She *needed* to be there for a while. It was her home, her refuge when she felt bewildered by events.

I wish I could give David the answer he longs for, she thought. With Oswald I had no doubts at all, but I was younger then, less cautious. I *do* love David, I know that, but something holds me back. If only Maud realised just how much Brother James feels for her. In her case, I just know love would grow . . .

She suddenly smiled. She would visit Mr Lozenge, who, despite being under suspicion by the authorities from time to time – for security was always paramount on the island Mr Lozenge himself had called a fortress – was still in his studio. She would have a new portrait made, especially for David. What would Esta say if he displayed it on his desk? she wondered.

Neither Tilly or Maud would have dreamed that, in seven years time, they would both still be single: that David and Brother James would still be waiting in the wings . . .

PART THREE

1914–1917

ONE

The letter arrived on 5 August. It was not the only one Tilly received from the Island. There was the usual weekly letter from Oswald's mother, now widowed. Tilly put that aside for later, and opened the other envelope.

My Dear Young Lady,

I beg leave to write to you on a most urgent matter. It is difficult to tell, but I am, without provocation, in the custody of the police. They say yet again that I am a spy, due to my habit of studying the ships in the harbour.

Of course, it is of interest to me that at present the warships gather, but that is all. Should I need a reference from a friend, will you oblige?

Your friend on London clay,

Heinz Rossel

Shaken, Tilly opened Mrs Relf's letter. Her mother-in-law told her that she intended to remain on the Island, although war would surely be declared very shortly; the agent who let the cottage for Tilly had cleaned and closed up for the duration, though everyone said this was just a flash in the pan. Tilly was not to worry, because: 'the military are in control here – already there are restrictions on movement to and from the Island'. She skimmed through a page or two until she came to the news she had guessed would be included: Mr Lozenge, in full view of government buildings, carrying his camera, had indeed been caught watching the ships of war gathering. Not only had he been taken into custody, but an ugly crowd had stormed his studio and the German photographer had already appeared in court. He had protested his innocence. After all, he had lived on the Island for forty years, he said – it was his home . . . 'They say if there is war he will be a prisoner-of-war, Tilly, and he'll be removed from the Island.'

How could a gentle old man like that be capable of spying? Tilly wept. Mr Lozenge had been her first friend on the Island, she thought. She must ask Petty what she should do about his letter.

In fact there was nothing she *could* do. The cutting from the *Sheerness Gazette* which Mr Arthur sent to Rosa reported the case in detail. Tilly's mother-in-law was right. Mr Lozenge was interned as an alien. The charge of spying was unproven.

It had been an eventful few years since Maud's return from Scotland – where, to everyone's surprise, Augusta and

Amy had remained. It seemed to the family that Augusta wished to cut herself off from them; letters had dwindled to one at Christmas. Maud was particularly hurt because they had parted on good terms.

It was 'All Change' in the wider sense too. Before the King's brief reign had ended, the Liberals returned to power, and that charismatic politician Lloyd George introduced the old age pension, for which Tilly's parents were grateful. In May 1910 the late King's horse and his favourite dog, Caesar, had been part of the funeral procession, following nine Kings, with the new King George walking alongside the German Emperor, which seemed ironic now. Coronation Day had seen the family joining the crowds in Whitehall to watch the royal coach pass by; drawn by those lovely cream-coloured horses, a sight Tilly would never forget. In the euphoria, she had overheard Brother James proposing yet again to Maud, and being turned down, though with a warm kiss.

There were still horse-drawn carts and bicycles in daily use, but motor vehicles were now dominant. Their noisy horns and fumes were overlooked because of their con-venience and speed.

Tenants had come and gone in Tilly's cottage – her own family, now they were better off, enjoyed an annual holiday there, which gave her much pleasure for of course they paid no rent. She had brought to her haven some she met through her salvation work, to convalesce in the bracing sea air and renew their strength to deal with life's knocks. Now the doors would be locked, Tilly thought, and for how long? When could she visit Oswald's grave again? She could always remember him so much more vividly on the Island.

Petty, Joe and Brother James were part of a vast, sombre crowd, waiting anxiously for official news in Whitehall. Fifteen minutes after midnight, on 5th August, an announcement was finally made: a state of war existed between Great Britain and Germany. They travelled back to Brixton together. 'Stay the night with us,' Petty invited B.J.

The womenfolk were waiting up for them. 'David kept us company for a while then he had to hurry back to his sister,' Tilly told them. 'He said Esta was worried for his safety because some of his old patients have turned against him for being German. She made him promise he would not go with you to hear the proclamation.'

The gravity of the news was enough for now; fortunately they did not hear what had befallen David and Esta until later.

When he reached home David discovered that the front windows of their house were shattered and Esta had barricaded herself in her bedroom. He felt terrible guilt at having left his sister on her own on this portentous night.

'You can sleep in Joe's room, B.J.,' Maud told him. 'The bed's made up. The lodgers are packing up already. Don't want to stay in London, they say.'

It was just as well that they were unaware that Nandy had already embarked on his ship.

A little earlier than usual the next day, after a sleepless night, Petty went along to his office only to find the windows shuttered and the doors barred. Another proclamation was nailed to the main entrance:

It is regretted that, in the present circumstances, the Management have decided to close these offices until the cessation of hostilities. Staff will be sent an official letter with all salaries due.

The notice was signed by the Managing Director, a charming man of German parentage who had lived in London all his life.

This was the third German known to the family who was a victim of public and, soon, official prejudice.

It was a complete shock; Petty stared at the notice for a few minutes then came to a sudden decision. He would go straight to the Admiralty and offer his services there as a retired naval officer.

'All those poor wives wondering where the next meal is coming from until their husband's Army pay comes through,' Tilly cried. 'That's what I joined the Salvation Army for, isn't it, to do all I can for others? All hands on deck.'

365

Tilly and Maud were clearing the breakfast table.

'Petty's old boss has been arrested, Tilly – taken to Olympia. Just imagine, a concentration camp in Kensington. I wonder how many of 'em really *are* spies?'

'About five per cent, they say,' Joe told them. He signalled wordlessly to Maud. She knew what he hadn't dared tell his mother yet – he was going to the recruiting office in his lunch hour.

'I'm worried sick,' Tilly confided in them, 'that David will be arrested too . . . '

'At least Petty's heard from the Admiralty, he's got an interview next Monday. Where's Rosa? I'd better get off to work,' Maud realised. 'Club tonight. Can you make me the usual buns, please?'

'Yes, we'll make the buns.'

'By the way,' Maud paused rather too casually by the door, 'I'll be in at two as usual, but B.J. is calling for me at half past, so I won't need anything to eat. We're going out for the afternoon . . . Cheerio!'

It was early closing day at the store where Maud had now risen to the heights of Supervisor, which was why she had chosen Wednesday for her club evening.

She had begun this venture at Brother James's suggestion. The majority of the children, she was cheerfully aware, attended her after school club to eat a good tea. Most came from poor homes, just a few were scruffy, but most wore clean, patched clothes and were well scrubbed in her honour – they were a lively lot, raucous at times, but willing to try anything Miss Searle suggested for their amusement. Brother James had negotiated with the vicar of a local church a nominal fee for use of the hall. There was certainly no need to advertise; the children passed on the good news from one to another. Tilly, naturally, had soon become involved, swelling numbers with her Sally Army contacts. 'You have so much to give to others, Maud,' Brother James had praised her quietly.

As she boarded her bus, she grinned to herself. Wouldn't they all have been surprised if they'd known where she was going – to see B.J.'s parents, no less!

TWO

The long line of men stood four or five abreast, stretching down the flight of steps outside the recruiting office, continuing for a fair distance along the pavement. There were bowler hats, straw hats, cloth caps, stiff wing collars, yellowing celluloid collars, smart business suits, well-brushed shiny jackets and trousers with frayed ends, hobnailed boots and patent leather shoes, yellow kid gloves and bare calloused hands – men from all walks of life, united in their resolve, cheerful and joking, prepared to wait all day if necessary to be asked briefly: 'Your age? School? Good eyesight? Any serious illnesses?' There would be the evasive answers, the downright untruths, but the majority would soon be undergoing three months' training, many still in their civilian clothes, improvising with broom handles where rifles were in short supply. Some would be advised to be at the ready but to stay at home until required.

Joe, to his bitter disappointment, was one of the latter.

'Don't worry, young sir, Kitchener reckons this'll be going on for at least three years. Get yer hair cut and yer affairs in order, eh?'

For his brother, Joe thought ruefully, the war was already a reality, serving in one of the Navy's Dreadnoughts. Of course, he didn't know that Nandy was already situated off Heligoland. Winston Churchill, the First Lord of the Admiralty, had ensured that the British Home Fleet was fully mobilised. Invasion was to be prevented at all costs, but the British were unaware that the German fleet had not the strength to make this challenge.

So Joe returned to his cubby-hole at Bartholomew's, the clock and watch specialists. He'd been working there for five years now, disappointing his parents by not opting to continue his studies and go on to university. He had started at the bottom, checking stock, and had progressed to packaging and invoicing, and now handled customers' compliments and complaints. With Maud's help, he'd taught himself to type and also studied Spanish, for he hoped one day to be sent to the firm's offices in Barcelona. That was Joe's dream, to see his grandmother's city.

'I'll be around for a while yet,' he regretfully told his colleagues.

'*I* won't, mate!' chimed in the cheeky office boy. 'I'm orf at the end of the week!'

Doris, the junior typist, redirected her hero worship from Joe to Fred. 'I'll knit you some socks, Freddie, if you like!'

Even Maud was momentarily at a loss for words when she opened the door with her usual flourish to Brother James and saw, parked outside their house, the splendid gleaming black Humber motor car, complete with imperturbable chauffeur.

'Your carriage awaits you, Maud!' Brother James was highly amused at her surprise. She gazed in further disbelief at his immaculate light grey suit, kid gloves, cravat and curly-brimmed hat: of course he wore a decent suit when he escorted her to concerts, she thought, but Maud had realised right from the start of their friendship that material possessions mattered not a jot to him.

'Well!' she remarked with feeling. 'I'm jolly glad I changed into something decent myself. Just come and say hello to the parents first, won't you?'

'Allow me to step over the threshold then, Maud.' He shook his head at her, laughing. He looked appreciatively, but not obviously, at her neat figure in a cool, simple tunic top over the new-length slender skirt in fine cream tussore. Quite the business lady nowadays, he mused, but she still walked with that tomboy bounce so that her black hair swung round her shoulders. She had a tendency to let her fringe grow too long so that when she was feeling earnest,

370

she would brush it back with her fingers, a gesture which Brother James found endearing – and disconcerting.

Rosa and Petty's astonishment at his appearance was much better concealed than Maud's.

Rosa beamed her approval, watching as Maud was handed solicitously into her seat. Maud gave a regal little wave with a simultaneous saucy wink, which prompted Rosa to say to Petty: 'She's hopeless!'

'I've several pieces of information to impart,' B.J. began as the motor car glided off. 'First, there is an invitation for you – and me – to attend a special wedding on Saturday week. Luisa Barbieri is to marry her fiancé now, rather than later this year as they had planned, because he expects to be sent to the Frontline very shortly. He was called up immediately, apparently, being a Territorial.'

'Luisa!' Maud exclaimed. 'I can't believe she is old enough to be married.'

'Oh, she must be nineteen or twenty,' Brother James told her. 'Don't forget, we are all ten years older than when we first met . . . '

'How long is it since we've seen her, B.J. – seen all the Barbieris? Five years?'

The family had moved up north to join prospering relatives in their hotel. This was shortly after Pino had returned to Italy. They had not seen him in the intervening years. By then, Pino's elder brothers had married, depleting the family ranks, and now there were just the three girls at home.

'I suppose it must be all of that. D'you suppose you will be able to take that Saturday morning off work?' he asked her.

'I'm sure I shall. But it's a long way to go just for a day, isn't it?'

'Luisa says we are not to worry about that, they will reserve rooms for us overnight at their hotel.'

Maud felt the supple leather upholstery appreciatively. 'This is real luxury, B.J. Come on, what else have you to tell me?'

'I am joining up, Maud,' he stated quietly, reaching for her hand.

'But—' She bit her lip hastily.

'You are surprised? I'm thirty-eight, that's not too old. No, you are thinking that I will never pass the medical examination, aren't you?'

'To be honest – and I hope I'm not being hurtful – yes, B.J. ' Maud was aware of the tightness of his clasp, the intensity of his gaze.

'Well, I realise naturally that I'll never make a fighting soldier, but there are other roles to be filled. I have been approached by an Army friend of my father's who believes I might be usefully employed as a welfare officer with the troops.'

'A sort of padre, you mean?' Maud queried. She was finding this hard to take in.

'Not exactly. But my legal training, together with my interest in the problems people have to face in life, is what I'm told they require.' Being Brother James, there was not a trace of vanity in this statement.

'Well, I'm really proud of you, B.J.,' she said, and meant it.

He withdrew his hand from hers and felt in his pocket. 'Maud, please don't say anything more until you've thought about it, but I'd like you to have this. It's up to you, my dear, on which hand you care to wear it, of course.'

Maud accepted the little case he proffered so diffidently, and wasted no time in opening it. The gold ring had a dazzling azure blue stone, flecked with golden lights: 'Oh, B.J.!' She was quite overwhelmed. 'How beautiful! Whatever is it – not a sapphire?'

'Lapis lazuli,' he said, almost poetically. 'Found in Persia, China, Siberia, Tartary, and – dare I say – Germany? And among the ruins of Rome . . . '

As the car swung smoothly round a corner, Maud slipped the ring on to her third finger, right hand. 'Just a shade loose, B.J., but not enough to worry about. I really don't deserve this.' She brushed back her fringe, and hoping that the chauffeur would not turn his head, leaned towards Brother James and shamelessly kissed him. His arms went round her, uncertainly at first, then tightened, and she was aware that it was he who was shaking, just a little. Then, she sat back and said earnestly: 'I know what you want this to mean B.J. You must realise how much I value your friendship – how very fond I am of you. I've told you so, enough times! I'm going to miss you more than you know. But for now I shall wear your ring on this hand. I'm sorry I still can't say yes, but I'm not saying no either, you see.' She surprised herself.

'Thank you, Maud.' His tender look told her so much. 'Here we are. Don't feel intimidated by the building, will you? My parents have been asking me to bring you along to meet them for years. I'm sure you'll like them just as much as I like Rosa and Petty.'

Their feet sank into the thick pile of the carpet as they climbed the wide stairs to the first-floor drawing room. There were oil paintings in hefty frames marching upwards on the walls, too, but Maud saw them in a blur for her usual cheerful bravado had deserted her. 'My grandparents, painted on their honeymoon in Paris,' Brother James told her, indicating the final portrait as they followed a manservant towards the door. Maud could not take in their formal smiling faces either.

Brother James's mother had already risen from her chair by the window from which she had been watching out for their arrival. Maud need not have worried. Despite the cut-glass accent and the conventional greeting, she saw at once that Brother James's mother possessed that same warm smile and kind brown eyes that he did. Maud realised immediately that Sophia Inkpen had noticed the ring on her finger. B.J.'s father was a tall, rather gaunt man, quite unlike his son, white-haired and fiercely moustached, with a grip which almost crushed Maud's fingers when he shook her hand heartily.

'So this is Maud, eh? My dear, do sit down and chat to Sophia before we have tea. Unpardonable, I know, but I have an urgent message for James and I do hope you won't mind if we retreat to my study for ten minutes?'

'Of course not.' Maud smiled. She really was rather relieved to see them go; she felt it would somehow be easier to talk to Sophia on her own.

'James has told you his news, I'm sure?' his mother asked.

'Yes, he has.'

'He thinks a great deal of you, Maud. Please don't be offended, my dear, but you have kept him waiting a good many years, and now I see that he still hasn't persuaded you into an engagement.' Sophia's voice was uncensorious.

'I know it will seem hard to believe,' Maud replied candidly, 'but honestly, until today, I hadn't realised just how serious he was – is that awfully naive?'

'Perhaps, but truthful, Maud. Now, as James isn't within earshot, may I ask you how you feel about *him*?'

'I regard him as my closest friend, I admire him tremendously, and he's been such a help and inspiration to me over my children's club.' Maud's cheeks were flushed.

'Is there anyone else? Don't be afraid to tell me,' Sophia asked.

'No. I *was* in love with someone – James knows – but it came to nothing. It was only ever on my side.' Perhaps this was the first time Maud had really acknowledged this to herself.

'Thank you for being so frank. Oh dear, Maud, am I making a great to-do of all this? I promise you, I didn't intend that! But may I just ask you one very impertinent question? Does James's infirmity trouble you?'

'Not a bit! I hope you don't think I am as shallow as that?' Maud's voice became heated. Sophia immediately looked distressed.

'My dear, I only wanted to be certain that you knew his condition is not hereditary. James was stricken with tuber-culosis of the spine at barely two years old and he was una-ble to walk again until he was seven. He was in a special spinal carriage until then. Nowadays I hear there is a con-troversial operation to correct any curvature, but really he has recovered amazingly well, and the thing I thank God for, over and over again, is that his lungs were not affected.'

B.J. had never mentioned a word of this to Maud.

'A cousin of mine died from consumption . . . ' she mur-mured, remembering dear Gussie.

'Now, Maud, we shall be friends, good friends, I hope? Of course James has led an independent life for many years now, but we would dearly love to see him married, and now I've met you, I realise why he has chosen *you*.' She rang the bell. 'The men should be back shortly. We'll take our tea now, as I understand you wish to be home by five in order to go to your club. Now, come on, I want to hear all about this cause of yours!'

Maud had consumed several cucumber sandwiches and was talking enthusiastically about her aims and ideals when Brother James and his father rejoined them.

'We approve of each other, don't we, Maud?' said Sophia, and smiled at her son.

THREE

Maud rushed indoors, changed hastily and dashed off again without displaying the ring to Rosa or Petty. In fact, she deemed it wisest to replace it in the box, close the lid with a snap and put it away in her handkerchief drawer.

Brother James would not be coming with her this evening, as he often did, but he had accompanied her home in the car this afternoon and kissed her goodbye with confidence.

Petty had already been along to the hall to set out the trestle table and to arrange the cups, saucers and plates of rock buns, sausage rolls and paste sandwiches. Maud paid for most of the ingredients herself, but Rosa and Tilly were always generous, and Joe often coughed up a welcome bob or two.

She filled the big kettle and set it to boil on the oil stove, then she emptied the bottles of milk into the tall enamel jug and allowed one of the early comers to tip the box of sugar lumps into the basin.

At the far end of the hall was a small stage concealed behind dusty plum-coloured curtains. Around the sides of the room there was an assortment of hard wooden chairs, begged or borrowed from many a local kitchen. The Armada Hall was attached to the church itself, and Maud was very grateful that B.J. had enabled her to have it. The club was open to all children, not just baptised members of the church – Maud had insisted on that, despite the vicar's initial hesitation – from nine to fourteen years of age.

The children were arriving in droves now, eager to be at the food. They had tried their hands at various craftwork, Maud reflected, as she took her place behind the tea pot. They had danced barefooted, waving silk scarves, and had learned to sing in parts – if not always melodiously. There were regular spring and summer outings to the country by bus where they all ate a picnic tea in a grassy glade, crushing the wild flowers they had picked so recklessly. Then there was always the nightmare of the journey home when some were sick from too much food or the excitement. Right now, they were rehearsing a musical play written by Joe – he would come along after work to coax a tune from the battered piano. The producer, naturally, was Maud herself, and she was also devising dance steps for the chorus.

Those who could not, or would not act, were planning and painting scenery – Maud had persuaded the vicar to appeal for old white sheets for backdrops, which had resulted in such a pile of long-hoarded linen she had been able to send some home with the children, as Tilly had quickly suggested.

'Here's Joe, Maud!' one of the girls called out, a little later. Maud had been busy arranging the stage for the evening's rehearsal.

'Good, he can help the boys shift the piano to the other corner,' she shouted back.

Later, pouring Joe some tea, for he had come without having had supper, Maud noticed: 'You look a bit down in the dumps, didn't your little enterprise go as planned?'

He was too disappointed to say much about that. 'Not exactly. What about you?' he countered. 'Will wedding bells shortly peal?'

'However did you . . . ' she broke off, shaking her head ruefully.

'*You* saw something coming, Joe, which was a complete surprise to me. Well, I'll only admit that I *was* asked – again! – but I still haven't made my mind up. Don't you *dare* say anything to Rosa, Petty or Tilly yet.'

Joe sat down and raised the lid of the piano. 'Cue for a song? 'Little Dolly Daydreams.' Where are the singers – where's the chorus?' He beckoned to a group of youngsters who climbed up on the stage, giggling and pushing each other.

'How you ring a tune out of that old Joanna, I'll never know,' Maud marvelled. His fingers flew across the yellow keys, niftily missing the dumb ones.

'Mother reckons you ought to get us all sewing comforts for the soldiers,' Elsie, a girl with a perpetual sniff, told Maud later.

'I'm afraid I don't have the slightest talent with needle and thread myself, Elsie – Joe can vouch for that – so it's not very likely I'd be able to organise a sewing party, now is it? I can't imagine there'd be any comfort in anything *I* made!' She winked at the earnest Elsie.

'She's speaking the truth, I *can* vouch for that,' Joe told them all wryly.

Maud was suddenly inspired: 'But maybe we could put on a *show* for the troops, how about that?'

'Good idea, Maud,' Tilly approved, looking in for a while as she often did. She had a sulky-looking lad in tow. 'This is Ben, Maud. I persuaded him that he'd have a wonderful time if he'd only give the club a try. Ben works in the ironmonger's in the High Street. His mum tells me he's got a grand singing voice.'

'It's breaking,' Ben said huskily. 'All prayers an' that 'ere, I reckon, ain't it?' he added rudely. He made a horrible face at a boy he knew from school days.

'No, Ben. Had your tea yet? I save a plateful for latecomers.' Maud took off the covering napkin, revealing an assortment of food.

He was forced to admit that he was rather peckish. They watched him wolfing down the lot.

'Be patient with him, Maud,' Tilly whispered tactfully. 'He gets in terrible rages, but has a hard time of it at home. His stepfather's a bully and often beats the lad, and at his work the boss is a real old tyrant. I promised his mum we'd turn the other cheek if he was naughty.'

'Well, we thrive on a challenge here, don't we, Tilly?' Maud said quietly. She took Ben firmly by the elbow. 'I'm Miss Searle, but you're welcome to call me Maud if you like. That's my brother Joe, playing the piano. We're going to put on a show for the troops.' Maud had already decided that, since most of her impulses were acted on. 'I reckon you'd enjoy painting some scenery, eh, Ben? This way!'

To Tilly's delighted surprise, Ben went meekly off with Maud.

'Miss Searle oughta get married and have kids o' her own,' remarked Dora, one of the older girls who liked to help. She was collecting the plates to wash up. 'Coo, look at this, Mrs Relf, he must've licked it clean!' She held up Ben's plate accusingly.

'You're right, Dora,' Tilly agreed. She didn't mean the plate, or Ben's lack of social graces.

'Roll your sleeves up, Ben, and pop this apron on,' Maud said, smothering a gasp as she saw the bruises on his thin arms. 'We use big brushes and size the sheets thoroughly first to stiffen 'em up for the painting – see? We're painting a bluebell wood for Dolly to dream in. Would you like to have a go?'

'What's a bluebell look like, miss?' he asked.

With a few, bold strokes Maud showed him. She kept her face bent over the painting. It wouldn't do, not at all, for young Ben to think she was sorry for him because he'd never had the chance to exclaim over a carpet of bluebells in a wood in the country. She never said to the club children when they picked bluebells with such abandon on their outings in the spring that she didn't like to see the flower heads hang limply from the long, white stalks after such a short while, for who was she to spoil such simple, precious memories? This wretched war! Would there even be a trip to a dreaming wood for Ben and the others next year?

FOUR

Tilly was alone in the house the next afternoon. There was an unexpected knock at the door.

The card, she thought in a fluster. Prospective lodgers, perhaps . . . She had been dusting the drawing room. Now she took off her pinafore and stuffed it behind a cushion, together with her duster.

Tilly really did not recognise the tall woman standing on the top step, holding the hand of a curly-haired child. She must have been staring for Augusta said: 'Have I changed that much, Tilly?'

The taxi-driver came up behind them and thumped down their cases. 'Thank you,' Augusta said. He touched his cap and retreated down the path, disgruntled at receiving no tip.

'Mrs Augusta . . . ' Tilly said in utter disbelief. She suddenly remembered her manners, opening the door wider and ushering them inside. 'Whyever didn't you let us know?' she said helplessly. 'Petty would have met you, of course – oh, I can't believe it's true. It's really you, after all this time.'

'We've been back two months,' Augusta stated calmly. She was much thinner. The clothes she wore Tilly recognised as pre-Scotland, and they hung on her now. And her hair, which had been so distinctive, was almost white. She looked an old lady, not like Mrs Augusta at all.

'Two months?' she repeated, stunned.

'Are you Mama's friend Tilly?' the little girl asked brightly. Tilly saw that she was small for eight years old, with a perky prettiness, which instantly reminded Tilly of Kitty.

Tilly nodded and ushered them wordlessly into the drawing room.

'You must excuse Mama, Tilly, she had a bad journey. We couldn't afford to stay any longer in the hotel so we thought of you and Aunt Rosa – Mama says you let rooms and we thought, oh, good, when we saw the card in the window.'

'Let rooms!' Tilly found her voice again at last. 'Whatever are you thinking of, Mrs Augusta! You're family, aren't you? You should have come to us straightaway. Of course you can stay here!' Tilly did not realise how indignant she sounded until she saw Mrs Augusta visibly flinch. She was instantly contrite. 'Do sit down and recover yourselves – I'll soon make you some tea.'

'Oh, *I* am perfectly all right, Tilly,' Amy Elizabeth told her. She hovered anxiously over her mother until Augusta was settled in Petty's comfortable armchair.

'They'll be home soon, I hope,' Tilly began. 'Petty's between jobs at the moment, I'm afraid, though he hopes to get in at the Admiralty. Joe and Maud are at work, of course, and Nandy's already gone off to war,' she added, prompting Augusta: 'Is that why you came home at last?'

'That was one of the reasons,' she said heavily. 'I shall tell you the rest later. The child . . . '

'Of course.' Tilly was grateful to hear a key turning in the lock. 'Here they are now; they *will* be surprised to see you! In here!' she called, her tone conveying a warning.

Like Tilly, Petty looked at Augusta uncertainly, then: 'My dear, whatever has happened to you?' he asked, bending to kiss her. Augusta did not respond. Rosa stood irresolute.

'Here's Amy,' Tilly put in. 'This is your Uncle Joe.'

'You might as well call me Petty,' he said, 'my own children do. It'll be easier for you, Amy, because you have a Cousin Joe too.'

'I know. I've heard all about you all,' she said, receiving a bear hug from her new uncle.

Tilly said, 'Shall I take your cases up, Mrs Augusta? There's the lodgers' rooms free – they've been empty since war started, though Petty thinks the halls will soon be packed again. Folks at war need entertainment. Will you come with me, Amy, then you can choose which bed you'd like, eh?'

'Good idea, Tilly,' Petty said.

She held out her hand to Amy who went with her, after glancing at her mother for approval.

'Yes, you go, Amy,' she said dully. Tilly hadn't changed; she was as intuitive and thoughtful as ever. It was time to talk.

'Wash your hands at the sink, dearie, then you might like to butter the scones,' Tilly said cheerfully to young Amy in the kitchen, a little later. 'Your Cousin Maud's going to be thrilled to see you again, you know – she looked after you when you were a baby,' she added.

'I know,' Amy said, dutifully soaping her hands, rinsing and wiping them, before taking the knife to the split scones. 'Mama told me. She said that Maud helped to bring me into the world, whatever that means, and that *you* were in charge of it all, Tilly. She said you helped my real mother when she was down on her luck, like *we* are now.' She looked hard at Tilly then added, 'Mama always says: 'Tilly is beautiful, inside and out.''

'Oh, I don't really know about that.' Tilly mustered up a jocularity she did not feel. 'I'm as old as the hills now, you know.'

'No, Mama is right, Tilly, you *are* beautiful, and I think you're very nice, too.' Amy put down the knife and quite suddenly her arms went round Tilly's waist and she said gruffly: 'Oh, Tilly, why did my real mother give me away?'

'She didn't want to part with you, really,' Tilly faltered. 'She thought you would be better off with Mrs Augusta – things were difficult for your mama then, you see.'

She hugged the clinging child tightly. It would be good to have a little girl in the house once more. Tilly had missed that.

'Your real mother, Kitty, was a singer – d'you like to sing?' she asked Amy.

'Yes, I do. But I've had to keep quiet lately, 'cause Mama has bad headaches and she's been so worried . . . '

When Tilly and Amy wheeled the tea trolley in, Augusta had already retreated upstairs. Tilly poured Rosa and Petty's tea and swiftly handed the cups around.

'We'll take Mama's to her, shall we, Amy, in her room?'

Later, bending over Augusta's prostrate form, she murmured, 'Don't cry, Mrs Augusta.' Tilly looked with concern at the shaking figure on the bed. 'Be brave for Amy – you must.'

'I was so foolish, Tilly. I was taken in by someone I really trusted – my Scottish solicitor. He invested my capital for me, or so he said. I've lost – everything . . . I think I'll get into bed, it's all been . . . too much.'

'Mama isn't well.' Amy's face was so concerned.

'I can see that, but we'll soon have her smiling again, don't you worry!' Tilly told her stoutly.

'It's good to be back,' Augusta murmured.

'And we're just as happy to have you here with us, too,' Tilly said.

'She's like Kitty, isn't she?' Augusta asked.

'Yes, she is – but it's you who have brought her up so well, Mrs Augusta, and you can be proud of her. A real help, she was, getting the tea. Come on, Amy, let's leave Mama to her rest and I'll show you round the rest of the house. If you're going to live here, you must know where everything is. I'll look in later, Mrs Augusta. Rest now.'

'*You* haven't changed, Tilly, I'm very glad about that. We can always depend on you, all of us, when things go wrong.'

'You've been family to me for a long time now – I need you all as much as you need me,' she replied softly.

FIVE

War did strange things to people, Tilly thought. In Sheerness poor Mr Lozenge had been arrested, here in London German shopkeepers were attacked in the street and now pathetic posters were appearing, pinned to doors: 'This is not a German shop – God save the King!' Their local baker was forced to put up his shutters. There would be no more delicious bread or pastries baked on his premises. Like Mr Lozenge, he had lived on British soil for many years – the baker had even married a Brixton girl and until the war had always been considered kindly and inoffensive. Two of his daughters were married to British servicemen. Where he and his wife had fled to was not known.

Now, Tilly was devastated to hear from Tom that David had been detained. They had been so busy with Augusta and Amy that Tilly had not been to see him at the surgery for several days.

Tom told her: 'They say that his sister and her late husband never legally adopted him, but fortunately David applied for naturalisation some months before war broke out.'

Rosa stood behind Tilly as she talked to Tom on the doorstep, for he was in a hurry; he was driving a tram now that the younger men had gone, and it was almost time for his shift. 'I'm sure that will stand David in good stead,' Rosa comforted Tilly.

Augusta had been very trying today. She kept to her room and had insisted that Amy keep her company. Rosa and Tilly had felt bound to tell her that the child should be at school and that enquiries would be made by the attendance officer. She must soon be enrolled, and in any case it would be better for her to be away from this atmosphere. Augusta had turned on them, and told them to keep their opinions to themselves. They felt this was really unfair especially since Tilly, and Maud when she was in, had been waiting on her hand and foot since her unexpected return.

'Rosa, I need your advice,' Tilly confided, last thing. She had been waiting for an opportunity to catch her friend on her own.

Rosa stifled a yawn. She was anxious to get to bed, and to talk over the problem of Augusta with Petty. He was Augusta's brother, after all, and might be able to put his weight behind the educating of Amy.

'Yes, Tilly?' She took in the anxious expression, the whitened knuckles as Tilly clasped her cup of cocoa.

'Should I go and see David's sister? I've never spoken to her, remember, since, well, you know when . . . She's not the only reason I couldn't make any promises to David, but—'

'I think you should go, Tilly. After all, you do care deeply what happens to him, don't you? You know how I feel about *that*. David needs his friends, especially you, at such a time,' Rosa told her.

Tilly banged on the door the minute she put her foot on the doorstep. It opened immediately, as if Esta had been anticipating this visit.

'Come in,' she said to Tilly, just as if they had met only recently. Things had not changed; the furniture was just as shabby and dustladen, the atmosphere as oppressive. But Tilly observed the tired seaming of Esta's face, the bleary, sunken eyes: her own hostility instantly evaporated, she knew it did not do her calling credit. Tilly handed her a letter.

'Please, Esta, will you give this to David when you manage to see him? A friend of ours, Brother James, has told his father about his trouble, and he believes he can help – thinks David could soon be released.'

Esta did not say that she would deliver the letter but she did not refuse to accept it. Tilly stood there, waiting for her to say something, anything. What transpired took her completely by surprise. Esta crossed over to the window, clutched at the curtains, and began to weep.

Tilly saw that angular body shaken by harsh, gasping sobs and instantly went to her. She did not touch Esta, just stood close by.

After a few minutes Esta turned to her, her face blotched and tear-stained.

'Tilly, I have to tell you something. I don't expect you to forgive me, but I think you will understand.' Tilly took her arm then and led her unresisting to a chair. She sat down opposite and waited for Esta to speak again.

'David is my son,' she stated baldly.

'I know.'

'My *real* son, I mean. *Not* my younger brother. Bernard knew this when he married me. It happened while I was still a student. My parents hushed it all up, and I went away with my mother for a while. When we returned home, she passed the baby off as her own. I was glad at the time, being so young and selfish, because I had not loved the baby's father – another Englishman, a fellow student – and I was ambitious for my career. I did not care for the baby then. But Bernard and I, we never had children of our own – it became my obsession, I admit it, to reclaim my son. But am I not my mother's daughter? Pride made me pretend we had adopted my *brother*. Tilly, I never told David! But now I must because I think it will also aid in his release – his real father is of this country, his stepfather, too.'

If only Esta had told her this at the start, thought Tilly bitterly. *I* would have understood. I never got *my* baby back. He is a man now, and may be fighting for his country. He could be killed and never know I am his true mother . . .

'Why did you try to part David and me, Esta, all those years ago?' Tilly asked abruptly.

'Ah, Tilly, I was jealous. I could not permit David to care for someone more than me.'

Tilly regained control of herself and swallowed hard. 'Please give him that letter. Do it *today*, Esta. I do forgive you . . . I must go now but I will come tomorrow, to see how things are. Between us we'll have him out of that place, you'll see.'

'I don't deserve your good will.' Esta looked at Tilly as if for the first time. She was humbled as she recognised the concern Tilly had shown for one who had been so unkind to her. 'Yes, please come tomorrow, Tilly,' she said huskily, and held out her hand for Tilly to shake.

David was released before the end of the week, thanks to the intervention of Brother James's father, who indeed had contacts in the right quarters. Mr Inkpen sent his motor to fetch David, and at his request Tilly was picked up too and driven to meet him.

Esta's confession had both confused and angered David. 'I *can't* go home, Tilly – I told her I wouldn't. May I stay with you, just for a few days?'

'Of course – there's a spare bed in Joe's room,' Tilly said instantly, while thinking wryly that here was another mouth to feed. Things were getting tight indeed since Augusta's return. However, Petty would be commencing at the Admiralty on Monday, which was a great relief.

'What will you do?' Tilly asked next.

'I have asked to be sent to a military hospital, Tilly. That is where I can be of the most help, I feel. Mr Inkpen is kindly arranging this, too. I do not feel I can go back to my surgery after this – is that cowardly of me?'

'No, David,' she said quietly. 'Never.'

'You will miss me, Tilly?' He gripped her hand tightly. He had been so good, she thought ruefully, had not attempted to kiss her since she had asked him if they might remain close friends, nothing more, for the time being.

'I will miss you, David. Oh, I will,' she said simply. Maybe the separation would give them both the chance to decide whether their relationship should deepen or remain as it was.

Amy opened the door to them and stepped back. 'Oh, you really *are* tall, Doctor David – Tilly said you were!'

He smiled down at her and said to Tilly perceptively: 'Now you are happy, dear Tilly, with a little one here to love and fuss over. She will keep you company while I am away.'

When David had gone, it was left to Tilly to tell Esta.

'I think,' she remarked dully, 'I have really lost him now.'

Then Tilly told her something which she thought might bring Esta a degree of comfort.

'David has asked me to look in on you from time to time, to see that all is well. I can give you news of him then. And, Esta, when he has got over the shock of all this, I will do all I can to help him to realise that you still need each other.'

'How can I thank you?' she asked.

How their roles had changed, Tilly thought. But the bond she and Esta shared was, of course, their love for a good and caring man.

SIX

'Slip your costume off, Maud, and lie down on the bed. Rest. The wedding is not until three. Drink your tea before it cools.' Luisa, not yet changed, her hair concealed by a rakish turban, knelt at her guest's feet and tugged off her constricting shoes. 'Oh, Maud, it is wonderful to see you again. I'm so happy you could both come for our great day! I shall tell Brother James to knock and wake you in good time! I shall see you later – looking quite different, I hope!' Then she rushed off.

It had been a long journey by train. They had decided against motoring here, for there was always the possibility of breaking down, and anyway the chauffeur had been unwilling to undertake such a lengthy journey without frequent stops. You knew where you were, travelling by railway, Maud thought.

They were now in the Quartiere Italiano of Newcastle: of the many Italian families who had emigrated to the North of England during the 1860s, a fair proportion had come from Southern Italy. The Hotel Barbieri was a modest establishment, and for this very special occasion, all the rooms were taken by the wedding guests.

'There will be such good food, much wine, music and singing *alla moda italiana* – we promise you that!' Celestina had greeted them.

Maud obediently subsided beneath the quilt and was soon dozing. She was not aware of the first tentative knocking, but when it was repeated, more firmly, she sat up with a jerk, staring at the door. Still disorientated, she padded on bare feet, clad only in her chemise, to open it.

'B.J.—' She broke off in surprise.

'It is me, Maud.'

She had not expected to see Pino. He was in Italy, surely, she thought, dazed.

'You may believe your eyes,' he told her, closing the door behind him.

Maud was suddenly all too aware of her state of undress. Before she could reach her robe, lying across the bottom of the bed, Pino was reaching out to embrace her. There was the familiar double kiss on her cheeks, and then an unexpected third kiss, more lingering, on her parted mouth. 'It has been too long, little Maud.' His voice was muffled, his face buried deep in her tousled hair. As it had been, Maud remembered with a sharp pang, the last day they had tried to comfort each other, the day that Gussie died. She felt the warmth of him, so close, experienced a surge of the emotions she thought she had quelled long ago, then somehow she disengaged herself from this disturbing, dangerous embrace.

He was broader and looked older, she saw. He sat down on the chair and stared quite openly as she tied her robe primly round her waist and hunted for her slippers.

'You're back,' she stated helplessly. What a silly remark to make, she thought. There was that familiar, endearing smile of his.

'Ah, Maud, how could I miss my little sister's wedding? But I return too for another reason: Italy is still neutral at present but I am anxious to help Great Britain's cause. Remember, I am born and raised here, this is just as much my country.'

'You never wrote,' she accused him, recovering from the initial shock and Pino's more than friendly greeting.

His smile vanished. 'There was always Gussie between us,' he stated slowly.

She sat on the edge of the bed, facing him.

'I don't understand, Pino.'

'I do not understand myself, but we three . . . ' He spread his hands expressively, searching for the right words. 'She and I, so close, you and she, so close – how can we ever forget?'

'I remind you too much of what you lost, is that it?' Maud asked urgently.

'Yes,' he said. 'She is always between us.' They stared at each other. They could never come together, Maud thought sadly, because they had both loved Gussie.

There was another knock and Brother James entered, looking searchingly from one to the other. 'You found her then, Pino?' he asked, his voice strictly controlled. Unselfish as always, he had given them their chance.

'I found her!' Pino rose, smiling broadly once more, in control of his emotions. 'And she has grown up into such a lovely little lady. You are a lucky fellow, Brother James.'

'I am the lucky one!' Maud had interpreted the look in B.J.'s eyes. She went resolutely to the dressing table, took the box from her toilet case, opened it, and slid the ring on to her engagement finger. She spun round and held out her hand, appealing to Pino: 'You see, Pino, *we* are to be married soon, too!'

His smile did not waver. 'I am glad,' he said sincerely. 'You are right for each other.'

'I know. I *do* know,' Maud repeated.

Brother James exhaled deeply. 'Shall we leave you to change now, Maud? Come down to the dining hall when you are ready. We should be at the church by a quarter to three.'

Pino slipped his arm around his friend's shoulders. 'We just have time for a drink together, old friend. We must hurry for I leave for the wedding before you. I am an usher.'

They left Maud on her own.

Emotional tears spilled from her eyes as she shook out the folds of her tussore costume. 'You've done the right thing,' she convinced her reflection in the mirror and brushed the fringe from her forehead, parting it firmly. 'Old married women don't have fringes these days, I believe,' she continued. Then she allowed the hair to fall back into place once more, and buried her face in her hands. A shaft of sunlight caught the golden freckles in the lapis lazuli.

The nuptial mass passed like a dream. The unfamiliar words recited in Latin, the mingled scents of flowers and of incense, of polished pews and well-rubbed brasses, the echoing footsteps of the bride as she was escorted proudly down the aisle by Carlo, portly now and greyer, but still as handsome. The bridegroom's wondering expression as he turned to see Luisa in her elaborate white gown and veil; the rich voices soaring to the pealing music; a young bridesmaid ducking to retrieve a posy; the proud Barbieris, shoulder to shoulder – such a family – all these were part of it.

Back at the hotel the food and wine were indeed unending. An elderly uncle played with verve on his accordion, feet stamped in time and bursts of singing made talking impossible. Maud sat with her new fiancé, aware of his arm around her back, drawing her comfortably close. Now and again they glanced at each other and smiled – a shy acknowledgement of their new status. Of course she loved B.J., Maud knew that, but was her love as great or unselfish as his? She doubted it. She felt warmth, drew comfort from him – but where was passion, she wondered.

'You won't keep me waiting much longer, will you, Maud?' he whispered, adoring her.

'Sorry, B.J. – what did you say?'

He motioned that they should leave the throng and go out into the foyer. They sat on gilt chairs placed there.

'When shall *we* be married?' he asked. There was an urgency in his voice which she had not heard before.

'As soon as possible,' she decided, impulsive as always. 'We can get a special licence, can't we? B.J. – *this*, Luisa and Bruno's wedding – is all so wonderful, but would you mind very much if we had just a small affair, just our two families? Church, of course, but no fuss. That's not my style or yours, is it?'

'Won't Rosa be disappointed?' he asked, adding diplomatically, 'If it is the money side, Maud, well, you must know that I am able to help with that.'

'No, B.J., it's not money, although Rosa and Petty are rather on their uppers right now,' she told him frankly. 'And there's Aunt A – she's even more impecunious than we are these days. We're all responsible for her and Amy now, but we don't mind because look at all she did for us in the past. And Joe hopes to be in the Army as soon as they'll relent and have him . . . But no fuss, no trimmings, that's what I'd like. Just the service and then back to our house for a piece of cake and a cup of tea, eh?'

'We'll see,' he said, loving her for her honesty in saying all that. 'I don't think I've ever been so happy in my whole life, Maud. I hope you won't regret marrying me – I'm hardly love's young dream,' he added wryly.

'Nor am I! All I want,' she said earnestly, 'is for *you* to be happy.'

'And what about yourself?' he teased.

'You fool! If I succeed, then I shall be perfectly happy too.'

'Maud darling, thank you.'

Pino, coming out in search of them, for the speeches were about to be made and the toasting to begin, observed the tender lingering kiss. He turned abruptly and left them. He too had made a sacrifice. For Maud's sake.

There were more hugs and congratulations back in Brixton: Rosa, as Maud had anticipated, was full of expensive notions that she was intent on quashing. But she had one request which she rather thought would surprise and please her family – actually it had been Brother James's idea.

'Now,' she said, 'you need some new tenants so how about B.J. and me? We haven't time to find somewhere else before he goes away and I don't much care for the idea of being on my own after that. We'd pay the going rate, wouldn't we, B.J.? And I intend to carry on with working, and with the club – no objections, please, Rosa, B.J. absolutely agrees. These are different times and women will be needed to do their bit while the menfolk are away. Just a quiet wedding first, I mean it!' she ended firmly.

'What will you wear?' Rosa was still worrying. It was typical of Maud, she thought, to make up her mind, just like that, and then expect everything to be accomplished in a rush.

'The tussore costume, don't you think? B.J. says it's the prettiest outfit he's seen me in, so what better? You can fashion me a posy of flowers, can't you? From the garden, if you like. And may we come back here afterwards, too?'

'If that's what you really want.' Rosa looked helplessly at Petty.

Tilly was bubbling with excitement. 'There's the rich fruit cake just made for Christmas – we got ahead of ourselves, Maud, thinking things might become short. Why don't we ice it? It'd make the perfect wedding cake, Rosa, wouldn't it?'

She nodded absently.

'We'll make ourselves scarce, shall we?' B.J. suggested to Petty. 'I think you should be aware of just what your daughter is taking on!'

'Good thinking, James.' Petty led the way into the dining room which doubled as his study nowadays. It would be difficult for them to drop the 'Brother', he thought, but one could hardly address one's son-in-law like that.

'If it's to be women's talk, I'm off too,' Joe remarked. 'May I just offer my condolences to the bridegroom?'

Maud aimed a cushion at his retreating back. 'We shall expect you to play the organ, Joe. You'd better brush up on your serious music!'

Maud, Tilly and Rosa settled themselves on the chaise-longue.

'One minute you're just good friends, going to another friend's wedding, the next you're planning a wedding yourselves!' Rosa sighed.

'You'll take it all in – eventually,' Maud assured them cheerfully.

'I'm not sure,' Rosa said, 'that I agree with you – carrying on working like a single girl, you know – oh, I know Tilly and I have always worked, but it's been within the home after all – although, of course, there's Tilly's welfare work, but that's not the same . . . '

'But, Rosa, B.J. will be off and away a few days after the event, and we're in no hurry to start a family. That reminds me, any advice forthcoming on that score from you two?'

'You must leave such things to your husband, Maud,' Rosa said primly, aware that Tilly was blushing fierily. 'Knowing you,' she added drily, 'you won't be too coy to broach the subject. Now tomorrow you must visit the vicar, eh, and I must telephone James's parents and invite them to come and see us.'

'You know, Tilly,' Maud said, not really thinking, 'we shall even surpass you! Your wedding was all arranged within a month, wasn't it?' She suddenly noticed that Tilly's lips were quivering. 'Oh, Tilly dear, I'm so sorry – of course it's brought all that back, I suppose.'

'Nearly twenty years ago, Maud – I'm just being silly.'

'No, you're not! I shall never forget what a beautiful bride you were, how happy you looked, and if we can be half as happy as you were in that short time, well . . . And I know you'll back me up, Tilly, about working, won't you?'

'You could never sit at home twiddling your thumbs, dearie, I know that. But I think, well – you should have a baby just as soon as you can.' She was blushing fiercely again. Maud squeezed her folded hands.

'We're at war, Tilly, remember? Oh, I love babies, I still think about the time I cared for Amy when she was so small, but I shall tell B.J. he'll have to wait a while to be a father!'

Tilly knows, she thought suddenly, *she* knows there's something behind all this hurry and excitement, but I can't tell even Tilly how I felt when Pino hugged me to him like that. It's a secret I must keep to myself forever.

SEVEN

Augusta was not told the news until the following day. The family decided that Tilly should be the one to do so.

She, along with Rosa and Petty, suspected that Augusta was very near a complete breakdown. Not at all surprising, they thought, after all she had been through. Together they planned a course of action. But would it work? Tilly was really the only one with whom Augusta would communicate: after the painful telling of her story, she had retreated to her room and remained there.

'Thank goodness Amy has taken such a fancy to Tilly,' Rosa said.

Augusta was sitting in her room, still in her gown, with her breakfast tray hardly touched, the food congealing on the plate. Tilly brought in a fresh pot of tea.

'Mrs Augusta,' she began firmly, 'you must make an effort – for Amy's sake, you know. I want your permission to take her along to the local school this morning. It would make all the difference if you would send her off with your blessing.'

Augusta said heavily: 'Now, Tilly, you know I would prefer Amy to have private tuition. When I feel more myself, *I* can be her teacher. How can you suggest a board school for my daughter?'

'You taught at board schools yourself, didn't you?' Tilly was determined; she'd been thinking what to say to Augusta during most of a sleepless night. 'You always said it was the teacher who counted, not the school or the lack of books. 'A good teacher will always inspire, help the child to make the most of his abilities.' I believed you, Mrs Augusta. My friend Sarianna's children go to this school, and they are doing very well.'

'All right, Tilly, I take your point. You may take Amy this morning, but I wish you to make it quite clear to the school that this is likely to be a temporary arrangement.'

It was not the time to argue, Tilly thought, so she said: 'Mrs Augusta, I'm sure you won't regret it. Thank you. Amy will be so pleased! Oh, and here is some very good news: Maud is to be married to Brother James in less than two weeks' time – before he goes to do his training then leaves for France. It's going to be a quiet wedding, that's what they want, but Maud will be very upset if *you* aren't there.' This was true, Maud had said as much.

'Maud, getting married?' Augusta mumbled. She'd hardly spoken to her niece since she had arrived here.

'Yes,' Tilly replied briskly. 'Now, Mrs Augusta, you can make a start by getting dressed and coming out of here! Rosa says she'd never have suggested you having a bed-sitting room if she'd known you actually intended to sit in it all day. D'you know, we'd rather have you as you were, poking your nose into all our affairs!' Tilly really had had to gird her loins to say such a thing, but she'd guessed right. Making Augusta furious was part of the shock treatment needed.

'How dare you!' she raged. 'After all I've done for you – *all* of you, in the past – how dare you accuse me of that! Of course, I'm coming to Maud's wedding, even though I expect Rosa doesn't really want me to, though I'm sure *Maud* does! You would all be surprised if you knew how close we were that time in Scotland – I did as much for her as if she had been my own daughter.' Then, realising what she had said, her face crumpled and she broke down. She did not resist when Tilly put her arms round her and rocked her soothingly, like a baby.

'I'm sorry, Mrs Augusta. I *had* to do it, you see . . .'

Tilly and Amy walked hand in hand to the school. They met Sarianna and her two children at the gate. 'This is my friend who got me into the Salvation Army, Amy. Remember Amy, Sarianna? Kitty's daughter.'

Sarianna was as bright-eyed and blithe as ever. 'Tilly was an angel of mercy to Kitty, Amy. Oh, you look quite like her, you know – she had such a pretty face.'

Amy said: 'D'you think Kitty thinks of me sometimes, Tilly?' Her voice was so wistful, Tilly gave her a quick squeeze and told her, 'Of course she does, dearie. You don't have a baby then forget it, even if you can't keep it yourself and know it'll have a better life with someone else.'

But she guessed that Kitty, if indeed she did think of the baby she had given away, would think of Amy as she was, tiny and helpless, just as she still thought of her own baby, Edward.

Tilly was very impressed with the nice young teacher who made Amy very welcome. Amy, being well ahead with her reading and writing, would settle in, the teacher assured Tilly. 'Stay a while and just watch from a corner, why don't you?' she suggested.

So Tilly sat there unobtrusively, as proud of Amy as if she had been her own small girl when she stood up to read in front of the class. She was glad she had shortened the skirt of the dress Amy wore. She had looked a real Polly-longfrock before. Tilly had washed the child's fine hair first thing, brushing up the soft curls all over her head. She was loth to leave but must hurry home, for before she knew it, she thought, it would be time to meet Amy to bring her home for her lunch. There seemed little likelihood that Augusta would be able to perform this task in the near future.

If I had married David seven or eight years ago when he wanted me to, she thought, as she slipped away from the classroom, I could perhaps have been bringing *our* daughter here to school today. But time is racing on, and soon I'll be too old for babies. David should look for another love, one who will give him the children he desires. I've been wrong to keep him hanging on in hope . . .

To Tilly's surprise and joy she found Augusta up and about when she arrived back at the house.

Rosa was already busy with preparations in the kitchen. It was strange not to see Petty around, Tilly thought, but it was good to think that, like Amy, he was making a fresh start. And Isabella would be arriving to stay this afternoon, to help with sewing for the wedding.

'Tilly!' called Augusta from the drawing room as she saw her through the open door, hanging her hat on the hall-stand. 'Can you spare a moment – I want to say something to you?'

In trepidation, Tilly faced her.

'No tears from Amy when you left her?' she asked.

'No, Mrs Augusta. She's made a friend or two already, it seems. The teacher is young and lively, I know you'll approve of her. She says Amy appears to be very bright and will soon settle in.'

'Good.' Augusta indicated the chair opposite. 'Sit down. I won't keep you long as you are always busy, I know, and Rosa tells me you have a meeting this afternoon. I will fetch Amy from school. Tilly, I owe you an apology for my rudeness this morning.'

'Oh, no, Mrs Augusta – it was me—' Tilly floundered.

'You said what you said, and it was the truth, because it was just what I needed to hear. I appreciate that, Tilly. Like Maud, I can make my mind up in a flash when the whim takes me. I believe you know that there is a trust fund in place for Amy? She will receive money when she attains her majority. She may wish to use this to train for a career. Not all girls marry nowadays, or believe in that institution as the be-all and end-all, you know. If anything happens to me before that date, well, Amy will need a guardian. Before you suggest Joe and Rosa, I will tell you that I would prefer someone younger – you, Tilly. Are you willing?'

'I – don't know what to say . . .'

'You are already fond of the child, aren't you? You are much better with young people than I am. Come on, what d'you say?'

'Yes,' Tilly said simply. 'But it won't come to anything because, Mrs Augusta, you'll go on forever!'

'Don't forget,' Augusta called after her as she excused herself to go and help Rosa, 'I shall want you to help me sort through all my things tomorrow. I may need something altered by Isabella for Maud's wedding, and as you are all likely to want her to sew for you, too, I intend to be first in line!'

'Don't look surprised, Maud!' Tilly tipped her the wink when she came in from work that evening.

There was Augusta laying the table in the dining room, assisted by Amy. Isabella was polishing up the best glasses, beaming.

'Celebration for Petty, eh?' Maud asked. 'First day with his knees under an Admiralty desk.'

'And for me, first day with mine under a school desk,' Amy piped up.

'I'm hardly domesticated, as you know,' Augusta said to Maud, 'but I gather we've a busy time ahead of us due to you, my girl. I understand that congratulations are in order?'

'They certainly are!' Maud exclaimed happily.

'She's back on form,' Tilly whispered, hugging the thought to herself that now she had a special role to play in Amy's life.

EIGHT

Maud clung to Petty's arm as they approached the bridegroom and best man.

'Joe's pulling out all the stops again!' she murmured to her father.

To please Rosa, she had allowed her to pin a coronet of fresh flowers in her hair, dressed by Tilly, and carried a bouquet of pink roses, just like the ones Brother James had sent her on their engagement. He had insisted on arranging this personally.

As she had wanted the church was half empty, merely the front few pews occupied. On the one side her mother, her grandmother and Tilly – and, yes, sitting right at the end of the third pew, by herself as she had preferred, was Augusta. Amy, the only one to have a new dress, followed Maud demurely as flower-girl. On the other side were James's parents, his sister, back from China, and his young nephew and niece. His brother-in-law stood beside him as best man. Maud smiled radiantly at each of them in turn.

'I, Maud Augusta,' she said clearly, in response to James's promise, 'take thee, James Albert, to be my wedded husband, to have and to hold from this day forward, for better, for worse, for richer, for poorer, in sickness and in health, to love, cherish and to obey, till death us do part, according to God's holy ordinance, and thereto I give thee my troth.'

Now the ring was on her finger, and they knelt together to pray. Petty read from the sixth chapter of the *Song of Solomon*. The congregation was very still and quiet as he asked:

'Whither is thy beloved gone, O thou fairest among women? Whither is thy beloved turned aside? That we may seek him with thee. My beloved is gone down into his garden, to the beds of spices, to feed in the gardens and gather lilies.'

His voice grew louder, his delivery more sure:

'I am my beloved's, and my beloved is mine . . . '

They came out into the September sunshine through the stone porch, and there, to Maud's delight, stood a Guard of Honour – her children from the club. Alternately, they bent low to hold coloured ribbons tautly for the bride and groom to step over, or stretched the ribbons high for them to walk under.

Rosa was certainly not the only one crying now, for Maud suddenly turned to her new husband and buried her wet face against his jacket. He supported her briefly. Then, 'Come on, Maud,' he reminded her gently. She composed herself quickly, smiled radiantly at the children, some of whom were looking anxious, thinking they had upset her in some inexplicable way.

'Oh, thank you – *thank you all*! I can't tell you what this means to me – us – but thank you!' she cried. 'I'll soon be back at the club, that's a promise, and Joe's standing in for me this coming Wednesday, aren't you?' she challenged her brother.

Joe had to admit that he was. The wedding car was waiting but Maud had other ideas.

'We'll walk back to the house, B.J. – it'll give us time to recover from the surprise! And I want *all* you children to come. We can feed them out in the garden, can't we, Rosa?' Followed by her bemused family and a skipping procession of children, Maud marched them up the street, not caring in the least that her satin slippers were gathering dust or that she had snagged her silk stockings. As the motor cruised slowly alongside, with Brother James's family inside, Sophia said laughingly to her husband: 'She's quite a girl, isn't she, our daughter-in-law?' And, of course, he agreed.

They had decided on a London hotel for their brief honeymoon, James being only too well aware that he was to report for duty the following Thursday.

'We'll want a few days in our rooms too – it was good of Aunt A to move into my old bedroom with Amy, wasn't it, saying we needed more space to be on our own. We need to settle in, so we really feel married,' Maud said.

'This is really grand,' she marvelled, as they were shown into their hotel suite. 'But you didn't need to do this to impress me, B.J.!'

'I know that, Maud. But you deserve it. I've ordered dinner for eight-thirty – does that suit you?'

'Could we have it up here?' She chose her words carefully for once. 'We have such a short time to be alone, and—'

'After all these years, we hardly know each other?' he teased. He judged that he was the more nervous of the two. 'I'm sure that can be arranged. I'd like it, too.'

She had chosen to wear the evening dress her parents had bought her for her twenty-first birthday, six years ago. It was in pink watered silk and revealed her smooth shoulders. As on that previous occasion she pinned three rose buds to the front of her bodice. They ate their meal by candlelight, hardly aware of the different courses, comfortable in each other's company as they had been, right from the beginning, in Little Italy.

When she had changed yet again into a clinging night-gown, again in pale pink – a gift from her new mother-in-law – she put her hands up to her burning cheeks and gazed once more into the mirror. I can't believe this is really happening, she thought. She smiled with her lips but her eyes gazed solemnly back at her, a little afraid. Then she became aware that James, having undressed in the bathroom, had come up behind her, and that he, too, was regarding her reflection. Maud answered his questioning look by turning quickly and holding out her arms to him. *She* must say it first.

'I love you!' she whispered, closing her eyes to the look of sheer joy on his face.

She was moping in her room after he had left when Joe came in to see her. 'Cheer up, Maud. You sent him away happy after all. Maud, I wanted you to be the first to know: I'm having a medical next week. Wonderful news, eh?'

'Not for me it isn't! I keep thinking about things – that terrible retreat through Mons, all those innocent people caught in the crossfire. Petty reckons we'll be in Flanders by now. Luisa's young husband and – Pino. *They* must have gone, too, by this time – and heaven knows where Nandy is. I hope they'll turn you down, Joe. It's more grief than glory!'

Noticing the hurt look on his face, she realised what she had just said. 'Oh, darling Joe, I'm so sorry! I'm having some sort of awful reaction to the events of the past few weeks: one minute war is declared and everyone I love best is intent on being involved; the next I find I'm *married*! I haven't even left home, I just have to go downstairs and I'm still

Maud, your sister, Rosa and Petty's daughter, Tilly's friend, Grandma Isabella's grand-daughter, Aunt A's niece—'

'Maud,' he interrupted, 'you need cheering up. Fancy coming to see Charlie Chaplin this evening?' Inwardly he wondered if she had been mistaken in marrying so hastily; he'd always secretly thought that one day she and Pino might somehow come together – not that old B.J. wouldn't be the best brother-in-law a chap could have, of course. Oh, Maud had never confided in him regarding this, even though they were close, but he had always known instinctively how she felt.

'I don't know. Well, I suppose so. I'll be pleased to be back at the office, I shan't have time to become morbid then.' Maud forced a smile. 'Let's see if Rosa and Petty will come, too, eh?'

Maud had brought along the wedding snapshots to show the children at the club. Joe had certainly caught the spirit of that occasion with his little box camera, even if the prints did not have the polish of Mr Lozenge's formal portraits. Clever Joe did his own developing, too. Maud shuffled through the pictures in turn.

The fumes from the oil stove were worse than ever. She began to feel quite nauseous. She sat down abruptly on one of the hard chairs. It was fortunate, she thought, that none of the others had yet arrived. Six weeks married and only those few nights with her new husband, but she was positive she was pregnant. She was determined not to tell a soul until it was obvious, not even B.J.; *he* could wait for his next leave to be enlightened, and goodness knows when that would be, she thought. She would just *hate* being fussed over, being told to rest, that she must give up work and not come here to the club.

'The children need this bit of fun and relaxation right now,' she told herself firmly.

Tilly had been waiting outside the bathroom that morning when Maud had emerged, ashen-faced, having been thoroughly, miserably sick. But dear Tilly wouldn't tittle-tattle.

Brother James's long, loving letters arrived daily, addressed to his 'Dearest Maud', but he was guarded about what he was doing and what training he was undergoing, though he had hinted he would soon be moving on.

'Are you all right, Maud?' Tilly had arrived with the milk. Her face betrayed her concern.

'Of course I am!' She sprang determinedly to her feet. 'Just feeling a bit down, that's all, wondering when I'll see B.J. next.'

Maud's instincts were sound. Tilly would say nothing.

NINE

Tilly picked up the telephone receiver with shaking hands: she had already seen the headlines in the newspaper. German Zeppelins had crossed the coast of Norfolk during the night to drop the first bombs on British soil at King's Lynn and Great Yarmouth. Twenty civilians were reported dead and forty had been seriously injured. A further shock was the fact that the bombs had only narrowly missed Royal Sandringham. This was a heinous beginning to New Year 1915.

Petty, Rosa and Augusta were in Norfolk on family business: brother Harold had died suddenly and Petty had the arranging of the funeral and the closing of the family home to contend with. He could ill afford to take time off from the Admiralty. Years ago Augusta would have taken this all in her stride, but now she leaned heavily on them.

'Are you there?' said Rosa's voice very faintly in the earpiece. 'Is that you, Maud, or Tilly?' She had rightly judged that Joe would already have left for Bartholomew's. He had been graded only 'C' at his latest medical and been advised to try again in the spring: 'When we may have to take what we can get,' as the recruiting officer had said bluntly.

'It's me, Tilly. Are you all right, Rosa? Those terrible bombs – I thought, you being that way . . . ' she babbled. It was cold in the drawing room, still dark and gloomy outside, and she shivered in her agitation, for some reason suddenly aware that she had forgotten to comb out her hair first thing and that it still hung in a thick rope over one shoulder. She felt a little tug on this now and then Amy, in her nightgown, was nestling up against her. 'Is it Mama, Tilly?' she whispered. Tilly's free arm went round her. The love she had felt for Kitty's baby in the early days had soon been rekindled. Amy adored Tilly too: she was tactile, unlike her mama and her Aunt Rosa.

'Shush, my love! No, it's Aunt Rosa,' Tilly whispered back.

'We didn't hear a thing, Tilly,' Rosa's voice was saying. 'Learned about it first thing, naturally. Dreadful business, eh? But don't worry, we'll be home this evening. Augusta sends her love to Amy. Take care of Maud, and reassure her, won't you?' Anxiety crackled along the line.

'Oh, I will, Rosa! Take care of yourselves, too. Goodbye!'

Tilly gave Amy a hug. 'Mama sends her love, dearie. They'll all be home tonight. Go and wash and dress now for school. I must go and rouse Maud.'

She went straight up the stairs and knocked on Maud's door. She seemed to come down at the last minute these days, eschewing breakfast, looking pale and distracted, only showing animation when there was a letter from Brother James, or news of Nandy or David.

There had been a letter this morning. They no longer arrived daily, for Brother James was now in France. Maud was ready for work, Tilly saw, her pregnancy well concealed beneath her tunic top; she had merely loosened her belt. She held the letter, a single page, as she opened the bedroom door.

Tilly explained quickly that all was well with the family: 'I wanted to tell you before you had a shock when you read the paper. I reckon Joe will ring home when he finds out. You look so pale, Maud, is there anything—'

'You know, don't you?' she challenged.

'I only guessed,' Tilly said softly. 'Maud dearie, have you said anything to Rosa yet?'

'No, but I will tonight. I suppose it's silly of me to be so secretive,' she admitted, then, 'Tilly, I didn't get a chance to tell B.J. on his last leave, and somehow it's so difficult to write about.'

'Maud dearie, don't be so foolish. You know how delighted he'll be.' Tilly scolded. She longed to cuddle her as she had Amy, but Maud seemed much too prickly this morning, she thought.

'Now, Tilly, don't start knitting and baby talk. It's ages yet. I know what you, Rosa and Grandma are like! Even Aunt A might start clucking, I suppose.' There was a glimmer of a smile, for Maud was secretly relieved at being found out.

'Just you be sensible, that's all I'm going to say for now. Brother James would blame us if anything happened now, wouldn't he? And rightly so. But he hasn't lived with you as long as we have.' Tilly's tone was wry.

'He hasn't really lived with me at all, if you think about it! I must go, Tilly, the war effort won't wait!' Maud ran down the stairs as if to show Tilly that she was still capable of doing so.

First Tilly must make breakfast for Amy, Grandma, who had stayed on with them, and herself. The housework must be flown through, a cold lunch prepared – Sarianna had volunteered to fetch Amy to and from school. Tilly would only manage an afternoon session with the Sally Army, whose welfare work was now so thoroughly appreciated, but she felt proudly that she was doing *her* little bit for the war effort. And there was Esta to call on later . . .

Whilst their menfolk went off to war, women had taken over on the workfront. Their chimney had recently been swept by their sweep's stout wife; indeed, Tilly thought that this lady had made a far better job of the clearing up afterwards. The coalman's daughters now pitched in to help their father, for their brothers were already at the Front. They wore the trousers the lads had left behind, and had cropped their hair to make for easy washing. City girls had offered eagerly to help on the land, and there was already a willing force making munitions. Tilly knew, from her brief married life on the farm, that working on the land was not her vocation. Rosa busied herself with her sewing guild, with Grandma's help, and with organising comforts for the troops. Even Augusta was threatening to knit socks and scarves to send to the Front.

When Tilly arrived home after seeing Esta, which nowadays was not a fraught experience, she found that Rosa, Petty and Augusta were already home, and that they had gratefully fallen upon the meal she had prepared for them before she left. Petty's broad grin said it all: like a small girl, Maud sat on his lap, her face pressed against his chest, and Rosa came running to meet Tilly with the good news. 'Isn't it wonderful, Tilly, Maud's going to make grandparents of us!'

'And an uncle of me!' Joe was obviously delighted, too.

'Shall I be an auntie?' Amy asked, obviously foxed by all the relationships.

'Aunt Amy E – I like it!' Maud giggled.

Seeing the relief written all over Maud's face as she turned towards her, Tilly pretended happy surprise and thought privately that she might well be able to champion Maud's cause by saying, if necessary, that she thought it would do her no harm to carry on working as long as she felt fit and well. After all, she thought, there would be no problem once Maud's employers realised the situation, since naturally she would then be forced to resign.

'Keep it under your hat, all of you, until B.J. knows. I'm writing to him tonight,' Maud said, then to her father and brother: 'If it's a boy he'll just have to be Joseph, after you two. Joe the third. I'm quite sure B.J. will agree! I'm seeing his parents this weekend, I'll tell them then.'

Joe fetched the sherry, the lemonade and the glasses. 'Let's celebrate!'

'So I'm to be Great-aunt A,' Augusta stated. She received the first glass naturally and raised it to Maud. 'My hearty congratulations, Maud. It's about time.' She was slowly recovering her old form. 'You'll have to calm down, of course.'

'Lemonade for Amy, Tilly and *me*,' Maud reminded Joe demurely, then rose from her perch and went to give Tilly a hug and a kiss. 'Thank you for not saying a thing! You were right, you always are,' she whispered in her ear.

Another baby, Tilly thought in gratitude – this *was* wonderful. But she must be resigned to the fact that it would probably never happen to *her* again. For now there was Amy Elizabeth to fill the gap, until she could cradle Maud's baby in her arms.

TEN

In February, British and French battleships bombarded the forts at the entrance to the Dardanelles. Nandy, unknown to his family, was involved in this strike. In April, the British, Indians and Australians stormed the heights of Gallipoli. In this month, too, a deadly and new weapon was employed by the Germans: mustard gas. Men fell in their thousands, gasping for air, lungs seared, blinded. Many would never fully recover. In the convalescent hospital, David and his fellow doctors were appalled when the first casualties were shipped home to their care. He had not been to London for months, but at Tilly's behest was at least writing to Esta again. Perhaps it was as well, he thought, though not really believing it, that he had never married and had a family, for now he could devote himself single-mindedly to his work.

Joe was exultant: at last he was among the hundreds of men drilling in the local parks, because the training corps was overflowing with recruits. It was now May, and the news was generally grave. On the eighth of the month the Cunard liner *Lusitania* was torpedoed off the southern coast of Ireland by a German submarine and over a thousand perished, though many others thankfully were saved. The street outside the Cunard offices was crowded by the anxious relatives of those who had been on board, waiting for news of survivors. '*Lusitania* sinks in 'alf an 'our!' cried the newsboys cheerfully.

Maud still had over a month of her pregnancy to go. She had reluctantly given up work at six months, when she could conceal her bulge no longer, but was still actively involved with the club every Wednesday. Tilly had promised to keep it going when she was actually confined, for Maud insisted that the children needed this break more than ever now, with fathers away fighting and mothers working.

'Tilly . . . ' Maud's voice sounded low and strained.

Tilly turned, instantly concerned. She had just been going downstairs and, preoccupied, hadn't noticed Maud standing awkwardly in her doorway.

'What is it, Maud dearie?'

'Ben. Poor Ben – the boy you brought to the club. His home was hit by one of the bombs last night. They dug his family out but Ben's been injured badly. Rosa and I went to the hospital to see him this afternoon. Oh, there were so many casualties, Tilly, it was awful. Ben knew me, although he could hardly see for all the bandages round his head. His mother is in a bad way, too, but they haven't dared tell him yet.'

'Don't go upsetting yourself, Maud, not now with Brother James expected any minute on leave.' She patted Maud's shoulder. She would have to warn Rosa to be at the ready. She didn't like the look of Maud, sagging like that against the door jamb. 'Go and have your supper, dearie – you must keep your strength up,' Tilly said briskly.

Maud managed a weak smile in return.

Brother James was not the only one to have some leave – Tilly had gone happily to meet David from the station. They were going straight on to see Esta, for David thought it would break the ice a bit if Tilly was there.

Tilly's last letter, the wording of which she had agonised over for hours, had finally made up his mind.

David dear,

Please go and see Esta when you next come home. Can't you see she made up for what she did when she had you to live with her after she was married? She loved you like a mother then. I never had the chance she did, to have my baby back.

That last sentence haunted David.

Now, as they walked towards his house, Tilly told him all the family news. 'Dear Joe left today – we'll miss him!' she concluded.

'What would they all do without you, Tilly? You're their rock.' As usual, they walked arm in arm.

'Rock of ages nowadays, dearie,' she told him ruefully. They were almost there. She squeezed his arm. 'Be kind to her, David. I won't stay too long, I'm on duty tonight – we keep the soup going all night. You see, we're needed more than ever now people are being made homeless through this awful bombing. But you will come and see me tomorrow, won't you, before you go back, to let me know how you got on?'

She looked up at him earnestly, and David thought how bonny she looked in her uniform still. She really was a saver of souls, his Tilly.

Esta opened the door, face betraying her anxiety, lips working. Tilly released David's arm, giving him a gentle push in Esta's direction. Then she stood back, waiting, while David enfolded his sister – for he could not yet think of her as his mother – in his arms. Tilly turned her gaze heavenwards, not wishing to intrude, murmuring a little prayer of thankfulness.

'Tilly!' Esta called joyfully. 'Come in, do!'

In uniform at last, Joe went out with some new pals to the Maidstone YMCA. In the hall there were refreshments served by friendly ladies, home-baked cakes and pies, good strong tea. There was entertainment of a passive kind from a massive matron, who reminded Joe of his long-gone old teacher on the Island, who played the piano with gusto, encouraging the soldiers to join in heartily with the singing.

There were games which required more active participation, like billiards which Joe always enjoyed. There was a quiet room off the hall provided for writing letters home. In yet another, the cinematograph was flickering away and a rival pianist, an elderly chap, provided accompaniment. A grey-haired clergyman moved diffidently among the assembly in the main hall, sitting to chat when invited, but having a word with each group of men anyway.

Joe went up to the counter for more tea. The girl lifted the lid of the giant teapot and said: 'A couple of cups still to go!' She reminded him of Maud, since she was dark, although her glossy hair was centre-parted and demurely knotted. When she looked up he noticed with surprise that her eyes were round and very blue, with long, curling lashes. He leaned against the wooden counter, ringed and stained by endless cups of tea, and asked her name. One didn't wait to be introduced in wartime.

'I'm Emily Rose. And you?' she asked. Dimples appeared briefly at the corners of her mouth.

'I'm Joe Searle. D'you always help out here, Emily Rose?'

'I do – and call me Emily, please. Rose is my surname, you see!' She was not in the least shy.

He stayed talking to Emily, between customers, for over two hours. Then the corporal, Jack, came over to remind him that it was time to return to barracks. He winked at Joe. 'A conquest so soon, eh?'

'Shall I see you again, Emily?' Joe had to know.

The dimples appeared again. 'Not after the end of this week, Joe. I'm going out with the YMCA to work in a canteen behind the lines. I'm a dancer by profession, and I expect I shall help to put on a concert or two as well.'

'We may meet out there, you never know,' he dared to say. He certainly hoped so.

'I'll be here tomorrow night, Joe Searle,' Emily whispered, more aware of Jack's knowing grin than Joe was. She rubbed hard at the counter with her dishcloth. She wondered how old he was. Early twenties? She was almost thirty, but rather hoped he thought her to be younger. Emily Rose had lost her fiancé with the Expeditionary Force.

There was a baptism of fire for Joe and his comrades that night. Zeppelins on their way to bomb London were bombarded by the gunners, but were tantalisingly out of range. The airships continued on their deadly mission unscathed.

Maud came heavily down the cellar steps to join her family. It was a dank, shadowy cavern, with its heap of coal by the chute, and the old chairs, each with a folded blanket, which they had placed there after the first air raid. Candles were lit and placed in the wall crevices. Isabella already lay on her camp bed.

Rosa wrapped the blankets round Augusta and Amy, who sat on her mother's lap. 'That's right,' she said gently, 'keep each other warm.'

'Tilly should be here,' Augusta said plaintively. To look after us all, she implied.

'I hope she's all right – that they take shelter . . . ' Rosa worried.

'Sustenance,' Petty told them, indicating a tin box. Inside was chocolate and biscuits.

Maud sighed. What time was it, she wondered, yawning, and leaned against her father, drawing support from his nearness. Augusta adjusted the blanket round her and Amy. It was true; it was a comfort to hold the child to her. Isabella slept on.

Maud spoke once, fretfully. 'B.J. should be here by now . . . '

They woke from an uneasy sleep, cramped and chilled. Petty went to investigate and reported that the alarm was over, the raiders gone.

Maud and Rosa re-folded the blankets.

'I hope Joe's all right in Maidstone,' Rosa murmured. 'Mother?' She gently shook Isabella's shoulder. 'Come on, old dear, back to your bed. I'll take you.'

Petty nipped out three of the candles and picked up the last one to light their way back up. He put a steadying arm round Maud, to help her, while the others went ahead.

'Wait a minute, 'til Rosa comes back,' Maud said to her father as they reached his bedroom door.

When Rosa arrived, Maud quite calmly asked, 'Rosa, may I stay with you, in your room?'

She took one look at her daughter's strained face. 'Petty – get dressed. Run for the doctor – quick!'

'Oh, I hope Tilly gets back soon! Don't tell the others, will you?' Maud gasped.

Her parents exchanged helpless glances, then together supported Maud as she staggered, in a haze of pain, towards the bed. Petty cried urgently: 'I'll be back as soon as I can! Hold on, Maud!'

ELEVEN

The doctor had already been called out to an elderly man who had taken a tumble down his cellar steps: they had obviously not been alone in seeking this particular refuge.

'And after that, I'm afraid, my husband was going on to the hospital, to deal with the casualties there – it was a bad night all round, wasn't it? He had your daughter booked for *next* month, didn't he? Do try not to worry, Mr Searle,' the doctor's wife added kindly, noting Petty's anguished expression. 'First babies are usually not in too much of a hurry, and I understand from my husband that you have knowledge of medical matters?'

'In the Royal Navy I assisted the doctor at all times.'

'Then I am confident that you will be a tower of strength until my husband arrives. I imagine you have contacted the midwife?'

'I called en route, but she has been called out too, to another confinement. Her daughter was unsure where, and you see, Maud's baby being so unexpectedly early . . . '

The doctor's wife smothered an exhausted sigh: yet another caller was propping up his bicycle against her gate post.

'Well, good luck, Mr Searle. You must hurry back home now! I'll despatch my husband immediately on his return – I promise.'

Once round the corner, Petty broke into an awkward run but was shortly defeated by the corpulence he attributed to Rosa's good cooking and to his sedentary working life since his departure from the Navy. The path was shining, darkly wet; there had been a short, sharp downpour of rain at dawn. He trod in his agitation through the sudden drifts of apple blossom, sharply reminded of the rose petals which Maud's 'children' had showered over her not many months ago. Many front gardens seemed to have a central, solitary apple tree. The streets were no longer swept by those patient men bent over their stout brooms; they, too, had answered Kitchener's call to arms.

Rosa held on to her daughter's arm as Maud slowly paced the room, biting her lower lip determinedly. When she paused, Rosa said: 'Maud darling, I must prepare the bed. It was lucky we kept all the things for the confinement down here – I couldn't leave you like this now, could I? Oh dear, wherever has your father got to – and why hasn't Tilly come back yet?'

As she tucked in the draw sheet, Maud clutched at Rosa's arm. 'I'm glad it's – coming – now – it's been intolerable, the waiting. Rosa, don't worry I'm – not—' A contraction caught her and she began to breathe shallowly. Rosa supported her as best she could. When the spasm subsided, she assisted Maud carefully on to the bed, turning her gently on to her side, where Maud indicated she felt more easy.

In a surprisingly loud voice, Maud went on: 'I'm not afraid. I saw Amy E born, remember? *She* came in a great hurry, too.' Her eyes screwed tightly shut as another strong contraction began.

'They're very close . . . ' Rosa muttered, trying not to panic. Then: 'Here's your father!' she exclaimed thankfully as they heard the front door open and close. Directly Rosa saw him, she realised he was alone.

'I'll fetch my box,' he said briefly. It was almost unbearable to him to think of his beloved Maud in pain. They rarely called the doctor for themselves, for Petty diagnosed their minor ailments and prescribed the appropriate remedies from pills and potions he stocked up with from the local chemist.

Rosa followed him to the door, whispering so that Maud could not hear: 'Have you ever delivered a baby?' Of course it was a vain hope.

'At *sea*? No, my dear! But you've been through this, haven't you? That will be a great help, if the need arises, and

Tilly must be here soon, surely? I thought a few drops of that stuff I gave Joe for his wisdom teeth – that might help to relieve her.'

'I don't think it's going to be easy, the baby's not down yet. She's in such agony, but nothing seems to be happening . . . '

'Then we must pray the doctor arrives soon,' he whispered back, tears in his eyes.

Their prayers were instantly answered, it seemed, by a knock on the door. But it was not the doctor they expected.

'Praise be!' Rosa cried, just as Tilly so often did. 'You've got your bag with you, David!'

'I left it at home when I went off in such a hurry last time. I just called to see Tilly, as I promised, before I go back to the hospital – rough night, eh?' He broke off, taking in their expressions. 'Is something wrong?'

'It's Maud, David! The baby, it's coming – and our doctor's been called elsewhere. The midwife, too. Please,' Rosa beseeched, 'you'll help, won't you, David? Tilly must be back shortly.'

'Of course I'll help. Take me to her now,' he said, even as they heard the welcome sound of Tilly's key turning in the lock.

Maud turned her head continuously on the pillow, her mutterings not making sense. David straightened up from his examination, and Tilly replaced the sheet over Maud's writhing form. Petty had his back to them, taut with worry. David joined him by the window, beckoning Rosa over.

'It's a breech presentation, I'm afraid. She's too far gone to move to the hospital. We must do the best we can here. I need steady hands to assist me.'

To her mortification, Rosa began to cry silently, her tired eyes spilling great tears. Her husband's arms went round her instantly.

'Go and get some rest,' he whispered. 'You're her mother so you're too close – don't stay. We'll do it, Tilly and I – I don't think Maud will mind my being here . . . '

'We'll call you the minute the baby's born,' Tilly promised.

David shook a ribbed bottle and uncorked it, pressing the neck on to a pad of cotton. A sickly, sweet smell began to pervade the room. 'Hold it, just so, over her nostrils, not too near her eyes and keep her mouth clear,' he instructed Petty. As Maud felt the first pressure of the pad, her eyes wavered open and she groaned.

Tilly had been close enough to realise just who Maud was crying for in her hour of need. 'She knows you're here,' she said to Petty, hoping that he would think that Maud had tried to say *his* name.

'Hold her there – and there, Tilly. Don't let her legs slip.' David patted her hands encouragingly. She was quite steady, despite her evident fatigue. 'Good girl,' he approved. Then, 'I'm going to attempt to manipulate the baby, and then . . . ' Both Tilly and Petty glimpsed the gleam of steel as he withdrew instruments from his bag and laid them ready. 'Keep the pad firmly in position – don't lose your nerve, either of you. I think we'll manage to get this baby born between us. Poor little Maud,' he added compassionately. 'She at least won't know a thing about it.'

There was a juddering sensation in Maud's ears, the oddest feeling of being lifted and then allowed to fall heavily. She attempted to raise her hands in feeble protest at the continued pressure on her face, then the blessed darkness took over.

'Maud, Maud . . . ' The echoing of several voices was dragging her back. Please go away, she thought. *Please* leave me alone. A hand was smoothing her fringe away from her clammy forehead, wiping her face so gently with a soft, wet flannel. Her eyes were opening gradually, although she was unable to focus properly at first. Her nose felt swollen, she was breathing through her mouth, but to begin with, she felt no pain.

'Maud darling, thank God – we haven't lost you . . . ' A familiar voice. Brother James, in his captain's uniform – so skilfully tailored that the curvature of his spine was hardly noticeable – sat beside her. He had knocked on the door at the very moment their baby was born. It had been five minutes before anyone let him in.

'Is he—?' she asked faintly. Brother James looked over at Rosa, proudly cradling her first grandchild in her arms. Tilly had fetched Augusta and Amy, for 'just a peep'. Petty had taken David to wash. It was time for the family to take over.

'The baby's absolutely splendid, Maud. Head just a little out of shape, from all the squeezing, but David assures us that this will soon disappear.'

'The baby's head?' she said clearly, with the quivering beginnings of a smile.

'No, Maud! They've all been wonderful, but you owe your life and the baby's to David, you know. If he hadn't arrived when he did . . . Such a lovely baby, small but perfect.' The first thing Brother James had felt had been the baby's pliable but straight back.

'Joseph . . . can we call him that?'

'Darling,' he said gently, 'we have a little daughter – you may call her just whatever you wish. All I – we – care about, is that you are both safe.'

Maud looked up into his face and what she saw there was enough.

'Joy,' she stated. 'She's brought joy to us – to us all.'

Rosa laid the shawl-wrapped bundle across Maud's breast and moved her flaccid arms to hold it tenderly. 'Thank you, Rosa,' she said, as her mother bent to kiss them both.

James fingered the shawl aside and Maud observed with dawning incredulous delight slate-blue eyes opening then closing, a thatch of almost black hair, still oily from the birth, tiny close-set ears. Her baby was indeed perfect.

'Hello, Joy,' she said softly. Then, 'Has anyone sent a telegram to Joe yet?'

'We've all been much too busy!' Rosa said drily. Here was Petty now, waiting his chance to kiss and congratulate his daughter. He was so proud of her.

'Thank you, Petty,' she said, as he touched the baby's little face.

Augusta brought Amy forward. 'Isn't she wonderful, Amy? Just think, you were as small as that once!' She was a little disgruntled at being shut out for so long, but it was not Maud's fault. Rosa had been so insistent.

Tilly came in, smiling, with Isabella. 'Here's something you didn't expect to see, eh, Mrs Barry – Maud with a baby!'

It was just as well that Augusta had departed because Isabella's opinion was: 'Ah, Maud dear – another little one – so *Spanish*!'

'Boot-button eyes, I guess,' Maud agreed. 'We don't let you down, Grandma, do we?'

Tilly lingered a moment. 'I must just have a word with David, then I'm going to fall into my bed, too, Maud. It was a long, hard night . . . ' In fact it had been *dreadful*.

'Tilly, thank you,' she said with gratitude. 'What d'you think of Matilda for her second name?'

'Oh, Maud!' Tilly breathed. 'Really? But what about Rosa – and Mrs Augusta?'

'Augusta's already much in use – don't I know it? – and Rosa's already given her blessing.'

Then Maud whispered to Brother James. He understood instantly. He lifted the baby and took her to Tilly, to place in the crib.

Maud held out her arms to David. 'And David – how can I thank you?' she asked, and gave him a grateful kiss. 'Thank you for bringing Joy into the world.'

'I was glad I could help, Maud.'

'Let's leave these three alone to get to know each other, shall we?' Rosa suggested. The room was still crowded, and Maud must be exhausted.

'Thank you all,' James said quietly as they filed out.

In the hall, David hugged Tilly and kissed her goodbye. It was right somehow to part now, he thought.

And in the bedroom, Brother James asked Maud: 'Can you believe, my darling, that we're a family?'

She turned her face to him so that their lips met briefly. It was enough for now.

TWELVE

Maud's mother-in-law was delighted with her new grand-daughter. 'Oh, Maud, how thrilled you both must be! Look, I'm glad to have this opportunity to talk to you on your own, my dear – you see I have a proposition to put to you ... My husband wishes me to go to the safety of the country while this wretched war is on. We have a house which was left to me by my father. It has been let in the past on a long lease. This has now ended and he has convinced me I should go there, together with our daughter and her children. Her husband would remain here in London, with your father-in-law.'

'That sounds very sensible,' Maud said, wondering what this was all leading up to.

'Well, it is a large house, and it seems to us that we could offer sanctuary to others. When you are back on your feet, my dear, will you join us with little Joy? I was also wonder-ing if your aunt and her daughter might agree to come too? I understand that she was a teacher for many years. If they say yes, well, there is a perfectly good schoolroom which could be used by our three young ones. You see what I am getting at, I'm sure? The house is rather remote and some miles away from the nearest school. There isn't the staff nowadays for the children to be transported there – and, Maud, if your mother would like it, I should love to have your grandmother with us too. We get on famously. You must have worried that you'd asked her here, thinking she'd be so much safer than on the Isle of Sheppey, and then all this bombing on London . . . '

'It's a wonderful idea. I know Aunt A will jump at it for she worries about Amy naturally.' (And she's such a snob! Maud thought wickedly to herself.) 'And as for Grandma – we'll do our best to persuade her!'

'And what about you, Maud?'

'I must decline gratefully, Sophia. I can't leave Rosa and Petty, or Tilly . . . '

* * *

Tilly had gone rushing over to Esta's first thing, for the postman had reported that there had been a direct hit on a house in her road. In David's absence Tilly took her responsibility for his mother very seriously.

She came home after some hours with terrible news, looking dazed and disorientated. It was Esta's house which had taken the full force of the bomb; she must have been killed instantly. She had disobeyed David's instructions to go down into the basement when there was a raid. Had probably been at her desk, busying herself with her endless translating.

'David will be devastated . . . ' Tilly wept to Rosa. Her only comfort was that he and Esta had eventually been reconciled.

'You must be thankful, Tilly, that you wrote that letter,' Rosa endeavoured to console her.

'Oh, Rosa, David doesn't deserve this, does he?' she asked sadly. She really couldn't see how she would comfort him – the police had already informed him of the tragedy when he was at his hospital. They told Tilly that he would be returning home as soon as he could make arrangements to leave.

'Tilly, you must tell David that he must regard this as his home – after all he did for Maud. If he needs us, and he certainly will need *you*, we'll always be here,' Rosa said softly.

So, after the funeral, Tilly brought him home. Rosa had taken her mother, Augusta and Amy over to Sophia's house for the afternoon – ostensibly to talk over the arrangements for the move to the country. Tilly was going to miss young Amy a great deal, she knew. As usual she had allowed herself to become too emotionally involved.

Maud was there, of course: she had not yet regained her full strength, and was very pale. 'Tilly, you don't mind if I leave you both for a while, do you?' she asked tactfully. 'Time for yet another feed. That baby of ours is insatiable.'

David said: 'I'm very glad she's doing so well. You, too, must rest when you can, Maud – you had a rough ride, producing your baby.'

He seemed quite composed, but Tilly knew he must be in turmoil deep inside.

When they were alone, she poured the tea and they sat in silence drinking it. Neither of them touched the cake.

'It will be difficult to carry on,' he ventured at last. The anguish in his eyes was apparent. Tilly gazed at him with concern.

'My dear David, I know,' she said, 'but it's the only way. I found that out when Oswald died. For years I thought I'd never get over it, but now I know I have: at some point, you begin to think of all the happy times you had together.'

'Is he irreplaceable?' he asked gravely. 'Won't you reconsider marrying me, Tilly?'

'I *do* love you, David, I always will – but I haven't been fair to you, keeping you waiting. Perhaps you should find someone else? Someone a lot younger than me, who can give you the family you need now that Esta is gone . . . But remember, David, I will always be here for you, if you want me.'

'I do want you,' he said. 'I don't want anyone else.'

Maud came back, her sleepy baby over her shoulder. Had they resolved their relationship at last, she wondered. They were both such special people. She felt a real bond with David since he had presented her with the miracle of her baby.

'You look so serious, Maud, since you became a mother.' David managed a smile.

'It's an awesome responsibility, especially with B.J. away,' she said. On a sudden impulse, she held out tiny Joy. 'Would you like to hold her, David? I'm going to tell her when she's big enough what a wonderful honorary uncle she has in you.'

He held the baby as tenderly as if it were his own child – which caused Tilly a pang, but reaffirmed to her that she had been right to say what she had.

'It's a comfort,' David said after a while, 'to remember that there is always a new life when one has ended.' His bearded face rested so gently on the baby's head.

'You see,' Tilly said to him, 'I was right. This is what you need, David, a family of your own.'

Tilly could see that Maud was puzzling over what she meant by this. She might confide in her later, but not today. Had she really given David up? How could she, when she knew she longed to lie beside him, to love him, to give comfort and experience them really being together as she had with Oswald so long ago? These thoughts, which she could not suppress, made her feel so very sad.

THIRTEEN

On a September day Maud and Brother James, carrying their baby, walked slowly along the streets of Little Italy. The next day he was due to escort those soldiers who had recovered sufficiently to rejoin their regiments, back in the trenches. He had been based in England since Joy's arrival, but not near home, comforting the wounded and their families. Now, he was enjoying a short leave with Maud and Joy.

Maud, glancing at him as he shifted the baby's weight to his good shoulder, noted that the lines on his face had deepened. We have both changed, she thought, grimacing at the reality of her rounded figure: despite her family's reassurances, she was convinced she was fat! It was strangely quiet all around, she noticed.

Now the barrel organs with their cheeky, nimble monkeys and the stolid German brass bands were no longer to be seen or heard on the London scene.

Even here, the usual noise and bustle had abated for the men of The Hill had gone to do battle. Already the piano organs were deteriorating in store and some would never be reclaimed. But of course there were the womenfolk and the youngsters, rushing out to embrace Brother James and touch his shining buttons, to shake hands with his wife and ask to kiss the baby, gazing curiously at them with dark eyes just like Maud's.

Joy wore a white muslin dress and starched bonnet to match. She was a strong baby, despite her early arrival, and Brother James could feel her digging her toes in against his chest as she attempted to feel her feet. He could hardly believe his good fortune.

'It's so sad, B.J.,' Maud murmured. 'The life really seems to have gone out of the place now so many have gone. And of course, the Barbieris aren't here anymore.'

'*Una bella statua bianco di marmo* . . .' Maud whispered to B.J. Who had said that so many years ago, when she was so young? Pino? Or was it Gussie? They were sitting in the cool interior of St Peter's, which they had visited by mutual, unspoken consent. A priest moved around the altar, busy with preparations for the next mass, then turned and came towards them, smiling. He of course recognised Brother James immediately.

'So good to see you again – and this must be your wife and baby? You have had news of the Barbieris?'

'Of the wedding – Luisa's? We were there. It was just before our own wedding,' they told him. He sat beside them in the pew, holding out his arms for the baby. Joy went to him willingly, her hands reaching out for the spectacles on his nose. He stretched his neck upwards so that she was thwarted. As she gave a protesting crow, the priest told them: 'Two terrible losses ... the young bridegroom leaving his young wife with a new baby, like this one, and just yesterday I have learned that Pino too is dead. He died of wounds so terrible that his family consider it a blessing. I am so sorry to tell you this news, my dear friends.' He returned the baby to her father.

They sat as if stunned. Then Maud asked in a choked voice: 'May we light a candle – is that what you do?'

The priest opened a box and fitted a candle into place amongst the rows of holders beside the marble statue. He lit the taper from an already burning candle and passed the brave flame to Maud. With a trembling hand she ignited the wick. Joy's expressive, eager fingers reached out again as she spotted the glow, and James moved away in order to distract her. She gravely regarded the statue of the Madonna and Child.

'We are to say a mass for Pino, and for his young brother-in-law, Bruno, at the request of the family,' the priest said. Adding, 'Do you wish to pray for them with me now?'

'Please. But, Father, I don't belong—'

'*Con tutti – vogliamo che con noi sentano la bellezza e la gioia del Vangelo, la Croce e la Risurrezione* ... With everyone – we would like the beauty that is the Gospel, the

Cross and the Resurrection . . . ' the priest intoned softly, motioning Maud to kneel beside him. As they prayed, Maud could hear the receding echo of footsteps as her husband took their baby out into the churchyard, in order that they should not be disturbed.

Later, as they took some refreshment with the priest in his study, Maud said: 'Years ago I came here with my cousin, Gussie, who was engaged to Pino Barbieri, my brother, Joe, and of course James.' She touched his sleeve in a fleeting caress as he nursed the baby who was now asleep. 'It was Procession Day,' she continued, eyes bright with tears, and with memories.

'Ah,' the priest interjected, stirring his coffee slowly.

'I've never forgotten – I never will – how happy we all were – how excited, how dressed up. How Pino was one of the bearers, how the flowers showered down, and the feathery doves, released from the cage . . . '

'You know, I have a newspaper clipping, a photograph of that day. 1905, wasn't it? His sister, you see, mentioned this also in her letter to me. I have something you might like to see . . . '

He rummaged in a desk drawer and withdrew a folded length of newsprint. 'Here you are.'

'B.J. – look!' Maud said. 'There's Pino, the Barbieri girls in the Procession, and B.J. – there *we* are, Gussie and me. And isn't that maybe the back of Joe's head?'

'You are holding it too close, Maud, I can't quite ... that's better. Yes, you're right, that must be Joe and myself to the left, I believe.' As always that quiet voice held an underlying warmth.

'You may keep it. The Barbieris, I know, have a copy,' the priest offered.

'Thank you, we will treasure it,' said Maud, re-folding the paper and placing it carefully in her bag.

For some time they sat quietly together on the journey home, Joy still sleeping but transferred to the crook of Maud's arm.

Then Brother James said thoughtfully: 'I feel as if I have just said farewell to a part of my life, to the Little Italy I have known and loved for nearly twenty years. You see, Maud, now I have you and Joy to care for, when this war is over I must find myself paid employment, ensure that you have a real home.'

'B.J., you know I will be behind you if you wish to continue with your work there. I don't mind living at home either, honestly.'

'I will, I'm sure, continue to be involved with and to care passionately about my many friends there, but this is a turning point for me – for us. We need to be on our own. Much as I admire and respect your family. And talking of families, I promised to pass this on to you, although I know what your answer will be. My mother asks if you would reconsider joining her?'

'I can't leave my family now, B.J. – even though some of 'em are with Sophia already. I'm not leaving Brixton until you are home again for good. I promise you I'll take every care, for Joy's sake, and that we'll descend to that wretched cellar the minute the alarm is sounded,' she assured him solemnly.

'Exactly what I told my mother you would say!'

* * *

Four-thirty in the morning and hungry cries were issuing from the crib beside their bed. Maud roused herself, lifted the damp baby, changed her napkin, then eased herself carefully back into her warm place. She turned up the wick of the nightlight, then unbuttoned her nightdress – she was back in serviceable flannel, she thought ruefully – and put the snuffling baby to her breast. Brother James leaned up to plump the pillows behind her for support. Then he lay, wakeful and watching, trying to forget that he would have to leave them within another three hours.

'Maud,' he said impulsively.

'Mmm.' Joy gave a protesting hiccup at her sudden movement.

'I wish I could paint you like this. You look so beautiful, so maternal—'

'For a start, B.J., you're no artist, and if you were, you'd need to be a Rubens and generous with the paint – just look at the size of me,' Maud sighed, looking ruefully at her full, white bosoms.

'I said you're *beautiful*. Perhaps I'm biased.'

'You must be.' She was purposely being flippant. 'I'm too short, too dumpy, too dark, too ordinary. I can't imagine what you see in me, you know!'

'I know your faults – and if you think you've just mentioned them, well, darling, you're wrong! Maud, I realise how sad you must be feeling about Pino.'

She positioned the baby against her shoulder and began to rub Joy's back with a gentle, circular motion. She had learned how to bring up a baby's wind in the Amy E days.

He thought she wasn't going to answer, then she said slowly: 'It's a tragic waste of a talented young life, B.J.. But I was thinking, when we were in the church, that it was meant to be. He hadn't got over losing Gussie – I just know he would *never* have done so. Now they are together again, wherever Heaven may be . . . '

She laid the drowsy, replete baby down again, and slipped back into his arms.

The bulky letter arrived as they enjoyed breakfast together, cooked and brought up to them by Rosa, who had nobly started frying at six o'clock. 'You don't want to waste precious moments slaving over a hot stove!' She departed discreetly, but was soon back to tell Maud: 'The postman just came. This is for you.'

'Any news from Joe?' she called after her mother.

'Yes, and one from Nandy, too. Oh, and Tilly's got one from David, so we're all lucky today – apart from Petty, who's grumbling, and asking why *he* gets all the bills?'

'It's from Luisa, poor girl, how sweet of her to write at such a time!' Maud exclaimed to B.J.. 'She even says she is sorry she did not write before to tell us about the baby. Well, we are remiss in that respect, too, aren't we? She has a little son, three months old, named Pino, for the uncle who would have been his godfather . . . Oh, B.J., she says the enclosure is something which Pino asked her to send to me if anything should happen to him.' She passed the small package to her husband. 'You open it, B.J., I – can't.'

Without comment, he passed to her the little gold wire ring with its single pearl.

'Pearls for tears!' Maud cried. 'This was Gussie's engagement ring.'

'I know.'

'D'you mind if I wear it in memory of them both, B.J.?' Maud wiped her eyes on the edge of the traycloth. 'Can't seem to find my hanky . . . '

'Of course you must.' He took her left hand, slipped free the lovely lapis lazuli ring she wore above her wedding band, smoothed the cheap little ring into its place, and then replaced the ring he had given her. 'There, will that do?' He looked searchingly at her.

'You said you were aware of all my faults, B.J. – but, d'you know, *you* haven't any at all!' Maud put the tray on the bedside table, and just as she leaned towards him, to hug him, there was a scream of protest from Joy in her crib, awake and hungry once more.

'D'you mind living up to your name, young lady?' Maud asked. 'Just you be joyful, while I give your darling father something to remember in the days ahead!'

And she did.

FOURTEEN

It was two days before Maud, who considered that there were far more exciting things to do in life, got around to cleaning their rooms following her husband's departure. As she dusted the mantelpiece, virtuously moving the heavy clock, an envelope which had been tucked right behind it was revealed. 'For Maud' she read in her husband's flowing, upward-slanting handwriting.

She smiled to herself. She had probably been intended to read the tender missive soon after he left, she thought. She shook her hair free from the confining cotton square and took the opportunity to sit down. The rattling of the crib had ceased at last. Lively Joy had fallen asleep.

The letter was folded within a stiffer sheet of paper, a typed document. Curious, she examined this first. It was a statement from their bank, to the effect that James Albert Inkpen had requested the transfer of £2,500 from his own account to that of his wife, and that they were pleased to report that this had been duly effected.

It was difficult to assimilate. Bemused, Maud turned to the letter:

Dearest Maud,

This is something I meant to do when we married, but somehow life seems to have been hectic ever since! The occasion of our first anniversary, which we were so fortunate to spend together, and the precious, wonderful gift of our daughter – our Joy! – reminded me to see to this before leaving for the Front. Maud, this is your share, as my beloved wife, of a legacy left to me by my grandmother. It had never seemed important to have this money, although I was grateful for the interest on the capital over the years as it enabled me to help, as I did in Little Italy.

This is yours to do with exactly as you wish. (Naturally, the rest would also come to you, as my wife, should anything happen to me.)

My darling, thank you for the great happiness of the past year and for the generous gift of your love.

I love you both so much and always will.

God bless you,

B.J.

'It's you who are generous, B.J.,' Maud thought aloud. 'I kept you waiting all that time because I suppose I was in love with a dream. That first time I told you I loved you

– did you know? And do you really believe me now? Oh, darling B.J., I do hope so!' Impulsively, she kissed the letter, then laughed at herself.

She showed it to Rosa, Petty and Tilly later. 'I feel I want to help someone else in our family to have their chance. Any suggestions?'

'I know Amy would dearly love to have singing and dancing lessons,' Tilly mused. 'Her natural talent is so obvious, isn't it? But just imagine what she might achieve . . .'

'What a wonderful idea!' Maud exclaimed, pleased. 'I'll write to Aunt A today and see what can be arranged. I *do* miss the club, you know, now we've had to close it because the evenings are drawing in and the children dropping off because of the raids. I must admit it was a responsibility, having that in the back of my mind, but I'll do something for children like those again, I'm sure of that.'

'I can't help wondering if Augusta's pride will prevent her from accepting,' Rosa said.

'I'll talk to her,' put in Petty.

'Oh, you can charm anyone; look how you got round Aunt A to allow Gussie to go to the Slade.' Maud had always marvelled at that achievement. It was something that had brought Gussie such satisfaction in her short life, she thought.

'Maud,' Petty asked, 'have you thought anymore about staying with Sophia? I know the raids seem to have eased up, but we've been warned they may resume.'

'I told B.J. I wouldn't leave you – but I've another idea. You remember Ben, Tilly – the lad you brought to the club, who was so badly injured in that first Zeppelin bombing?'

Tilly said, 'Of course I do. Tom gave me news of him the other day – the poor boy has been left with some degree of paralysis.'

'That's right. Well, they've not discharged him from hospital because his family can't cope, apparently.'

'Tom mentioned that he might have to go into an institution until he recovers, but they think he will, given time, care and good food.' Tilly felt guiltily that she should have visited him again.

'You know we would have had him here,' Rosa said instantly.

Petty chuckled. 'We should call our house 'the elastic-sided boot'!'

'Of course, I *knew* you'd say that,' Maud said to Rosa. 'But I'm going to ask Sophia if she and Aunt A will have him there – I'm sure she'll agree, don't you? And then, while they're busy getting Ben all better and educated, 'cause he left school hardly able to read and write, you know, well, they won't have time to worry about Joy – and *me*!' Maud paused for breath.

'It's been a worrying time for all mothers, don't forget. Well, how could you?' Rosa realised what she was saying, and smiled despite the seriousness of it all. '*She* has a son at the front – well, we've *two*. Poor Nandy! That latest girlfriend of his, Edie, blowing hot and cold like all his girls seem to do. He's never been lucky in love.'

'It's hard to keep track of what you two are saying, you keep changing course . . . ' Petty murmured.

'Oh, she'll change it yet again, when she sees old Nandy in the flesh. No girl can resist him,' Maud joked.

'Maybe not,' Petty remarked drily, 'but none of them *marry* him!'

'One did!' winked Maud. Petty gave a yelp as Joy tugged unexpectedly at his beard.

'Your daughter, Maud, is a right chip off the old block,' he told her, giving Joy a hug to show that he'd forgive her anything.

None of them noticed that Tilly had gone very quiet. She, too, had a son after all, to whom anything could have happened and she would never know.

FIFTEEN

The second Christmas of the war was a simple one. They all huddled over a small fire, bearing in mind the greater need of industry for coal. There was a large chicken for dinner, gratefully received from Sophia, who had failed to prevail on them to join her family in Wiltshire. Rosa had made a plain steamed pudding, and as Petty said, there were memories of the gargantuan feasts of pre-war days to sustain them.

Superstitiously, Rosa insisted on places being laid for absent members: for Joe, Nandy, Brother James and David, though as Tilly said, with an unaccustomed droop to her mouth, 'I don't know if he celebrates Christmas – and he certainly wouldn't feel like it this year, not after losing Esta.' It was a time they had never spent together.

After dinner, Tilly changed into her uniform, tied her bonnet firmly under her chin and added a warm shawl around her shoulders. 'I'm off then – there's others that want their dinners.' She was going to spend the rest of the day feeding and cheering those less fortunate.

They had made the hall as cheerful and welcoming as possible. Plates were piled high, and even if there were more vegetables than meat, the meal was as hot as they could make it, to warm those who sat, hungrily expectant, at the tables.

Tilly ladled out potatoes with a smile. She pitied the poor fingers, with itching chilblains, reaching for the gravy jugs. She came upon Kitty quite suddenly. Recognition was not immediate, for Kitty had aged considerably, her features coarsened.

'Kitty?' she asked uncertainly.

'I hoped I'd see you, Tilly,' she replied calmly.

'I'll be back,' Tilly said quickly, 'later, when I've done with dishing out – I'll talk to you then.'

Some time later they sat side by side while carols were sung. Kitty was not in the terrible state that she had been when she and Tilly had last met in similar circumstances, ten years previously. She was thin and poorly dressed, it was true, but not down and out and hopeless.

'I'm married, Tilly. He's not a bad sort – poor, but honest, as they say. We've given up the halls. I never was much good on my own, and he never had any talent to speak of. He was taken to hospital two weeks back, and I didn't have the heart to cook for myself today. We only have a couple of rooms in the East End where he was brought up, so I came here. I thought I might have some news from you of Amy. Oh, don't worry, I'd never claim her back. I'd hate her to know she had a mother who looks like this. Anyway, there's no room for a child in my life. There never was, as you know.'

'It's a long story,' Tilly said gently, and reached for Kitty's hand. 'It's best if I tell you about Amy as she is *now*. She is living in the heart of the country, well away from the threat of bombing. Mrs Augusta is teaching again, and Amy is one of her pupils. She's a bright girl, Kitty, and looks very like you, you know. We think she has a gift for singing, too. You would be proud of her, as Mrs Augusta is. As we *all* are.

'You did the right thing, Kitty, when you gave her up. You knew you couldn't put heart and soul into motherhood, didn't you?' Tilly was speaking from the heart here, thinking briefly of David and herself, and her own relinquishing of bonds.

Kitty nodded. 'You will give her a kiss from me, when you see her next? Tilly, I never sent it to you but here it is now. The money I owed you – what I took from your purse when I left.'

'Please give it to someone who needs it more than I do,' she said swiftly. 'But I'm so glad you remembered. Kitty – what happened to George?'

'It didn't last long – our getting back together. He died a while back, I heard. My Sam is a better man than George ever was. He's been very ill, bronchial, you see, but he'll be back with me soon. And he has a grown-up daughter who is very good to us both. She wanted me to be with them today, but I said I was visiting friends . . . Didn't you get married again, Tilly, to your nice young doctor?'

'No, Kitty, but we're still great friends. I couldn't leave the family, you see,' Tilly told her.

'It came upon the midnight clear, that glorious song of old,' the motley assembly sang, and suddenly a clear voice was heard, true as a bell. Kitty could still sing like a lark.

'We'll keep in touch, won't we?' Tilly asked as she and Kitty parted. A little of the old sparkle was back in Kitty's eyes.

'Dear Tilly, just leave it that we *may* see each other from time to time, eh? I think that's best. You won't want to keep secrets from the family, that's not in your nature. No, I walked away from my baby for good that day.'

They exchanged a warm kiss. 'Happy Christmas!' they said to each other. Then they went their different ways.

At home, Rosa produced the Happy Family cards, the old ones that Maud had designed in the Sheer Necessity days. They were battered and discoloured, but she'd always treasured them. 'Here, Maud, you sort these out and see if they're all there. Then we can have a game later. Grandma –' Isabella had joined them for the festivities – 'why don't you have a turn with the baby? Petty, you can start the washing up. I told Tilly it'd all be done when she returned.'

'Now, Maud,' Rosa said confidentially as they sat side by side on the old sofa, 'what's this surprise you promised to tell me about?'

'I shall be weaning Joy – she's doing very well with real food now, and has four teeth after all.'

Rosa was scandalised. 'Oh, Maud! I nursed *you* for almost a year. Joy's barely seven months. You're surely not thinking of going back to work, are you?' she asked reproachfully. She wouldn't put anything past Maud.

'Rosa, you're not nearly as sharp-eyed as Aunt A in her hey-day! Well, I might as well come out with it. My surprise is – I'm expecting again . . . '

'Well!' Rosa really didn't know what to say for a moment, then: 'I realised you were putting on weight, but I thought it was just contented fat, being married and having such a lovely baby. But *when*?' She did some rapid mental arithmetic.

'June, I suppose, unless he or she makes an early arrival like Joy.'

Petty stood eavesdropping, having come in to place a handful of the best knives and forks in their presentation box.

'Well, I'm surprised at Brother James – you've hardly had time to get over Joy's birth. Didn't you have a word with him, Joe? I asked you to.' Rosa turned to Petty who instantly wished he had stayed in the kitchen.

'I did not! I told you it's none of our business. Just look at Maud, Rosa, this motherhood lark suits her! Well, I'm pleased for you, my dear, but don't make too much of a habit of it, or you'll never hear the last of it from your mother.' He dropped an affectionate kiss on her head. Maud stretched up and pinched his cheek in a familiar gesture.

'Thanks, Petty, I knew *you'd* be nice about it. And there's not much chance of a baby a year if this war keeps grinding on and James doesn't get home too often.'

Trust Maud to be John Blunt, Rosa thought. She had to give in gracefully. She patted her daughter's stomach. 'We'll look after you while he's away,' she said gruffly, and looked fully at Maud and saw what she must have shut her eyes to. She was unashamedly pregnant, and happy as could be, despite the worries of the menfolk being away at war.

'B.J. should know by now,' Maud said, answering her unspoken question.

Chuckling over the cards took Maud back to the cottage: to William sitting with Joe, and the simple remembered pleasure of combing out her grandmother's hair.

'Can I let your hair down, Grandma?' she asked, and saw at once that Isabella was remembering that other Christmas, too.

'And her Spanish hair was hanging down her back!' sang Petty.

Maud stood behind her grandmother, gently pulled the crinkled hairpins from the coronet and then loosened the plaits. Isabella closed her eyes at the sensuous strokes of the brush, drifting away into a happy, elderly lady's after dinner snooze as Maud busied herself.

'I reckon she only takes it down once a month!' Petty murmured.

'Shush!' Maud grinned.

Rosa had rocked Joy to sleep a few minutes before. Now she laid her face wistfully, possessively, against the baby's hair, as black as her great-grandmother Isabella's. So many years since she had been delivered of her last baby in the cottage under the sea wall . . .

Tilly came in then, her face glowing from the cold air outside, and as if reading Rosa's thoughts remarked: 'What a blessing babies are!'

Rosa said proudly: 'Maud has told us some good news. She is expecting another baby next summer. Let's pray the war will be over by then, and all our loved ones safely home with us.'

Tilly looked over at Maud and smiled. Of course, *she* had guessed. Maud smiled back.

'I'll just go and see if Petty has made that pot of tea, shall I?' Rosa said. 'Here, Tilly, your turn to hold the baby. Then how about a game of Happy Families?'

SIXTEEN

The Allies' transient foothold on the Gallipoli beaches was over: the troops were evacuated in January, 1916. There was continued stalemate on the Western Front.

Corporal Joe Searle drove his lorry, crammed with men who had scrambled through the mud and rain, deafened by the thundering of the guns – men who had not slept, eaten, bathed or changed clothes in weeks – lousy, stinking, but still able to rouse a cheer at the sight of the lorries and the prospect of a precious few days' leave. Crumpled cigarettes were passed from hand to hand, treasured photographs displayed.

An aeroplane was flying erratically overhead, obviously homing in on its base behind the lines. Wings were fluttering ragged ribbons, engine sputtering loudly, having been hit by German fire once too often, yet still there was an audacious salute from the pilot to his comrades travelling along not so far below. The soldiers waved back. Reconnaissance aeroplanes were a common sight. Vital information regarding troop movements on both sides was garnered daily.

'Crazy beggars!' the sergeant commented, sucking noisily and disgustingly on his empty pipe. He was a few years older than Joe, a regular soldier and solid as a rock. 'Hoping to see your girl?' he asked. Sarj reckoned that Joe was a natural, a good driver and a dependable mate, but an innocent so far as the ladies were concerned.

'Hoping,' he agreed amicably. They were not out of danger yet. He swerved to avoid a crater, and the consequent jolting of the men in the back led to a fresh outburst of swearing.

''Aven't told the boys the shockin' news yet – Kitchener, y'know,' Sarj confided in a low voice.

'It'd lower morale,' Joe agreed. Kitchener, on his way to Russia, had been drowned, along with all hands, when *H.M.S. Hampshire* had been sunk west of the Orkney Isles on 5 June. Five days before this, at the naval battle of Jutland, fourteen British vessels had been sunk – the British officers and men killed or taken prisoner far exceeded the German casualties, yet the German High Sea Fleet was demoralised and would not again contest the British command. Joe, naturally, was unaware that Nandy's ship had been one of those seen going down in great belching clouds of smoke and scalding steam, and that, with other survivors, his brother had leapt overboard to be picked up, by a stroke of real luck, by a limping, badly damaged sister ship. The war was over for Nandy – his active naval career, like Oswald's, had been brought to a premature end. Before long his relieved family would learn that he was back in Blighty, but he would be in hospital for a considerable stay. His hands and chest had been severely burned.

It seemed incredible, Joe thought, as he swerved this way and that, that there were still tourists visiting the parts of France which were untouched by war. Here, in the Frontline villages, the only visitors were the soldiers on leave. The YMCA canteen and bath houses were a veritable godsend to the troops between spells of duty in the foul trenches. They walked slowly, on dragging feet, between the piled-up sandbags into heaven. Here, too, was the hospital, staffed by those brave nurses from home. The lucky ones were those with minor injuries, able to rest and recuperate for a few weeks, looked after devotedly by these angels of mercy.

Hot water, soap, the delousing of bodies and clothes, soggy feet finally freed from stinking, cracked boots and thick, woollen socks stiff with mud and sweat; a mirror, a stropped razor, camp beds with cotton sheets, and the luxury of a hot, cooked meal ... the British Tommy was revitalised by all of these things. Then there were the concerts, some impromptu, some put on by professional singers and other artistes, for those who were not venturing further afield in search of more lascivious entertainment – and Joe would not have presumed to sit in judgement on them.

Before he succumbed to blessed oblivion, he always sat down to write letters home. He sometimes despaired of finding anything to say; it was better to ask questions than to provide the answers they must be hungry to hear. But there were the private notebooks, grimy and dog-eared, which he kept in his breast pocket with a stub of pencil, in which he poured out his longing, his frustration, despair, and his love for those at home. The cruel end of those who had been his mates for a brief time was recorded, together with an address if he knew it, for if he got through himself, Joe felt he owed it to them to find their families and try to explain how it was. Sometimes, he would score out a vivid description he'd just written. The words might be obliterated, but he could not forget.

He could let Maud know that he had seen Brother James quite recently: they had chatted briefly, Joe had been told the good news that all was well with Maud and the others, then he had seen his brother-in-law go off further down the line.

Emily was there – she'd been there all along, landing in France even before he did. She was cool, clean, compassionate. Untouchable. She sat opposite him at the small table, pouring tea for him and the Sarj. Her slim hands were bare of rings, her nails cut short. Joe endeavoured to remember to eat the savoury stew with both knife and fork, not to shovel it into his mouth as they had all become accustomed to, digging into a tin of meat, tearing at dry, sometimes mouldy bread with filthy hands.

'Heard from your family recently, Joe?' He told her between mouthfuls that he had: that his sister was expecting her second baby very soon, that 'Tilly who lives with us – I can never remember a time when she didn't!' was busy in her work with the Sally Army, with all the unmarried girls the soldiers had left behind them and their babies. There was real help given, no time wasted in censoring those who had given into the urgency of the boys home on leave. Who knew when they might be blown to bits? He told her that Maud, despite her advanced pregnancy, was busy arranging for orphaned children to stay with her mother-in-law in Wiltshire for weeks at a time; that these children were being taught by his indefatigable Aunt Augusta; that his parents had welcomed into their home Belgian refugees, two aristocratic (one, autocratic!) ladies.

The Sarj wiped his plate clean with his bread, belched politely behind his hand and asked Emily: 'Any more tea, lass?'

'And what about you, Sarj – what news from home?' she asked politely.

'Wife's just had another. Bloody miracle if you'll excuse my French, Miss Rose. Eleven months since I was 'ome . . . But, turn a blind eye, as they say. She's always been a grand wife to me, and she had the guts to write and tell me. And *my* little lad, she says 'e's the spittin' image of yours truly. I owe 'er somethin' for 'aving 'im.' And Sarj puffed contentedly on his replenished pipe.

'You're a saint,' Joe said to him admiringly.

Emily Rose volunteered no information about her family but said, as she piled up their empty crocks, 'You'll both come and see me dance tonight, won't you?'

'Rather,' Sarj said enthusiastically. Joe was unsure. He didn't want to share Emily Rose with the other Tommies, roaring their appreciation of scanty costumes and unladylike songs. He could not really imagine how she had become a dancer – remembering some they'd had as lodgers in the past. Rosa had kept a very watchful eye on that sort, he smiled wryly to himself, with his virtue ever in mind!

There was a stout lady singer, reminding him of Kitty with her girlish curls and Irish voice. The makeshift curtains had been drawn back, the little stage spotlit thanks to the expertise of a youthful lieutenant, and at last Emily Rose came drifting on to the stage, exquisite in a froth of ballet skirts, dancing delightfully on her toes. Her dark hair was drawn back in a ballerina's knot and even her dimples were suppressed. Joe understood now. The whole audience was hushed, following every delicate movement; the pianist, who could thud away many a musichall ditty, toned down his playing . . . then came the deafening applause.

When later Joe and Emily sat holding hands, oblivious to Sarj guarding their privacy in avuncular fashion so that other admirers would not approach, Joe said quietly: 'I never dreamed you could dance like *that*, Emily.'

And she leaned towards him, looking demure, and invited him to kiss her. It was the first time. 'Thank you, Joe,' she whispered, while Sarj gave a whistle of approval.

SEVENTEEN

'Mrs Relf,' Madame said sharply in her faultless English as Tilly passed her the plate of steaming scrambled eggs on toast, 'we were awakened very early, too early, by Mrs Inkpen's child. My daughter needs adequate sleep if she is to perform at her best tonight in concert. The very cream of Belgian talent will be appearing to a *most* select audience.'

Madame, Tilly mused, is an inveterate snob. It had seemed such a brilliant idea at the time to offer to take refugees from Belgium, about whose plight so much had been written in the press, and their advertisement in *The Times*, courtesy of Maud's schoolgirl French, had been answered almost immediately. They had indicated their preference for those with a theatrical connection. Madame was a widow and she and her daughter had found their initial refuge not to their taste. Fortunately, Madame had reserves of money over here, so was able to pay well for the accommodation.

She began grumbling on the second day – initially she had bowled them all over with her regal charm! Their room was too small for the two of them – oh, and *when* would it be possible for Marie Claude to have the drawing room to herself, and the piano for her practising? And the food! 'Ah, my cook, *her* meals were consummate!'

Now she looked disparagingly at the rather runny eggs. 'I do not believe this was my choice,' she stated. Her reddened lips, which left their mark on the cups, to Tilly's distaste, made a disagreeable moue.

Marie Claude, thoroughly in sympathy with Tilly, mouthed at her across the table: 'What is?' Then she asked sweetly, 'Please may I have another cup of your delicious tea, Tilly?'

Tilly blessed Marie Claude for her kindness. There was not yet rationing but frequent grave government warnings. By using one egg between two, and adding milk but no butter, they were doing their bit. The standard loaf was yet to come, but bread did not taste the same as pre-war . . . and the tea! Well, Petty had a rude naval expression to describe it and asked how had it managed to crawl from the pot?

'Just off to the doctor's.' Maud looked in. Madame glanced at her with distaste. It was not seemly to go out in daylight, so hugely pregnant. And carrying her baby like that on her hip! No nursemaid, despite the fact that Maud was well connected by marriage.

'Hello, little Joy, how are you?' Marie Claude asked, smiling at the little Dutch dolly of a child, just the same as Maud had been, with her dark bob and wide eyes. Joy grinned back, dribbling down her clean front.

'Joy's on top of the world, aren't you, sweetheart? She's cut that wretched tooth at last.' Maud approved of Marie Claude, they were of an age.

Rosa appeared behind her daughter.

'I won't be back before you set off,' Maud told her mother. 'Best love to old Nandy, and tell him when I've shed this load I'll be coming to cheer him up – just you bully him to get better. Cheerio, all!'

'Tilly will be back from work in time to cook dinner for you ladies tonight. I'm afraid I must leave you now,' Rosa said. 'I am visiting my eldest son in hospital.' A tattoo on the front door meant her cab had arrived.

'You are staying overnight?' Madame enquired.

'Yes. I will be back some time tomorrow afternoon, all being well.'

'I shall see to your needs in the morning, too,' Tilly said demurely.

Rosa added: 'I wish you good luck for this evening!'

'Thank you! And good luck to you and your son, too. We hope you will find him improved,' Marie Claude said warmly.

As they said goodbye at the gate, Rosa said to Tilly: 'However did that old toad produce a nice daughter like that?'

'Now, Rosa!' Tilly hugged her. 'Give Nandy my love.'

She found Marie Claude clearing the table, to her mother's evident disapproval.

Marie Claude, Tilly thought, was a handsome girl: tall, full-busted, with a tiny waist and small hands and feet. Whilst her mother was frantically preoccupied, before they fled with concealing their valuables, Marie Claude had cut her hair decisively into a short crop, shaking her head in relief at losing the weight of dusty-blonde coils of thick, curly hair. Her eyes were rather narrow, dark blue, and she had a perpetually amused expression. Her voice, as the family had soon discovered, was a rich contralto. Madame, in the past, had also been an opera singer of some repute. Marie Claude's career had just been taking off when Belgium was invaded.

Along with thousands of others, the well-to-do, the bewildered poor, priests and nuns, they had desperately sought a place on one of an assortment of vessels which had come to their rescue, from great liners to skiffs. Jostled and sea-sick, all too aware that they could be blown to bits by the mines lurking in the depths below, they had mercifully escaped the atrocities.

Now Marie Claude whispered her nightmare to Tilly, instinctively knowing she would not repeat it. 'There was a young girl, Tilly, wrapped in a blanket, her face quite blank, unable to cry although she had been violated . . . It haunts me. I still seem to hear the hopeless sobbing of her mother. who was powerless to give comfort.'

Tilly, instantly reminded of her own terrible experience, put out a soapy hand to Marie Claude. 'You can always talk to me, if it helps.'

There was the letter in her apron pocket which she had only had a chance to read briefly, with all the bustle first thing:

Tilly, my darling girl,

Can you meet me at the station at 10.30 tomorrow morning? I have been sent on leave with instructions to rest. Will you give me refuge?

My love as always,

David

She would have to make her excuses at the soup kitchen, she thought, and said now to Marie Claude: 'I will be back earlier than Mrs Searle suggested – I shall have a friend with me – but we will not interfere with Madame's arrangements, of course.'

The train was crowded as usual. Tickets were collected at the other end by a plump girl with wispy hair escaping from the oversized cap set saucily on her head. Women were very proud of the various uniforms they wore; some even wore trousers where a flapping skirt would have been a hazard.

Rosa struggled with her heavy bag. Not a cab in sight, she sighed, feeling hot and dusty as she toiled up the long drive to the hospital. The June roses were in full bloom.

Nurses were walking the paths, wheeling patients, and despite their bandages and disabilities there was an air of optimism, Rosa could sense it.

The heavy doors stood open, revealing the mosaic floor of the hall. There were exquisitely arranged flowers in a cut-glass bowl, polished furniture, and that overriding odour of hospitals everywhere: carbolic. A young nurse, white-gowned and coiffed, crackling with starch, answered the pulling of the bell.

'Mrs Searle? Lady Evelyn is expecting you.'

Mr Arthur's daughter-in-law had opened her country home at the Government's request to receive wounded naval personnel, and, determined to do the job properly, had undergone nursing training herself. She had specified the hospital would welcome all ranks and had recruited a band of young VADs.

'But as fast as I train them they up and leave us for the battlefields,' Lady Evelyn sighed. Her drawing room was now the nurses' rest room. Here they wrote letters or sat by the french windows, which looked out on to the sweeping, formal gardens beyond.

'I'm sure you will wish to see your son before luncheon – we have a light meal on the terrace at twelve-thirty. But first I will show you to your room. Not a very illustrious one, but you won't mind that?'

Rosa followed her at a brisk pace along a corridor and up a side staircase to what had once been the servants' quarters. Lady Evelyn told her: 'My nurses do every-thing – cooking, cleaning, washing, as well as nursing. The servants were mostly conscripted. The horses too! At least we have been allowed to keep our motor for essential journeys.'

Rosa asked after her husband, who had been her employer's young son when she worked at Mr Arthur's house in Cheyney.

'A letter today. He sounds in good spirits. A nurse will come to take you to the patient. I must return to my duties!'

Nandy was out on the balcony, propped up on a day bed, his lower half covered by a scarlet blanket, his upper body bare but for the wide bandaging round his chest. His arms were swathed in white bandages, his left hand concealed in a mitten, but his right fingers just showed enough to grip a spoon or pen. Without his beard, he looked boyish and vulnerable.

'Good to see you,' he said simply. Rosa bent to kiss him.

'Sorry I can't give you a filial hug ... ' But his voice betrayed no bitterness.

He studied the photograph of Maud with Joy on her lap. 'So this is my little niece – just like Maud, isn't she? Has she her mother's temper to match?'

Rosa smilingly shook her head. 'A new baby expected any minute.'

'Once old Maud makes up her mind to do something, she has to go the whole hog!' It seemed remote, that childhood in the cottage, with both of them determined to have the last word.

'Writing paper, thanks. I was running low . . . '

'The books are from me. Tilly sent the fruit, and I made the cake.'

'It's good of you, all of you. I had a long epistle from Aunt A. She seems to have taken on a new lease of life in the country, eh? You must be pleased to have her off your back at last, Rosa?'

'Yes and no,' she admitted. 'Tilly says we're both mellowing in our old age! The money from the sale of the farm has enabled us both to be independent of each other, of course.'

'Joe been in touch?'

Rosa sighed. She showed him a letter. 'From some young lady, a Miss Rose. Says she's a friend of his and I'm not to be worried if we don't hear for a bit as he's in hospital with a fever . . . Both my boys laid low! Miss Rose says he might even be shipped home to convalesce. I do hope so.'

'At least he's not in the firing line right now.' Suddenly, Rosa saw a tear sliding sideways from one eye. 'And he has a girl who cares enough to write,' he mumbled. 'Comes to something when you can't even brush away your own tears, Rosa.'

'When you're well enough, you will come home so I can take care of you, won't you?' She was fighting back tears herself.

'Where else would I go?' he managed to joke. 'Are you going to reply to Joe's girl?'

'I don't think you should call her that. Maybe she's just his nurse?'

A VAD appeared: 'Time for your lunch, Lieutenant!' She spooned clear broth into Nandy's mouth, which he opened and closed obediently, like a baby. 'Your lunch is ready now, Mrs Searle. Lady Evelyn is waiting.'

Lady Evelyn discussed with Rosa her ideas for entertaining the patients. 'Keeping up morale is as important as mending broken bones,' she said.

Rosa, enjoying fresh fruit from the greenhouses, mentioned: 'We have a young Belgian lady staying with us, an opera singer. If you can wait a few weeks, my daughter Maud, I'm sure, would be happy to oblige on the piano.'

'And I can rustle up some local talent,' Lady Evelyn mused. She glanced at her watch. 'You must excuse me, time for the medicine round. And your son will be wondering what on earth is keeping you!'

EIGHTEEN

Tilly had smuggled David upstairs to Joe's room, not wishing to be waylaid by Madame, who was in the drawing room.

He had hardly spoken since he stepped down from the train, and she had instantly realised he was suffering from complete exhaustion.

'Hungry, dearie?' She helped him remove his jacket, and hung it up. He sat on the edge of the bed, head in hands.

She sat beside him, hugging him to her. 'Get undressed, David, straight into bed, eh? I'll bring you up a nice cup of tea.'

When she returned, he was already under the covers and asleep. She put the saucer on top of the cup. Smoothed the sheets, tucked his arms under. He had trimmed his beard, she saw; his thick hair was cut very short. For a few moments she looked down on him with love, then bent and gave him a swift kiss. He did not stir.

'Sleep the day away, David, if you want to . . . ' she whispered, and left him alone.

Tilly took a plate of sandwiches up to Maud's room. Marie Claude was in the kitchen, heating up last evening's leftover soup for herself and her mother. 'See you later, Tilly,' she said meaningfully, for she had observed that Tilly's friend was a man, and had heard them going upstairs. Not that one would ever suspect Tilly of being improper.

Maud had her feet up. Joy wriggled on to Tilly's lap, and bit into a sandwich. She was so lucky, Tilly thought, to be able to share Maud's little girl. It was wonderful to be needed, as she still was.

'Had a few twinges, Tilly,' Maud remarked casually. Tilly looked at her sharply. Then: 'Oh, my waters have broken!'

'I'll run for the nurse! David's upstairs, but I daren't waken him, Maud.'

'Quick!' Maud gasped. She almost crawled to the bed, hauled herself on to it and lay gasping a little. 'I'm all right, Tilly, don't look so alarmed. Nothing like last time – I – I assure you.'

Tilly scooped up Joy. 'I'll ask Marie Claude to look after her. I'll be back as fast as I can! Are you sure you want me to go?'

'I said – no pains, hardly, honestly – just go! There'll be – plenty of time, Tilly!'

Marie Claude was practising on the piano. 'Of course, leave her with me. Mama, fortunately, is resting!'

'I wouldn't mind a dozen like that!' Maud beamed. She had delivered her son all by herself as Tilly ran upstairs with the nurse in tow. Their expertise had been needed thereafter, of course, but Maud was feeling so relieved and so euphoric that they had to persuade her to get into the bed when Tilly had changed it. 'Won't Rosa be amazed? Don't ring her, Tilly, or she'll rush back and cut short her visit to Nandy, and *he* needs her now – you'd better break the news gently to Petty, too.'

Absurdly, Rosa felt cheated. 'Maud,' she said reproachfully, 'couldn't you have held on until I got back?' She joined in the general hilarity as she cradled her first grandson in her arms. Then she held him at arm's length and looked him over critically.

'Oh, he's all there, I checked,' Tilly said. They were all crowded into Maud's room, drinking tea. Joy had crawled under the covers, to be near her mother.

Maud cuddled her close, heeding Tilly's wise words: 'Don't let Joy feel left out, Maud, will you?'

'Would you mind?' she said softly. 'I know I always said a boy'd be Joe, but when I saw him, with B.J. not being here and that the only thing spoiling it all, I thought – well, James, after his father. But he can have Joe as his second name, of course.'

Tilly knew that Rosa had been counting on a Joe to keep up the family tradition. She gave her a little nudge.

'He looks like a James anyway,' she said generously.

'David's here – sorry, Rosa, I should have told you right away ... He's completely exhausted, been asleep more or less since he got here. I hope you don't mind if he stays for a while?'

'Tilly dear, of course I don't. He's your David, isn't he?'

An acid voice called up the stairs: 'Have you all forgotten *me* and Marie Claude?'

Tilly sat on the edge of another bed, holding David's hand. He was awake now, still lying down, regarding her gravely.

'I don't know when I can go back there, Tilly ... I don't think I had time to grieve properly for Esta – it all seemed to overwhelm me. You understand, don't you? I am to take indefinite leave, they say. But they need me at the hospital. How can I?'

'You can and you will, dearie. You're no good to anyone while you feel as you do. I'll take care of you until you're fit enough to have a little break. I know just the place, if you'll agree to go!'

'Will you come with me, Tilly?'

'You never know – I just might!'

NINETEEN

'1 July, 1916: ceaseless gunfire for over a week, awful air of anticipation,' wrote Joe in his notebook. It was the first time he had managed to sit up, let alone write anything. His fever was down today.

Apprehension made the patients lie quietly, smothering groans, catching brief glimpses of the nursing staff as they scurried to and fro, making up beds, rolling bandages and moving any soldier who felt unable to stand on his own two legs but who was otherwise in a reasonable state, by ambulance to a safer place. If one could call it that. It was a convent which had been heavily shelled in the early days of the war, but which the nuns, aided by nurses newly arrived from home, had since turned into a creditable hospital.

'Ready, Joe?' Emily Rose, who had volunteered to join the nurses, having done the demanding VAD training before she left for France, had been nursing Joe through his second bout of rheumatic fever. She had skated over the truth in her letter to his mother: at the height of his delirium, there had seemed little chance that he would survive. He had cried out for his mates, desperate to be back with them in the trenches, answering unheard calls, sweat constantly soaking his bed. His face was thin and stubbled, his eyes staring and distorted.

At what had seemed the end, to Emily, she had almost lain across him, holding him down desperately as he thrashed about, trying to stifle the awful cries which were disturbing the other patients – her face against his damp one, her tears flowing and mingling with his sweat. She echoed Rosa's cries over the little Joe long ago: 'Joe, don't leave me! Joe, I can't go through it all again … ' Then the sister-in-charge had lifted her and led her away, not unkindly, telling another nurse not to allow her back until something had happened, either way.

The pain and weakness were still there in his limbs, crushing his chest when he breathed in. 'Are they taking me, Emily?' he managed.

'Yes, Joe. You're going to the nuns. You'll have the chance to recover properly there and you won't be so aware of what's going on.'

'You're coming! You will come, won't you, Emily?' he begged.

'I'm coming with you, Joe,' she reassured him. No need for him to know that she had promised to return here. The word was that the boys were going over the top today – heavy casualties were inevitable. They were as ready for this as they could be.

Wave after wave of brave men, shoulder to shoulder, rose up and went forward over the divide towards the enemy lines. The big guns on both sides pounded pitilessly; there was the ear-splitting screeching of shells; the swollen observation balloons floated in the early morning mist, now seen, now obscured from view. Smoke billowed. There was wretched coughing and retching. Aeroplanes soared then swooped low. Ambulances squealed into action on worn tyres, the brave men marked with the Red Cross leapt out with their stretchers in a desperate search for fallen comrades: some were killed instantly, some mortally wounded, some blown to eternity. Back came the wounded to the clearing station to be assessed.

Brother James went from bed to bed. The hospital was overflowing with bodies. He knelt by stretchers on the floor, comforting, listening, quietening, helping the Padre to administer the Sacrament or the Last Rites, whatever the religion might be of the poor fellow at his last gasp.

The reek of death, the blood slippery underfoot, the inadequacy of the medical supplies, the hollow ring of spades urgently turning over the sods for a quick burial, the laboured, rasping breathing of those who would soon need this service – this was a disaster of real magnitude. This was the horror, the unspeakable truth of the Somme.

An ambulance driver was half carried in by his mates. He had been hit in the face by a bullet. A replacement driver was urgently required. Brother James did not hesitate to volunteer. A nurse with a lovely face and smooth centre-parted hair took from his steady hand the little canvas wallet containing his personal effects and made him a solemn promise.

'You must be Emily Rose, surely?' he exclaimed. 'Joe Searle's friend?'

'Yes, and you're his sister's husband. I should have realised, when they called you Brother James.'

There was so little time to talk. He merely asked: 'How is Joe? Give him my best.'

'He's doing well but I dread to think they'll send him back to this. I lost my fiancé right at the start,' she added helplessly, although she was aware that he was already gripping her hand in farewell.

'God bless you, Emily and Joe,' he said gently.

She dashed after him. 'You must come back!' she shouted urgently. 'For Maud and your babies . . .'

Four times she saw the ambulance return with its wounded, then early on the third day she waved to the Captain, the brave man they all knew as Brother James, for the fifth and last time. When they brought him back and she took off his jacket, determined to perform the last offices herself, Emily Rose saw his deformity and gave a desolate gasp. It was something Joe had never mentioned.

'Nurse,' said the sister, 'come. We must tend the living first.'

Joe lay, not unpeacefully, on his narrow bed, the sun filtering through the grille set high in the cold stone wall of the cell he occupied. Outside he could hear the geese quarrelling, the creak of the pump handle as the nuns filled their buckets with clear spring water. Was that thunder he could hear, rumbling in the distance?

'I shan't come with you. I'm sorry but young James is such a glutton I would have to keep dashing off, but I'll think of you and look after things here,' Maud told Rosa.

This was a last-minute decision on her part. The party for the hospital entertainment was already assembling. Madame had unexpectedly offered her services. 'I shall play the piano then I can chaperone Marie Claude.'

'She was coming anyway, I think,' Marie Claude said softly to Maud. 'All those men in their déshabillé, you see.'

Marie Claude wore a pretty dress in sea-green silk, with a necklace dangling to her waist. Despite her efforts with water and a stiff brush, her hair had sprung back into a fuzzy mop, but it really was quite attractive, even though she did not appreciate this.

Rosa ushered them all outside, turning to kiss Maud's armful of babies and telling them: 'Grandma will be back late this evening, and here's another kiss in case you're both asleep then!'

'Really, Rosa,' Maud smiled, 'who'd have thought you'd be such a doting grandparent?' She kissed her mother. 'I hope you all have a wonderful time, and that the audience doesn't disappear under the chairs – or beds – or whatever!'

'You can manage on your own, Maud?' Tilly asked ten minutes later. 'I just want to pop down to see one of my girls. Her baby's only five days old, and she heard from his mother yesterday that her fiancé is a prisoner-of-war. I won't be long,' she added.

'Oh, you must go, Tilly, of course – poor girl!' Maud agreed. Tilly had been very busy with her young mothers since David had returned to the hospital. He was still not over his exhaustion but had been sent for urgently. Something must be up, they'd all thought.

Maud stayed downstairs in the drawing room to feed the baby as Tilly had suggested, putting her feet up on the chaise-longue and watching Joy playing with her bricks on the tray of her little chair.

'I love you, James. I love you, Joy,' she said aloud. 'To think that two years ago I wasn't even married and you two weren't even thought of . . .'

She didn't hear the first knock on the door as she wasn't expecting a caller. The postman had already been early, as usual. Then the knocking was repeated more urgently. Maud buttoned her blouse, frowning, laid the baby on the couch and wedged him with a cushion to prevent him rolling off, then went to the door.

The telegraph boy stood there, the yellow envelope in his hand. Maud stared at it. Please God not Joe, with Rosa not here, she thought.

'Mrs Inkpen?' The boy cleared his throat. 'Sorry, mum.'

Maud took the telegram from him. He waited for a long moment, then repeated: 'Sorry, mum.' He remounted his bicycle and rode away.

She was still sitting by her children, the envelope unopened, when Tilly returned – alarmed to find the front door open.

TWENTY

It was to be an open-air concert. Volunteers had trundled the piano onto the terrace which would provide the stage, the audience sat on the lawns below, in wheeled chairs or supported on camp beds, with a nurse between every two patients. Despite the crutches, sticks, and varying degrees of disablement, they were a cheerful, responsive crowd.

The local rector had come along to act as MC, and had a practised line in patter with an infectious laugh. He had rounded up half a dozen of the ladies of the parish, some talented, some not so, but all appreciated, even though three of them would not see fifty again.

'Twenty minutes!' Marie Claude whispered to Rosa, who was acting as dresser and prompt behind the drawn curtains of the rest room.

When Marie Claude appeared, a great cheer went up. Madame repeated the opening bars of the music, and she began to sing. There was tremendous applause as she swept into a low curtsey at the end. Biting her lip, she was urged back for an encore. She had never known an audience like it.

Even Madame rose to the occasion when the request was for that favourite: 'Sister Susie's Sewing Shirts For Sailors'.

The finale was led by Marie Claude, with the company around her, her vibrant voice soaring above the rest in 'There's No Place Like Home'.

When Marie Claude thanked the audience for their response, she told them that this song was particularly poignant for her, because she too was far from home.

'Wonderful!' Lady Evelyn enthused. 'You must have tea before you go back.'

They went to see Nandy: he and a companion had listened to the concert from their balcony. 'We couldn't see anything, but we heard every word,' Nandy said.

Rosa introduced Marie Claude: 'Hers was the beautiful voice you heard singing 'No Place Like Home',' she told her son.

Nandy looked at Marie Claude and Marie Claude considered Nandy. Then, before her mother could demur, Marie Claude leaned over him and planted a kiss on either cheek. He looked right into her laughing eyes. 'I'm defenceless,' he murmured.

'What a pity!' Marie Claude whispered back.

'A kiss for the brave sailor – surely you cannot object, Mama?' Marie Claude challenged Madame. Taking in the extensive bandaging, Madame's haughty expression softened. To everyone's surprise she, too, presented the double kiss to Rosa's son.

'I shall see you again, I hope?' Nandy said to them both, but his eyes were on Marie Claude.

Tilly and Rosa came slowly downstairs together, leaving Sophia with Maud. Petty had gone in late to work, after meeting Sophia and Augusta off the train. Madame and Marie Claude had tactfully decided to visit a fellow countrywoman for the day.

Tilly thought that Augusta had comforted Sophia as best she could. She despaired of any of them getting through to Maud. She had been still and quiet ever since the telegram, obediently swallowing the sedatives the doctor had given her, accepting the baby passively when he was brought to her for his feeds. Tilly had slept with Maud, her arms around her, but she had cried, just once, murmuring: 'Oh, Tilly, *why*?'

Augusta said to them: 'It's an inconsolable time, I should know. Is there any way I can help?' Once she would have given money. Now they were all equal in that respect.

'She will appreciate your coming,' Rosa said, meaning it. The only good thing to come from this dreadful war was the easier relationship with Augusta.

'I often think that was the best thing I ever did,' she said, 'taking *you* in, Tilly, and then sharing you with Rosa and her family.'

What would they all do without Tilly, who helped so unobtrusively in such practical ways, who prayed for them all constantly?

'I imagine we've had more than our fair share, Augusta,' Rosa said.

'I'll make some coffee, shall I?' Tilly offered.

'No, I'll do it,' Rosa told her. 'You sit and talk to Augusta.'

'D'you intend to marry your doctor friend eventually?' she asked unexpectedly as Tilly rocked little James in her arms. Through Sophia, Augusta was learning tolerance for those of different classes and creeds. You were never too old to change, she had realised.

'No, Mrs Augusta. I suppose I've decided to devote myself to my work. Poor David, he had such a shock, too, his sister being killed like that. But we think of him as part of our family now, you know. He's been working so hard, we were really worried about him. But he had to go back. So many more needing him after . . . this.'

'Amy sent her best love. Tilly, you've no idea how glad I am that I took that child into my life. She has kept me going through all the bad patches. Of course, sometimes I can't help worrying if she will turn out like her mother later on.'

'Kitty wasn't a bad person, Mrs Augusta, she just loved unwisely. You and Amy are lucky to have each other.'

It was no good, Tilly realised, the little chap in her arms was not going to settle until he had been fed. Thank goodness, she thought, that Joy was so good about her morning and afternoon naps.

'Excuse me, Mrs Augusta – oh, good, here's Rosa with the coffee. I must just take the baby up to Maud. He's hungry again.'

She found Maud sitting holding her mother-in-law's hand. As Tilly came in with the baby, she looked at her in anguish. 'Oh, Tilly, will *you* hold on to me, too?' She laid the fretful baby in his crib immediately.

After a long while, Tilly gently reminded her that she must put the baby to her breast. She hoped that the shock had not turned Maud's milk.

'I must go down to Rosa and Augusta,' Sophia said. She had been brave for Maud's sake, and now she knew she must go quickly before she broke down in front of her daughter-in-law.

'Maud,' Tilly said quietly, 'remember when we lost Gussie? You cried for her. Now you must grieve for your husband.'

Then there were two for Tilly to rock in her strong arms.

TWENTY-ONE

Emily Rose sat in the drawing room, straight-backed, hands gripping her bag, on Rosa's little prayer chair. Tilly had departed tactfully for the kitchen and the making of the usual pot of tea.

A small girl appeared in the doorway, sucking her thumb. This must be Maud's daughter, Joy, Emily realised, smiling encouragingly at her. The toddler came forward a few steps, then stopped and stared at the strange lady again. Maud followed, shooing her gently forward, then came Rosa, carrying baby James.

Maud was much thinner and tinier than Emily had expected: she recalled the vivacious girl in the family photograph Joe had showed her, arms linked with her brother and her husband. This girl looked much older.

'Emily, so here you are at last.' Maud smiled. 'We had your letter weeks ago. We've had one from Joe since and he asked if we'd met up with you yet. He sent his love! This is my mother Rosa, of course, this as you can see is Joy – and here is little James.'

Rosa smiled at Emily as she said: 'Hello, I'm so pleased to meet you. Thank you again for that kind letter you wrote to me when Joe was so ill, and we've heard so much about you from him, you know. Maud, shall I take the children out into the garden? Tilly'll bring you yours in here, but we'll have ours outside, it's really very mild for October. I look forward to having a chat with you later,' she added to Emily.

'Bless you, Rosa,' Maud said. Joy clung to her grandmother's skirts as she took the children out again.

'Joy is going through one of those shy stages,' Maud told their visitor. They waited for the arrival of the tea and had a little chat with Tilly before Emily opened her bag and gave the precious parcel to her.

'I won't look at it now, if you don't mind,' she said in that quiet, calm voice, 'but I'm very grateful to you, Emily, for keeping it safe. Did you know my husband well?'

'I really only knew him just those last two days, but I'd heard all about you – all of you – from Joe. Maud, I must tell you – Brother James was so brave. He never flinched. The soldiers still talk about him, even those who came afterwards. It seems he is quite a legend.'

'He's irreplaceable!' she cried with sudden passion. 'Emily, we were so happy, and it was so cruel! It was such a short time, and the thing I can't forgive myself for is we could have had ten years together, not just a few weeks in the last two.'

Emily replaced her cup on the tray, rose impulsively and went to Maud, standing beside her, one hand on Maud's shoulder.

'It might help you if I tell you that I have suffered the same guilt. I put my career first, my dancing. I became engaged to a young man I'd known since I was a child, but made it plain to him that he came second in my life. It was a shock when he told me he'd been called up with the Reserve. I'm going to tell you something now, but it must be kept a secret between us – will you promise?' She gazed earnestly at Maud.

'I promise,' Maud said immediately.

'We didn't have much time left, just two days – so we went away together. When I heard he'd been killed, oh, Maud, I prayed to have his baby. But it wasn't to be. And I'd wasted all those years!'

'Then you do understand!' she exclaimed. She motioned to Emily to sit beside her on the sofa, as if they were old friends. 'What about Joe, Emily? He seems so fond of you, how do you feel about him?'

'I believe I love him, Maud – but I'm not sure if it's the way I felt for *him*. And anyway, if Joe found out what I've just confided in you – well, he wouldn't want me, how could he?'

'Then you don't really know him at all, Emily!' Maud reproached her. 'But as I promised, I won't ever say a word. Don't let him go, Emily. You see, he needs to believe you're waiting for him.'

'I won't disappoint him,' Emily promised.

'Thank you. I'm so glad you came, and that we could talk like this.' Maud sprang to her feet. 'Ah, here's my other brother. We've only had him home a week. His fiancé was walking him gently to the park. I'll just let them in, eh?'

Nandy, one arm in a sling, came in to be introduced.

'Emily, this is my brother Nandy,' Maud said. 'And this is Marie Claude, his fiancé, and this is—'

'Madame de Lusy, Ferdinand's future mother-in-law,' Madame proclaimed. Despite Nandy's present disabilities and uncertain future, Madame had decided that as an officer he was quite suitable for her only daughter, much to everyone's surprise – and Marie Claude's delight. It really had been love at first sight for these two. Madame had naturally accompanied them to the park, as she had thought it improper for them to sit there alone together.

'I'll call the others in. And I'll ask Tilly to make some more tea, shall I?' Maud went out, with the little bag tucked under her arm. She would pop up to her room first, leave it there and look at it tonight, she thought, when she could be alone with her sadness, and the children were asleep.

She hoped very much that Emily Rose would marry Joe, for Maud thought that they too were the perfect match.

EPILOGUE

1919

Tilly hung laughingly on to Joy's jacket as the four year old bounced up the three whitened steps to the stout front door of the cottage under the sea wall. Maud, with James, stood chatting to the young officer who had met them at the station and driven them here.

The door swung open almost immediately, and David, as bushy-bearded as ever, scooped Joy up into his welcoming arms.

'Aw, Uncle David – your whiskers are all bristly!' she said, dodging his kiss.

'Hello, David,' Tilly said simply, feeling warm inside as she always did when she saw him again. Then it was her turn for a hug and she looked up into his eyes and saw his happiness at holding her close, even if it was in a chaste, brotherly embrace. She was so glad to see him well and obviously thriving here, in this place which was so much loved by them all.

'Whyever didn't you write to let me know you were com ing?' he asked, then hesitated before continuing: 'Are you staying?' There were only the two tiny bedrooms, after all.

'Not here, don't worry, David. The cottage is yours, remember?' Tilly told him. It had really not been such a hard decision for her to make. When the war ended, six months ago, David wanted, needed, a complete change. When the compensation for the house he had shared with Esta at last came through, he was in a position to buy a small place of his own. Tilly, with Rosa and Augusta's blessing, had offered him the cottage. Rosa and Petty intended to retire back to the Island fairly soon, but there was Isabella's cottage, of course, now temporarily occupied by Nandy and Marie Claude, for he had been fortunate enough to have been retained by the Navy in a clerical capacity in Sheerness. Tilly hoped secretly that David, too, when he felt the time was right, would want to set up in practice again here. Shades of dear Dr Box, she imagined fondly. And, strangely, of Mr Lozenge, too.

Maud came over the threshold now, and was warmly greeted. 'Maud,' David said, 'how good to see you – and James. How the lad has grown, eh?' James was already tug- ging at his hand, wanting to play.

'We are staying with Uncle Nandy and Aunt Marie Claude,' Joy said importantly. 'Maud sent them a telegram this morning.'

'Oh, it's so nice to be back!' she exclaimed. 'It's all *just* the same!' She considered the whitewashed walls, the pitted beams, the latched doors. Maud always seemed young and carefree here.

'Ah, thanks to Tilly I don't have to watch out for the water cart, as you all used to do – but those stone jars Nandy talks about are still ready under the sink! He tells me and Marie Claude so much about those good old days.'

'What news of old Joe, eh! Married to Emily Rose – we can hardly believe it! He should be back in Blighty soon, one of the last,' Maud informed David. 'Rosa was most indignant that she missed out on the wedding.'

'I think it is very good news indeed,' he said. 'How long can you spare now for me?' He looked at Tilly.

'We thought we would leave our cases here, if you don't mind? Nandy can get them picked up later, if we ask him nicely. Would you walk with us to Mrs Barry's cottage?' Tilly asked.

'It will be my pleasure!' David said gallantly.

Marie Claude, too, welcomed them warmly. 'I wrote to Mama, you know, and asked her to visit, but she said she was much too busy at the hospital, and that Lady Evelyn could not spare her! How happy I am to think of her so well occupied there still – what good fortune that she came with us when I met my darling Nandy, then Lady Evelyn writing to ask if she might help if they became desperate.'

'How does Nandy feel, being back at work after so long?' Maud asked.

'He seems to be coping very well, quite content to be a landlubber.'

Later, Maud took Joy upstairs to show her Grandma Isabella's old bedroom: 'This is where you and James, and Tilly and I will sleep tonight. You and Jamesy top to toe in that small bed, Tilly and I in the big bed. Fun, eh? One day I'll walk you and Jamesy along to the old Ship on Shore and I'll tell you a story I told your Uncle Joe when he was a small boy.' She sounded dreamy at the memory.

'Tell me *now!*' Joy demanded. Maud could see herself, quite clearly, in this determined small person. She sank down on the bed and took her daughter on to her lap. 'Well—' she began. She was looking better, although she had remained very thin.

'You don't miss your singing, Marie Claude?' Tilly asked downstairs. David had taken James along the lane to see Mr Arthur's remaining horses.

'Oh, I sing all the time, Tilly. Sometimes Nandy complains – he says this place is too small to contain such a voice! Now, at the barracks, I am to have use of the piano if in return I will sing sometimes for the Navy!'

'No thoughts of a family yet?' Tilly enquired blushingly on behalf of Rosa, as instructed.

'A family?' Marie Claude teased. 'But I have a family – all of you, and Mama.'

'You know . . . ' Tilly told her affectionately.

'Ah, I know – we shall be the most elderly parents, I fear! But we do intend to one day, you may tell your dear friend Rosa that!'

Maud and Joy came downstairs. 'Maud,' Joy said, wriggling uncomfortably. Maud had, of course, decided that her children should address her informally, as she had her own dear Rosa, but Tilly was secretly pleased to hear Maud call Brother James 'Papa' when she talked to them of their father.

Maud asked Marie Claude: 'I presume it's still out in the garden?' And it was.

'Tilly!' David's face really lit up when he saw who was at his door the next morning.

She pulled gently back from his embrace to look at him and see how he was really feeling nowadays. 'David dear, you look so much better,' she approved.

'You prescribed the right medicine! Sending me here, to your cottage under the sea wall,' he teased. 'The only thing it lacks is a family.' He smiled, but his glance was wistful.

He had put his mark on the place, Tilly thought. Books and medical journals everywhere, dust on the mantelpiece. He was so dear to her, she thought, with a catch in her throat. She took off her hat. 'I'll tidy up for you, shall I? Show you how a bachelor should look after himself.' Her tone was purposely light.

David touched her hair fleetingly. 'I'm glad you haven't cut your crowning glory, Tilly. All the ladies round here seem to have been shorn!' Perhaps she had kept it long for him, he thought . . .

'More white than fair now, David,' she sighed. 'Fetch me a brush and pan, there's a good fellow!'

Tilly soon set the dust flying and had the cottage to her satisfaction. She sat down finally with a happy sigh. 'Once a maid-of-all-work, always one, I suppose, David!'

'More like a good wife . . . ' he said, removing the duster from her clutches. 'Now, perhaps we can talk. I hope soon to open a surgery here, to treat the poor people as I did in Brixton. Not in the cottage, of course. I shall rent rooms near the docks.'

'Oh, David dear, I'm so glad – it's just what I was hoping for. You could be another Dr Box!' Tilly exclaimed fondly.

'He is the one that Nandy talks of – the one you all knew, when he and Maud and Joe were young?' he asked.

'Yes, he was a wonderful man. Loved his work and his patients, as you do – did – when we first met. Can that really be nearly fifteen years ago? He died at the same time as my Oswald. They were buried on the same day.' Tilly's voice was soft, remembering. He sat beside her, taking her hands in his.

'Tilly, is it any use my hoping you might join me here? Oh, I understand you have always felt your place was with Rosa and her family – with your Mrs Augusta – but they don't need you in the same way now, and soon Rosa and Petty will be living nearby, they tell me.' He tightened his clasp unknowingly.

'Maud – the children – they—' He had caught her off-guard.

'Dear Maud will marry again, I hope. She should have a husband and the children a father. Maud is an independent lady, and a strong one. She would say: "Tilly, be happy for *yourself*." I know this, and so do you.'

'My work with the Salvation Army . . . ' she floundered.

'You need not give that up. You will be fulfilled here, too.'

His arm went round her shoulders; he was tilting her flushed face tenderly to kiss her cheek. 'Oh, Tilly,' he said gravely, 'don't you think it is time we are together at last? I love you, and I believe you love me. Perhaps I can never live up to Oswald—'

'David,' her lips were trembling, 'how could I be so selfish? It's probably too late for me to have more children. You should have a family of your own. It's not fair if I marry you *now*!'

He took the pins slowly from her hair, letting it fall past her shoulders. She sat there, unresisting, not looking at him.

'I only ever wanted *you*, Tilly, from that moment we first met,' he whispered. 'Family? Don't we have family? There will always be children to come here and stay with us, under the sea wall.'

Her arms slid around his neck. It was as if the years rolled clear away.

He told her, as he almost squeezed the breath out of her: 'No rainbow light shining on you here, Tilly, as when we embraced in the hall at Brixton. But to me you are just as beautiful – as desirable – as you were, then.' They had not kissed in that way since, but now her lips parted.

The beard did indeed prickle, as little Joy had candidly remarked, but Tilly didn't care. She was swept along by the sheer passion and sweetness of their embrace.

'Oh, Tilly,' he said, releasing her at last, 'what a generous spirit you have. How *loving*.'

She bundled up her hair with trembling hands, her eyes shining. 'Don't tell the family yet, David. I have to get used to the idea. But I'll stay here – not in the cottage, of course –that wouldn't be proper until we've tied the knot, as they say! I won't *ever* leave you again, I promise. I don't know how I'll face Maud, though. I reckon she'll guess!'

'You've made me so happy, so proud,' he said, and reached out to her again.

Mr Arthur had sent the old pony with the creaking governess cart. Most of his horses had been commandeered for the war effort. It saddened him to think that many of those beautiful beasts, whose glossy coats had been curry-combed by the son of Old George, who had inherited his father's empathy for the horse, had been slaughtered in the cause of war between men. And Young George, the wrong side of forty, had been called up at last and lost his life within three months. What a waste! He had been a simple, gentle fellow who had lived for his charges; had not even been one to fight with his peers at school.

The old house looked rundown, Maud thought. Rooms had been closed, furniture shrouded in dust sheets, grimy themselves. Food was no longer prepared in the cavernous kitchen, the steps no longer echoed to the busy scurrying feet of the servants – Mrs Arthur was reduced to cooking for herself on a portable stove in the corner of the dining room where the couple spent most of their time, particularly in winter when it was impossible to heat the whole house.

Mrs Arthur had made an effort with the table, laying it in style, lighting the candles in the beautiful silver candelabra. She had so wanted them to come to dinner before Maud and the children returned to London.

There was port to follow the simple meal. Tilly naturally refused, but Maud enjoyed her glassful – it warmed her. She tried not to think of the little ones. Marie Claude and Nandy had insisted that practice in looking after them would be good for them.

Mr Arthur lit a rather bent cigar, after asking in his old-fashioned way if the ladies present objected. They sat on in the candlelight, reminiscing. Well, Tilly seemed lost in thought.

'The books,' Maud asked. 'What happened to all the books?'

'We had them crated up and sent to Richard and Evelyn at the beginning of the war. We didn't know then how long we would have here, anything could have happened. Got shot of most of the antiques at the same time. Just kept a few favourite things to remind us.' Mr Arthur broke off abruptly, reflecting on the changes the war had wrought. He looked more than his seventy-odd years.

'We've decided to leave, you know,' his wife said sadly, playing with the silken tassel on a faded velvet cushion. 'Evelyn keeps urging us to sell up and join them in Richmond. It is depressing living like this, you see. It should be a place for younger people, with children.'

'Richard doesn't want the house – anyway it's not what it was,' Mr Arthur observed. 'We'll have it auctioned, I suppose, cut our losses.'

'You'll like it in Richmond,' Maud tried to console them.

'Yes, but we'll only be happy if the right people move in here,' Mr Arthur sighed.

There was a renewed spring in Maud's step as she walked along to the Big House the next morning. Tilly and Marie Claude hadn't minded a bit being asked to look after the children again while she pursued a sudden bright idea. 'I'll let you into the secret if it all comes off!' she had promised.

Mr Arthur was gardening in a rather haphazard manner – the young boy who was helping him seemed to have more idea as to what was what. The heavy wooden wheelbarrow was overflowing with great clods of earth clinging to the clumps of weeds. He was glad to stop and dust off his hands in the traditional way on the backside of his breeches. The boots, which had belonged to Young George, made his corns throb. Mrs Arthur was drifting about, snipping a bloom here, a bud there, laying them in her flower basket, a chiffon scarf tied under her chin to keep her hat in place on a breezy day.

They sat out in chairs sipping sherry, which was easier to come by than tea. Mrs Arthur batted at the gnats with her gloves. 'A plague of them, it seems – something to do with that pond needing clearing, I believe.'

'I'll come straight out with it, and I shan't be offended if you say no,' Maud said in her forthright way. She brushed her fringe aside so that they could see she was in earnest. 'I would like to know, please, how much the house is valued at, and if it is not more than £2,000 – well, I would like to buy it!'

Mr Arthur looked at his wife. She gave an amused nod. This was not really far short of the figure the local agent had quoted.

'May I be indelicate enough to ask, Maud, where you came by this large amount – in your present circumstances?' Mr Arthur asked.

'I don't mind telling you. My husband made this gift to me on our first anniversary, to do with exactly as I wished. There is enough other money for our future, for the children and me – but, you see, *this* would be for them too!'

'It's a big house to run, Maud. Without servants, quite impossible.'

'For what I have in mind, this house will be just right,' she said firmly. She was bubbling inside. She was going to do something positive, she realised happily, after being in limbo since the loss of Brother James.

Mr Arthur held out his hand to her. 'If you want it then you shall have it, my dear. There'll be a deal to arrange. It'll take time, you know.'

'We must have another glass of sherry to seal the bargain!' Mrs Arthur cried, pouring out further generous measures. They raised their glasses to each other.

'A holiday home for deprived children from London?' Even Tilly sounded unsure.

'If Sophia and Aunt A can do it with their school, well, think how we could complement each other! There must be a way to raise funds. I'll talk to Petty about it when we get home. I'd have to rely on volunteer staff to help me, I realise that.' She bounced James up and down on her knee to keep him happy.

Tilly hadn't yet told Maud that she would be with her on the train to help with the children when it was time to return to Brixton, but that after she had seen Rosa and confided her exciting news, she would be returning that same day. Come to that, she hadn't asked Marie Claude and Nandy if she could stay on with them until she and David were married!

Marie Claude sat by the open window, smoking – she had been given her first cigarette on the refugee boat, and one now and then helped to calm her.

'I will help you, Maud,' she offered, 'so long as we are here. I wished to train as a kindergarten teacher, but Mama insisted I must not waste my voice. When you are ready, I shall come to assist with the cleaning and the changing around.'

'I will, too, of course,' Tilly added. 'And don't forget, I shall send you some of the Army's waifs and strays.'

There was a tapping at the window. Nandy's grinning face looked in on the domestic scene. 'Has the kettle boiled, woman?' he asked Marie Claude through the glass.

She rushed to open the door to him, kissing him so eagerly that both Maud and Tilly averted their gaze tactfully. Nandy's left hand was still covered, but with his right he was now able to manipulate most things, although the skin was still angrily red and puckered. However, he could manage a very satisfactory one-armed hug. He still couldn't believe his luck in meeting and marrying the wonderful Marie Claude, and was determined to keep her happy.

'I hope you have eaten, Nandy, we did not expect you at this time!' his wife scolded fondly.

Maud could not help feeling a few pangs as she watched her brother and Marie Claude together. It was she who had urged Nandy: 'Marry the girl. Don't wait until the war has ended as Madame insists – do it *now*!'

'Come and sit down, Nandy, and hear just what amazing things your sister is up to,' Marie Claude told him.

'Mr Arthur is selling the land separately, but he says I could have that lovely paddock where the horses used to be, and the stables, and the greenhouse with the kitchen garden. We could grow all our vegetables and fruit,' Maud enthused.

'Fatten pigs – scatter corn to the hens – have a house cow, eh?' Nandy was amused at the very thought of old Maud sitting hopefully with a bucket positioned under a cow. 'You could have boy scouts visit with bell tents,' he suggested. 'They could set up camp in the paddock, why not?'

'You're going too fast – putting even more ideas in her head!' Tilly warned him.

There was that soft murmur of voices from the next room, then Tilly heard Marie Claude's throaty chuckle. She was nursing a fretful James in her arms. Too much sun today, she thought, but the little toad resisted wearing a hat, just as his mother had done! Joy slumbered peacefully on, her hand cupping her chin on the pillow. Maud turned over in the other bed. The candle was burning low, flickering erratically then dying out, but moonlight streamed through a chink in the curtains.

There was no sound now from the other room. She pictured them sleeping, comfortably close, and thought shyly that was how it would soon be between her and David. She had missed unbearably, she realised now, the solace of arms around her, a husband's love. She laid James carefully down at his end of the bed.

As she climbed into bed, she saw Maud looking at her. She knew instinctively that Maud had been thinking as she had. Thank goodness *she* had the children, Tilly thought – yes, this project was a good thing, Maud needed to feel positive again.

'Maud dearie,' she whispered, 'I've got something to tell you, too . . .'

Tilly laid the flowers on Oswald's grave. She rubbed at a patch of moss on the headstone. 'I know you would be happy for me,' she whispered. She took one last look at his resting place then turned to Rosa, who was waiting, and they walked arm in arm back to the cottage. Rosa's pleasure at her news had set the seal on Tilly's happiness.

Rosa and Petty had brought Mrs Augusta and young Amy with them. As before, Tilly would spend her wedding eve in the hotel.

'We'll all soon be here together, isn't it wonderful?' Rosa said. 'And Joe and Emily will be with us by this evening.'

'The family under the sea wall,' Tilly said. 'That's what we are, Rosa.'

Tilly lay in bed, waiting for David to join her. He had his back to her, busy at the washstand. She listened to the surge of the sea and her heart beat fast. She wore another special nightgown, the shimmering pale pink silk which Maud had worn on *her* wedding night.

This was where her story had really begun, she thought, when Augusta had despatched her so impulsively to care for Rosa and her family in their hour of need. Now, things seemed to have turned full circle: she would still have dear Maud and her children nearby – yet she was glad that she had made up her mind to marry David before Maud decided to settle here again, for it was important that he should know that she had not taken this into consideration before she finally said yes. Rosa and Petty would be in Isabella's cottage in a few months' time, and Nandy and Marie Claude hoped to stay in Sheerness for some time to come. Joe and his Emily Rose were to settle in London, of course, but they would visit often, Tilly was sure of that. Emily had confided a delicious secret when she greeted Tilly with a kiss: another little one for Tilly to cherish! She smiled happily at the thought.

'I'm glad you wore the amber,' Augusta had said, in her gruff way. Both she and Amy Elizabeth were thriving, and full of their school.

Tilly touched the beads on the bedside table. Still warm from her throat, coiled in a golden glow.

Her arms, bare and still smooth, hugged the coverlet to her, for she thought that the extravagant nightgown was really meant for a young bride. She had not the least idea how beautiful she looked to David when he slowly turned and looked down at her. Dear Oswald had shown her that there was no need to be afraid. But she must not think of him tonight. Except . . .

'Come to bed, David,' she said simply. How blessed she was, she thought, to be given a second chance.

The satin straps slid down her shoulders as she cradled his head to her breast. 'David, I love you,' she murmured. And offered a silent prayer that they would be together now to the end of their days.

This was their place. It would always be their home. Under the sea wall.

Tilly would have cried with happiness if she could have known that, at forty-five, it was not too late. There would be three new arrivals early next year: two more little girls, red-haired like Great-aunt Augusta, one born to Joe and Emily, one to Nandy and Marie Claude – and to Tilly and her David, a tiny baby boy, blonde like his mother, and dark-eyed like his father.

Now the little house sighed and creaked around them. Despite the ravages of time, its exposure to the elements and the sea, in another hundred years there would still be a family under the sea wall.

ACKNOWLEDGEMENTS

What made me want to write about Tilly and her family under the sea wall? My Father, all through my childhood told me such vivid stories of his own early days in Sheerness, and later, in Brixton around the turn of the century. I would like to thank the many interested folk I spoke to when I visited the island with my husband John, who helped so much with the research, and those who corresponded with me. I am grateful for their enthusiasm and encouragement. These include Sheerness Library, Mrs Iris Gwatkin, Ashford Library, the Local History Society, the Museum staff, Mrs Sheila M. Judge (author of the splendid *ISLE OF SHEPPEY*) and Mrs Pamela Mears. The wonderful, wordy old local newspapers really helped me to soak in the atmosphere too.

I am also indebted to Mr Dick Playle of the British Music Hall Society, so knowledgeable, who suggested the character of B.J. As for Little Italy, I was enthralled by all the information generously provided by Mr Pino Maestri for whom I named a character!

My thanks too to my fellow writers for spurring me on. They know who they are!

Last, but certainly not least, I must thank my friend Mrs Bertha Barter, a lifelong Salvationist for telling me about that caring organisation.

All these ingredients were duly stirred into the novel which my Dad said I must write, for although it *is* a novel, peopled through my imagination, I like to think how happy he would have been with the result.

S.N.

Welcome to the world of *Sheila Newberry*!

Keep reading for more from Sheila Newberry, to discover a recipe that features in this novel and to find out more about what Sheila is doing next . . .

We'd also like to introduce you to MEMORY LANE, our special community for the very best of saga writing from authors you know and love and new ones we simply can't wait for you to meet. Read on and join our club!

www.MemoryLane.club

Meet Sheila Newberry

I've been writing since I was three years old, and even told myself stories in my cot. So it came as a shock when I was whacked round the head by my volatile kindergarten teacher for daydreaming about stories when I was supposed to be chanting the phonetic alphabet. My mother received a letter from my teacher saying, 'Sheila will not speak. Why?' Mum told her that it was because I was scared stiff in class. I was immediately moved up two classes. Here I was given the task of encouraging the slow readers. This was something I was good at but still felt that I didn't fit in. Later, I learned that another teacher had saved all my compositions saying they inspired many children in later years.

I had scarlet fever in the spring of 1939, and when I returned to our home near Croydon, I saw changes which puzzled me – sandbags, shelters in back gardens, camouflaged by moss and daisies, and windows re-enforced with criss-crossed tape. Children had iron rations in Oxo tins – we ate the contents during rehearsals for air-raids – and gas masks were given out. I especially recall the stifling rubber. We spent the summer holiday, as usual, in Suffolk and I remember being puzzled when my father left us there, as the Admiralty staff was moving to Bath. 'War' was not mentioned but we were now officially evacuees, living with relatives in a small cottage in a sleepy village.

On and off, we returned to London at the wrong times. We were bombed out in 1940 and dodging doodlebugs in 1943. I thought of Suffolk as my home. I was still writing – on flyleaves of books cut out by friends – and every Friday I told stories about Black-eyed Bill the Pirate to the whole school in the village hut. I wrote my first pantomime at nine years old, and was awarded the part of Puss in Boots. I wore a costume made from blackout curtains. We were back in our patched-up London home to celebrate VE night and dancing in the street. Lights blazed – it was very exciting.

I had a moment of glory when I won an essay competition that 3000 schoolchildren had entered. The subject was waste paper, which we all collected avidly! At my new school, I was encouraged by my teachers to concentrate on English Literature and Language, History and Art, and I did well in my final exams. I wanted to be a writer, but was told there was a shortage of paper! True. I wrote stories all the time and read many books. I was useless at games like netball as I was so short-sighted – I didn't see the ball until it hit me. I still loved acting, and my favourite Shakespearian parts were Shylock and Lady Macbeth.

· MEMORY LANE ·

When I left school, I worked in London at an academic publisher. I had wanted to be a reporter, but I couldn't ride a bike! Two years after school, I met my husband John. We had nine children and lived on a smallholding in Kent with many pets (and pests). I wrote the whole time. The children did, too, but they were also artistic like John. We were all very happy. I acquired a typewriter and wrote short stories for children, articles on family life and romance for magazine. I received wonderful feedback. I soon graduated to writing novels and joined the Romantic Novelists' Association. I have had many books published over the years and am over the moon to see my books out in the world once again.

There Was Always Room at the Inn

The old Swan Inn was a magical place to a small girl with a vivid imagination. This was where my grandmother was born; it was our family home for nearly 200 years. Once it had been one of three village inns, where carriages rattled to a stop in the courtyard, patrons made merry, travellers sank wearily on to feather mattresses, horses snorted and stamped in the stables, the fire blazed a welcome in the winter and beer quenched summer thirst.

My Nanna, Isabella, married Ernest when she was twenty-one. The youngest of her family, she had been orphaned young, and in her teens assisted her eldest brother in *The Swan*. The newlyweds moved to *The Buck*, in a nearby village, with the support of her mother in law Emma, who cared for the children. Isabella was responsible for the day to day running of the inn, while Ernest had a butcher's shop in the courtyard. Isabella managed both businesses when Ernest was called up in WW1 aged forty. My mother, Bella, six years old, accompanied her mother when they delivered meat to outlying villages. After that war, with the loss of so many young men, trade at *The Buck* declined.

My grandparents retired in the mid 1930s, and returned to *The Swan*, now a private dwelling. Isabella was a determined little lady, plump and smiling, with soft hair curling all over her head and gold rimmed half-moon glasses. The first Christmas I recall at *The Swan*, in 1939, at the beginning of WW2, we arrived in our Austin 7 and pulled up by the pump in the back yard where at dawn every morning, my uncle Hedley enjoyed his 'morning shower', be it June or December. Isabella waited while I was lifted, pale and wobbly, and put down on the cobbles. 'Come you on inside,' she said in her soft Suffolk voice as she took her travel-sick grandchild in hand.

Christmas began with the welcome from my grandparents. Ernest had been busy in his shop opposite when he saw us arrive. He was of Irish descent, over six feet tall, with brilliant blue eyes and a mop of silver hair. It was his moustache which held my attention, bristling like Lord Kitchener's and ginger like the hair on his arms. My delight at seeing him was mingled with fear of the moustache, for it prickled my face as he kissed me. 'What ho! My owd sugar lump!' he laughed.

The Swan was rambling, cosy and draughty in parts, with rooms unexpectedly up here and down there. The pantry cum kitchen was dominated by an enormous table and a glowing black range with sooty kettle on the boil. Tea stewed thick and strong in a huge teapot. I disliked that tea but I loved the cups, delicate bone china with a bluebird pattern. Bella and Nell, her sister, who'd also arrived with her family, helped Isabella with the Christmas baking. Their young sister Myrtle, newly-wed, would join us later, as her husband was awaiting his call-up papers.

The parlour was cheerful and bright, with a good fire crackling and comfortable chairs with plump cushions. We decorated in here and dust was shaken from ancient paper chains. There was a speaking tube in the wall through which we children called our orders to the kitchen!

The following Christmas, 1940, my mother, brother and I, having been bombed out of our home near Croydon, were already living in Suffolk with Nell, Ralph and little Glenys in a two up, two down cottage, eight miles from *The Swan*. My father was with the Admiralty in Bath. Ralph delivered essential food supplies in East Anglia. While our mums cycled merrily along, Ralphie, as we called him, transported the children to *The Swan*. A lovely surprise, my dad arrived late on Christmas Eve.

I shared a bed with Glenys in a room under the eaves. My parents slept the other end under a picture which frightened us – of an angel, bending over a sleeping child. Uncle took Derek up the bell tower to watch him bell ringing; Glenys and I peeped out of the window at stars shining over the old church. Downstairs, the hustle and bustle went on.

Christmas morning and it was still dark. The adults were asleep as they had been to Midnight Mass. We felt for our pillowcases, bulging, wobbly, AND FULL! A whistle was blown downstairs in the snug, where my grandparents slept. 'Granddad's opening his stocking – oh please!'

Soon would come the cheerful call to the land girls and cowman billeted there, and frozen fingers must fumble over the milking. 'Rise up bor – rise up you gals – thass half-past four!'

Afterwards we had opened our gifts by torchlight, and wished Granddad a happy Christmas when he brought in a tray of tea. 'Thass got a little extra for you,' he said to my parents. Was it a warming dash of whisky?

Yawning at the breakfast table were the land girls, in heavy jumpers and breeches, their hair steel curled for Christmas afternoon frizz. We ate tender pink ham and soft-boiled eggs. The goose had been returned to our oven. The giant pudding rocked away and we anticipated finding a silver threepenny piece for each of us hidden in its dark fruity depths. We couldn't do justice to all the wonderful food that day, which must have meant months of economising in those difficult times.

After dinner we played a new game, such as Housie-Housie, or were absorbed in our new books. This was when Isabella and Ernest took up the big holly wreath and made the long pilgrimage to the grave of a little son, who passed away when he was only seven.

We sang round the piano in the evening and lubricated our throats with dry ginger wine.

Many years later, when we visited *The Swan*, when Hedley was there by himself (though later he was joined by his sister Myrtle) I half-expected to see them. Ernest swinging down the stairs and Isabella rolling pastry in the stone flagged pantry – and was the goose still hanging on the back of the door?

They all live on in my heart, especially at Christmas.

· MEMORY LANE ·

Recipe for Farmhouse Griddle Scones (1894)

'Come in, my dear – of course you must be Tilly. Don't stand on ceremony!' Oswald's mother was short and as round as the butterballs she shaped so expertly in her dairy, with a weather-beaten, smiling face. She wiped floury, pudgy hands on her coarse apron . . .

In her big, sunny kitchen, she welcomed visitors with scones and a welcome cup of tea. On this occasion she baked the scones in the oven, but when she had more time she made Griddle scones on the range hotplate*.

Ingredients
- Eight oz plain flour – add a teaspoon of baking powder
- A dessert spoon of caster sugar
- One oz melted butter
- 1 egg – whisked well and added to a quarter of a pint of milk
- A pinch of salt
- A few plump sultanas – on special occasions

Method
- Mix all ingredients to make a soft dough ball, then roll out on a floured board. This makes eight scones.
- Place four scone rounds on a hot griddle.
- When the first side is cooked (golden brown) and the scones have puffed up, turn with a spatula and repeat the process.
- Serve warm, split, with butter, or strawberry jam and cream.

Enjoy!

*Nowadays, if preferred, use a shallow frying pan, with non-stick base.

· MEMORY LANE ·

Don't miss Sheila Newberry's next book,
coming May 2019 . . .

THE FORGET-ME-NOT GIRL

**When her family is torn apart, can she find her
place in the world?**

Emma is growing up in the beautiful Norfolk countryside
with her family. Life seems idyllic, but little does
she know things are about to change.

Soon she finds her family split. Her younger siblings are
destined for the workhouse whilst Emma takes a job
as a cook in a wealthy London household. Then she
meets a dashing young fireman. As Emma marries
and her family grows, so does her happiness.
Until tragedy strikes.

Will Emma turn her life around once again?
And can she finally find her happily ever after?

Sign up to MEMORY LANE to find out more

· MEMORY LANE ·

Introducing a new place for
story lovers – somewhere to share
memories, photographs, recipes and
reminiscences, and discover the very
best of saga writing from authors you
know and love, and new ones we
simply can't wait for you to meet.

· MEMORY LANE ·

A new address for story lovers

www.MemoryLane.club